T0374175

Witch Hunt

Witch Hunt

L. M. BRIGANT

WITCH HUNT

iUniverse books may be ordered through booksellers or by contacting:

iUniverse
1663 Liberty Drive
Bloomington, IN 47403
www.iuniverse.com
1-800-Authors (1-800-288-4677)

Because of the dynamic nature of the Internet, any web addresses or links contained in this book may have changed since publication and may no longer be valid. The views expressed in this work are solely those of the author and do not necessarily reflect the views of the publisher, and the publisher hereby disclaims any responsibility for them.

Any people depicted in stock imagery provided by Getty Images are models, and such images are being used for illustrative purposes only. Certain stock imagery © Getty Images.

ISBN: 978-1-5320-6728-0 (sc)
ISBN: 978-1-5320-6730-3 (hc)
ISBN: 978-1-5320-6729-7 (e)

Library of Congress Control Number: 2019900946

Print information available on the last page.

iUniverse rev. date: 02/05/2019

Prologue

Max huddled under the overhang, feeling the cold wind cut through his light uniform jacket. The small extended roof over the doorway protected him from most of the rain, but as the wind shifted, he swore as a thin stream of very cold water managed to find the exact spot where the back of the jacket bent away from his neck. He cursed the stupid law that prohibited smoking in any public or office building. Just yesterday, Jeffers had sneaked a cigarette in the staff bathroom, but—no surprise—their pencil-pusher supervisor Bronson had caught him and written him up. With child support due to two ex-girlfriends, Max couldn't afford to lose this job. At least the benefits made up for the working conditions. His pocket vibrated as his phone let him know his break was done. Bronson probably analyzed all the security records to see who went in and out and exactly when.

Max flicked his cigarette end away, watching the tiny red spark as it arced away from the pool of light by the door to the exercise yard. The cracked asphalt was gleaming where the security lights made the wet surface shine. Though the sky was attempting to lighten in the east, the heavy clouds prevented much light from breaking through. A black shadow that moved across the surface managed to avoid the pools of light as if it were flowing around them. Max didn't notice it.

The sheeting rain drowned the lit end of the cigarette before it could land in a puddle. Max slicked his wet hair away from his face and turned back to the door, where he held his security pass to the card reader and then pressed his forefinger on the fingerprint scanner. The door clicked. He swung it open wide and stepped through. Lightning lit up the sky brilliantly behind him and flung his shadow in sharp edges against the opposite wall. Max jumped as shadows leaped up in front of him and then jerked around, as the lightning danced behind him. He blinked the afterimage away from his eyes. After the brilliance, the dim security lights in the narrow corridor made it nearly impossible for him to see anything. He pulled the heavy-duty flashlight off his belt, feeling foolish as he flicked it around. What was he looking for, the monster under the bed? "Must be gettin' old. Jumpin' at my own shadow now," he muttered. But the flashlight was a comforting weight in his hand, and he didn't hang it back on his belt.

In spite of his tightly strung nerves, he didn't notice the amorphous black shadow that slithered in behind him, clinging to the wall as the door swung shut.

Max strode to the next security checkpoint, his booted feet sounding loudly against the concrete floor. The well-lit area sent a wash of relief over him, though he was embarrassed to admit it, even to himself.

"Hey, Max." Tom Jeffers looked up to check who had come through the door. "Do the riot gear check, would ya? Then you can get some chow and watch the monitors after roll call."

"Yeah, sure."

Max stifled a chuckle as Jeffers leaned his chair back on two legs and clicked a remote at an overhead TV to find a more interesting show, ignoring the other monitors which showed row after row of featureless darkened corridors, iron staircases and barred cells. Jeffers would never change.

Neither of them saw the formless darkness that dogged Max's steps. It fell behind in the space before the security door but slipped in close at the checkpoint, and then it disappeared beyond him into the area lined with cells.

"Wait a sec, Max. Would you sign off on my perimeter check first?"

"Yep." Max glanced through the checklist and scrawled his initials and the time.

"Hey, that's kind of weird." There was a thud as Jeffers' chair dropped back onto four legs.

Max looked up to see his colleague staring intently at a large monitor showing the view from several security cameras.

"What's weird?"

"Three of the monitors kind of went dim just for a second, one after the other. I wouldn't even have noticed if I hadn't just been looking right at them. They didn't turn off or anything, just sort of faded a bit and then came back, but it was weird that it was one right after the other."

"Odd," Max agreed, staring at the monitors also. "Maybe we should have those cameras looked at?"

"Yeah, wouldn't hurt. I think those are the ones that just had those newer night vision LEDs installed."

"I'll just add that to the day list," Max said, scrawling a note at the bottom of the paper. "Okay, I'm gonna check the riot gear. You're off after roll call, right? See ya tomorrow?"

"Got three days off," Tom said with a grin. "I'll be back Sunday."

"Lucky you—at least if this rain stops. Have a good weekend, man."

Beyond the checkpoint, the oily blackness slipped silently toward cell block C7 and glided soundlessly up the metal staircase to the second level. As it slithered along the corridor, it paused briefly in front of each barred cell, creeping a few feet up the bars and then leaching back downward to move on to the next cell. After repeating this behaviour half a dozen times, it changed its method, and instead of flowing onward to another cell, it seeped inside the cell and drifted up onto the bed, where a sleeping man lay covered with a standard-issue grey blanket. The man jerked once and made a slight gurgling noise, just enough to make his cellmate stir and turn over in the upper bunk, and then all was silent. The grey blanket lay twisted on the empty bed.

Moments later, the black shadow, now twice the size and moving more slowly, slid between the bars to disappear down the corridor.

Nobody was near the janitorial closet to see the shadow seeping under the door, and the predawn stillness outside was too dark to see it leaking out of the tiny barred window and down the rough stone wall, even if anyone had been looking there.

Passing back through the security points, Max strode toward the weapons vault, which contained the riot gear as well as extra weaponry. He greeted another officer and unlocked the heavy steel door under the other guard's watchful eyes. He didn't look up as the hooting wake-up alarm was broadcast over the PA system, though the sound of tramping footsteps grew louder and then passed as the morning shift went to conduct roll call.

He was just finishing the task and locking the vault door when the alarm sounded again, but this time it was the alert, and the red lights were flashing.

"Shit, what now?" he and the vault guard said simultaneously, both tensing in alarm. Both sets of eyes swung to the overhead set of security cameras, but most of them showed only numerous prisoners standing in front of their cells as required and evenly spaced rows of guards facing them. The two men's uncertainty did not remain unsatisfied for long.

"Code 10-57, C7, 213," a crisp voice announced over the PA system.

Max closed his eyes and sagged against the wall for a moment. "Missing person?" He translated the code easily, recognizing that the announcement also identified the cell block and cell number of the absent prisoner. "Fuck me! *Another* one?" The icy shiver that went down his spine was worse than when the cold rain had found the gap in his jacket. Heads were gonna roll for sure. He just hoped his wouldn't be one of them.

Chapter 1

Natalie Benson frowned as her cellphone vibrated, making a rattling noise against the granite countertop. She glanced at the backlit clock on the stove and saw that the time said 6:30 a.m. Constance's "wake-up call" still had her off balance. Being awakened by a powerful telepath was like getting unexpectedly doused with a bucket of ice water. Not a great way to start the day.

But Constance didn't communicate by text message. *What now?*

Taking a deep breath, Natalie picked up her phone and saw that the message was from Rajit Naresh, the lawyer whom she worked most closely with. The two of them reported to the same partner, a man whose tendency to panic often added stress to an already stressful job. "Disaster alert. JB's gonna freak. Take a look at the *Sun.*"

Natalie frowned at the display. Was this some kind of a joke? Raj had a weird sense of humour sometimes. The *Toronto Sun* was not the newspaper he usually read, and it seemed extremely unlikely that James Behrman would read it either. What the hell was Raj doing reading the *Sun* at 6:30 in the morning? Given that the two of them typically worked late into the evenings, neither of them was an early riser, by choice.

She picked up her tablet from where she'd left it the night before on the coffee table and walked out onto the balcony, trying to tuck her blouse

1

into the waistband of her skirt one-handed. She was a tall, lean woman, her eyes a striking shade of blue, with strawberry blonde hair and a pale complexion. The expensively tailored suit skirt had a matching jacket, which was currently lying across the back of the sofa.

It had been raining earlier. The leaves of each of the plants making up her container garden were glistening with diamond-like water droplets as the early-morning sun poked through the dissipating clouds. Natalie took a deep breath of the fresh-smelling air, enjoying the rare quiet of a city that had not yet begun its day, wishing she'd had more time to put herself together. Her shower had been rushed; it felt like the water had barely had time to get her wet before she was hurrying to get dressed. With everything on her plate today, she'd just have time to take care of Constance's request and then grab a cab to work. There wasn't even going to be time to do her makeup, though she hated going to work looking less than her best.

Turning on the tablet, Natalie typed *Toronto Sun* into the search box and clicked on the resulting link. Her eyes widened as she saw the headline that her colleague was surely referring to:

LOCAL LAWYERS IMPLICATED IN PRISON BREAKS

Natalie glanced down toward the main road visible off the right side of her balcony, while a view of the lake stretched out on the left. A lone streetcar rattled past, a delivery truck and a couple of cars passing in the other direction a few moments later. Since her expected visitors had not yet arrived, she touched the icon representing the article and began to read.

Catching sight of the name of her firm in the first sentence, Natalie swallowed hard. Was her worst fear about to come true? Mostly she had been able to keep her two worlds from colliding, but there was always the fear that one day, it would become impossible. She sank into a chair, ignoring the damp surface, and began to read:

> A possible link has been found between Toronto law firm
> Mason Sullivan LLP and some of the recent prison escapes
> in the Toronto area, says James Matheson, member of
> the RCMP task force created to investigate the growing
> number of prison breaks. It is widely suspected that many

of the escapees are either mages or assisted by mages, since there are rarely clues on how the disappearances were effected. Since the notoriously secretive magic community has neither confirmed nor denied their involvement, the public is left to assume the worst.

Natalie groaned as she went on to read that several of the most recent AWOL inmates were people accused of fraud, the one kind of crime that often had a civil lawsuit as well as a criminal case related to the same set of facts.

Where there are non-criminal court cases, the party on the other side of the lawsuit was represented by Mason Sullivan LLP, in many cases. Mason Sullivan, a large law firm in downtown Toronto, does not practise criminal law. Several of those who have recently disappeared from jail were named in Anton Piller orders obtained by Mason Sullivan on behalf of its clients prior to the arrests. Similar to a search warrant, for non-criminal matters, an Anton Piller order grants rights to enter private premises and seize computers and electronic data as evidence.

She read the rest of the article with growing dismay. She, Raj and James Behrman did almost exclusively fraud litigation, so this accusation was levelled straight at their department, even if they weren't personally named.

The newspaper article continued to suggest that her firm was in some way involved with the steady trickle of prison escapes that dominated the news. The reasons were fairly vague and, to Natalie's mind, quite far-fetched. But that wouldn't matter. Just a sliver of doubt would be enough to make someone hire a different law firm. Everyone hated and feared mages and anything to do with them. Natalie and her sister had been aware of that since they were children, when their parents had told them what they were, and what they would be when they grew up. What to do, what not to do, how to hide it—their lives had been a continuous smokescreen.

And what would happen if the partners ever found out that one of their junior lawyers did occasionally have something to do with those prison breaks? That could easily be the end of the career Natalie had worked so hard to achieve. It's not like she would be permitted to explain what she did and why. Thinking of several recent hate crimes that clearly targeted suspected mages, she felt her heart rate speed up as she contemplated consequences even worse than the ruination of her career.

Glancing up to see a cab pulling to a halt just outside her building, Natalie struggled to pull herself together. She stood up and saw three men emerge from the back seat, one after the other, all wearing sombre-looking business suits. One of the men glanced up and nodded at her slightly, as though there weren't fifteen storeys separating them. These, then, were the people she had been told to expect. Seeing an ambulance pass the driveway entrance, she thought of her sister, who worked as a paramedic, a job where she was actually able to use her magical abilities to save lives. Natalie sighed, thinking she should have chosen a different career path, and turned back inside just in time to hear her buzzer sounding.

How long would it take before this one hit the news? Constance hadn't bothered to identify the parties involved, of course. Her mental contact had been abrupt as always, and she had closed down the communication before Natalie was awake enough to ask questions. What if it was another one that could somehow be linked to Natalie's firm? Each time she was involved in one of these situations, it increased her risk.

On the other hand, how could she justify her wish to be left alone? With great power came great responsibility, a truism she had heard more times than she cared to think about.

"Yes?" she said in a neutral tone after she'd pressed the response button.

"It's LEO," came the expected answer. "Is it okay if we come up?"

"Sure." With a sigh, she pressed the release button and glanced around to make sure the place was presentable. She flicked on the TV and switched to CP24's rotating headlines before muting the volume. Sometimes these situations were fairly awkward; having an excuse to look at the TV could be useful.

Within minutes, there was a knock on the door. Natalie opened it, stepping back to let the men enter. One of the three walked stiffly, with a blank, almost frozen look on his face. Though these three men were strangers to her, this was an exercise that had been repeated many times in her condominium unit.

The two men flanking the third were doubtless police officers, though one of them did not particularly look the part. The stiff-faced individual was a prisoner, and the fact that he was moving in exact synchrony with the officer wearing jeans and a rumpled T-shirt made Natalie shudder. Even though she knew that the situation warranted it, she couldn't help but feel uneasy seeing coercive magic being practised right in front of her eyes. To all but a select few, using coercion magic was almost the worst crime a mage could commit. The thought of taking away someone's free will bothered her on a primal level.

As she was stepping aside, she remembered that all three of them had been wearing suits when they got out of the cab. Looking more closely, she noticed that the one worn by the prisoner didn't quite move in a natural way. It was like bad CGI, and Natalie could easily spot the illusion. So the red-haired man's suit had probably also been an illusion, which he had dropped once it was no longer needed.

"Good morning, Ms. Benson." The officer who spoke was the one still wearing a suit. Natalie noticed that his broad shoulders strained the fit of his jacket. Probably no illusion there. He had large hands and a buzz cut. Even with no uniform, his entire appearance broadcast his occupation. "I'm LEO Marcus Keane. My partner is LEO Jon Forrester. Our … guest … is Peter Lassiter. Thank you for assisting."

"Not like I'm really given much choice." Natalie sighed. "I just wish I could be given a bit more notice, you know? Surely this was planned way sooner than 45 minutes ago?"

Marcus sighed. "Well, yes," he admitted. "But there's been a series of problems that made it necessary to request your assistance. I assume the Chief called you?"

"No. Councillor Constance Reeve gives me the orders. To be honest, I can't stand that woman invading my head. Especially not when she wakes me up at six in the morning. Being woken up by a phone would be far more pleasant."

"No kidding," Marcus agreed. "I'll be sure to mention it to the Chief when we get there."

"I'd appreciate it."

"Speaking of getting there, though, that's part of the problem. I'm afraid there's going to be a slight delay."

Natalie tensed. "I don't have a lot of time," she warned.

Marcus pulled a cellphone from his pocket and sighed as he looked at the screen. "The original plan was for us to remove this guy while he was en route to his hearing this morning. Then we would have taken the court vehicle out to the nearest portal in the east end and returned the vehicle later." He referred to a method of long-distance travel that was used by most mages since it was quicker than ordinary transport. "But we learned they had increased the security even more for courthouse appearances from that prison, which was why Jon got brought in. Jon's been on the go for, what is it, 21 hours straight?" He looked toward the red-haired man, who nodded without speaking. Natalie opened her mouth to ask why the increased security meant that this particular law enforcement officer needed to be involved, but Marcus continued before she could ask. "So then we were instructed to ask you to send us to the Sioux Lookout portal since I understand you can handle that distance. But the LEO who was going to meet us there has had some kind of family emergency. Now they're sending a replacement, but we need to wait for his signal that he's there."

Natalie's heart sank as she thought about the inevitable delay. "You need three of you? Even at this point?"

"Two," Marcus clarified. "Jon can't travel to Sioux Lookout and back; he's about to fall over. So we need to wait for the other LEO to get there. That's the rules. Except in extraordinary circumstances, whenever coercive magic is used, there has to be at least two LEOs, who have to file separate reports. God help us if our facts don't match."

"Ah."

"Speaking of which, do you mind if we release it? We're supposed to use it as minimally as possible."

Natalie glanced at the other officer, who still hadn't spoken. His look of drawn exhaustion added years to what should have been a young face. Given that he was still standing with the exact same posture as the prisoner, it was clear who was operating the coercive magic. She noticed that one of his hands was covered with a black leather glove, though the other was bare. A prosthetic, maybe?

She nodded. Jon sighed with relief and made a slight gesture with an unusual-looking octagonal coin held in his hand. Immediately the prisoner staggered a little and then started swearing in a loud and very angry tone.

"Keep it down, please," Natalie told him sternly. "I have neighbours, you know." She raised an eyebrow at Marcus, whose jaw tightened.

Marcus spun around in a circle, gesturing with something he held in his hand, and suddenly Natalie could feel an oppressive pressure in the air, although it faded to a less uncomfortable level quickly.

"Nobody will be able to hear anything now," he told her.

"I could barely breathe, you fu—" The prisoner's words cut off, and Natalie saw that Jon had raised his strange-looking coin, which had blurred and turned into a deep green stone. With his gloved hand, he pulled a small business card from his pocket. Peter, who was staring at the stone with obvious trepidation, took a step backward in shock when the card turned into a pair of handcuffs.

"That's your own fault, mate," Jon retorted, a strong British accent evident. Peter began to struggle as Jon pulled his arms behind his back and secured both wrists. Natalie sensed a surge of magic as he did so, making it evident that the officer was using both physical and magical effort to ensure the prisoner's co-operation.

"If you weren't trying so hard to resist arrest, it wouldn't've been so hard. Waste of time anyway. We're LEO." Peter didn't speak, just sucked in a deep breath and glared at Jon. Marcus stepped closer, frowning menacingly at the prisoner.

"Can you place a block?" Marcus said in a low voice to Jon, who sighed. "Sorry, man, I've never been able to do that one."

Jon raised his green stone and moved it around in a pattern that caused Natalie to briefly feel a wave of nausea and a hint of a headache. The symptoms faded quickly, but she recognized another magical tool restricted to police use only, which prevented the target from being able to perform any magic. Though she had never experienced it personally, she had been told that it could cause a migraine-like headache if used for too long, particularly if the person so bespelled was trying to do magic in spite of it. She had not previously known that some constables were not able to perform this spell and was surprised that an officer could be sworn in without that ability. Still, she was aware that LEO was understaffed.

Though the prisoner looked surly, he did not appear to be aware of what had just happened.

Jon looked around for a chair and sank down into one, rubbing his forehead, though he didn't take his eyes off the prisoner either. He did not look nearly as much like a stereotypical police officer. He was tall and fairly thin, but there was an impression of whipcord strength in the long-fingered hand that rested on the arm of the chair. Though he was obviously exhausted, there was nonetheless a slight tension to his body that suggested he would be capable of springing into action very fast, should it become necessary.

"You can drop the illusion now, mate," Jon said, looking at Marcus.

"Oh yeah," Marcus answered. He raised his stone again and frowned at Peter. As he moved it around in a noticeably different pattern from that which Jon had used, Natalie recognized that he was using the crystal to help with removing an illusion.

Immediately, Peter's face appeared to melt. His tightly curled black hair straightened and turned a dull sandy brown as his poor complexion improved and his face lengthened. At the same time, his suit turned a dull orange colour and was revealed as a one-piece coverall with a seven-digit number blazoned across his upper chest.

"What's up with this LEO thing? Is it some kind of code? And where the hell are we?" Peter asked belligerently. It sounded to Natalie as though he were trying to cover his obvious nervousness with bravado. He appeared to be unaware of his changed appearance, though he stared warily at the small prism Marcus was holding. Peter took a few steps back, away from the large, grim-faced man, turning his head to look behind him along the hallway that led to Natalie's bathroom and bedroom. Natalie thought it looked as though he were going to try to run if he got an opportunity. Marcus evidently came to the same conclusion.

"Freeze!" he ordered. "Do not move, or I will ensure you can't."

"What the fuck does that mean?" Peter snarled. He ignored the instruction and took a few more steps away from the officer.

Marcus moved his prism around in another pattern that Natalie recognized, and suddenly Peter froze. She was intrigued to realize that his head still appeared capable of movement; it was only from the neck down that he was immobilized. His face began to turn red as he presumably attempted to break free of the spell, without success.

"It means you stay put voluntarily, or you stay put because I make you," Marcus answered the question, although it was already obvious at that point.

"LEO stands for law enforcement officer," Natalie answered Peter's earlier question, frowning as she glanced at the clock on the stove. "Our kind of cop."

"*Our* kind? And who are you?"

"Think of me as a taxi service."

"Who the hell *are* you people? I was asleep in a jail cell, like, five seconds ago. What the fuck is going on?"

Natalie looked at Marcus, puzzled by the prisoner's evident confusion.

"You're being transferred to the magical justice system," Marcus explained in a clipped tone. "You were taken from the mundane prison system because they can't handle magically talented criminals."

"That's a load of bull. As soon as they throw that kind of accusation around, you don't get any kind of fair trial. Or bail."

"You'll get a fair trial where you're going," Marcus said. "Whether you like it or not."

"I am *not* a—"

"Don't waste your breath, mate," Jon advised drily. "We're all mages here, and it's perfectly easy to tell when you know how."

"What, all of you?" Peter seemed to be a lot more nervous now, his eyes flicking around between the three of them.

Natalie thought it was odd that he actually sounded like he might believe he wasn't a mage. Sure, you could be uncertain when you were only a few years past puberty and your abilities were just starting to emerge. That was even truer if you were from a non-magical family. But this man was clearly old enough that he couldn't have failed to figure it out. Still, she unfocused her eyes and looked past the side of his head to make sure. To her surprise, the glow that always identified a mage to those who could see it was a murky yellow colour, like nothing she had ever seen before. With a shiver, she remembered having been told that's what coercive magic looked like.

"How long does the yellow tint last?" she asked, trying to conceal her reaction.

"A few days at least," Marcus said. "Sometimes even a few weeks. It depends how long the coercion was held on the person. Illegal coercion is not the kind of thing you get away with. We can only use it in very limited circumstances, for a short time, with plenty of rules and regs."

Natalie tried to shake off her discomfort. At least the measures to control the use of the highly distasteful form of magic made sense. "It's a pity it's not visible on the person who did the coercing," she commented. At Marcus's puzzled look, she clarified. "You said you can't get away with it. But, in fact, the person who set the coercive magic might get away with it if you can't figure out who that was. You can tell this guy was coerced, but not by whom."

"True, but—" Marcus's counterargument was interrupted by Jon.

"Bloody hell, that was quick," Jon muttered, gesturing toward the TV in explanation when the others looked at him in silent question. A red banner reading Breaking News was passing across the bottom of the screen. The scene switched from a newsroom to a view of a reporter standing in front of an institutional-looking brick building with wire crisscrossed over the windows, all of them closed except for the small ventilation openings at the top.

Natalie picked up the remote and turned the volume up to audible levels.

"David Rogers reporting live from the Don Jail, where another escape took place early this morning," the reporter said with a grim face. "The missing man was being held on remand. He was present in the cell at lock-up yesterday evening but was gone this morning before roll call. His cellmate, who was asleep in the bunk above him, saw and heard nothing."

"Death penalty for mages!" was heard yelled in the background. The camera angle widened to show a group of protesters waving signs behind a metal barrier.

"Animosity continues to rise against the magical community in light of the persistent trickle of jailbreaks and crimes that can only have been committed by non-natural means," the reporter continued. "The escapee, Peter Lassiter, was scheduled to attend a prehearing this morning at City Hall."

A mug shot of the missing prisoner appeared on the screen, easily identifiable as the man now standing in Natalie's living room. Natalie nervously glanced toward her balcony, which faced another high-rise condo tower that was the twin to her own. Though the two towers were a few hundred feet apart, binoculars or a telescope could potentially make the distance insignificant, and her blinds were open. She made a gesture in the direction of the blinds, and the vertical panels rotated to block any view from the other tower. She noticed that Jon raised an eyebrow at her action, but he didn't say anything.

Marcus sighed. "We've got to stop doing this. The Council needs to realize it's causing a huge problem."

"Stop doing what?"

"Transferring criminals from their system to ours without telling them."

"What? What would happen to people like me and Ms. Benson if they knew about us and what we can do?" Jon objected.

"No offence, pal, but you First Circles make up less than 1 percent of mages. This is screwing things up for all of us. We've hidden you guys for centuries. I'm not saying we should tell them what you can do."

"What can you do?" Natalie put in, reminded that she had been wondering why Jon had needed to be brought in to help. She glanced toward Peter, who was still standing to one side of the living room. He was looking back and forth between the three of them as they talked, appearing as though he wished he were anywhere but here.

"Jon's a metamorph," Marcus answered for him. "First Circle, like you." He shuddered. "I totally get why nons would be terrified if they knew about people like him. He scares the hell out of me, and I'm a mage myself."

Natalie's mouth fell open as she thought about what that could mean. "So, can you turn into an animal?" she asked Jon.

"I can turn into anything I can visualize. And I've got a vivid imagination." He grinned.

"What about size?"

"Doesn't matter. I can literally be a fly on the wall. Except that would be pretty dangerous. Flies have lots of predators."

"So, do you become a jail guard for these things?"

Jon shook his head. "I'd be caught on camera that way. Too many problems. I become smoke for the jailbreaks. When I take a non-corporeal form, I can turn someone else into it with me."

"Wait, what?! You turned me into *smoke?*" Peter's voice came out in a strangled squeak as his eyes looked like he was attempting to check his lower body. His inability to move anything other than his head limited what he could see. Natalie's mouth had dropped open as she also contemplated being turned into smoke.

"You've still got all your parts, mate," Jon told him, smirking a little.

"That is terrifying." Natalie realized this was why Marcus had identified Jon as a First Circle. That was the name given to those few mages who had one particular magical skill that was significantly more powerful than what most mages could do. There was plenty of variation in skill levels, both due to practice and simply natural talent, but First Circles were in a class by themselves and were very rare. It was bad enough being a mage in a world that hated mages, but she was a minority within a minority. Prior to today, she had only met one other First Circle, a woman whom she thoroughly disliked.

"So is being able to transport people instantaneously over great distances. Imagine if the military got hold of you."

"Um, no thanks."

"The point is, what about the rest of us?" Marcus said. "Did you hear about that gang-rape case a year or so ago?"

"Uh, no." It was Jon who answered, though Natalie grimaced, knowing the story Marcus was referring to.

"I guess it didn't make the British news. It was somewhere in upper New York State. A 21-year-old woman was seen doing something magical, and four guys jumped in and beat her nearly to death. Then they gang-raped her while she was barely conscious. The police dragged their heels and did as little as possible. They finally arrested one of the attackers, but he got off on a technicality. Tell me that would have happened if the victim wasn't a mage. And she's not the only one, either."

"Nons have always hated mages," Jon pointed out, though he looked a bit sickened by the story.

"I don't think it's been this bad since the Salem witch hunts." Marcus checked his phone as he spoke, frowning and jiggling his foot impatiently.

Natalie assumed that he had not yet received the hoped-for communication from the officer scheduled to meet him at Sioux Lookout.

"And you think this is all due to the prisoner transfers?" Though Jon was arguing the point, Natalie thought his tone sounded strangely neutral, as though he was not really disagreeing with his colleague but was simply curious to understand his reasoning.

"Well, maybe there's other reasons, but I'm betting that's the big one. We've been doing this for nearly 25 years now, and the hate has been getting worse every year."

"It's a Council decision."

"Hey, I follow orders, but I don't have to like them. Look at those protesters." Marcus indicated the TV. The screen had switched back to the newsroom, but there was still a picture of the crowd of protesters in one corner. "It's not just a few nut jobs anymore. Public opinion is seriously swinging toward bringing the death penalty back. We haven't had that problem in centuries."

"That's true here," Jon said in a grim tone, now sounding more engaged in the debate. "But not so much in the Middle East. I've taken people out of facilities over there, and you don't even want to know what those hellholes are like. The antimage attitude isn't about escaping prisoners over there; it's a religious thing. I've made some memory stones."

Marcus shuddered. "I think I'll skip those, thanks. I had to do a ton of those historical stones before I got my badge. Gave me nightmares for months."

Natalie was surprised to hear that the law enforcement officer had been required to experience numerous memory stones before being authorized as a constable, but she approved of the idea. Generally, memory stones were thought of as entertainment, but their value was incalculable in learning history. Reading about situations in a history book or even seeing a movie re-enactment could not compare to experiencing the memory of a person who had been involved. Memory stones permitted the person to experience the memory with all sensations, including feeling the emotions that the creator had felt during the actual events. Being stone, they did not deteriorate over time. She vividly remembered the stone she had experienced many years ago of one of the witch hunts in the seventeenth century. It had been created by someone who had watched a young woman

L. M. Brigant

being dragged from her home by a mob and burned alive. Though the girl was probably barely sixteen, and doubtless the spectators had known her their entire lives, her screams had elicited no sympathy. Experiencing the recorded memories made it clear that the maker had been desperately afraid that the mob's fury would turn on him as well. Guilt as well as terror had permeated the experience. The memory still haunted her dreams sometimes.

Natalie glanced at the clock, trying not to let her impatience show. Luckily, at that moment, Marcus's cellphone chirped.

"Finally!" he exclaimed as he read the text. "Our contact has arrived. We can go now."

Natalie stood up then and drew a deep breath, holding a silver pen on her flat palm. It shimmered and turned into a deep blue jewel-like stone. The stone helped to focus the mental energy required in constructing the complicated spell, just as using a magnifying glass would make it easier to read tiny print. It would be possible to do this or any other magic without a focus object. But using one required less effort. Frowning slightly, Natalie moved the prism in a complicated memorized pattern.

A shimmering white shape began to take form in the centre of the room, its edges becoming firmer in moments. It resembled an archway, but instead of wood or stone, its edges were pulsing, glowing strands of twisted light.

"That's the brightest one I've ever seen," Jon murmured. "I reckon I'm lucky I don't have to make up excuses why I'm exhausted after I do my bit."

"Okay, let's go," Marcus said as he waved his prism, releasing the immobilization spell, and immediately grabbed the prisoner's arm in an iron grip. Peter began to struggle violently, trying to back away from the brightly glowing arch.

"Jon?" Marcus said.

Jon raised his green focus stone. Moments later, Peter's resistance evaporated, and his arm, which had moved up to mimic Jon's position, mirrored Jon's action as he slipped the stone back into his pocket.

"You go through first," Jon suggested, "then I'll send him through with the coercion on him. You're on your own at the other end. Bear in mind the block will be gone too when I'm not right there."

With a nod to Natalie, Marcus stepped through the arch and disappeared. Jon moved toward the glowing arch, moving in exact synchrony with the prisoner. But then he stopped short while Lassiter stepped through like an automaton. Natalie shuddered as she thought about that sort of total control. She collapsed her gateway as she saw Lassiter stagger slightly on the other side.

"Right. Well, I have to get to the office," she said to Jon. "Are you staying at a hotel?"

"I would imagine they've booked me one. Hang on," he said, scrolling through e-mails on his phone. "Ah, here. Marriott Eaton Centre?"

"That's not too far from my office. We can share a cab if you want."

"Brilliant, thanks."

Natalie picked up the remote to turn off the TV but stopped as her attention was caught by the reporter who had begun a new segment. This time it was a woman in the studio reporting, and the small picture in the upper corner of the screen showed a small wooden log house engulfed in flames.

"A fire at a cottage in Muskoka has claimed two lives in the early hours of this morning," the reporter said. "The local fire department believes the blaze may have been caused by a poorly maintained chimney which had not been cleaned in several years. The fire marshal is investigating. Two men perished in the fire."

The inset picture changed to photographs of two people as the reporter continued. "Thomas Makowski, 28, of New York was visiting friends in Muskoka. The other victim was 29-year-old Christopher Narcourt of Moose Jaw, Saskatchewan. Several other young men were able to escape the blaze with minor burns. Nobody was acquainted with Mr. Narcourt, who was not part of their group. It is speculated that he may have seen the fire and attempted to assist before becoming a victim of the flames.

"Efforts to reach Mr. Narcourt's family were unsuccessful. However, enquiries made of the Moose Jaw Police Service revealed that Mr. Narcourt had been reported as a missing person just over two years ago, and no reports had ever been received that his whereabouts had been ascertained."

"That guy's name seems familiar," Natalie commented, a frown marring her forehead as she tried to remember the thought the name had triggered.

"Who, the bloke nobody knew?" Jon asked.

"No, actually, the other one. Makowski." She picked up her phone from the kitchen countertop and tapped the name Thomas Makowski into the search box. The first several hits referenced the fire, but the fourth one was different.

"Oh my God," she said as she read the summary part of the fourth hit. "He was one of those gang rapists that Marcus was just talking about, the one who got off on a technicality. What are the odds?"

"I thought that other name rang a bell, but I can't think why," Jon mentioned.

"Well, horrible though it is, I've got to hurry." Natalie switched off the TV and used her Uber app to summon a cab.

Given Jon's evident exhaustion, Natalie decided to drop him off first and then go to her office. When he got out of the cab with a wave, she noticed that a folded section of a newspaper was sitting on the car seat, although she was unsure whether he had brought it or if it had been left by a previous passenger. The last paragraph of the article she had read earlier was at the top, just under the fold. Her stomach felt queasy as she reread the ominous final words:

> The Ontario College of Legalists, the governing body of lawyers and paralegals in the province, will be conducting a full-scale investigation.

Turning on her phone again, she reread Raj's text: *Disaster alert. JB's gonna freak.*

It was going to be a long day.

Chapter 2

Mikyla Burton's entire body jerked spasmodically as the alarm clock made an unmusical squawk when turning itself on. Deep in a dream, she was *not* ready to wake up. What kind of sadistic person had decided that school should start at 8:00 a.m.?

As her mind swam sluggishly up from unconsciousness, Mikyla realized that she wasn't hearing music like she would have expected. Instead, she was hearing the measured tones of a newscaster. Mikyla grumbled aloud to herself. The stupid clock radio was probably running slow again if they were already doing the news segment, which meant she couldn't even take the time to try to pry her eyelids apart slowly.

Like most of her possessions, Mikyla's alarm clock had come from a second-hand store, so it had seen better days. If it had lost time at a reasonably even pace, she could have made a habit of resetting the time once every few days, but instead it would go slow at random and totally unpredictable intervals. She pulled the old cellphone her friend had given her from off the cardboard box that served as her bedside table and squinted at the cracked display as she fumbled with the power button. Too bad she couldn't use that for her alarm, but it no longer made any sounds except through earbuds, and she couldn't sleep with those in her ears. Though she didn't have money for mobile phone service, it worked for telling the time and playing music. Since there was Wi-Fi most places these days, she could get e-mail, use Messenger, and surf the Web almost as much as if she had a data plan. It was only one corner of the screen that had a spiderweb of cracks; she could still see most of the display.

"Shi-i-it!" she mumbled to herself as her bleary-eyed gaze registered on the numbers informing her that it was already 7:05. If she didn't catch the streetcar at 7:20, she wouldn't make it to school on time.

As she rolled off the mattress that was her primary piece of bedroom furniture, Mikyla staggered to her feet, still trying to get her eyelids to remember how to open up all the way. She pushed her long brown hair out of her eyes and glanced toward the dirty window, wondering if the rain from last night had let up. The old cotton sheet that served as her curtain fluttered in the draft from the poorly fitting window. That window opened onto a narrow alleyway, so the chances of seeing enough to figure out the weather weren't that good anyway.

Thick layers of off-white paint all but obscured what had once been detailed moulding on the frame, though it was more visible where the paint had chipped off. The adjacent walls were riddled with cracks where she hadn't covered them up with pictures torn from old magazines. Some of them were of boy bands or even Disney movies she had long since outgrown, but looking at them was better than seeing the leprous colour of the walls, which looked as though a chain smoker had inhabited this room for fifty years, turning walls and ceiling the same dull greyish-yellow colour.

Mikyla started reaching for the clothes she had dropped on the floor last night, but she froze as the words the news reader was saying penetrated the sleep fog.

"… another jailbreak that took place early this morning. Peter Lassiter, being held on remand at the Don Jail on charges of assault and possession of child pornography, was present at roll call yesterday evening but was gone when officers opened the cell doors this morning."

Mikyla was suddenly wide awake. Peter Lassiter was the name of her mom's latest ex-boyfriend, and the assault that had led to the charge mentioned by the news reader had put Tina Burton in the hospital for nearly three weeks. Mikyla herself had sustained a black eye and a badly strained wrist trying to avoid getting caught in the altercation.

Her two younger brothers had been put into temporary foster care while Tina was out of commission. After one night in another foster home, different from the one her brothers were placed in, Mikyla had evaded Children's Aid and stayed at the apartment by herself, coming home only late at night in case the authorities had continued to look for her. Being in foster care was something she had hoped never to experience, and her first night in a foster home had confirmed her opinion. The foster parents' son had clearly believed any fosterling owed him something in exchange for the privilege of staying in his house. He made it clear what compensation he expected from a female. Only the fact that he had suddenly developed a migraine headache had enabled Mikyla to escape his attention. Besides, at 16, she was perfectly capable of looking after herself, as long as she had a place to sleep.

And now Pete was back out? He was probably mad as hell at anyone he considered responsible for putting him behind bars in the first place. Mikyla didn't know whether he would know who had called the cops that day, but it would have been obvious it wasn't her mother.

Mikyla's heart-shaped face was pale from the startling information, and her eyes, wide with shock, dominated her face. She hadn't known anything about child porn charges, but she wasn't particularly surprised. Her mother was scraping the bottom of the barrel in her choice of boyfriends lately.

"The public is getting increasingly angry at the magical community as the number of unnatural jailbreaks grows," the reporter continued. "There is no way this escape could have happened without magic. Lassiter's cellmate, asleep in the bunk above him, had not been awakened. No explanation has been found for the man's disappearance from a securely locked cell. The lock was not damaged. Footage from a security camera trained on the corridor immediately adjacent to the cell showed nothing."

"No freakin' way!" Mikyla muttered to herself, a cold sweat breaking out on her forehead. A pissed-off ex was bad enough, but a mage? How was that even possible? He had seemed like every other lowlife creep Tina had ever brought home. If he was a mage, that would be way scarier.

Her stomach was roiling too much to want to eat any breakfast, even if she had had time. Fortunately, she always kept a stash of granola bars in her locker since she was rarely up early enough to eat breakfast. Mikyla hurried to the bathroom and hastily scrubbed her teeth, then made some attempt to drag a brush through her tangled hair. She grabbed her backpack that was sitting by the door and left before her mother got up. Her thoughts were on the child porn charges, and suddenly she wondered whether she or her brothers featured in any of the images that had been found. If that creep was a mage, he might not have needed a camera, and who knows if she might be missing a few memories? Nobody knew what those people could do.

Mikyla slouched low in her seat on the streetcar, earbuds in her ears playing music she didn't hear, still breathing heavily from having to run to the bus stop. Maybe having gotten a window seat this morning hadn't been such a lucky break after all. Sliding into the seat with her mind elsewhere, she had bumped her head on the window frame, not hard, but enough to feel her still-fading black eye throb. The discomfort triggered the memory that had played through her head like a bad movie many times over the past three weeks.

Her mom had been fighting with her boyfriend again. They were both shouting and swearing at each other. It was a near-daily occurrence, and Mikyla had initially just tried to ignore them. Usually she stayed in her room as much as possible. She wished she'd done the same this time. She didn't even know what had triggered his incoherent rage. Considering he was drunk whenever he wasn't high, irrational rage was not unusual. Mikyla had attempted to get out of the way when Pete had started hitting her mother. Tina was knocked over from the force of a punch. Pete had moved forward to hit her again, just as Mikyla tried to go in the same direction. After being backhanded into a corner, hitting the side of her head on the rickety coffee table in the process, Mikyla had crept away as quickly and quietly as she could.

He was between her and the front door, so there was no way she was going to be able to get out without him noticing. The living room was crowded with mismatched furniture, mostly obtained from Goodwill or, in the case of the stained couch, left in the apartment by the previous tenant. If it hadn't been for the frayed edge of the rug that she had tripped on,

Mikyla probably wouldn't have hit her head on the coffee table. That was likely what had given her the black eye.

Most of Pete's attention was on Tina, and he was yelling too loud to hear Mikyla's slightly unsteady progress anyway. Her heart was hammering so loud that it seemed like everyone should be able to hear it. She snuck a glance in his direction as she stealthily picked up the cordless phone from the floor, where it had fallen when she knocked the coffee table over. Tucking it into the sleeve of her hoodie, she darted toward the bathroom.

Mikyla's 6-year-old brother Ben was crouched in the doorway of the boys' bedroom, whimpering, his lower lip trembling with fear. Mikyla grabbed his arm and pushed him ahead of her toward the bathroom, jerking her head at Noah, two years older, who scrambled to follow. The bathroom door lock was weak, but it was better than nothing. The boys' bedroom door didn't even latch closed properly. It wasn't the first time they had hidden in the bathroom, though she had never before seen Pete get quite this violent. As quietly as possible, she locked the door from the inside before giving Ben a towel to muffle his cries. She was doing her best to fight the urge to burst into tears herself. No question that if she did, both boys would lose it.

Pulling the phone out of her sleeve, she hastily dialled 9-1-1 and whispered "Police, and ambulance" when the operator asked her which emergency service she needed. Judging by the violence of the punches she had seen so far, if an ambulance wasn't necessary yet, it would be soon. Hastily she had whispered the address and told them Peter was beating up her mother. Ignoring the operator's instructions to stay on the line, she had disconnected the call and hidden the phone in the cabinet behind the cleaning supplies. If Pete finished up with Tina and decided to bust his way in there, no way did she want him finding out she had called the cops on him.

The three had waited, huddled on the chipped edge of the bathtub, for what seemed like an endless amount of time, though it was probably only five or ten minutes, before a loud hammering on the front door was audible throughout the apartment.

"Open up. Police!"

Peter's cursing cut off abruptly for a brief few seconds, but it sounded as if he must have punched Mikyla's mom again, because Tina called out for help, but it turned into a yelp. *First smart thing she's done all day,* Mikyla thought. That was enough to ensure the cops weren't going to stand passively outside the front door, waiting to be invited in. A loud thud from a boot was easily enough to break the cheap lock on the door. Mikyla tensed in alarm as she heard the sound of running feet coming closer, but in the next second she heard a muffled thump and the sounds of a struggle, with two voices yelling at Pete. Pete's swearing was loud enough to drown out most of whatever was going on, but Mikyla breathed a sigh of relief when she started hearing the sound of the police reading Pete his rights in a voice loud enough to be heard over the swearing. His curses didn't stop throughout the recitation. Mikyla closed her eyes and pulled in several deep breaths, trying to reduce the pounding of her heart. Ben's sobs had turned into hiccups while silent tears rolled down his face.

She also heard two other voices, a male voice, deeper than either of the two that she assumed were police officers, and a softer female voice. Both sounded more distant than the cops, who were probably in the hallway just outside the bathroom. Perhaps the other voices belonged to paramedics? They both sounded more soothing than the officer's sharp tones as he recited the Miranda rights that Mikyla had heard many times on TV. Still, she waited a few more minutes, hoping that Pete would be removed from the premises before she and her brothers emerged so that he wouldn't associate her, or the boys, with his arrest.

She only opened the bathroom door once she heard Pete's swearing moving away. Even then, she peeked carefully through the crack to check out the situation before moving out. She saw Pete still struggling violently, in spite of being handcuffed, and in the grip of a police officer significantly taller and bulkier than he was.

She gestured to the boys to stay behind her and waited until Pete and the officer had gone through the front door before she opened the door fully. Her brothers' fear was enough to make them unusually obedient. Ben hung onto her hand like a lifeline.

There was one police officer still in the hallway, who had just been peering into one of the bedrooms as the three kids emerged. Mikyla felt a trickle on the side of her head and reached up to touch it. Her fingers came away bloody. She must have cut it when she hit the coffee table. She hadn't noticed until now.

"Are you kids okay?" the cop asked gruffly. "Is there anyone else in the apartment?"

"Yeah, we're all right," Mikyla answered for the three of them. "Nobody else here but our mom and you guys. Is she hurt bad?" She glanced toward her mother, but it was hard to see much past the pair of bustling paramedics, one a large black man with a shaved head and the other an incongruously small ice-blonde woman. Still, she pulled Ben into her side, hoping to shield him from the sight of their battered mother and maybe spare him any more trauma. There hadn't been any sounds from their mother since the well-timed yell for help. Was she unconscious? What if she was dead? Several ominous scenarios ran through Mikyla's head before the cop responded.

"She's badly hurt, but she'll be okay. She's your mother, you said?"

Mikyla nodded.

"I'll need her name, please, and an adult next of kin?"

The paramedics had carried Tina out by the time the police officer had finished making notes of Mikyla's answers, but the blonde EMS woman had returned.

"You need some patching up yourself," she told Mikyla as she came up to her and gently turned her head to look at the cut. She cleaned away the trickling blood from Mikyla's forehead with gentle hands. Mikyla thought she felt an odd tingling sensation at the same time, but ignored it. The woman stuck a bandage over the swelling cut, telling Mikyla it wouldn't need stitches. Then she asked Mikyla to tell her how many fingers she was holding up, tell her the date and time and recite her address, and then asked her if she felt dizzy or sick at all. Satisfied with her answers, the ambulance attendant told her she should call 9-1-1 if she started feeling nauseous, in case she had a concussion.

Mikyla had no intention of doing that, already calculating how she could evade being delivered into the hands of Children's Aid. The paramedic looked a bit unfocused for a second, but then she pulled a small card out of her pocket, along with a pen. The card was printed with "What to Do in an Emergency" instructions with the emblem of Toronto EMS on the front. She scribbled a phone number on the back, and handed it to Mikyla. "I'm Suzanne. You call me if you need any help, okay? Whatever you need." She seemed unusually insistent, and Mikyla thought it was strange that a paramedic would give her what looked like a personal cell number, as well as reminding her to call 9-1-1 if she needed it, but she nodded and took the card.

"You kids will need to come with me," the police officer said. "We'll follow you to the hospital and have CAS meet us there," he added, addressing the paramedic, who nodded. Mikyla's heart had sunk as she realized her hopes of avoiding the foster care system were dwindling.

Now, nearly a month later, she was remembering the paramedic's intense look, and she noticed that the card was poking out of the torn pocket of the backpack on her lap. It seemed dumb to consider calling a paramedic for advice, but she wasn't at all confident that Tina wouldn't let Pete back into the apartment, even assuming she was given a choice in the matter. And if that happened, she'd probably need a funeral director, not a paramedic.

She wished she'd thought to leave her mom a note in case she wouldn't end up listening to the news.

Chapter 3

Natalie was walking toward her office, reading e-mails on her phone, when she heard a familiar voice behind her.

"You don't *look* much like James, but give it 20 years. You are two peas in a pod."

Natalie spun around and her mouth fell open as she registered Rajit's words.

"What?! I am nothing like James Behrman!"

Raj grinned at her mockingly. Though five years older than Natalie, he was technically junior to her in the firm since he had worked in the insurance industry for several years before obtaining his law degree. A wiry man, he rarely sat, seemingly possessed of endless energy. He had been one of the first in the office to get rid of his ordinary desk and move in a standing desk, a trend that had started to get popular.

Raj was of Indian ancestry, with deep brown skin and black eyes, but spoke with barely a hint of an accent, having lived in Canada since he was an infant. The two of them reported to the same partner in the department that dealt mostly with fraud lawsuits.

"Could've fooled me," Raj said.

"How am I like James, then?"

"You panic. And worse, you immediately assume everything is all your fault and your whole world is going to come crashing down around your ears."

Natalie's eyes narrowed. She didn't want to acknowledge how accurate Raj's assessment was. "James doesn't tend to assume it's his fault," she pointed out. "And anyway, this is evident how?"

Raj laughed aloud. "I know you, Natalie. And I've never seen you with your shirt hanging out before. Or without makeup."

A flush crept into Natalie's cheeks as she reached for her waistband and found that her blouse was half untucked.

"Says the guy who sent me a text at 6:30 in the morning that said 'disaster alert,'" she growled. Turning into her office, she put down her laptop bag, purse and coffee cup and rapidly straightened her skirt and tucked her blouse in properly.

"It doesn't hurt to be prepared, knowing what James is like. But it's not the end of the world."

"Did you read the same article I did?" Natalie tried to keep her face expressionless, though she was remembering how she had felt seeing the firm's name in the first line of the article.

"Of course, and I agree James is gonna want answers, fast," Raj said.

"The whole management committee will," Natalie retorted, "but clearly this is aimed straight at our department, with the Anton Pillers and fraud cases. Especially if there's going to be an investigation."

"Let's wait until we actually get a notice from the College of Legalists before we worry about an official investigation, shall we? Right now, it's just a reporter who is incredibly good at taking a few isolated facts and presenting them in a way that implies a lot of stuff that he can't back up."

Natalie paused in the action of bringing her coffee cup to her mouth, realizing that the cup was already cold. In the face of Rajit's air of unconcern, her fears were starting to seem excessive. But then her eyes narrowed as she remembered the points made in the article. Raj was using his courtroom argument skills to persuade her, and she was accustomed to using those skills herself. Putting on an air of absolute confidence was vital to making an effective argument before a judge.

"You're manipulating me," she accused him.

Raj grinned. "Yep," he acknowledged without remorse. "But admit it, you're calming down and thinking more constructively now."

Natalie grumbled under her breath, then picked up her silver pen, held it near her coffee cup and twirled it in a motion that looked like she was just fidgeting. She brought the now steaming beverage back to her lips, sighing as the hot liquid relaxed neck muscles that had gone unusually tense.

"At least we can be thankful the *Sun* isn't one of the more popular newspapers in the business community," Natalie admitted as she sipped her coffee, trying to keep her stress in check.

"You don't check your Twitter feed, do you? It's trending. That's how I came across it."

"What? I thought you were going to tell me why I shouldn't be panicking!" Natalie felt her heart rate speed up.

"Well, not this accusation specifically. It's the whole hashtag jailbreak thing that's trending, so since there was an escape this morning from a local jail, this article is getting more attention. Did you hear about the escape?"

Natalie gave him a dirty look. "I'm not completely clueless. I saw it on TV this morning. I don't know how you have time for social media."

"I hardly ever watch TV." Raj shrugged. "I'm sure someone will bring it to James' attention if he didn't come across it himself. He's going to get hauled in by the management committee within the hour."

"We need to have something for him before that happens," Natalie agreed, glancing up as one of the first-year associates strode briskly past her office door. "You know how he is if he goes off the deep end."

"At your service, madam." Raj flourished a piece of paper at her.

"And that is …?"

"Each of the actual statistics quoted in this article."

Natalie's eyebrows rose as she looked at the fairly short list.

"There are three names in that article. I checked them. They're right. We did do Anton Pillers involving two of those people, though one of them was two and a half years ago," Raj explained. "The third one was not an Anton Piller though, and it's completely ridiculous. I looked up the guy's name. The firm acted on a real estate transaction four years ago. We were acting for the vendor. This guy was the purchaser. Last year, he was charged with something to do with getting private financial information off one of those ATMs you see in bars and making fake bank cards. Us handling the house purchase has absolutely nothing to do with his criminal activities. And he wasn't even our client."

"You're kidding me! That's really reaching." A phone rang shrilly, somewhere among the assistants' desks. Natalie looked toward her desk clock with a frown. Though she was rarely here so early, she was fairly sure phones wouldn't usually be ringing at 7:30 a.m. The thought reminded her of the to-do list she had been mentally compiling before her morning visitors had arrived. Clearly her day was going to go all to hell and it had barely started. She pulled her mind back to the problem. Raj had been right, though she didn't want to admit it. When she started panicking, she was less focused, and then she would get nothing done.

"It's all like that," Raj said. "Look at this." He pointed to the first item on the sheet of paper. "It says there have been 773 fugitives in the past year. That's for all of Canada, not just Toronto. Then it later says that 41 percent of those remain at large." He raised an eyebrow as he quoted the latter statistic.

"Huh, which means that 59 percent of them got caught again," Natalie said with a disgusted snort, picking up on what Raj was implying with his reference to 41 percent. "So if the escapes are because of magic, how come they're getting caught again? More than half of them?"

"To be fair, it does talk about some escapes happening at night, with nothing caught on security cameras," Raj said thoughtfully. "Those sound like they'd be magically aided."

"Yeah, maybe," Natalie agreed. "But then it's not saying how many of the escapes are taking place at night, when the cells are locked, just that some of them are." She drummed her fingers on the desk and forced herself to stop the nervous gesture as she heard her nails clicking against the wood.

"Exactly. It just implies it's all or a majority of them, but for all we know, it could be a bare handful. Stirring the pot sells newspapers. And here's another totally vague one: 'several' of the recent escapees were in for fraud. Then 'many' of those have civil lawsuits," he added. "Not all of them. How many of our fraud cases involve convicts, anyway?"

"Probably not that many. We don't do criminal law here; they got that part right. What were you saying about all of Canada?"

Natalie turned to her computer and rapidly called up the article, skimming through its contents again.

"The article quotes the total number of missing fugitives in all of Canada, but then it's alleging that we have some connection to recent escapes in the Toronto area," Raj clarified. "But this whole jailbreak thing is everywhere. Not even just Canada. I read somewhere that the numbers are way higher in the States. So how are we implicated with numbers in Toronto, when this is an international situation?"

Natalie opened a second browser window, paused with her fingers poised over the keys for a moment, and then typed a phrase in the search engine. "Here's something about jailbreaks generally, rather than specific ones," she said after she had read the summary parts on several hits that did not look like what she was looking for. "It says here, 'Why don't we hear about more of these when they happen? Because most of them aren't predawn jailbreaks with no natural explanation. Dramatic, Hollywood-style escapes are rare. Often, it's a person serving a suspended sentence who goes AWOL, or an inmate at a minimum-security facility, many of which are overcrowded and understaffed, who slips away without being noticed.'" She had a suspicion that a mage was involved in writing this Web site. It carefully did not say anything about magic, but it clearly went against the growing trend of assuming mages were behind all the prison escapes.

"Isn't a suspended sentence when you just get probation? You don't actually have to go to jail," Raj said.

"Yeah, I think so, unless you reoffend or something. It's been a long time since I took criminal procedure in law school."

"So those numbers aren't just jailbreaks, then; they also include people who missed an appointment with their probation officer?" Raj's tone was clearly irritated. "That puts a whole different slant on it, too. Missing an appointment is a whole lot less significant, at least in my mind, than busting out of jail."

"I don't think too many people would disagree with you," Natalie agreed. "And maybe that's why they're able to get so many of them again. They just show up for their next appointment with an excuse for the missed one. That doesn't require an accomplice, magical or otherwise." She began to entertain the hope that they could turn this around quickly and make the damning article a brief blip, quickly submerged in the media's constant search for the next big story. "So when it says that 26 percent of the escapes are from the Toronto area, it's implying that that's 26 percent of 773, which is about 200 people. But if that 773 number includes all of Canada and includes people on probation, those aren't escapes. The real numbers might be hardly anything."

"It would still be extremely easy for this to get blown all out of proportion," Raj admitted. "Any scapegoat will do. You know what the general public attitude is toward mages. What if we do have one here? Or more than one? And how many clients might just transfer their files elsewhere on the basis of this article alone? It's not like we can complain about that. They're entitled to retain whatever lawyers they want."

"Still not doing a great job of persuading me not to panic," Natalie said drily, dropping the volume of her voice as several administrative assistants passed her office door. "You're exactly right about a scapegoat, though. It's much easier to blame the scary mages than to actually do some digging and figure out what's really going on."

She frowned at the computer screen for a minute and then added thoughtfully, "I've got another question: What's our motive? How does this firm benefit if our opponents have help getting out of jail, presumably to continue committing the crimes that our clients got stiffed by in the first place?"

"Now that's a really good point, and definitely one we should make in a media release. Which we ought to get out as soon as possible." Raj frowned at the ceiling as he thought out loud. "We should get something up on our Web site too, right away, right on the home page, so that if people read this and start looking stuff up on the Web, our response is one of the most relevant hits—including the hashtag."

"You should be in PR." Natalie chuckled, jotting down a note about his suggestion.

"Crap. Actually, I just thought of an answer to that motive question, not that I like it. Presumably if the people stiffing our clients are getting out of jail and can keep stiffing our clients, that means we get more business."

Natalie thought about that with a grimace. "That's disgusting. Wait a second—no, you're wrong. Our clients aren't going to issue another fidelity bond to someone who was caught committing a crime before."

"Oh yeah, that's true. But then sometimes we subpoena that person at trial, or the evidence from their criminal case. If they've gone missing, our civil case potentially drags out longer, which a really suspicious person could argue means more revenue for us. And it would definitely make a College of Legalists investigation more likely."

"Ugh. You could have a point. And again, it's the kind of accusation that would be really hard to defend." Natalie was silent for a while as she thought things through, tapping her pen against her lips.

Just then the phone on her desk rang shrilly. "Right on time." She sighed. The caller ID identified James Behrman's assistant. "At least we've got enough to stop an impending heart attack."

"Let's hope."

Natalie took one look at James Behrman's pale face, which he was blotting with a handkerchief that was already damp, and inwardly cringed. When he wasn't blotting his forehead, he was twisting the handkerchief in his hands and muttering to himself.

The department's senior partner was a perpetual worrier. Actually, Natalie was fairly sure his stress level was an actual anxiety disorder, but she was aware that he had a fear of doctors, among other things, so if there was anything medical science could do to help, he was too scared to find out. While the nature of the group's work often dictated sudden priority changes and rush court filings, a significant part of Natalie and Raj's interactions with James Behrman involved calming him down and assuring him that they had matters under control.

Though he was not yet 50, the small amount of hair James still had, had been grey for as long as Natalie had known him and was liberally sprinkled with white now. He was overweight, likely due to a habit of nervous eating. Natalie suspected he drank quite a lot, too.

She had been considering a comforting approach, but sometimes James needed more of a jolt to shock him out of panic mode. She needed to hide her own concerns about the impact of the newspaper article and put on an act of assured self-confidence. In spite of the fact that she had to do just that when arguing in court, somehow it was always far more difficult when dealing with her boss, particularly when she was in sympathy with his fears.

Closing the door behind her, she saw that James had a hard copy of the newspaper on his wide mahogany desk. He was looking between the newspaper and his floor-to-ceiling windows as though contemplating whether to jump.

"This is bad. This is really bad," James said before either of them could speak. "Clients are going to start transferring their files if they think there are mages here."

Raj frowned and spoke before Natalie could do so. "James, these allegations are ridiculously vague, with hardly any actual facts to back them up. The idea that we have acted on the opposite side of a handful of matters where someone is wanted by the police or has escaped doesn't prove we've got someone here helping people evade justice."

"You don't get it, Rajit." James sighed. "It doesn't matter if we've got someone helping people escape from jail. It matters if we've got a mage here. No matter how unfair that might be, people hate mages," he replied. "Worse than they hate lawyers," he added, a ghost of a smile crossing his face but quickly disappearing. "If clients start transferring their files, or not opening new ones, we stop having any work. We have to start laying people off. We'll probably start having problems collecting outstanding invoices from those who have taken their work elsewhere. We could go bankrupt!"

Natalie was pleasantly surprised to hear the senior partner suggesting that the antimage prejudice was unfair, but she hoped that jumping from a damaging single newspaper article to speculating that the firm was going to go bankrupt was a bit of a leap.

"You make a good point, James, but one of the things we ought to do, as soon as possible, is get information out there, perhaps on our Web site or in a press release, pointing out the circumstantial and inaccurate aspects of this newspaper article. It's full of implications that aren't supported by the facts. Totally misleading. If we acted on a civil lawsuit involving someone who escaped and got caught again, or even someone who was never arrested in the first place, that does nothing whatsoever to tie us to prison escapes. The public attitude against mages is at an all-time high, and this reporter is just cashing in on that, any which way."

Natalie pointed out several more of the vague and misleading points in the article that she and Raj had already discussed. "If our response makes it clear this is just an attempt to get on the front page and that the article is full of nonsensical allegations, we manage to squash the suggestion that we've got mages here without actually having to address that."

"Maybe we need to address that," James said heavily.

"How?" Raj asked bluntly. "Nobody knows how to identify mages."

"And you're right when you said that it's unfair." Natalie decided to take a gamble on seeing whether the partner's views on mages were really as open-minded as his comment seemed. "I actually know a few mages, and I've talked to them about why they're secretive. It makes total sense. People are afraid of them and hate them, so if they admitted it, they'd probably lose their jobs at a minimum. Or get lynched."

"You know some?" Raj was startled.

"Yeah. They're perfectly normal people," Natalie replied with a shrug. "They just happen to be able to do a few things that non-mages can't— move things with their minds, and stuff like that."

"So can you tell who's a mage?"

"Even if I could, I wouldn't," Natalie replied flatly. "I wouldn't want to ruin somebody's life because of a completely BS allegation like this. An ethical mage has just as much right to be a lawyer, or an employee of a law firm, as an ethical non-mage. Or, you know, whatever their job is," she added hurriedly, afraid she might be giving herself away.

Raj was still looking surprised at Natalie's revelation, but James' worried frown was now even more pronounced.

"I don't know how we can avoid addressing the mage angle." He sighed. "Phillip is going to be all over that one." He identified the managing partner.

"No doubt," Raj agreed. "But you know, I just figured out another thing that's really reaching." Raj was now frowning at his phone, on which he was evidently rereading the article. "The woman who was involved in that Anton Piller from two and a half years ago? Not only did we provide the evidence that got her arrested in the first place, but also the prison she escaped from is in Niagara. It's ludicrous to suggest that Niagara is in the Toronto area."

"I wonder how many correctional facilities there are in southern Ontario, if you include as far away as Niagara?" Natalie mused. Raj nodded, tapping something into his iPhone. He leaned back against James' credenza as he spoke and jumped as he knocked over one of the numerous family photographs that dotted the polished surface. He hurriedly righted the picture of James' wife, not looking at her pale-faced husband.

"And what percentage of all Canadian jails that is?" he added to Natalie's question, moving aside to lean against the wall, where he was in no danger of knocking anything else over.

"Let's just jot down some angles to take a look at, rather than trying to do this research ourselves," Natalie suggested. "We've got to get a response out fast, and a media consultant probably has a better idea than we do of where to search. So, what percentage of jails in Toronto?" she muttered, opening a notebook she had brought with her. She pulled her silver pen from where she had tucked it behind one ear and scribbled down that note. "What's the population of Toronto and southern Ontario versus the whole of Canada?" she added, writing the word *population* followed by a question mark underneath the first note, frowning at the paper as she thought out loud. "I'm sure it's one of the bigger cities, so maybe it's not so out of whack that 26 percent of the escapes are from around here."

"What are you two talking about? Why do we care how many jails there are in Toronto?" James asked in a confused tone. He had been looking back and forth between them as they spoke, his puzzlement evident on his face, but Natalie had been too focused on Raj's point to notice.

Natalie looked up from the notepad. She was accustomed to the way that Raj often tended to be on the exact same wavelength as her, understanding her thoughts barely before she had articulated them. It was disconcerting to realize that James had no idea why she was even thinking about statistics.

"The article indicates that there are more escapes in Toronto than anywhere else in the country," Natalie pointed out, "and goes on to very pointedly imply that the reason they're higher is because it's an inside job in this city. Then they point a finger at us. That's a load of BS. The numbers are higher in Toronto because it's one of the most populous cities in the country. Of course we've got more criminals. Add in the fact that they've included a very large area in their definition of Toronto, and no wonder the numbers look so bad."

James' eyes narrowed and his breathing sped up as a new fear evidently occurred to him. "It's a ruse," he said. "A ploy to get us to go chasing after a mage or mages in our midst and flush them out for them. They don't care if they ruin the firm's reputation or make us close up. They just want to use us to get at them!"

Natalie frowned. Getting James out of panic mode was their goal, but getting him started on a conspiracy theory was probably not useful either. "Could be," she agreed slowly. "But then, even if we do have mages here, that still doesn't prove that this firm, or anyone in it, has anything to do with prison escapes. The only thing we can do, should do, is defend our reputation, make it obvious that this is the same kind of witch hunt that's happened over and over again throughout history. And not limited to mages, either. Innocent people have been made scapegoats in all kinds of situations, probably forever."

"I wonder if these statistics have changed much over the last, say, 10 years?" Raj asked thoughtfully. Natalie nodded and jotted that question down too.

James brightened. "That's a good one," he agreed. "If the escapes have been relatively steady, that also makes it less likely that someone here is an accomplice, particularly if we weren't on the record for any related party."

"I don't suppose there's any way of figuring out how many civil lawsuits involve incarcerated persons?" Natalie murmured, nodding in answer to Raj's question, while she posed another.

"I doubt it," Raj said. "But what about splitting up those numbers into actual prison escapes versus probation, like we talked about? If we could get that information?"

"Probation?" James repeated, clearly baffled again.

Raj explained the thought he and Natalie had come up with, that some of the missing fugitives, particularly those who had been arrested later, might just have been people who missed probation appointments.

James scrutinized the article again. "Forty-one percent remain at large," he muttered after he'd found the part they were talking about. "This *is* BS."

"Exactly," Natalie agreed, relieved to find that James was now more focused on that aspect. "I wonder if we could split up the actual escapes by which kind of jail? I'm sure if people were escaping from maximum security, it would be all over the news."

"There was one," Raj said, frowning at the ceiling as he tried to remember the details. "I'm pretty sure it was that psychiatric facility up north. You know, if someone is found to be not guilty by reason of insanity but they're clearly dangerous? They go to a place like that."

"Oh, I remember that one. It was a few years ago, wasn't it? He'd murdered the president of a Montreal newspaper, I think," Natalie said.

"Yeah, but he kept insisting throughout the whole trial that he had no memory of anything. I think some witnesses, family or friends, reported that he had completely disappeared for a few years right before it happened, too, and there turned out to be records from various mental hospitals in the States where he'd been admitted."

Natalie pursed her lips. Raj's reference to the man's disappearance for several years had reminded her of the news story from this morning, about the victim from the fire who had been missing for two years prior. It dawned on her that both of them might have been arrested by LEO, which would explain why no non-mage knew where they were. Her heart sank at the thought that there might actually be another magical connection, in addition to LEO's involvement with inmates going missing. "Wait, didn't he get found again, though, after he escaped?"

"I think so. Yeah, I'm pretty sure the police tracked him down in a small town out in British Columbia, but when they had him surrounded, he blew his brains out. It was only a few weeks after he'd escaped, I think."

Natalie chuckled. "You have a memory like a steel trap," she said. That was a relief. It wouldn't be possible for someone arrested by LEO, if convicted, to be outside a magical community just a few weeks later.

"Well, there again, there's no incriminating tie between us and an escaped convict who was almost recaptured and then killed himself, particularly given he committed the murder in Montreal, got imprisoned in northern Ontario and was later found in British Columbia. None of those places is anywhere near Toronto."

"This doesn't help us," James said in an irritable voice. "I don't give a damn about some murderer who shot himself in the head out west! Good riddance. What I care about is how this firm is being implicated in this crap and how to disassociate ourselves from it."

"What about libel?" Raj suddenly said.

"What, against the newspaper?" Natalie asked in surprise.

"Offence as a form of defence?" Raj grinned.

"Sue-happy much?"

"Occupational hazard."

"I think we should hold that thought," Natalie mused. "Let's figure out where we're at first. Attacking too quickly could also be seen as a cover-up."

"What about the mages?" James demanded, his former fear having clearly turned to anger now. Natalie watched as he stood up, almost knocking his chair over in the process, and walked over to the window, still breathing heavily. Anger was better than panic, but clearly their efforts to redirect his thoughts had not been as effective as they had hoped. He was still focused on the mages and no longer focused on the misleading and circumstantial nature of the newspaper article.

"What about them?" Natalie shrugged, determined to maintain her tone of calm reasonableness, though she had no idea what she would do if James continued to concentrate on the possible presence of mages at the firm. "We can only work with facts, not speculations."

"Being linked to any of those people is a problem for us," James snapped. "Even if it is playing into the hands of whoever is behind this, we've got to find them."

"How?" Raj asked bluntly, though his eyes flickered toward Natalie as he spoke. "If finding mages was easy, they'd have been identified a long time ago. Before we can even begin to worry about that, we need to clear the firm's name so that we don't start losing clients. That's the priority."

Natalie wondered if she might have caused herself more problems by telling her colleagues that she knew several mages. She had a feeling Raj's thoughts were continuing on the track of whether she knew how to identify a mage.

"That woman who escaped from the Niagara prison, her employer was Fidelity Insurance's client," Natalie said. "We're on the record for Fidelity, who paid out the loss for whatever it was she did. But the claimant was trying to inflate the claim way out of proportion, so we acted for Fidelity in the lawsuit to sort out what was really owed. If it's all random connections like that, then it starts to look a whole lot more like a smear campaign."

James turned around. "You think someone's got a vendetta against Mason Sullivan specifically?"

"It's also a possibility." Raj shrugged. "Just as likely as the idea that someone just randomly latched onto using us to try to unmask mages. Who've we pissed off lately?"

"Who the hell knows?" Natalie answered the question, although it was directed at James. "Could be anybody we've ever acted against. Or won against anyway. But what about Fidelity? They're a big client."

"Clearly we've got to get Marketing on this. They better have some PR people they can call," James said. "I'll call John Marsden at Fidelity, find out if they're reacting."

"We should call the paper," Natalie added her suggestion. "See if they'll give us more details. We're going to want to have something in there as soon as possible responding, either way. I wonder if we can get the names of all the Toronto escapees? That ought to be publicly available information. They're usually on the news as soon as they escape. Do we have any connection with that guy who escaped this morning?"

"No," Raj answered. "He was in for domestic assault and child porn."

Natalie nodded, reflecting that the man she had met that morning could easily be the kind of person who would commit assault without thinking of the consequences. He certainly hadn't considered how pointless it was to try to look for escape possibilities while handcuffed and while a solidly built mage police officer was between him and the door.

"So if we get all the escapees' names and run those in our client database, we can respond on matters where we actually can find some connection to the escapees," she said. "Really, the fact that we're on the record for some lawsuits involving convicts who are still in jail is completely irrelevant. We can't really address this effectively until we know the facts. As Raj said, we haven't been involved in very many matters that end up involving criminal convictions."

"All right," James agreed, though he was still clearly agitated. "Figure out who to call at the *Sun*. Get those names. I want something solid before this escalates. Ifs and maybes aren't good enough."

As Natalie followed Raj out of James' office, she heard the partner mutter, *"Mages.* What the hell am I supposed to say to Phillip?"

Chapter 4

"Would you get a drink already? You're so tense, you're making *me* jumpy." Mikyla could barely hear her best friend's remark over the music blasting from the speakers, her head throbbing in time with the beat.

"I have a drink." Mikyla lifted her can of Coke.

"You know that's not what I meant."

Mikyla wrinkled her nose. "Yeah, well, you know I don't like any of them. Beer is gross. I hate lemonade, and vodka coolers are usually lemon flavoured. Rum and Coke tastes like puke. I'm out of luck." She didn't mention that watching her mother go through two or three 24-packs a week reduced the appeal as well. You could always tell how long it had been since the last welfare cheque by the stack of empties beside the front door.

Still on edge over the news about her mom's ex, home was the last place she wanted to go. But she wasn't really in the mood for a party either. Mikyla scanned the crowd, many of whom she recognized from school.

"I think I saw some of those peppermint coolers in the kitchen. You like those. Want one?"

"Yeah, okay."

As the girls moved toward the stairs, the door leading up to the kitchen opened, and a tall young man started down, a six-pack of beer cans hanging from a plastic strap from one finger. His black leather jacket was hanging open, and the white T-shirt underneath was straining over his pecs. A tattoo of a Chinese symbol twined up the side of his neck. Suddenly, he paused, looked back over his shoulder and then reversed direction and left the basement.

"Who was that?" Mikyla asked her friend. "He's hot." Maybe this party hadn't been such a bad idea after all.

"Jake Conrad. He goes to our school. Same grade as my brother." Tara grinned as they started up the stairs. "Good thing Tom's not here; he can't stand that guy."

"Why?"

"'Cause he beat him in the tae kwon do finals." Tara smirked. "When they were, like, 12. Plus he's some kind of computer genius. He hacked into the school's network and then went and told them how to improve their security, apparently. Tom thinks he's an arrogant ass."

As the basement door swung shut behind them, the pounding of the music was cut off abruptly.

"Weird. Is the basement soundproofed or something?"

"Must be." Tara shrugged, but Mikyla shuddered at the thought.

"That's kind of creepy. Anything could happen down there, and nobody would hear you."

"You watch too many horror flicks," Tara said with a laugh. "It's just because Mike has a band. Plus, how else could he have these parties and not get busted by the cops for noise complaints?"

Tara found one of the coolers and held it out to Mikyla, but she was looking around for Jake, who was not in sight.

Suddenly they heard a thump from the upper floor, along with raised male voices.

"She said no, dude. You got a problem with that?"

Muffled cursing got louder as it came nearer. Mikyla and Tara were looking toward the front hall, which was visible from the kitchen, in time to see Jake pushing another guy ahead of him down the stairs. The second young man was bare-chested, one hand holding his shirt up against his nose. The other arm was being tightly grasped in Jake's fist. Mikyla saw blood spreading a stain on the white shirt.

"Yeah, anytime," Jake responded to an unheard comment. He opened the door, pushed the other guy outside and shut the door behind him.

"I think I disagree with your brother," Mikyla muttered under her breath to Tara.

"You and me both," Tara said with a grin. "Not like that's new territory. When did I ever agree with Tom?"

"I'm not feeling so great, though." Mikyla sighed. "And those coolers are kind of sickeningly sweet. Is there any ginger ale?"

Tara put the peppermint cooler back and pulled a dripping can of ginger ale out of a large plastic tub half full of ice cubes and water. Mikyla splashed the ginger ale into a cup, swearing as it fizzed up and threatened to overflow.

"Somehow I don't think you have a future as a bartender," Tara teased her.

"Nah, I plan on becoming a brain surgeon." Mikyla's light tone hid her inner tension, but she looked down at the fizzy ginger ale, wishing it was flat. That would do more to settle her stomach than another pop. She swallowed hard as the bubbles rising up through the cup abruptly dissipated, leaving the surface of her drink calm and unruffled. All the froth from the overflow had disappeared. What the hell had just happened? She poured the rest of the can into a cup, and there were still absolutely no bubbles.

Mikyla looked up from her strangely uncarbonated pop, her face pale, in time to see Jake glance at the two of them as he walked back into the kitchen. He had a sharply chiselled face and eyes that seemed to hold deep secrets. Mikyla thought for a moment that he hesitated slightly, looking at the cup in her hand. But maybe that was her imagination. He nodded at them as he picked up the beer that he had left on the counter and went back downstairs. The wave of sound as the door opened instantly brought back Mikyla's headache, which continued to throb even after the door closed and cut off the noise.

"Seriously, Ky, what is wrong with you? You've been acting weird for three days now."

Mikyla closed her eyes and rubbed her aching forehead. There was no reason not to confide her stress to her best friend. "You know that asshole who beat up my mom a couple of weeks ago? He's the one that escaped from jail on Wednesday. And they're saying he's a mage."

"Shi-i-it!"

"You got that right."

Before Tara could react further, the basement door burst open again, but this time no loud music blared out. Agitated voices reached the girls instead, and Mike, the party's host, ran into the kitchen, yanked the phone on the wall off its cradle and quickly pressed three buttons.

"Yeah, um, ambulance please. ... I don't know, this girl, she's unconscious. And puking. And kind of, um, jerking around."

While he was anxiously describing the situation, several people ran up the stairs and out of the house.

Mikyla's heart rate increased. "Tara, get out of here. You're underage, and if the cops come and you get busted, your parents are gonna freak."

"So're you!"

"Yeah, but I haven't been drinking. And my mom wouldn't care anyway. Go!"

Without waiting to see if Tara was going to take her advice, Mikyla darted down the stairs, avoiding more fleeing partygoers. Her lip curled in some disgust, particularly at the seniors who were running away from a medical emergency to save their own skins.

Down in the basement, she saw Jake Conrad kneeling behind a girl who was jerking spasmodically and had thrown up already. He was attempting to hold her upright, which was evidently not an easy task, but he also had his face turned away, having clearly been made nauseous by the smell.

Mikyla darted over to an office area in one corner of the basement and came back with a garbage can, which she placed in front of the girl. Then she found the bathroom, which was predictably a total mess. She grabbed several towels and shoved one under the tap.

Jake breathed a sigh of relief as she used the wet towel to clean up the pool of vomit. He brightened further when he heard the sound of an approaching siren.

"I hope that's the ambulance," he said in a worried tone, casting his eyes upward as though he would be able to see through the ceiling. Then his eyes refocused on Mikyla as if he hadn't initially noticed who was helping him. "Most of the others couldn't get out of here fast enough," he said to her gratefully. "Not you, though, huh?"

Mikyla shrugged. "Sadly, this isn't the first time I've cleaned up after a drunk. Do you know her?"

"No. You? I hope she's gonna be okay."

"I bet she didn't eat much today," Mikyla said, looking at the girl's petite frame. "She looks vaguely familiar. Is she one of the cheerleaders? Drinking on an empty stomach maybe? Bad idea."

"Could be." Jake nodded. "Do you think it's a bad sign that she's still unconscious?"

"It's a bad sign that she was having a seizure or whatever," Mikyla pointed out. "Alcohol poisoning or something? I dunno, but EMS is coming, so we've done what we can."

"I guess. Thank God she's stopped puking."

Suddenly shy, Mikyla kept her eyes on the unconscious girl but sneaked a sideways glance at Jake. She jerked sideways in shock at what she saw—a bizarre flickering glow around his head, like a halo that was shorting out.

"What?"

"Um, nothing. I'm just, I dunno, kind of freaking out today. Lots of crap going on."

"No kidding. Hey, what grade are you in?"

"Ten."

"So you're, like, 16?"

"Yeah."

"And you've cleaned up after a lot of drunks before?" In his surprise, Jake may have relaxed his grip on the unconscious girl a bit as she slipped sideways. He grabbed her limp body and moved her more upright again. "Shit, I'm probably giving her bruises."

Mikyla grimaced. "Not a lot of drunks, just one drunk, quite a few times. And I think bruises are the least of her problems right now."

"Yeah, true. So, bad home life, huh?"

"You could say that."

Mikyla took a deep breath and gathered her courage to look straight at him. Now he looked perfectly normal, no flickering lights. *I am seriously losing it,* she thought. She looked away again and flickered her eyes sideways as she had before. Again, she saw a weird flickering glow. What the hell?

Jake looked around as if to confirm that the other people still in the basement were some distance away, except for the unconscious girl. "So, if your home life is shitty, I guess you had to grow up when you were, like, 10. So maybe you have this whole mage thing figured out already?" He spoke in a voice too low to be heard by the onlookers.

Mikyla's already agitated heartbeat sped up even further. Had he said "mage thing"?

"What—what are you talking about?"

Before he could answer, however, noises heard through the open door at the top of the stairs indicated the paramedics had arrived.

Mikyla looked up as two ambulance attendants came hurrying down the stairs. She sucked in a startled breath as she recognized the same two paramedics who had been at her house a few weeks ago. The blonde woman did a double take, and she nodded at her.

"Mikyla, right? We really have to stop meeting like this. What's going on with this young lady?"

"I'm not really sure. Alcohol poisoning maybe?" Mikyla was trying to remember the paramedic's name. Susan? No, Suzanne. That was it.

Suzanne nodded. "Perhaps. Anybody know if she has any medical conditions? Diabetes?"

Mikyla looked toward Jake, who shrugged.

"Sorry, I don't know," he answered. "I don't even know her name."

"Uh, her name is Marie Sanderson." A girl who had been in the corner moved forward to identify the patient. "I don't know of any medical conditions. I don't think she's diabetic."

"How old is she?"

"Um, 17," the girl said with a bit of hesitation, which Mikyla assumed was probably because the patient was under the legal drinking age.

"Do you have contact information for her parents?" the other paramedic asked, fitting an oxygen mask over the unconscious girl's mouth. "Airway's not blocked," he added to his partner.

"Blood pressure 110 over 69, quite low," Suzanne replied as she checked the monitor she had strapped to the patient's arm. "Pulse 60. Do you know if she uses antidepressants or antianxiety meds at all?"

"Um, I don't know. I think I have her brother's number," the girl who knew the patient replied to both questions. "I'll call him."

"Thanks." The male paramedic, whose name tag read "D. Timmons," turned to the party's host and asked him if he could help bring the gurney downstairs.

Mikyla noticed that Suzanne's name tag also said Timmons, although of course her initial was *S*.

Suzanne removed the blood pressure monitor and was tucking it back in its case. As she did so, she looked up at Mikyla, and it looked as though she flicked her eyes to a spot off to the side of Mikyla's head, then beside Jake's head, and then back at her. Suzanne looked surprised, but she said nothing. She adjusted the oxygen mask, and Mikyla gathered up the dirty towels and took them toward a laundry room that she had spotted earlier. Her mind was churning madly. What was that weird flickering glow around Jake's head? She could only see it when she wasn't looking directly at him, but she had seen it twice, so it wasn't just her imagination. And why did Suzanne look at her indirectly as well? Had she seen Jake glow too?

As Mikyla came back into the main part of the basement, the two paramedics were just lifting the patient onto the gurney. Jake was staring at Suzanne with a look of surprise on his face.

Taking a deep breath and tensing her stomach muscles, Mikyla unfocused her eyes and looked at a point off to the side of Suzanne's head. Her breathing sped up as she saw an unmistakeable steady glow, not bright, but just as if there were a light somewhere behind her. Straight on, there was nothing visible.

Suzanne turned her head toward her. "I really need to talk to you, Mikyla. I have to go, though. You still have my number?"

"Um, yeah?"

"Okay, call me. Please?"

"O—okay," Mikyla stammered.

Suzanne nodded and started up the stairs, holding one end of the gurney, which was behind her. Her partner glanced toward Mikyla with a slight frown on his face, and then he shrugged. Mikyla tried looking indirectly at him but saw no glow. He held up the other end of the gurney, high enough so that the patient would be level even though they were climbing a staircase. His muscles bulged with the effort. Mikyla looked at Suzanne one more time and noticed that she didn't even seem to be straining to lift her end. Admittedly, she wasn't holding it as high as her partner was, but she didn't look particularly muscular either. Mikyla noticed that this time the glow was even stronger, sort of pulsing. She was conscious of a slight feeling of dizziness. What did this weird stuff mean?

"Wow, that lady is strong," Jake muttered.

"No kidding," agreed Mike, the party's host, who had come back into the basement with the ambulance personnel. "I guess you have to be, to be a paramedic. You've got to be able to lift people and stuff. I'll just go let them out. Thanks for helping, you guys."

"So you know that lady?" Jake said to Mikyla, as Mike followed the paramedics up the stairs.

"Well, we met a couple of weeks ago. She, um, came to my house."

"That's probably not a good thing," Jake noted.

"Not really." Mikyla looked away and did not elaborate.

"I need to talk to you." Jake had moved to stand very close to her and spoke quietly.

Mikyla looked up at him. He had his hands in his pockets but was looking kind of tense.

"So, talk," Mikyla said, increasingly uncomfortable. Why was everyone saying they needed to talk to her?

"Maybe, uh, not here," Jake said, glancing around at the small number of partygoers still in the room. Most of them had stood around helplessly while the unconscious girl had been lying on the floor, but at least they hadn't run away like the rest. "Walk with me?"

Mikyla shrugged and headed up the stairs. Mike was still standing by the front door.

"Hey, thanks again," he said to them as they approached. "Mikyla, right?"

"Yeah."

"Glad you came. Thanks, Jake."

"No problem."

"There's, um, some dirty towels in the laundry room," Mikyla said. Mike made a face.

"Yeah, I better put those in the wash before my mom comes home and smells that. I hope that girl will be okay."

Jake nodded sombrely, and Mikyla preceded him out of the front door. They walked in silence halfway down the block before Jake spoke.

"I don't really know how to ask this, so I'm just gonna come out with it. I have loads of questions, and I have no clue who to ask, but you seem to already have some of this stuff figured out."

"Me? What makes you think I've got anything figured out?" Mikyla said glumly. "If I had things figured out, I don't think my life would be such a mess."

"Well, since you're one too, even if you're just starting or whatever, I was hoping maybe you could give me some pointers," he said, now speaking in a hopeful tone. "I've never met another one. That I know of, I mean."

Mikyla stopped abruptly like she had been slapped. Jake took a few more steps before he realized she was not keeping up with him. "Since I'm one what?" she demanded.

Jake looked at her sharply. "Oh shit, you haven't figured it out yet? Oh my God, I am such an ass." He put his head in his hands.

"I'm one what?" Mikyla repeated in a harder voice.

Jake sighed. "You're a mage. I'm sorry, I just assumed you had to know already. I wouldn't have said it like that if I realized ..."

Mikyla swallowed hard and squeezed her hands together, her knuckles turning white. "How do you know if I'm a mage?" she demanded. She firmly squelched the rising panic she was feeling. As if her life wasn't complicated enough! If she was honest with herself, the thought had crept into her mind, even before the ginger ale. Just last week, there was that fight with her mother, when Tina's beer had inexplicably fizzed up and overflowed its bottle, even though the bottle had been half empty. And then that other time, when Tara's feet had slipped out from under her on the wet staircase, but somehow, impossibly, she had regained her balance. Mikyla had almost passed out as a wave of dizziness had overcome her after that, and she was sure she had somehow done something. She just didn't know what.

"Well, okay, I don't actually know for sure." Now Jake sounded uncertain and more nervous. He glanced around as if to make sure nobody was near enough to overhear their conversation. "It's just, you made that ginger ale go flat when you weren't feeling good. And then that girl stopped puking as soon as you got there."

Mikyla's eyes widened. "I didn't make her stop puking!" she exclaimed.

"But the ginger ale?"

"I … I don't know what you mean." But she had turned her face away, sure her cheeks were flaming. What was that with the ginger ale? It had been normally carbonated when she first poured it into the cup.

Mikyla was breathing in short gasps. Then she swallowed hard and unfocused her eyes as she looked at nothing past Jake's head. Sure enough, just like before, there was a flickering glow around his head.

She screwed her eyes tightly shut.

"Um, what? You did that before, too."

"You, um, kind of glow," Mikyla muttered, her eyes still closed.

"I what?"

"Like there's a light behind your head. Except it's sort of flickering, and you can only see it indirectly, not straight on." She sighed and opened her eyes.

Jake's face took on an expression of discomfort, and Mikyla fought the urge to giggle. "Yeah, I know. It sounds insane. Maybe I'm crazy." Suddenly, she wished the ground would open up and let her sink out of sight. How embarrassing. Why had she told him that? But then she took a deep breath. Hadn't he just told her he was a mage? And that he thought she was one too? Maybe it was all connected. "Look, try looking off to the side of my head with your eyes kind of unfocused. Do you see anything weird?"

It took a few seconds before Jake tried it, only he crossed his eyes while he did, which made Mikyla giggle. Her laughter died as his mouth fell open and his focus sharpened back onto her face.

"Did you see something?"

"Yeah."

"And? Don't keep me hanging here."

"Just like what you said. A glow that sort of flickers. Really faint, though. If it wasn't for the flicker, I wouldn't have seen anything."

Mikyla's eyebrows rose. "Yours is brighter than that."

"What does that mean?"

"You're asking me? I haven't got a clue. About anything." Mikyla shuddered and closed her eyes again. She felt as though she were in a snow globe that someone had just picked up and violently shaken with no warning. Her thoughts spun around uncontrollably, flashes of potential scenes of horror playing out in her head: her mother kicking her out to live on the street; fighting off drug addicts and wannabe pimps; being attacked by former friends once they knew what she was.

Finally, she opened her eyes and looked at him, her expression haunted. "I was starting to suspect," she admitted in a hesitant voice. "But I didn't know, not for sure."

"You want to get a coffee?" Jake gestured toward a Tim Horton's across the street. "I could sure use one."

"Sounds good to me."

They were silent as they walked slowly toward a nearby park. Mikyla had a small iced cappuccino in her hand, while Jake had gone for a large coffee, double-double. He had forestalled her attempt to buy her own and paid for them both.

Mikyla followed as Jake led the way toward an empty bench. Her thoughts were turbulent as she stared at the unoccupied swing set, the scorched ground underneath each swing packed solid by the feet of all the kids who had played there. The grass around the edges was yellow and sickly looking, although the City's maintenance program prevented any overgrowth or weeds. Still, the park was not one of the more attractive ones around; it played host more frequently to drug dealers and their customers than to playful kids. Whenever Mikyla had brought her brothers here, she carefully combed the ground under the playset for old needles before she let the boys run loose.

Could she trust this guy? She barely knew him. What if he was trying to trap her? But there was that glow. And he had said she had it too.

"You know the paramedic? The woman? She has that glow too. But she doesn't flicker. I'm thinking that's how you tell who's a mage."

"God, they're, like, all over the place." Jake looked around nervously.

Mikyla had to laugh. "*They* are us," she pointed out. "Why are we scared of people who are like us?"

"Good point. I still am, though. They could be anywhere; you don't know."

"Well, if we all glow, then we *can* tell."

Mikyla took a deep breath, stunned to realize that they had both just admitted to each other that they were mages. Then she realized she had the opportunity to ask questions of someone in a similar position. Screwing up her courage, but trying to make her voice sound casual, she asked, "So what kind of weird stuff happens to you?"

Jake shrugged. "The first thing was when stuff started floating."

"Floating?"

"Yeah, like I'd be lying on my bed and the stuff on my floor would start floating, like there was no gravity. Then when I would notice and freak out, it would all fall back to the ground."

"God, that would make me think I was going crazy."

"It kind of did at first. Then I was sort of mad, and I—I dunno, I started trying to move things deliberately. Without touching them, I mean. And it worked! It was really hard at first, but it got kind of easier."

"Easier how?"

"Just less effort. At first, if I intentionally tried to lift one single thing off my floor, it felt like I'd just run a mile. But it bugged me, so I kept trying. Now I'm just really lazy." He grinned. "Like, I'll be lying on my bed and want my iPod that's on the desk, so I just make it float over to me."

Mikyla was looking at him with an astonished expression on her face. "I can't do anything like that," she told him. "I just seem to make drinks overflow or go flat. What the hell use is that?"

"Different mages can do different things?"

"Oh sure, you can pick things up without touching them, but I just get to ruin people's drinks. That *sucks*."

With a frown, Mikyla took a key ring with two keys on it out of her pocket and put it down on the bench, looking around to ensure that nobody was close by. She angled her body to hide the keys from the view of anyone passing behind the bench anyway. Then she frowned at them fixedly for a few minutes, but nothing happened. Finally, she sighed and looked at Jake with a raised eyebrow. He shrugged and looked at the keys, and without any visible effort on his part, they started floating upward, moved toward Mikyla and dived back into her pocket.

"How?" she demanded.

"I can't really explain it," Jake admitted, spreading his hands helplessly. "I just think about it moving, and it does. Oh shit!" His gesture had accidentally knocked the coffee cup off the bench. Mikyla sucked in her breath as the cup froze in position, hovering sideways in the air, with light-coloured coffee spilling out of it. Then in the next moment, it flipped right way up, and the coffee flowed back up and into the cup like a movie clip played backward. She looked up at him, startled, to see that he was breathing hard and there was a sheen of sweat on his forehead. She also glanced around again and was relieved to see that nobody was looking in their direction, so the unnatural behaviour of the coffee had not been noticed.

"I'm pretty sure it ought to be easier, though," Jake grumbled. "What use is it if it's a huge effort just to catch a paper cup and some coffee? What about when you made the pop go flat? You didn't look like you just ran a race after that."

"I was just thinking fizzy pop would make me feel sicker, and suddenly it went flat," Mikyla admitted. "It just happened, you know? But the other day I was mad at my mom, and suddenly her beer fizzed up and overflowed all over the table. I took off. I kind of knew I did that, so I was freaking out."

"Did this stuff only just start to happen to you?"

"As far as I know."

"So I guess things were kind of floating for a few weeks for me before I even started to figure it out, and it was way longer before I worked out how to do it deliberately."

"What good is it though?" Mikyla demanded in a disgruntled tone. "Even if I can learn to do stuff other than ruin people's drinks. I already know what people think about mages."

"Yeah. That's the part that really sucks."

"So I'm thinking maybe my dad might have been a mage, 'cause I never knew him. What about you?"

"I know both my parents. There's no way they're mages, and I'm not adopted." Jake shrugged. "Maybe it's just random? Normal people just pop out a magical kid sometimes?"

"Like having a disabled kid, I guess." Mikyla sighed. The thought that her dad might be a mage was a strange thought, although not an entirely unpleasant one. It would be nice if he wasn't as much of a dead end as her mother.

"Well, it's an extra ability, not a disability."

"Yeah, but one we're gonna have to hide for our whole lives."

"I guess we just have to hang out with people we don't have to hide it from." He smiled at her, and a slow smile spread across her face as well.

Suddenly Mikyla was feeling a whole lot better.

Chapter 5

"All rise. The Honourable Justice Burns presiding."

Natalie rose to her feet, straightening the short jacket she wore under her court robes as she did so.

The judge took his seat behind the raised desk at the front of the courtroom and straightened some papers sitting in front of him. Then he nodded to the registrar.

"You may be seated," the registrar said.

Since it was her client who was bringing the motion, Natalie was the first to address the court, so she moved to the podium in the centre of the room facing the judge with her binder of notes. She began her introductory statement, explaining the nature of the order her client was requesting and summarizing the grounds it intended to rely on. The motion was for summary judgment, an attempt to have the case dismissed based on a lack of evidence presented by the plaintiff. Being able to dismiss the case at this early stage would save her client a lot of money, but it was always a bit of a gamble. If judgment was not granted, her client would be liable for the costs of this failed proceeding, for both parties.

She spoke in a calm, well-modulated voice, easily heard throughout the wood-panelled courtroom, a room designed for good acoustics. Her outward calm in no way reflected how she was really feeling. As she reached for her copy of the documents filed in court in preparation for the motion, which was sitting beside her on the table for the defendant's lawyers, there was a vibration in her head. She tensed in panic and had only about a quarter of a second's warning before a mental voice loudly stated, *Mage Benson, the Council requires an explanation of the communication you sent to LEO headquarters last evening.*

Natalie winced at the volume. It seemed impossible that the other occupants of the room could be unaware of it, yet clearly they were oblivious. A wave of fury filled her at the typically abrupt communication originating from Constance Reeve, a member of the governing Council of Mages and a First Circle communicator. The unique skill which made Constance a First Circle mage was the mental communication which she was able to achieve with any mage anywhere in the world. Natalie could only initiate a mental communication with someone after intentionally creating the connection, which required some kind of physical contact. Constance could do it after merely having seen a photograph of a person. Unlike most mages, she did not appear to be at all limited by distance.

Constance regularly acted as though she considered herself entitled to a great deal of deference. Natalie was not sure whether this was because of her age, her First Circle status or her position on the Council. Possibly all three.

"I would ask Your Honour to refer to tab 3 of the motion record," Natalie began aloud, and then responded mentally in an angry tone: *This is not a good time. I am in court. Contact me after business hours.*

"Paragraph 14 of my client's affidavit—" she began, but she was cut off as the mental voice boomed in her head again.

That will not be acceptable, Mage Benson. Law enforcement is a high priority for this Council.

I. Am. In. Court. She grated the silent words individually, gritting her teeth.

"Is there a problem, counsel?"

Natalie jumped as she realized that she had stopped in the middle of a sentence, as far of the rest of the occupants of the courtroom were concerned.

"I apologize, Your Honour. I seem to be getting a migraine. In paragraph 14—"

Mage Benson!

"Mr. MacLaughlin is describing the business relationship which existed between his company and that of the plaintiff—"

Mage Benson!

Natalie jerked backward and gasped at the strength of the mental intrusion. Her fists clenched as she was consumed with anger at the mage politician.

"Counsel, do you need a break?" the judge asked, a concerned expression on his face.

"Actually, Your Honour, could my colleague take over?" Natalie now spoke in a strained voice, attempting to disguise her anger at Constance Reeve's unbelievably arrogant and inconsiderate behavior.

"As you wish, counsel."

Natalie nodded at Jeffrey Stiles, the junior lawyer sitting at the table to her right. He looked a bit alarmed, but he had helped to draft each of the documents that had been submitted to the court, including having prepared over half the written argument before she had ever reviewed it.

Jeff cleared his throat as he stepped up to the podium. Natalie resumed her seat at the table and closed her eyes. Though she kept her face expressionless, she directed a blast of absolute fury at her mental intruder and had the satisfaction of sensing the woman's shocked reaction.

Natalie picked up her silver pen and rested it against her forehead. She could not properly trace the pattern that she needed and yet still make the action appear to be random. Still, just pointing it in the right direction provided a little assistance with what she wanted to achieve. It was always possible to do magic without any assistance; her sapphire prism, even in its customary disguise as a pen, simply made it easier, particularly when doing powerful magic. Keeping her eyes closed, she concentrated on building an impenetrable wall around her mind, brick by brick. Natalie could sense growing anger from her mental intruder as it became apparent what she was doing, and she heard a furious demand for an explanation before the wall was finished. Once it was as solid as she could make it without anything being visible to the non-mages in the room, she drew a deep breath and slowly opened her eyes.

Having caught a glimpse of the suspicious, narrow-eyed expression on the face of one of the plaintiff's lawyers, before he averted his gaze toward the judge, she sighed. Since the newspaper article three and a half weeks ago, rumours of magery at Mason Sullivan were fast spreading throughout the legal community. Another newspaper article about magic interference with a court decision had appeared in the same newspaper, written by the same reporter, last Friday. Although this one did not specifically mention Mason Sullivan, there was a widespread assumption that it was about her firm as well.

If Natalie appeared to miraculously recover from a wicked migraine, it would not help her firm's reputation. With a slightly theatrical wince, she reached down for her purse and found a small container of Advil pills. The headache she had claimed was actually developing, and she suspected that her mental wall was being attacked. The painkillers would help prevent the headache from blooming, but on the other hand, they might make it a bit more difficult to maintain her barrier if that obnoxious woman was determined to try to breach it. She would not have any difficulty blocking an ordinary mage who was attempting to communicate with her mentally, but it was a different matter with a First Circle communicator. Reaching for the glass of water that sat on the table in front of her, Natalie swallowed a pill and then repeated the action to make it appear that she had taken two.

Unfortunately, as she was able to pay better attention to her immediate surroundings, she became aware that Jeffrey was not presenting the prepared arguments nearly as smoothly as she had hoped. He was speaking too fast, and his nervousness was evident in his almost monotone presentation. When the plaintiff's lawyer jumped in with an objection, it was obvious that he lost his place in his notes. Then he had to spend several agonizingly long seconds trying to reorient himself.

Natalie estimated that the Advil pills might have taken effect after twenty minutes. She lifted her chin and opened her eyes from their previous squint after that period of time. The headache had, in fact, eased a lot as soon as she had gotten the shield up, although every now and then there was a lance of pain, possibly another attempt by the mage politician to breach her protection.

At a questioning look from Jeff, Natalie nodded and smoothly took over the second half of the presentation.

The motion was a lengthy one. It was nearly lunchtime before court was adjourned, with the judge having indicated that he would provide his decision within 48 hours. Although Natalie had hoped for a decision on the spot, it was not unusual for a judge to reserve his decision on a matter this technical. She hoped that Jeffrey's difficulties while she was incapacitated had not caused any damage to the case.

"Thanks for covering for me, Jeff, I appreciate it," she said quietly after the judge had left the room. Though his presentation skills clearly needed work, that topic would be better addressed later.

"That was terrible," he groaned. "I messed up. I'm just glad our client wasn't actually here for this one. Do you get migraines a lot?"

Natalie sighed. "Sometimes," she told him untruthfully. "They've been getting a bit worse lately. Unsettled weather doesn't help. I've heard it has something to do with barometric pressure."

"Stress probably doesn't help either," Jeffrey commented.

"No, I'm sure it doesn't," Natalie agreed wryly. "But what can you do?"

They were silent then as they packed up their papers and left the courtroom. Since the court was not far from their office, the two lawyers from Mason Sullivan walked back, each pulling a wheeled cart with a box of their materials and their court robes, with their laptops strapped to the tops of the boxes. As they exited the building, Natalie looked up and was dismayed to see that the sky was bright blue with not a cloud in sight. So much for her story of the weather affecting the headaches. She sighed as she donned dark sunglasses.

A large black crow sat on the branch of a spindly tree outside the gleaming tower that held the law office of Mason Sullivan. Certain members of the magical law enforcement organization were no doubt wondering why numerous e-mails sent to one of their best undercover operatives had received no response, but Jon had decided he didn't care. He had been running from one side of this continent to the other for over a month, with only a single day off here and there, and it looked like the next few months were going to include more of the same. What were they going to do, fire him?

The sun was pleasantly warm on his black feathers, which made sitting in the tree no hardship. In fact, it was a nice change from his recent punishing schedule. He had briefly considered being a smaller, less noticeable bird, but birds of prey were always a possibility even down near pavement level. Evading an attack from a swift-moving hawk would be far more conspicuous.

After waking from twelve solid hours of sleep the last time he had been in Toronto, Jon's thoughts had returned immediately to the blonde gatemaker who had transported two people, seemingly effortlessly, from downtown Toronto to a point in the far northwest of Ontario, which was probably over 600 miles away. The brightness of the gateway and the smoothness of the transition bespoke her skill. Lesser gatemakers whom he had worked with would not have been capable of a fraction of that distance, particularly when transporting more than one person. She had not even seemed tired after what should have been a herculean effort.

She kept popping into his head at odd moments over the next couple of weeks. Out of curiosity, he had googled her name, not really expecting to find much information from such a mundane source, especially since her name wasn't all that unusual. To his surprise, one of the first hits included a photo, leaving no doubt it was the correct person, and a biographical entry that was part of a Web site for a Toronto law firm. Having had initially assumed that such a powerful gatemaker would be a prized LEO employee, he had been puzzled by her reference to going into the office. At the time, he had written his confusion off as the result of his exhausted state. If she was actually just doing that on the side, in addition to what was likely a demanding career, then that was astonishing. It also explained the irritation she had displayed at the delay.

Besides, in spite of her poised, professional appearance, it had not been hard to see the vulnerability, particularly when she had instantly closed her window blinds as soon as the news segment identified the missing prisoner who was then standing in her living room.

Skilled, clearly highly intelligent, attractive *and* possibly a little bit scared—all traits which immediately woke his protective instincts. He had not been able to stop thinking about her. Thus, the crow perched in a tree not really strong enough for its weight, waiting to see if she would emerge from the building that housed her office. There were many other options, of course, but being a potted plant in her office felt a bit too voyeuristic, and impersonating someone who could legitimately visit her office and actually getting in to see her might seem a bit pushy, considering they had met for barely 15 minutes three weeks ago. He was content to wait. There was a Starbucks that had an entrance inside the building's north lobby. It also had an exterior entrance and a nice outdoor patio. A seemingly coincidental meeting had some potential.

Jon idly watched the patrons of the Starbucks, a rapidly changing crowd, until his hopes were rewarded when Natalie appeared, although she'd arrived from somewhere outside the building. She was dressed in a severe black suit with a white blouse featuring an unusual neck adornment rather like an old-fashioned cravat. It seemed vaguely familiar, and it took him a few moments to recognize part of the outfit barristers sometimes had to wear in court, minus the billowing black robe. It seemed odd to picture Natalie dressed like that, and he could not recall whether lawyers wore wigs in this country as they still did in some cases in England.

A young man beside her raised a hand in farewell and continued on toward the elevators, but to Jon's relief, Natalie strode to the Starbucks counter to take a place in the short line. Quickly, the crow launched itself away from the tree and into a nearby shipping bay which he had scouted earlier, where a tall man had a reasonable chance of appearing out of thin air without being noticed. When he strode back around the corner and into the Starbucks, however, he was a bit disappointed to notice that Natalie was sitting at a table with another woman, whose back was toward him. Her dark blue shirt was imprinted with "Toronto Paramedic" in large font across the back, but as his eyes flicked toward Natalie, it was immediately apparent from her relaxed posture that the other woman was not there in her professional capacity.

"… doesn't even help us. Just the one has been a complete disaster for us. It could cause the firm to go bankrupt, or—"

"Ms. Benson?" Jon was hesitant as he interrupted what seemed like an anxious conversation.

Natalie visibly tensed as she looked around to see who had called her name. Jon was relieved to see that she relaxed and smiled as soon as she recognized him.

"Jon?! I didn't realize you'd be back in Toronto. And call me Natalie, please." Jon carried the cup of coffee he had just purchased over to their table. "Are you in a hurry, or can you join us?" A wrapped sandwich sat untouched in front of Natalie, though her large coffee had already been partially drunk. A folded piece of paper that looked like a copy of a newspaper article sat beside the other woman's cup.

"Free as a bird. I've got about 48 e-mails waiting for me, but I haven't had a day off in a fortnight, and none of them is urgent, so I've decided it's my weekend. Maybe I'll play tourist." He grinned as he glanced with deceptive casualness at those closest to their table. Scrutinizing his surroundings was such an ingrained habit that he was barely aware of doing it.

The table chosen by the two women was in a corner, furthest away from the counter, and separated from the area not claimed by Starbucks by several small trees in tall planters. Another potted plant further shielded them from the attention of the only other occupied table, currently in use by four young people who each had headphones in their ears and seemed to be paying far more attention to their phones than to each other. Those who simply took their order away with them did not pass close to the table. He approved on all counts.

His gaze swung back to Natalie, and he was startled to see that, close up, she looked pale and a little ill. Signs of strain were visible in her slightly reddened eyes and her tense upright posture.

"Jon, this is my sister, Suzanne Timmons," Natalie introduced him. "Suzy, Jon—um, Foster, wasn't it?"

"Forrester. Close enough." Jon smiled and shook Suzanne's hand.

"Jon's a LEO," Natalie explained in a low voice to her sister. "We met a few weeks ago when, well, you know."

"I heard about it." Suzanne nodded. "In fact, oddly enough I was at the scene when that guy was arrested."

Natalie glared warningly at her sister. Jon pulled an odd-looking octagonal coin out of his pocket and appeared to play with it among his long fingers. Immediately a sense of slightly oppressive air appeared around them and quickly dissipated. He grinned as he put the coin away.

"Won't that be kind of obvious?" Natalie asked in a low voice. Suzanne looked confused.

"Not at all," he answered in a normal volume. "It makes our conversation sound like a muted drone, as if we're talking too quietly to actually hear. Plus there's a bit of an inclination to not really be too curious."

"Wouldn't that count as coercion?" Suzanne's eyebrows had shot up.

Jon shook his head. "I know those regs backward and forward. Since it's just a slight encouragement not to care enough to want to investigate, it's acceptable. It would actually be really easy to override, even for a non-mage. If someone was particularly curious about us, they could brush it aside without even being aware of it."

"And then they'd hear us?" Natalie asked.

"Nope, then they'd just hear the muffled buzz of a conversation too low to decipher. They might realize something weird was going on, but they still wouldn't hear us."

"That's a useful sort of spell," Suzanne said admiringly.

"Totally. I wouldn't mind learning that one," Natalie agreed, but Jon noticed that her cheerful tone sounded forced. "Are non-LEOs allowed to?"

"Absolutely. I'd be happy to teach you. It'd have to be someplace more private, though. It's a bit hard to be subtle when you're showing someone else." He lifted his coffee cup and moved it around in an exaggerated pattern, similar to the way mages often sketched a pattern with their prisms. It did look a bit odd.

"Line of duty?" Suzanne asked curiously, nodding toward Jon's black leather glove-encased hand, wrapped around his disposable coffee cup.

"Yeah," Jon replied, looking at the glove himself. "I usually tell people it was a car accident and that it's two prosthetic fingers."

"Can't you make it *be* two prosthetic fingers?" Natalie asked. "Or real ones, for that matter?"

"No," he replied with a sigh. "You're stuck with Boadicea's curse; d'you know what my Achilles heel is?"

"Salt, isn't it?" Natalie asked, while Suzanne looked baffled.

"That's it," Jon confirmed. "You know every First Circle mage has a weakness?" he added in explanation to Suzanne. "Boadicea's curse is for gatemakers, yeah? They can't go through their own gateways. Mine is salt, of all things. If you throw salt at a metamorph while he's in another form, he's going to freeze into that form. Permanently. And if it's a form that can't eat or drink …" He drew a finger across his throat with a grimace.

Then he snapped open the tab on his coffee cup and took a long drink. Perching in the tree for almost an hour had left him very thirsty. Though it had been fairly cool the last time he was in Toronto, today the weather was more like summer.

"But why two fingers?" Natalie asked with a confused look.

"A metamorph?" Suzanne spoke at the same time, her eyes growing huge. "You mean a shape-shifter?"

"It wasn't thrown at me. There just happened to be a tiny bit of salt on the floor, and I oozed over it," Jon explained, nodding in answer to Suzanne's question. "I was using a smoke form. Makes it easier not to be noticed, since I can't go totally invisible or anything like that."

Suzanne suddenly started coughing, her face turning red. After a few seconds, she managed to wheeze. "Smoke?!"

"Jon's a First Circle metamorph," Natalie explained. "He can turn himself into absolutely anything. Gives whole new meaning to *undercover*. What's your favourite form?" she asked curiously.

"Birds. God, I love flying," Jon said. "It's brilliant. And oddly enough, when I turn into something else, I'm intact, but as soon as I turn back into me, bam, back to fingers made out of smoke. I'm lucky it only affected those two fingers, but they're smoke now, and they won't even hold the shape of fingers without the glove. Imagine if my mum saw that?" He bent the two offending fingers all the way backward with his other hand and then let them go. They did not immediately spring back to a more normal-looking position until he frowned slightly and used a touch of magic to fix the position of his hand.

"So, ah, you can tell me to mind my own business if you like, but I couldn't help noticing that you seem upset about something."

Natalie looked torn for a moment and then sighed.

"There have been two newspaper articles in less than a month." She gestured toward the folded paper by her sister's cup. "The first article was actually the same day we met. It specifically named my firm and alleged that we are assisting with the prison escapes."

"What?!"

"It mentioned people escaping from jail who are part of cases that my firm has acted on." Natalie sighed. "My practice group, in fact. The partner I report to is livid, and there are rumours of an investigation from the lawyers' professional society."

"Are you in any danger?"

Natalie shifted in her seat, looking uncomfortable. "Depends on what kind of danger you have in mind. I mean, it didn't name me personally, so I'm not too likely to get beaten up. But it definitely mentioned fraud cases, and that's the kind of stuff I do. My career could crash and burn."

"What is the second article about?" Jon asked.

Natalie picked up the paper and unfolded it. Jon saw that the headline read "ISP Forced to Release Personal Info."

"It suggests that magic was used to make a judge grant a certain kind of order recently," she explained, sliding the paper toward him. "It required an Internet provider to reveal the identity of an account holder who created several inflammatory Web sites. It's a libel thing. The thing is, it doesn't actually give the name of the law firm involved in getting that order. But after the previous article, people are assuming it was Mason Sullivan as well, even though it actually wasn't."

"That doesn't even make sense," Jon said in a confused tone. "Even if magical coercion wasn't completely illegal, you couldn't coerce someone and have that stay put after you weren't holding it on them anymore."

Suzanne snorted. "They don't know that," she pointed out. "In fact, *I* didn't know that. Most of us poor ordinary mortals don't have a clue about how magical coercion works. It's against the law, that's all I know."

"Actually, I know that you couldn't possibly miss it if someone tried it in court," Natalie said. "The person being coerced takes the exact same posture as the person doing the coercing. They're like robots who mirror every movement. It's super creepy. And there's that yellow glow thing." She shuddered as she peeled back part of the plastic wrap covering her sandwich. Jon was surprised at the description she gave, since it was usually him doing the coercing. He hadn't thought about how it would look to another person.

"Well, that's not entirely true," Jon said. "It's just a whole lot harder to try to make the person act and move differently from me, so if I'm not in a public place, I don't bother. One thing I can't change, though, is the person's voice. If they speak, they're gonna sound like me." He shrugged.

"With your accent?" Suzanne laughed.

"Yep. And my actual voice. Say I was doing coercion on a woman; her voice would sound deeper. Maybe not exactly the same as mine, because her vocal cords might not actually be capable of that, but it definitely wouldn't sound like her own voice."

"Weird. And even more creepy." Suzanne shuddered and took a swallow of her coffee, looking as though she wanted to wash away a bad taste in her mouth. "Anyway, the fact is, non-mages don't even know exactly what we can and can't do," she said. "If anything, they seem to think we're all-powerful and can actually do far more than we really can."

"Hmm. Um, did I hear you say something about your firm going bankrupt?" Jon had turned toward Natalie as he asked the question.

"It could happen," Natalie admitted. "A month ago, I would have said no chance, not in a million years. When my department's partner suggested that, I thought he was way overreacting, since he does tend to do that. We're a large successful law firm. But clients have already started transferring their files, and we've lost nearly a quarter of our staff just in the last three weeks. Most of them just stopped showing up for work, no notice, nothing. Like rats deserting a sinking ship." She sighed, a slump to her shoulders that Jon thought suggested she was more stressed than she was admitting.

"I don't get it. Why?"

"Because nons hate mages. Remember that other LEO—Marcus, was it?—was saying the hate has been increasing? He felt it was because of the prisoner transfers. He might have a point. Any hint of magical activity and everyone panics and overreacts. They seriously hate us."

"Not quite all of them," Suzanne murmured.

"Your husband is an extremely rare exception," Natalie told her sister.

"You're married to a non-mage?" Jon was startled.

"Yeah."

"He knows you're a mage though, right?"

"Yep. He told me he was absolutely terrified when he first started to suspect, but, well, he changed his mind. Long story."

"One I'd like to hear sometime," Jon noted thoughtfully. "I don't want to sound like I've got anything against the nons, but I couldn't imagine having a relationship where you had to keep that secret. And if you did, and then they found out later, I can't imagine it not falling apart." He looked away for a moment, thinking of how his siblings would likely react if they ever found out the truth about him.

"Oh, I agree," Suzanne said.

"I have to admit, Marcus made some valid points, even though I argued with him. I'm from a non-magic family. I have two brothers and a sister who are police officers, and I certainly hear a lot of antimage comments. My dad used to be a copper, too. I haven't told any of my family what I am." He sighed.

"So why'd you argue with him then?" Natalie asked.

"That's another long story. It's not nearly as black and white as Marcus was suggesting."

"Go on," Natalie encouraged him.

Jon paused to gather his thoughts. "LEO was founded just over 60 years ago," he said. "Do you know the background of that?"

"Not really," Suzanne admitted, while Natalie shook her head.

"I'm sure there were plenty of reasons, but the real catalysts were three murder trials that happened widely spread apart, between 1950 and 1956. One was in Canberra, Australia, one in Valencia, Spain, and one in Massachusetts, somewhere near Boston. Those places all still had the death penalty at the time. Very different fact situations, but the accused in all three cases were mages who were actually innocent. They each made memory stones that proved their innocence, but not surprisingly, the non-magical authorities wouldn't accept those as reliable evidence."

Natalie sighed. "Unfortunately, I have to admit that makes sense. How would they know it's impossible to fictionalize a memory stone? If they even knew what a memory stone was?"

"Right, but the thing is, virtually everything about all three cases was botched. Circumstantial evidence, deliberately falsified or withheld evidence, crazy media circuses that prejudiced the juries, who weren't sequestered. The worst was the one in Spain. The mage was convicted of abducting and murdering a 6-year-old child, even though no body had been found. He was executed in spite of the fact that the case had holes you could drive a tank through. The child showed up four years later, perfectly fine. She had actually been abducted by her father, who had allegedly not known anything about the trial even though it was all over the news. The mother had told the court she had been happily married to her then current husband for 10 years and that he was the child's father. In fact, she had divorced the first bloke when the kid was 2."

Natalie looked bewildered. "How hard is it to look into a person's marital status?" she asked.

"That's just one of the many glaring shortcomings in the way the trial was handled."

"Did the authorities know the accused were mages?"

"Oh yes," Jon confirmed. "Back then the Council wanted to co-operate and assist the mundane authorities as much as possible. They didn't want people getting away with crimes because of magical help any more than the nons did. But obviously they knew those three were innocent and they did everything they could to get proper justice. They got blocked at every turn."

"I had no idea," Natalie said. "To be honest, I kind of thought the Council had always been dominated by isolationist types."

"Well, that's partially true," Jon agreed. "We've always had the huge divide between the isolationists and the ones who want to live in the real world. Those trials took place just before an election, so you can guess what happened."

"They cleaned house and voted in a set of councillors with completely different views?" Natalie guessed.

"Hole-in-one. LEO was formed, and we started investigating our own bad guys. We used to be a whole lot more subtle about it, though. If a mage had been arrested and was imprisoned, we just kept an eye on things, with some of our people working for the police and as prison guards. It was only about 10 years ago that we started removing mage criminals from mundane prisons."

"I thought Marcus mentioned 25 years."

"He was wrong. The Council passed a law 10 years ago that said LEO was to use all means possible to ensure that all magical criminals were tried in our own justice system. In fact, that bill was tabled by one of the two Canadian councillors, and it was pretty hotly debated."

"Let me guess," Natalie said drily. "The Canadian councillor was Constance Reeve, right?"

"Yes, I believe so. She's a bit of a nightmare, that one, in my opinion. I mean, obviously, I'm a cop; I'm all for getting the bad guys off the street. But she's like a right-wing fanatic."

"Actually, I know why she's so over the top," Natalie told him. "Her son was murdered. It was totally a wrong-place-at-the-wrong-time kind of thing. He got in the way of a bar fight and got knifed. He fell into a dark corner and bled out before anyone realized he was seriously injured. His assailants got convicted of manslaughter, rather than murder, and were released on good behaviour after something like four years."

"Huh, I can see why that would impact her views on law enforcement," Jon said thoughtfully.

"Was that when they also made the law that says that once convicted, you can't leave a magical community?" Suzanne asked.

"Yep."

"What, ever? Even after you've done your time?" Natalie was startled. She had been just about to take a bite of her sandwich but pulled it away from her mouth as she spoke.

"Yeah. The conservatives, especially Constance, argued that if your moral compass is poor enough that you'd use magic to commit a crime, you pretty much can't ever be trusted again," Jon explained. "The liberals argued for the Character Test, which I guess they figured was a decent compromise."

Suzanne made a face at that, so evidently she knew about this, even if her sister did not.

"What's that?" Natalie asked, confirming Jon's guess.

"A kind of intense mental examination. It requires the person's consent since it's way more invasive than normally allowed, and there's another pile of rules and regs about that one. There have to be two examiners, and they're only allowed to look into certain things—stuff like that. But it basically determines if the person is likely not to reoffend. If you pass, you're as free as the rest of us."

"Wow, I had no idea."

"Did you say you were at the scene of that arrest, Suzanne?"

"Yes. It was a domestic assault, and actually I was the one who called it in since I saw he was a mage."

"I'd wondered how that bloke was tagged," Jon said. "Are you often in a position to report these things?"

"Well, not often, but there's been a few. Drunk drivers and assaults, mostly. If I can see some obvious criminal offence, particularly if they get arrested in the ordinary way, and if I can tell they're mages, then I report it."

"So I guess you've been asked to testify a few times?"

"Yep. I just tell them it has to be on my day off, or some time when I'm not on shift. *Some* of us know how to say no."

Natalie snorted at her sister's remark. Jon raised an eyebrow, realizing that there was meaning to the pointed remark that he was not privy to.

"Funny you should say that, because I did say no, last night," Natalie said. "I e-mailed the North American chief LEO and told him no more gateways, not until this whole thing with my firm is resolved. I've got too much on my plate."

She rubbed her head as she said that and closed her eyes. A crease appeared between her eyebrows, and she appeared to wince.

"Are you sure you're not sick, Nat? You took terrible." Suzanne voiced the concern that Jon was feeling, but he had been unsure how it would be received coming from him.

"Constance Reeve apparently does not approve of my resignation," Natalie said in a clipped tone.

"What's it got to do with her?"

"She seems to believe LEO is her own private army, and apparently I'm an enlisted flunky with no right to resign."

Jon made a low growling noise under his breath. "You've got that right. The private army part, anyway. Did you know she's managed to make three North American LEO chiefs quit in the last ten years? Seth Turner has lasted longer than any of them, but even he can't stand her."

"Yes, I know. Although it was Seth who told me about her son, so I guess he gets why she's the way she is. Anyway, she interrupted me in court this morning, wanting an explanation of my e-mail to Seth. My e-mail was perfectly clear. I told her I was in court and couldn't talk, but she wouldn't take no for an answer."

"So, what happened?" Suzanne asked.

"She kept trying to yell at me about it, so I shut her out."

"How does one shut out a First Circle communicator?" Jon asked. "Now that's a trick *I'd* like to learn. That woman has jarred my concentration a time or two. No bloody manners at all, that one."

"I just sort of visualized a solid brick wall, and when she kept trying to get through, I put steel over top of it. Anyone else would take the hint, but she keeps trying. It's like a migraine. Or maybe a steel spike being driven into my skull."

"That is assault," Suzanne said angrily. "She's got no right."

Jon nodded. "I agree with your sister. That is completely unacceptable. I would recommend you make a memory stone while it's fresh in your mind. Evidence, even if you want to take some time to think about whether you want to press charges. I wonder what her First Circle weakness is?"

"Press charges?" Natalie was startled.

"Why not?" Jon asked. "Suzanne is right. That's assault. And you should demand more money."

Natalie laughed but shook her head. "I'm not on the payroll."

"What? You mean to tell me you do all this for free?"

"Well, yeah. I guess I figure since I have this freakish ability, it's only right."

"I have a freakish ability too," Jon pointed out drily. "But there's no chance I'm working for free. They pay me very well. You're letting them walk all over you."

"I've been telling her that for years," Suzanne observed.

"I'm just hoping there aren't going to be any more 'escapes' around here in the near future."

"Not that I know of. But then I've got those 40-odd e-mails that I need to look at …"

Natalie grimaced sympathetically.

"That reporter is great at twisting things around," Suzanne pointed out. "I bet if there were absolutely no escapes in the Toronto area for the next few months, she'd imply that her allegations were making the person responsible lie low, so it's proof that she's right."

"I can't win." Natalie groaned.

Jon frowned. "I could probably let you know if I hear of anything nearby, but I can't do anything to postpone it. And for that matter, it's entirely likely I might not hear of it. I usually only get called in for the ones that need my special abilities."

"You must travel all the time?" Suzanne asked. Jon nodded. "How do you explain what you do to your family?"

"I tell them I'm in the military," he answered, chuckling at Natalie's startled look. "It's the last thing I'd want to do, really. With LEO, I can use my abilities to their fullest extent, but since I'm not dealing with non-mages, I don't have to worry about the ethics of the thing. The story fits, though. I supposedly do some kind of counterterrorism top secret stuff. Hence, I can't talk about it much. And if anything ever were to happen to me, well, counterterrorism's a dangerous job, isn't it? It also explains why I sometimes have sunburn at odd times," he added. "I'm ginger, I burn easily."

"You miss them?"

"Sometimes. I've got quite a big family, and they've all got kids, so we're a big, rowdy lot. Family parties are brilliant. Pity I'm going to miss my brother's fortieth. It's a week Saturday, but I'm on a three-month rotation around North and South America."

"All right, I'll make you a deal," Natalie offered.

Jon wasn't sure what she was suggesting. He gave her a confused look.

"I'll get you home in time for your party and back the next day, but in return I want some information, maybe classified."

"You can do that?" Jon asked, his mouth dropping open. "Send me to England?!" His fingers slackened a little on his coffee cup in surprise, and he slopped a little coffee on the table accidentally, before firming up his grip.

"Nat hasn't found her limit yet." Suzanne grinned.

"I don't want to try," Natalie retorted. "Can you imagine Constance's reaction if she knew I could send someone across the sea? Besides, it's illegal to bypass border security. But obviously you're legally allowed to be in England. And Canada. Are you okay with bending that law?"

"LEOs are actually allowed to do that," Jon said. "If I use a border portal, I just have to flash my badge and I'm through. I'm an ordinary person at airport security, but on the mage side, I've got top clearance. So what kind of information are you looking for?" He still felt stunned and was mulling over the possible implications of such a powerful ability.

"It's about that allegation linking my firm to prison escapes," Natalie replied. "I don't really know what the reporter's sources might have been, so it's a bit hard to fight when I don't know exactly what I'm fighting. But it would make my life easier if I could have accurate information on magical criminals taken out of the ordinary justice system in the last year, at least from Toronto-area jails. In fact, if possible, even arrests of people who were on the mundane wanted list, or are on parole, since those are all counted among 'missing fugitives.'"

Jon pursed his lips. "A lot of that is confidential information."

"As you saw that day, it's usually on the news in under an hour after each escape," Natalie pointed out drily. "So how confidential is it, really? What if you just gave me the information of those who were actually convicted in the magic system? Wouldn't that be effectively public information? Public to mages, anyway?"

Jon thought about it for a moment. "Yes, you're probably right. Sorry to be a stickler for the rules, but ..."

"You're a cop; you're supposed to be a stickler for the rules." Natalie smiled. "It's just, if I know who really escaped and who didn't, it helps me figure out what to fight, you know? I'm convinced it's complete BS anyway. If anyone really had reason to suspect me, I'd have the police at my door, not an investigative reporter pointing fingers at my firm."

"All right, I reckon I can do that."

"Excellent. Here's my number," she said, jotting it down on the napkin. "I imagine you can get back to my condo next Saturday? I'll have to do it from there. You saw what one of my gateways looks like. They're not subtle."

"I noticed." Jon laughed. "I'm still blown away at the thought of someone who can build a gateway over thousands of miles! And across the sea. The portals can't do that; I have to catch a plane for the ocean crossings."

Natalie sighed. "I'd be grateful if you didn't tell anyone about that. Do you have a picture of somewhere private I can send you?"

"Don't think so. Can you just grab something off the Internet?"

Natalie shook her head. "Can't. Most places online are too public. The gateway's just as obvious at the other end."

"How about London headquarters?"

"No way, my secret would be out. LEO does *not* know my range, and I want to keep it that way."

"Huh." Jon pulled out his phone and started scrolling through pictures. "Hey, here's one. In my kitchen," he suggested, showing her the phone. "My sister took it a couple of months ago. We were just mucking around, being silly." He looked a little embarrassed as he passed over the phone to show a picture of himself wearing some kind of puffy-looking hat with a Union Jack on it and making a face.

Natalie grinned. "Yeah, that's enough detail. I can see the window and the side of the stove. Nobody will be there?"

"No, I live alone," Jon confirmed.

Just then Natalie's phone buzzed. She glanced at the e-mail that was being previewed. Her face paled and she swore as she clicked it and read the whole thing.

"The College of Legalists has sent investigators to the firm, and they're asking for me. I need to go upstairs," she explained. "I'm really going to need that information, Jon."

Chapter 6

Natalie's step faltered as she entered the main reception area of the firm, to find the managing partner waiting for her. Phillip Mastersen was usually a jovial man with a booming laugh and a ready smile, but not today. The main reception area of the firm was spacious and well-appointed with several clusters of couches for waiting visitors and a fantastic view from the 24th-floor picture window. But today it was empty except for the waiting managing partner and the receptionist, the latter of whom was studiously ignoring them.

"Natalie, there you are. Please go to the McClure meeting room."

Natalie looked toward the small meeting room he had indicated, noticing that the doors to other interior meeting rooms along the corridor were all closed, with the signs indicating they were in use. Though the firm had clustered its meeting rooms in the same area, it was odd that so many were in use simultaneously. Were there multiple investigators interviewing numerous people at once? A shiver ran down her back.

"Are these all investigators?" She waved her arm weakly at the closed doors.

"They are," Phillip Mastersen said in a tone so devoid of expression that she felt her heart sink even further. "This is a bad day for Mason Sullivan. Please do your part to turn this around for us."

"I'll do what I can."

Natalie pushed aside the door that stood slightly ajar and walked in, feeling awkward about the fact that she was holding a disposable Starbucks coffee cup. It made it clear that she had been off getting a coffee rather than working in her office when her presence was sought.

"Good afternoon. Ms. Benson, I assume?" The speaker was an older woman with a narrow face and prominent cheekbones, old-fashioned half glasses perched halfway down her nose. She was wearing a flowered blouse that had probably gone out of fashion thirty years ago. Natalie was immediately reminded of a particularly picky teacher she had had in grade school.

"Yes. I apologize for keeping you waiting," she added politely, holding out her hand for a handshake. "Unfortunately, I wasn't aware you were coming."

The woman visibly hesitated before extending her hand, and the handshake was very brief. She did not smile or wave aside the apology.

"My name is Meredith Baxter. I am with the Investigations Branch of the Ontario College of Legalists," she said, introducing herself.

Natalie nodded and took a seat, but she said nothing as she waited for the woman to continue. The reason for the visit was immediately obvious, but Natalie felt it would not do her any good if she went on the defensive. Her heart rate sped up a little, and she tried to will it to return to a regular speed, hoping that the investigator was not an astute reader of body language.

"The College has received a complaint, and we wondered if you could shed any light on the situation."

"What situation would that be?" Natalie asked blandly.

The investigator gave her a pointed look, but Natalie merely raised an eyebrow in response.

"The allegations of magery at Mason Sullivan, including the possibility of magical interference with the operation of the court and the connection with jailbreaks in the greater Toronto area, among other matters," Meredith Baxter clarified in a disapproving tone.

"My knowledge of those allegations is not particularly in-depth," Natalie told her with a deliberately casual shrug. "I am aware that both allegations were made in two newspaper articles which appeared in the

Toronto Sun within the last few weeks. Neither article appeared to have a great deal in the way of factual evidence to support it."

"Nonetheless, the College's mandate is to ensure the integrity and ethical practices of its members. These are allegations of great severity and concern," Meredith responded in a frosty tone.

"These are allegations with virtually no substance," Natalie contradicted her bluntly. "We've got a reporter seeking to make a name for herself by cashing in on the rabid antimagic prejudice to get on the front page. Do you honestly mean to tell me that the College of Legalists has initiated a formal investigation based on nothing more than what was said in those two articles?"

The investigator did not respond but only raised her own eyebrows. Natalie gritted her teeth and tried to suppress her growing irritation. Just at that moment, another lance of pain hit her temples as Councillor Reeve attempted to breach her barrier and re-establish mental communication. A wave of fury flooded Natalie, though she irrationally felt just as angry at the College investigator as she was with Constance. She closed her eyes momentarily and took a deep breath, trying to gain control of her temper and also attempting to solidify her mental barrier. Suzanne's suggestion of an assault charge was gaining appeal.

Opening her eyes again, Natalie focused her gaze on the view outside the window momentarily and then looked down at the highly polished wooden table in front of her. Having realized that she had unconsciously clenched her fists, she made a conscious effort to relax as she met the investigator's eyes once more.

"If you insist, I will try to respond to these allegations, but considering there were only a lot of vague implications in them, that's a bit hard," she said in a clipped tone. "I assume you are a lawyer yourself? A litigation lawyer?"

"I am," Meredith replied. "I practised commercial litigation for 25 years before joining the Investigations Branch."

"All right then. So you know that fraud is the one area that tends to have both a civil and a criminal component. Considering that the hot button item in the media these days is all the prison escapes, it's a bit hard to tie that to a firm that doesn't practise criminal law. But a firm with a large civil fraud practice is going to be your best option if that's your intention."

"I hardly think that the reporter is coming up with an allegation first and then trying to figure out whom she can attach it to," the investigator said in a scathing tone.

"It's completely illogical to suggest that the firm which obtained evidence that helped put two people in jail must have something to do with the fact that both of them escaped. If it weren't for us, they wouldn't have been in jail in the first place. What possible motive do we have to help them get out? So they can continue stiffing our clients?"

"You are suggesting that your firm got two of the people named arrested?" The tone now was disbelieving. Natalie sighed.

"In a manner of speaking. That is actually about the only unequivocal fact in the entire thing. The article named three specific people who escaped from jail. We acquired an Anton Piller order against two of them. I don't know for sure, but it's possible that some of the evidence we seized may also have been used by the police. The third person was someone the firm acted for in a real estate transaction, which had absolutely nothing to do with his criminal activities. In fact, we didn't act *for* him; he was the purchaser, and we were acting for the vendor."

"And you know that how?"

"Because we ran the names from the article in our client database, of course. We're not going to completely ignore something like that, even if it is vague and circumstantial. It did mention Anton Pillers, and we do a fair number of those."

Meredith raised an eyebrow. "Anton Pillers, huh? It takes a lot of convincing to get a judge to order one of those."

Natalie didn't like her tone. "What do you mean by that?"

"Oh, I don't know. A little magery might just help grease the wheels."

Natalie's anger flared. "Please. We have at least three boxes filled with documents for each order. You want to paw through them? Be my guest."

"Doesn't change the possibility."

Natalie took a deep breath, trying desperately to control her rising temper. "If you have any evidence of a mage having messed with a judge's mind, I'd be delighted to hear it. We have all of the documentary evidence at hand on which the judges made their decisions in both of those cases. It's not reasonable to jump to the conclusion that there was magical coercion involved unless, at a minimum, the documentation is lacking."

"If mages weren't so obscure and secretive, maybe people wouldn't be so fast to jump to conclusions."

"Back when it wasn't socially acceptable to be gay, how many people openly admitted that they were?"

"What does that have to do with anything?" Meredith Baxter seemed genuinely confused at the turn the conversation had taken.

"It's exactly the same! I can't blame mages at all for not wanting to openly admit what they are. It would be practically like sticking a giant target on their backs." Natalie paused, afraid she might have been too obvious about her sympathies. But what was she supposed to do, pretend to be as antimage as everyone else? Hiding the truth was hard enough. Lying was out of the question.

"You have strong opinions on this subject."

"I do. I don't like discrimination. That goes equally for racist, homophobic, sexist or antimagical discrimination."

"Are you a mage, Ms. Benson?"

"That is a completely inappropriate question, Ms. Baxter. Just as inappropriate as asking about my bra size, my sexual orientation or my religious beliefs. What are you investigating, exactly? Whether there's a mage at Mason Sullivan? Or whether there is someone at Mason Sullivan who has breached the Code of Ethics? An ethical mage has just as much right to be a lawyer as an ethical non-mage."

"Those people are not to be trusted."

"Some people believe all Moslems are terrorists. That prejudice doesn't make it true. The business of law deals in facts, figures and evidence, not speculations and prejudice."

"It is a fact that large numbers of people have escaped from jail, many of them obviously utilizing magical assistance."

"So I hear. But this firm needs solid information in order to investigate and either rebut the allegations or determine if there really is some wrongdoing within this firm. Presumably, so does the College. I can't think of anything I can do about it in the absence of solid information."

"You can sign an undertaking to voluntarily cease practice while the investigation is under way," the investigator suggested, her tone cold.

77

"What?!" Natalie sat bolt upright in her chair, her face clearly expressing her fury. "What possible justification is there for asking me to do that?"

"The rumours are rife within the legal community, Ms. Benson. You have to be aware of that. Your firm is losing clients and respect."

"The rumours are utterly baseless allegations made by a newspaper reporter who has much to gain by getting a story on the front page. What have I done wrong? Are you suggesting the whole fraud department ought to quit? And leave our clients hanging? Do you consider that ethical?"

"This is going to be a long and thorough investigation, Ms. Benson. Uncooperative behaviour on your part will only make it worse."

"There is no way in hell that I am going to voluntarily cease practice, unless or until you people get some actual facts on your side. Come see me when you have some evidence against me. Right now I'm way too busy for this crap. Good day."

Natalie got up and left the room, ignoring the managing partner who still stood in the reception area, now talking to another of the senior partners. They both fell silent as she walked past them toward her office.

Just as she approached her office, Raj stepped out of his adjoining office, his face utterly devoid of its usual humour.

"There you are. We need to go talk to James."

"Right now?"

Raj gave her a strange look. "I don't think it can wait. That was the most brutal meeting I've ever sat through. I think I'll have a whole lot more sympathy for a witness being cross-examined from now on."

"The whole thing is absolutely ridiculous. The thought that this firm could be in actual danger because of completely BS allegations makes me want to bite somebody's head off. And I have a headache from hell, but I already took two Advils, so I'm gonna have to stick it out until my four hours is up." Of course, she hadn't actually taken two Advils, but the real reason she didn't want to take two was for fear that the painkillers might weaken the barrier she was holding against Constance's continued attempts to breach her mental defences. That was the last thing she needed to deal with, on top of everything else that was going on.

Natalie took a deep breath and tried to reduce her irritation. She certainly couldn't take out her frustrations on James.

"All right, let's go talk to him." She stalked ahead of Raj and walked toward James' office, not looking to the right or the left. Even without looking directly at anyone, she found it impossible to avoid noticing that the tension in the air was thick enough to cut with a knife.

Natalie saw that James Behrman's face was even paler than it had been the morning of the first newspaper article, but this time she was too irritated to worry about his state of mind.

"You wanted to see us?" she said in a clipped tone, pulling a seat further away from in front of James' desk so that she could stretch her legs out comfortably. Raj, as was his usual habit, did not even take a seat but propped himself against the wall partially behind Natalie, with his hands in his pants pockets.

"Do you still think I was overreacting?" James asked in a hopeless tone. "This is even worse than I feared."

"This investigation is a load of crap," Natalie said angrily. "Doesn't the College have to meet a reasonable standard in their evidence before launching an investigation?"

James raised an eyebrow. "I'd say they've got enough to warrant an investigation," he contradicted her, looking a bit puzzled by her vehemence.

"Who else did they question?" Raj asked. He rubbed his eyes as if he, too, were suffering from a severe headache.

"So far, virtually all of the partners, and every senior associate who was specifically named on the record of any one of the cases they are looking into," James responded with a sigh. "So what do you propose we do about it?"

"Wait, what cases are they looking into?" Natalie asked, jolting to a more upright position in surprise. "That woman was just asking me about those idiotic newspaper articles, as if they had any substance or factual basis."

Raj snorted. "How long were you in there?"

Natalie swivelled around to look at him and saw that he was looking at her with a baffled expression on his face. "About 20 minutes or so, why?"

"I was being grilled for an hour and a half. What did you do, walk out on the investigator?"

"Uh, yeah," Natalie admitted. "With my head already splitting open, I had no patience at all for it. I did try to explain to her how much evidence has to go into getting an Anton Piller. I offered to give her copies of the supporting motion materials so that she could see for herself how much evidence you need."

"Do we need client permission?"

"I guess it wouldn't hurt to ask. If our clients are really starting to jump ship, we don't need to piss them off worse, if we can help it."

"If?" James repeated heavily. "Considering that not one single new file has been opened in a week, there can be no doubt how the clients are feeling about this situation. Who were the clients on those Anton Pillers in the article?" he asked.

"One was for Fidelity Insurance," Raj responded. "The other one was for Alpha Pharmaceutical."

Natalie closed her eyes and rubbed her temples.

"What is wrong with you?"

"Migraine."

"Since when do you get migraines?"

"Not very often, fortunately. But no surprise now. I've been trying every which way to find any kind of connection or actual solid fact whatsoever and coming up completely empty, since there aren't any."

"Let's back up a second," Raj suggested. "Nat, you seem to be under the impression that the College of Legalists is investigating based on nothing more than those two newspaper articles. Right?"

"Uh, yeah?"

"Brace yourself." He took a deep breath. "We've been served with a Notice of Application from the College. There are fifteen wildly different lawsuits or legal transactions mentioned in this thing. They all involve someone missing from jail or for whom there's a warrant out for their arrest, all of them with Mason Sullivan on the record representing one of the parties."

James jumped in before Raj could continue.

"We almost always seem to have acted for the other party, not the missing person, but the sheer number and variety is definitely enough to warrant an investigation. This is not a completely bullshit witch hunt; this is a total nightmare for the entire firm." He blotted his shiny forehead with a much-abused napkin as he spoke.

Natalie's mouth dropped open as she looked at the senior partner in horror. She felt as though she had been running along a completely solid path, pounding her irritation out with each footstep, only to find she had suddenly fallen off a cliff whose approach she had failed to notice.

"I'm not surprised we're losing staff," Raj added gloomily. "Hell, I would go look for another job right now if I had that option."

Natalie looked back and forth between the two men. "She never mentioned any lawsuits, except for those Anton Pillers mentioned in the article," she protested.

Raj gave her a sardonic look. "Did she, by any chance, make a leading remark about the newspaper articles and then just let you ramble on?"

"Well, um ..."

"And you call yourself a trial lawyer," he scoffed. "Oldest trick in the book. Ask a broad, open-ended question, and see if the witness will spill their guts about anything and everything. Way to go, Nat."

Natalie felt her face getting hot. She wanted to sink through the floor. Raj was right, it was a common approach. How could she have been so stupid? Even the resignation suggestion was probably just a ploy to see if she would react in a way that suggested guilt.

"What are some of the wildly different lawsuits then?"

"The list is insane. A mortgage fraud case, several small insurance fraud matters, a thing about a pro golfer who was accepting bribes to lose certain matches, a lottery thing where there were really two winning tickets but one went missing, along with the store owner."

"It's not even just the litigation departments," James put in. "Corporate was acting for a health food company that was found to have been mislabelling some of their products. The CEO got a 15-month prison sentence, was out on a day pass about six months in, and disappeared. Wills and Estates had an estate administration matter with an absconding trustee. A few million dollars went missing with him."

As the list went on and on, Natalie felt more and more as though the ground was washing out from under her feet, and the more she tried to catch her balance, the faster the ground was being swept away. She was entirely speechless and felt more helpless than she ever had in her life. Then she suddenly winced and grabbed her head as another wave of pain lanced through her brain. Anger flooded back in as she recognized another attack on the mental wall she had built to exclude Councillor Reeve.

"You look like your head is going to explode," Raj said, a frown on his face. "Maybe you should go home."

Natalie made a disgusted noise in the back of her throat. "As if I can go home with all this going on."

"Natalie!" Raj said in a sharp, loud voice. She winced and jerked backward in her chair so hard that the chair rocked, which caused her to clench her eyes shut and grab her head with both hands. "Yeah, that's what I thought," he added in a quieter voice. "Your head is about to split into 17 pieces. Quite frankly, you are no use to us in this state."

"Raj is right," James agreed with a sigh. "We need you and everyone else on top of their game. Go home, go to bed, let things simmer in the back of your head and see if something occurs to you. Preferably before the College shuts the entire firm down."

"As long as people aren't going to read something into that as well."

"Not much we can do about that. There's a whole line of cabs sitting out front of the hotel on the other side of the road," Raj noted, looking down through James' plate glass floor-to-ceiling window. "You can be home in 10 minutes."

"Go," James ordered. "Raj, let me know what the clients say about giving those Anton Piller materials to the College. And get Duplicating to start making copies anyway. I can't see the clients refusing permission. Natalie, we'll talk tomorrow. Get some rest."

"Thanks, both of you."

Natalie slid into the back seat of one of the waiting cabs and gave the driver her address. As he put the car into gear, she was surprised to hear him exclaim, "Oh my God! Jeez, I've been sitting here for 15 minutes and I didn't even notice."

Puzzled, she looked up, to see that he was not looking at her but toward the courtyard area in front of her office building, which contained several benches and planters in a geometric pattern. On the side of each, facing toward the street, spray-painted graffiti was visible. Someone had painted a hanging figure in a noose on the largest planter. Underneath, in dripping red letters, had been written, "Mages, get out!"

Chapter 7

Suzanne opened her eyes slowly and stared at her sister with a look of horror on her face.

"And I thought I knew what a bad day was," she muttered. She looked at the green quartz stone lying in the palm of her hand as if it were a live snake. "If I didn't know that memory stones can't be fictionalized or exaggerated in any way, honestly I would have a hard time believing she was that incredibly aggressive. She looks like a harmless old lady." She put the stone down on Natalie's coffee table and deliberately pushed it as far away as she could reach. Then she picked up her drink and drained it in a few swallows.

"Aggressive doesn't come close," Natalie replied sourly. "She is the most obnoxious person I have ever met. You've only seen her in public mode, like when she's campaigning to be re-elected."

"That's true. Every time there was an extra pulse of that awful headache, was that her attacking again?"

"Probably," Natalie confirmed. "She didn't give up until about midnight. I tried to keep the shield up the next day, but it was really exhausting. Fortunately, it seems like she finally gave up."

"She kept actively attacking you for *over 12 hours?*"

"On and off," Natalie said grimly. "That's why I took Jon's advice and made the stone. I wasn't about to rely on my word against hers. I plan to complain to the Council next time I'm in Neekonnisiwin. I'm going to demand that she never be allowed to contact me again. If they want me for something, there's no reason the chief LEO can't phone me."

Natalie had not been able to get any sleep the day she had left work early. She'd just lain on the couch with a cool cloth over her eyes. At least she was able to keep the cloth cool without actually having to get up.

"Good. Look, Nat, the thing that worries me even more is that I hadn't realized the kind of stress you're under. You do far too good a job of hiding all that and looking cool and professional all the time. What are you going to do about this College of Legalists thing? And what can I do to help?"

Natalie grimaced. "God knows. I am still in shock over it all. I was being my usual stubborn one-track-mind self, determined that it was a load of crap and only based on those stupid newspaper articles. And now I found out it's way more serious."

"That's the part I don't understand," Suzanne said. "Did the newspaper articles trigger the investigation? Or were they already investigating your firm anyway, and the articles were just a coincidence?"

"Your guess is as good as mine. But I'm sure you've heard about Bill 409 put forward by our least favourite MP, Daniel Baxter?"

Suzanne made a growling noise in the back of her throat. "The one about requiring all of the evil mages to identify themselves to their employers? It's the stupidest thing I've ever heard. How would they expect to enforce it? Not to mention it completely contradicts the Charter of Rights."

"You said it. I might just as well resign as tell the firm I'm a mage. Especially now."

"So what's that got to do with the investigation?"

"I googled the investigator who was questioning me. She's his wife."

"The MP's wife?"

"Yup. And it was pretty clear during the interview that she is as adamantly antimage as he is."

"Did she launch the investigation?"

Natalie shrugged. "No clue, but locating evidence to help hubby get his pet bill passed is a possibility, wouldn't you say?"

"Huh, could be. So, um, have you heard from Jon since that day?"

Natalie gave her sister a mocking look. "Very subtle. Are you trying to matchmake?"

"I'd have to be blind not to have noticed that he was interested." Suzanne grinned, unabashed. "I'm not so sure that meeting was as coincidental as it seemed."

Natalie's eyes widened. "Really? I didn't think of that."

"Question is, what about you? Interested?"

Natalie smiled. "I might be. We had dinner on Tuesday."

"How come he's in Toronto so much? Not exactly a hotbed of magical crime around here, is it?"

"He travels constantly, and I do mean constantly. He'd been to Argentina, Guatemala, Brazil, a few places in the US and somewhere else, I think maybe it was Puerto Rico, in the time between when we met him at Starbucks and when we had dinner. One week."

"Good God."

"Sounds like he knows the portal network as well as I know the subway system. Probably for the whole world. Fortunately, it's not exactly hard for us to get around fast."

"Did he get you that list?"

"Yeah, it was great. It goes back five years and lists every single person arrested in Canada, what they were charged with, whether they were convicted and whether they were taken out of jail or just arrested somewhere else."

"What do you wanna bet it wouldn't have been that detailed if you were 55, male and bald?"

Natalie chuckled but did not answer.

"But more seriously, how many of them match your College Notice?"

Natalie sighed. "Nine. So more than half, really, are magical criminals. And I'm not going to be able to produce any evidence about them. I was kind of hoping more of the ones named in the Notice of Investigation wouldn't be on Jon's list so that I could maybe dig and find out that they were people who missed parole appointments or something. Check this out though: I came across something really weird, nothing to do with my College thing."

Natalie bounced off the couch and went into her den, where she unlocked a drawer with a wave of her hand and pulled out a red file folder. She pulled a spreadsheet out and flipped through the first couple of pages to reveal a line that she had marked with a yellow highlighter, pointing it out to Suzanne as she handed her the sheaf of papers.

"Remember that guy who tried to kill Baxter last year?"

"Yeah, that was a strange story. Didn't he die of a brain aneurysm right as they were arresting him? And he was supposed to have been an escapee, so I guess they got that wrong."

"No, they didn't."

"What?"

"He was taken out of jail by LEO. Here." She pointed to the highlighted line where the name Paul Dasovic appeared, with details of having been removed from a prison in Alberta in March 2017 and convicted on charges of break and enter. Having already served some time for the crime, his sentence was for 18 months.

"Wait, when was that thing with Baxter?"

Natalie pulled another piece of paper from the folder and showed her sister a printout of a newspaper article. "May 2017."

"How could he have been out and attempting to murder Baxter two months after being given an 18-month sentence? They don't do parole for good behaviour or anything like that in the mage system."

Natalie opened her mouth to respond, but the phone rang. She reached over and picked up the receiver. Her mood instantly changed as soon as she heard the voice at the other end.

"What?" she said flatly. She listened for a moment, and even Suzanne could hear the tinny sound of the angry voice at the other end. After a couple of seconds, Natalie sighed heavily and just held the phone away from her ear, waiting for the shrill voice to wind down. Once there was silence, she brought the phone back to her ear. "Are you done? Now *you* can listen to *me*, and I suggest you listen closely because I won't be repeating myself. I quit! I have absolutely had it up to my eyeballs with you. You are the most inconsiderate and rude person I have ever met in my entire life. Henceforth, my services are not available to you, or to any member of the Council, or to LEO, and when they ask why, you can tell them it's all your fault. Do not ever contact me again, by any means. That includes phone, e-mail, Canada Post, mental contact or freaking carrier pigeon." She slammed the phone down.

Suzanne started clapping. "There is hope for you yet!" she exclaimed. "I never thought I'd see the day that you would actually unvolunteer."

"I don't think I ever did volunteer," Natalie pointed out. "I got volun-told."

"But you put up with it; that's the whole point," Suzanne crowed.

The phone started ringing again. Natalie glanced at the call display.

"I shouldn't even be surprised," she said in tones of disgust, and she turned away to the sideboard to pour herself a drink. The phone rang until the answering machine clicked on, but the caller hung up before the message finished. Moments later, the phone started ringing again. Natalie leaned down and pulled the cord out of the wall plug. "How old is she, five?" she asked rhetorically.

"She doesn't have your cellphone number, I hope?" Suzanne asked.

"Not bloody likely," Natalie responded. "Nor my work number, or even the name of the firm I work at. For that matter, she probably doesn't even know, or care, what I do for a living. It's outside the mage world; therefore, it's irrelevant. Thank God she wouldn't have a clue how to search for me on Google or LinkedIn or something."

"Too true. Now I am going to introduce you to what normal people do in the evening," Suzanne changed the subject with a grin, although the expression didn't reach her worried eyes. "It's called relaxing. It can involve such activities as watching TV, reading a book, going to a movie or going out to a bar with friends. In other words, *not work*."

Natalie rolled her eyes and picked up her cellphone, but Suzanne snatched it out of her hands. "That includes *not* checking your e-mail. Sit! This little device here is called a remote control. Use it wisely, Grasshopper."

Natalie laughed and gave in. She flopped onto the couch, put her feet up on the arm and turned on the TV. Suzanne poured herself another drink and then made a big bowl of popcorn, being far too generous with the butter and salt.

Two hours later, while eating a pizza that Suzanne had ordered, Natalie noticed that her cellphone started vibrating on the table beside her sister's chair. Suzanne picked up the phone and looked at the display with a narrow-eyed gaze. "Huh, long string of numbers. International call?" She tossed the phone to her sister.

Recognizing the number, Natalie pressed the call answer button and held the phone to her ear. "Hi, Jon. You're ready to come back already? Kind of early, isn't it?"

"Not in England; it's two in the morning."

"Oh, of course. Are you back in your apartment?"

"Yep. And, um, I just got an odd text from Seth. Er, is everything all right?"

"Well, not exactly," she admitted wryly. "What have you heard?"

"That you don't want to ever have any contact with LEO again?"

"Oh God, I shouldn't even be surprised. I told *Constance Reeve* that *she* was not allowed to contact me again."

"Good for you," Jon said.

Natalie picked up her prism from the coffee table and traced the familiar pattern in the air in front of her. Within seconds, the glowing arch revealed Jon standing in his kitchen, just turning around after having evidently reached up to put something on a shelf in the cupboard. He had his cellphone pressed to his ear and a chipped mug of steaming liquid in his hand. Reaching upward had caused his shirt to ride up a bit, revealing a strip of flat stomach above his low-rise jeans. Natalie's eyes fixed on the ripped muscles with just a hint of hair below the belly button. She pulled her eyes away quickly, afraid he might have noticed where her gaze went.

"I wonder what happens if I step through with my mobile still connected to yours?" he said with a grin, and proceeded to walk forward through the glowing portal, staggering slightly as he stepped into Natalie's living room. "It went dead. Makes sense." He slipped the phone into his jeans pocket and smiled down at Natalie, before noticing that there was someone else in the room.

"Ah, hello, Suzanne."

"How was your party?"

"Brilliant. Though I'm attempting to sober up. My brothers have the alcohol tolerance of a herd of rhinos. I brought my tea with me," Jon replied with a grin, holding up his chipped mug. His gaze swung back to Natalie. "How are you? You look like you've been getting aggro from all sides."

"You could say that," Natalie agreed. "Here, I'll give you the full version." She scooped up the stone from the coffee table and offered it to him.

"I should be sitting down for this, I reckon?" he asked in a more serious tone, immediately recognizing the memory stone for what it was.

"Definitely," Suzanne answered for her sister. "That stone needs to come with a warning label!"

"Sounds like fun." He grimaced. Putting his tea down on the table and taking a seat, he closed his left hand over the stone and traced a pattern over his closed fist with the other hand, which was still encased in its black leather glove. Then his face went blank as he sank into the experience Natalie had embedded in the stone. While he was unaware of her observation, Natalie kept her gaze on him, noticing how the golf shirt he was wearing in place of his usual rumpled T-shirt strained over a very well-developed chest, and how a vein pulsed in his neck when he tensed in reaction to the feelings he was experiencing.

The stones permitted the observer to experience something in a much more compressed period of time than the events really took to unfold, without seeming unduly rushed while experiencing it, so it was not long before his eyes opened again.

"Bloody hell," he exclaimed, with the same look of horror that Suzanne had worn earlier. His face immediately hardened though, and he bounced out of the chair. "Right, I need to borrow your computer. Uh-oh." His face turned slightly green, and he grabbed the back of the chair for support.

Suzanne laughed and pulled out her own, smaller prism, which currently looked like a key chain medallion. She traced a pattern in the air in front of Jon, and his face immediately resumed a normal colour as he straightened up.

"Blimey, what was that?"

"Paramedic skill number one," Suzanne said. "A.k.a. Sober Up Fast. Having people throw up on me is not one of my more enjoyable experiences."

"Brilliant. Do I also get to skip the hangover?"

"Drink some water."

"Be nice," Natalie told her sister. Turning to Jon, she asked, "Why do you need my computer?"

"Because you are going to press charges of assault and mental battery," he said firmly. "I can log on to LEO headquarters in Switzerland and file the charges on the spot. Then I'll just duplicate this memory stone and take it with me when I head over to Neekonnisiwin tomorrow."

"Okay, no hangover," Suzanne conceded, moving her prism around again.

Jon grinned at her. "And you said we're not nearly as powerful as the nons think. Imagine how much you could get for an instant hangover cure?"

"Pity I can't sell it online," she agreed. "It will make you tired, though. I basically sped up your body's own ability to process all those toxins, but your liver's still doing the work."

Turning to Natalie, Jon's face grew more serious. "I don't know how much I can help with your professional investigation, but I am not going to let you get it from both sides when you don't deserve it from either."

"My laptop is over—no, wait, that's my work computer," Natalie said. She gestured toward the small den which was almost entirely filled with a wraparound desk, custom built for the odd-shaped space. "I might be getting paranoid, but let's do it from my own computer, just in case. I'd rather not have any Internet history record that links to some strange unidentifiable remote log-in site."

Jon preceded her into the den, and she waved him toward the chair.

"What if they seize this computer?" Jon suggested.

"Good luck to them. I don't really know what a forensic examination on a computer that was logged on to LEO headquarters would turn up," Natalie replied drily. "Probably just that it was an IP address that they can't identify. A week ago, I would've said there's no way in hell they could come in and seize my stuff, but I'm honestly not so sure anymore. Regardless, the other laptop belongs to them, so they could probably do a forensic examination on that one, even without a court order."

Jon booted up the computer and called up the Web browser, tracing a pattern with one hand over the keyboard to navigate to the magical law enforcement agency's remote access site, an intranet stored on servers located in the various magical communities scattered around the world. There was no Web address to be typed in, so it was impossible for a non-mage to access or hack it. Once logged in, he rapidly located a form for pressing charges and filled in the details. Natalie was astonished to see that he typed with only the first two fingers of each hand, but he did so as rapidly as she could type with all ten fingers.

She leaned against the desk and watched his face, noticing that his jaw was tense. A faint shadow of beard darkened his chin, and she wondered what he would look like with an actual beard. She thought it might suit him.

"Right, read that over and see what you think," Jon said, pushing the chair back from the keyboard to allow her room.

Natalie read through the form, then raised her eyebrows at Jon. "Compensation for all the gateways I've built for LEO? And punitive damages?"

"Absolutely," he said firmly. "Even if this assault hadn't happened, it is still ludicrous that you do so much work for them with no compensation. The fact that she has the nerve to assault you for not being willing to interrupt your income-earning work is twice as bad considering that you do so much for them for free."

"But how can I now demand payment for something that I've clearly willingly done for free to this point?"

"This is about more than just you," Jon told her with a frown. "They should never have even asked a private citizen to expend time and energy on their behalf any time they knock without offering compensation. That's abusive right there. So then I have to ask myself, who else are they abusing?"

"I agree with Jon," Suzanne called from the living room. "Just because you've let them walk all over you for years doesn't mean you have to keep letting them."

"You're a lifesaver," Natalie said with a smile. "I would just love to be a fly on the wall when she gets hauled up to respond to this." She grinned vindictively but then sighed. "Of course, a lot of people apparently feel the same way about me right now, or at least about the unknown mage at Mason Sullivan."

"You don't need to be a fly on the wall. There will be a hearing, and you'll need to attend as the complainant."

A slow smile spread across Natalie's face. "A hearing. Even better."

Just then, the door buzzer sounded. Suzanne walked over to the monitor set into the wall near the door.

"Indian guy, carrying a laptop bag, looks miserable," she told her sister. "I think it's that guy from your memory stone. Raj?"

"You have to know things are bad when Raj is looking miserable," Natalie commented. She checked the monitor and pressed the button. "Come on up, Raj."

He waved into the camera and then disappeared from view as he came inside the building.

Natalie slid the papers from Jon and the newspaper article back into the red folder, which she put back into the drawer in her den. Then she picked up another folder from beside the computer and flipped through it quickly. When Raj arrived a few minutes later, he handed her an envelope.

"Here's the Carsons outline," he told her.

"Thanks, but you could have just e-mailed it," she said, giving him a strange look. "Come on in."

"Oh, you've got company. Sorry, didn't mean to intrude."

"Don't worry about it. This is my sister, Suzanne Timmons, and my friend Jon Forrester." Jon was just shutting down the computer as she mentioned his name. He came over to shake Raj's hand.

Raj didn't smile as he greeted either of them, which was drastically out of character.

"All right, Raj, spit it out. What else has happened?"

"I'm that obvious, huh?"

"Open book."

"Good thing you didn't come back to the office yesterday after your meeting. I didn't want to tell you over the phone, or in an e-mail or something, although I wasn't sure if you might've heard it on the news." He paused, and his eyes flicked toward the TV, which was now playing the evening news. Then he sighed heavily and met her eyes with a solemn gaze. "The building had to be evacuated yesterday afternoon. There was a bomb threat."

Natalie's jaw dropped. She stared at him in shock. "Did they find anything?"

Raj hesitated for a moment before answering. "No," he said slowly.

"You don't sound terribly confident about that," Jon suggested, raising an eyebrow.

"They didn't find any evidence of a bomb, or anything in the office, but there was vandalism in the parking garage," Raj explained.

"What kind of vandalism?"

"Spray paint on cars. There are some reserved parking spots. I guess you pay extra to have one that's reserved for you, and quite a few of our senior partners have them. Each of those spots has a sign with their name."

"Oh my God," Natalie said in a breathy voice, guessing where this story was going.

"Every single one who is from our firm and had a car there got paint sprayed on their car. Plus a P. Smythe from the Royal Bank, because we have a P. Smythe."

"Paul Smythe is a junior associate. I know for a fact he rides his bike to work most days and takes the subway if it's raining. If he has a car, he doesn't drive it to work. And those reserved signs don't say the firm name," Natalie pointed out with a frown.

"The guess is that the vandals knew the garage had the names, looked up our lawyer directory on our Web site, and had a list of all the names, then went around the garage looking for matching names. P. Smythe from the bank was unlucky enough to have the same initial and last name as Paul."

"Nice to know how pathetic our security is," Natalie said in a disgusted tone. "That must have taken plenty of time. Nobody got caught?"

"Nope. It was at the same time as when the building was being evacuated, so I'm sure that wasn't a coincidence. There's some security footage, but the vandals were all wrapped up like ninjas, so none of them could be identified. And 15 more staff members handed in their notice, by e-mail, later on. Apparently, they're not even waiting until they get another job. They just want out quickly."

Natalie sighed and closed her eyes, one hand covering them.

"I'm kind of wishing I could just quit myself," Raj admitted. "Our entire careers could be heading straight down the toilet, and we did nothing wrong. But nobody's going to hire a lawyer who just left Mason Sullivan. I apologize for accusing you of panicking unnecessarily. Looks like you were right on the money."

"Don't feel bad. Panic doesn't help anybody, and you got me thinking constructively, which is exactly what I needed to do." Natalie took a deep breath and lowered her hands, which she clenched into fists. "We can't run away from this. We have to meet it head-on and fight it and make it obvious to everyone that it's complete and utter bullshit. Do you want a drink?"

"I'd like to drink until I don't even remember my own name, but sadly I know that wouldn't help." Raj sounded completely defeated.

"Well, I might have something better for you," Natalie told him.

"Dealing drugs now, are you?"

"Funny boy. Here, a list of every prison escape that's been on the news for the Toronto area for the last year. All 167 of them. That's within the actual GTA, and not pretending that Niagara is part of Toronto."

"You say 167? And the College's Notice lists 15? Where did you get this?"

"Gotta love Google." Natalie did not admit that her searches had begun with Jon's list, but it was true enough that she had quickly been able to locate additional information online from various media sources. Even when it wasn't front page news, prison escapes were enough of a hot topic in the media that it wasn't hard to find details. She had also found, and printed out, a detailed press release from the federal police that had been particularly useful.

Natalie handed Raj a bottle of beer she had retrieved from her fridge, although she couldn't remember how it came to be there. She wasn't much of a beer drinker herself.

"Cheers." Raj cracked open the bottle and drained about half of it in one go, though his expression no longer looked quite so defeated.

"That girl looks familiar," Suzanne suddenly said in a puzzled tone.

Natalie turned to see who her sister was talking about and realized she was staring at the TV with a frown. The screen to the right of the news reader contained a photograph of a young woman and a much older man. The photo of the man showed him with an arm raised and his mouth open, looking like he was giving an impassioned speech. The young woman, on the other hand, was almost as expressionless as if it were a police mug shot.

"Corbin Jamieson, the well-known televangelist, was found dead in a motel room in Philadelphia early this morning. His death appears to have been caused by a drug overdose, but it is not clear whether it was intentional," the news reader said. "Witnesses state that a young blonde woman, who has been identified as Serena Pryor of the State of New York, was seen leaving the motel room late in the previous evening, close to midnight. Ms. Pryor's body was found later this morning. She was also killed by a drug overdose."

"That's the mage, the one who was beaten up and then gang raped," Raj said grimly. "Although I kind of have to wonder about that story now."

Natalie was reminded again of Raj's excellent memory for faces and facts. Though she had been thinking of that story mere days ago, and even though she had, in fact, experienced a memory stone made by that young woman, she had not recognized the photograph.

"What do you mean, you wonder about that story?" Jon asked curiously.

"Allegedly, she was gang raped, but there was a media ban on the court proceedings on that, and her attackers were not convicted. Now she's found in a seedy motel with a fairly wacko preacher old enough to be her father? Doesn't seem likely she was getting spiritual counselling, does it?"

Natalie felt as though a bucket of ice cold water had just been dumped over her. She had experienced a memory stone of the vicious battering and rape and knew the facts were true without question. But Raj's point was equally valid. Why on earth would that traumatized young woman be with a well-known televangelist in a seedy motel late at night, barely a year after that attack? For that matter, it didn't seem all that likely that she would have even wanted to leave the isolated magical community she had moved to after the trial. The stone had left no doubt how devastating the experience had been, though the court case had been, in some ways, almost worse than the original assault.

There was something decidedly peculiar about this story. Natalie struggled to overcome her feelings of empathy for the victim to try to figure out how the facts could fit together.

The news reader went on to identify Serena Pryor as the alleged victim of a beating and rape and implied the same doubt that Raj had expressed. Natalie felt a slow burn of anger. Regardless of the truth of these events, Serena had definitely been the victim of an incredibly vicious assault, and her attackers had not been punished. And now she was being slandered after a tragic death. Though she did not personally know her, Natalie felt the injustice keenly.

A memory of the words spoken by Jon's temporary partner from the previous week crossed Natalie's mind: *We've been doing this for nearly 25 years now, and the hate has been getting worse every year.*

Here was a clear indication of the depths of that hatred.

But further, as Natalie thought of Raj's defeated tone and the employees quitting the firm with little or no notice, she suddenly realized that there were two things that she had stubbornly refused to recognize or accept recently, without making much effort to consider either. Not only had she just jumped to the conclusion that the College's investigation was based on nothing more than the newspaper articles, but also she had been similarly blind about Marcus's opinion. If the Mage Council would be willing to admit the existence of magical law enforcement to the regular criminal justice system, Mason Sullivan would be cleared and nobody's career would be in any danger. All along, she had focused on the idea that the purpose of the secrecy was to protect the First Circles, but as Marcus had said, the abilities of the First Circles had been successfully hidden for centuries; the increase in magical law enforcement activities was far more recent.

"This is very helpful," Raj said, pulling Natalie's attention back to the list she had given him. She was startled to see that he had already dismissed the news story from his mind, as though it were an insignificant series of events. Before she could get offended, however, she reflected that when she had seen the news of the tragic deaths of two young men in a fire a few weeks ago, she had not spent much time considering that two young lives had been tragically cut short. It was easy to write off horrifying events reported in the news as if they didn't matter when you were not personally affected by those events.

The list Raj was looking at was actually a spreadsheet, which also included some details of each person's case and the URL of the Web site she had found that had provided the information. "This is way more names than were mentioned in the Notice of Investigation."

"Does it help, though?" Suzanne asked with a frown. She had been silent for a long time, but her face was pale and Natalie knew her sister was extremely worried. She suspected Suzanne's worry had more to do with the bomb threat and the possible danger to her than with any reaction to the news story. But then she did not think Suzanne had experienced

Serena's memory stone. "It does nothing to defend the accusations about links between escapees and your firm, except to point out that there's more escapees than links."

"True," Raj agreed. "But I've been focusing on the ones in the Notice. More than half of them involve somebody going missing who didn't actually escape from jail."

"Like that CEO James mentioned who disappeared while he was out on a day pass?" Natalie asked. "That doesn't need to involve an accomplice." Though still troubled by the reported deaths, she forcibly pulled her mind away from that story to focus on the situation that was likely to have a much more immediate impact on her life. She also picked up the remote and turned off the TV as she spoke.

"True, although we did act for the company in that one. You could make an argument for us having a motive there. But that estate trustee who disappeared with the money? We were acting for the estate administrator. Having the trustee disappear with the money was terrible for our client. So what's our motive?"

"How does your professional association plan to prove these allegations, anyway?" Jon asked thoughtfully. "They don't just have to prove motive; they have to prove actual guilt. Don't they?"

"You'd think," Natalie agreed. "Innocent until proven guilty and all that. But with the damage that's already been done to the firm's reputation, we just can't afford to be complacent."

"But with these names, and especially the cases where our link with the fugitive is purely circumstantial, we can put in a solid fact-based defence to the College," Raj said thoughtfully. "The facts might not clear us 100 percent, but they sure as hell show how weak the evidence is."

"Plus we tell them about the vandalism and the bomb threat," Natalie added. "And the graffiti from earlier this week. Now that we're talking personal danger to the employees of Mason Sullivan, surely this puts a different spin on it? It's not about protecting mages. It's about protecting everyone who works at the firm."

"You need to get that information to the media, not just your College," Suzanne said. "Getting some public sympathy is going to do more to keep your employees safe than shutting down the investigation. The public probably doesn't care that much about the College of Legalists, if they've even heard of it."

"Good point," Raj agreed. "And the public doesn't know about all the allegations in that Notice, either. They only know about the newspaper articles."

Jon suddenly yawned and looked embarrassed. "Mind if I make myself another cuppa, Natalie? I need some caffeine badly. It's been a long week."

"Of course." Natalie walked into the kitchen herself and filled the kettle from the tap. Jon frowned at the cupboards for a second before unerringly finding the one that contained a box of tea bags hidden way at the back.

Raj gave Jon a curious look. It did not take much for Natalie to guess that he was wondering about her relationship with this man she had never before mentioned. Although Natalie realized that Jon has used magic to locate the tea, it must have looked like he knew exactly where to find things in her kitchen cupboards. And he clearly wasn't making any move to leave even though he had just complained of tiredness. She did not bother to give Raj any explanation. Let him think there was something between her and Jon. Natalie had once wondered whether dating Raj was a possibility, given how in tune their thoughts often were. But Raj had made his dislike of mages clear. She wasn't willing to keep her secret from someone she was dating.

Natalie offered Raj another beer, but it seemed he was suddenly feeling like a bit of a fifth wheel in spite of the fact that Suzanne was also in the room. It was not long before he bid them all good night and left.

"You weren't joking about that spell making me tired," Jon remarked to Suzanne, blinking eyes that were looking distinctly red. "I feel like I'm about to fall over." He pulled out his cellphone and ordered a cab from a long list of saved contacts, providing the name of the hotel he was staying at.

"I'll duplicate the memory stone for you," Suzanne offered. She found a blank piece of quartz in a box in Natalie's bookcase. She went and sat at the table, put the two stones side by side and cast the spell that would make the second stone identical to the first.

Natalie retrieved Jon's list of arrests from the den, together with the file folder that had several more printed pages in it.

"Before you go, I wanted to see if you could look into something that's decidedly odd," she said, pointing out the highlighted name again. "According to your list, this guy was removed from a prison in Toronto in March 2017 and sentenced to 18 months in our system." Then she pulled out several newspaper articles and laid them out on the coffee table.

"But he's the same guy who was all over the news in May 2017." She pointed to the points as she made them. "Paul Dasovic, whom they identify as an escaped inmate, attempted to kill MP Daniel Baxter while he was giving a speech at the West Ottawa Board of Trade." She grimaced. "Baxter is extremely conservative. Antimage, antiabortion, anti–gay marriage, the whole bit. Total asshole, in my opinion. There was a strong police presence because that guy has plenty of people who don't like him. The police were able to prevent anyone from getting hurt and arrested Dasovic."

"But if we transferred Dasovic to our system and convicted him, what the hell was he doing in Ottawa two months later?" Jon asked.

"Exactly what I was wondering," Natalie confirmed.

Suzanne handed Jon the duplicated memory stone. He thanked her and slipped it into his pocket, still frowning at the newspaper article.

"Hey, that's the guy you were talking about, the one who tried to kill Baxter and then died of an aneurysm, right?" Suzanne asked.

"What's an aneurysm?" Jon asked.

"Burst blood vessel in the brain," she explained. "Instantly fatal, and usually totally unpredictable."

"That happened before they even got him out of the room," Natalie said, pointing to the relevant paragraphs of the article.

"Was there an autopsy?"

"Yep," Suzanne confirmed. "And in fact there was a mage at the Ottawa coroner's office who was involved. But you can't tell if someone was a mage after they're dead. He didn't notice anything out of the ordinary. And they were looking because there were accusations that it was some kind of police brutality thing and they were lying about the cause of death."

"Very strange. I'll look up our records on this bloke in Neekonnisiwin tomorrow."

"Sorry to drag you into this. You've already done a lot for me."

"Don't be daft. If there's something dodgy going on at the mage's end of things, then sorting it out is my job. Besides, you got me to my party, *and* your sister prevented a killer hangover. I think I owe both of you."

The door buzzer rang. Suzanne went over.

"Jon's cab is here," she said, then answered the buzzer and told the cab driver his passenger would be right down.

Just before Jon left the apartment, he ducked down and kissed Natalie's cheek. "Keep your chin up. You'll get through this," he told her firmly.

She had a slightly goofy smile on her face as she shut the door. Suzanne wisely did not comment.

Chapter 8

Jon stretched his long body and groaned as he twisted around, causing his back to make some cracking noises. A glance at the clock beside the king-size bed told him he had been asleep for 10 hours straight. No wonder he was stiff!

He was extremely thirsty, too, and grabbed a bottle of water from the mini fridge before stepping out onto a small balcony. Being slightly claustrophobic, he liked finding hotel rooms that had some outdoor space, or at least large windows. The morning air was cool, but it felt like it might get hotter later on. Suddenly remembering that he ought to have had a hangover this morning, he grinned as he realized he felt fine.

While shaving after his shower, his thoughts were more occupied with a certain blonde lawyer than with the task he did every day. She continued to intrigue him, particularly the unexpected combination of strength and vulnerability. Why would someone as clearly self-confident as she was put up with years of being used? It was almost as if she considered it to be some sort of moral obligation. The experience of Constance's attack reminded Jon of two occasions when the forceful councillor had abruptly contacted him at inconvenient times. He had found it irritating, but at least he had actually been on duty on both occasions. The councillor's casual assumption that she had the right to demand answers at any time infuriated him, and not just on Natalie's behalf. There had been a few times when demands had been made of him that he had resisted. Just because it was easier to use the skills of a metamorph did not mean that was the only option, particularly when he was short of sleep and had not seen his own home in months. Maybe such inconsiderate treatment was more widespread than he had realized.

Suddenly, with senses honed by his years in magical law enforcement, Jon sensed an exercise of unskilled magic nearby. For him to sense it from any more than a few feet away suggested an adolescent untaught in the use of his abilities, and such a person usually could not maintain a magical effort for very long. The surges that he sensed suggested some kind of sustained effort. Concerned that the young mage might either be attacking or being attacked, Jon used a quick shape-shift to make the rest of his chin smooth.

Shortly afterward a large crow flew out of the hotel window, in the direction from which the sense of inexpert magic use had originated.

As he flew toward it, however, the magic use ceased. Jon continued in the direction it had come from but found nothing. When he saw a parked police car, he landed in a nearby tree that bent under the weight of the large bird, unnoticed by the two officers in the car. Invisible among the leaves of the tree, the crow became an owl, with hearing strong enough to hear a twig crack 75 feet away. He could now easily listen to the police officers' conversation.

The officers both stopped talking as the radio crackled to life and a brisk feminine voice advised that a report had been received of an altercation involving a knife. The witness thought that someone had been stabbed but was unsure. When the dispatcher identified the area, both police officers got out of the car.

"That's just behind here," one said, while the other used the radio attached to his shoulder to advise Dispatch that they were looking into the report.

Moments later, three young men emerged from an alleyway, two of them clearly supporting the one in the middle. The owl's sharp eyes saw blood dripping from the figure in the middle, but he unfocused them enough to look for the telltale mage glow and did not see it. So that suggested that the adolescent mage might be the attacker.

Since the two police officers were clearly going to intercept the injured young man and his friends, Jon lifted himself silently into the sky and resumed his search for the mage he had sensed.

His head whipped around as he felt another surge of inexpert magic use and heard a thud against a metallic object. Silently, he altered his flight direction and saw a young man jump from the top of a Dumpster, over a wooden fence and into a narrow laneway that was lined on one side with garages. The other side was blank brick walls at the backs of commercial buildings. The young man was dark-haired and tall, likely no more than an inch shorter than Jon, and wore a plain white T-shirt and jeans. A tattoo that looked like some kind of Chinese symbol decorated the side of his neck. He was breathing heavily, and sweat dampened his hair.

There was no sound except the young man's footsteps as the owl circled above his head, though the sight of an owl flying in a peculiar pattern, and during the day, would have looked strange had anyone been watching. Suddenly the young man stumbled slightly, and his face grew panicked as he stopped, looking wildly around him. Then he began walking forward and sideways, altering direction rapidly, so that he made very slow, roundabout progress to the end of the alley, bumping into the fence a few times.

The owl flew ahead and landed on the fence near the end of the alley, where its ability to turn its head almost 180 degrees allowed Jon to quickly ascertain that nobody other than the young man, still feeling his way slowly along the alley, was within sight.

He resumed his own form just as the dark-haired young man reached him. Flipping his octagonal coin in his fingers, he watched without speaking as the young man jerked to a halt, looking wildly around him.

"What the fuck? There were loads of alleyways, and they were moving or something." His voice trailed off as he focused on the coin in Jon's fingers. Then he looked up and flicked his eyes to the side of Jon's head. "You did that, didn't you?"

"I did," Jon confirmed. "It was a confusion hex. Would you mind telling me what you were doing before you jumped the fence, and whether it had anything to do with the bloke dripping blood over on Dundas Street?"

"That wasn't my fault. It was an accident!" He clamped his mouth shut as he realized he had said too much.

Jon raised an eyebrow. "Jon Forrester, magical law enforcement," he abruptly introduced himself. "And you are?"

"Jake."

"Got a surname?"

"What do you mean, magical law enforcement?" Jake demanded, not answering the question.

"Exactly what it sounds like. Magic police. Who track down people who commit crimes using magic and deal with them."

"I didn't commit a crime."

"But you did use magic to do something."

Jake shifted uncomfortably. "It was self-defence."

"Self-defence and an accident, yeah? There was a report of an altercation involving a knife, and a bleeding victim was helped out of the other end of that alley by his mates, which tends to corroborate the report. So, would you like to tell me what happened? Last chance to exonerate yourself."

"What about my right to remain silent and all that?"

"I haven't actually arrested you. Yet. And the magical law enforcement organization works a whole lot differently from what you've seen on TV."

"You don't have a gun."

"You think I need a gun?" Jon asked mockingly. His phone chirped, and he pulled it out of his pocket. As he had anticipated, as soon as his attention was diverted, Jake attempted to run. Jon sighed and held his disguised prism between two fingers as he quickly traced a pattern in the air. Once again, Jake started altering direction and not getting very far.

"Now you're under arrest," Jon told him. "The charge is assault with a weapon. Would you like to add resisting arrest to that?"

Jon looked at his phone. "How's your head?" the text message asked.

"No hangover. Your sister's great," he texted back.

"Did you get a chance to look up that Dasovic guy?"

"Just woke up. And just about to make an arrest." He glanced up and smirked at the sight of Jake still stubbornly attempting to make his way down the alley. He had managed to travel about two feet away from Jon in total as he kept going in several different directions.

"No rest for the wicked, huh? Need a gateway? I found two more really weird situations."

"I was going to portal, but if you don't mind? I'd have to bring this kid with me."

"I can handle two. Just don't tell Seth."

"Be there in 10."

Jon could hear muttered cursing coming from where Jake was still standing, facing away from him.

"Okay already. Would you get rid of this?"

"I'm still waiting to hear what happened," Jon told him, not removing the hex.

"I stopped that asshole from pretty much raping his girlfriend at a party last week. It wasn't the first time. Dunno why she doesn't dump him. So then he came after me with a friend, told me he wanted to 'teach me a lesson.' I held them off. I do martial arts. So then he came back with two friends. And a knife. I'm good, but I'm not that good. But when I pushed the guy with the knife off balance, the other guy got cut."

Jake spun around as Jon traced a pattern, the reverse of the previous one. "What *is* that?"

"Confusion hex," Jon replied casually. "Makes it so you can't tell where you're going. Did you use magic to push the guy with the knife off balance?"

"Yeah." Jake sighed.

"All right, sounds like it might possibly have been self-defence, or an accident like you said, but you're going to need to tell that story to my superiors. Not up to me to decide. Let's go." He pulled Jake's arms behind his back and secured his wrists together with an invisible restraint. Then he set a quick illusion that would make it appear to any observer that Jake's arms were by his side. Since Jon was not wearing a uniform and would need to take a cab to Natalie's condo, it would look odd if he were seen leading someone in handcuffs.

"Where? And what about my parents? They're gonna freak if I just disappear for a while."

"You're 18." Jon shrugged. "If you get off, you'll be home by this afternoon, so I'm sure you can come up with some story."

"That fast? How'd you know I'm 18?"

105

"Maaaagic." Jon dragged out the word in a mock spooky tone and then spoke normally. "And if you don't get off, you'll get a phone call."

"Can I see some ID? You don't look like a cop."

"Sure." Jon pulled a typical-looking police badge out of his pocket. When he held it out to Jake, though, the photograph became more like a 3-D hologram which spun around, clearly identifying Jon though the picture was a few years old.

"International Magical Law Enforcement Organization," Jake read. "I never knew there was one."

Jon took Jake's arm and walked to the end of the alley and then back around to the same street where he had perched in a tree. The police car was still there, and the other three young men were still with the officers.

"Shit," Jake muttered. Jon quickly altered his illusion so that the two of them appeared to be two women with linked arms. To avoid questions, he set it so that he and Jake did not see the illusion on themselves.

"Don't worry, they won't recognize you or notice that you're wearing handcuffs. And to answer your question, non-mages don't know about us. Are you from a non-magical family?" Jon saw that there were no cabs in sight, but he wanted to put some distance between them and the officers in any event, so he started walking south.

"Yeah. How does that work? I'm not adopted or anything." Jake's tone was a curious mixture of sullen irritation and curiosity, with the thirst for information clearly winning.

Jon shrugged. "Nobody really knows why it happens. A very small percentage of non-magical families manage to produce a magical kid. My family is non-magical as well."

"Can I learn to do what you did?"

"Some of it," Jon answered. "As long as you don't end up with a criminal record. Some of it is for police use only."

Jake sighed. "Where are we going, anyway?"

"A magical community located out on the west coast."

"Whoa, what? How the hell are we getting all that way and back by this afternoon?"

"You're gonna see some really impressive magic," Jon told him.

Jon motioned for Jake to precede him into Natalie's apartment, which the younger man did in silence. His eyes darted around the room, looking puzzled, but Jon did not bother enlightening him as to what was going to happen.

"Jacob, meet Natalie," Jon introduced them casually. "You never did tell me your last name, by the way."

"Conrad," Jake said after a slight hesitation.

"Hi." Natalie held out her hand but then dropped it as she realized that her visitor was handcuffed.

Jon noticed that Natalie was barefoot and had no makeup on. There was a silver pen tucked into the twist of hair at the back of her head, while the rest of her hair hung loose. He thought the slightly dishevelled look suited her much better than the stiff hairstyle and suit she had been wearing at the coffee shop a couple of weeks ago. Although the figure-hugging dress she had worn when they went out for dinner had been very attractive too.

"What on earth is *that*?" Jon's appreciative gaze was jolted away from Natalie as Jake's startled question drew his attention to what looked like a large spreadsheet floating in mid-air, with various rows highlighted in different colours. To the right, there were several rectangular glowing boxes hovering in the air, filled with writing. He glanced at Jake and saw that the younger man was also staring at the floating spreadsheet with a baffled expression on his face.

"Oh, that's just a sort of, um, virtual monitor," Natalie said with a sheepish look on her face. "I'm kind of visual. It's easier for me to put stuff together if I can see it and manipulate it, you know? But my laptop screen isn't big enough, so I just sort of made it 3-D."

"A virtual monitor," Jon repeated slowly. "Sure, why not?"

"I got the idea off the *Iron Man* movie," she admitted with a laugh. "You know, where Tony Stark is designing something and it's 3-D all around him, and interactive? All I really did was to expand what's on the laptop. At work, I generally have two good-sized computer monitors, but my laptop screen is really small. So I started doing this when I'm working at home, a long time ago. See, look, it's all right there." She pointed to a fairly small laptop that sat on the table, and Jon realized that the diagram on the screen actually was the same as the one floating around him, although the laptop showed multiple windows overlapping each other, which were more spread out in the air.

He noticed that Jake looked back and forth between the laptop and the floating windows as well, his eyes large and his mouth hanging open.

"So, is it a problem if you delay leaving for a few minutes? I won't take up much of your time," she said, her eyes flicking toward Jake, who closed his mouth with a slight gulping noise, clearly trying to hide his discomfort.

"Shouldn't be a problem," Jon agreed. "Right, I'm going to take the handcuffs off," he told Jake. "You already know how effective it's gonna be if you decide you don't like being my guest."

Jake just sighed. He flexed his hands once they were free.

"Have a seat." Jon gestured toward the couch.

"Coffee?" Natalie offered, sipping from her own oversized mug.

"Sure, thanks," Jon accepted for both of them. Natalie pulled the pen out of her hair and waved it at the cupboards. They opened, and two more mugs came sailing out, to sit on the countertop next to a container of sugar. Natalie poured the coffee manually and pulled a small box of cream out of the fridge.

"Just a bit of cream, thanks," Jon said.

Natalie looked questioningly toward Jake, who cleared his throat uncomfortably. "Um, double-double, please."

Jon realized that, as a young mage from a non-magical family, Jake was probably not accustomed to casual displays of magic, and he recalled how jumpy he had felt about it when he had first been introduced to the magical world. Fortunately, his introduction had not involved getting arrested.

Natalie made the two coffees and gave a mug to each of them.

"So you remember the thing with Dasovic? I found another two things last night. I was hoping you could look into these too." Her gaze flicked toward Jake. Jon immediately figured out she was not sure of the protocol in discussing things in front of someone whom Jon had identified as someone he had arrested.

Jon winked conspiratorially at Natalie as he took his octagonal coin out of his pocket and flipped it around, producing the now-familiar sense of stifling air that dissipated quickly.

"Perfect," she agreed, as it was evident that their conversation would now not be overheard by the young man sitting a few feet away. Since the spell also made people nearby disinclined to be curious about the conversation they could not hear very well, there was an additional layer of protection.

"You don't need to do that block thing too?" She referred to the magic which could be used temporarily to prevent a mage from being able to perform any magic.

"He's new to his talents," Jon said with a shrug. "I doubt he can come up with anything I couldn't counter quickly."

Jake pulled his phone from his pocket and was soon texting with impressive speed. Jon watched him for a moment, thinking over the security implications of the prisoner texting someone, but then he shrugged and decided it wasn't an issue.

"So, first, do you remember the day we met, after Marcus had left, and the news reported a house fire with two victims?"

"Uh, not really," Jon confessed. "I was pretty much sleepwalking by the time Marcus left. The only part that stuck in my mind was a certain very attractive woman ..."

Natalie smiled but looked a little embarrassed.

"Well, there was a fatal house fire that day, up in cottage country, with two victims. There's a really bizarre similarity to the thing with Dasovic. I thought when the story came on that the name of one of the victims sounded familiar. Turns out he was actually one of the rapists from that case Marcus had mentioned, because I googled the two names."

"The same rape case they mentioned on last night's news?"

"Yeah. In fact, this guy was the one who was arrested and tried but released on a technicality."

"What kind of technicality?"

"Uh, I think it was something like tapping a phone without a warrant or something. Makes my blood boil for the victim. Her attacker goes free because the police acted inappropriately. How is that fair?"

Jon opened his mouth as if to argue that point, but she made a "never mind" gesture and continued. "Anyway, the other victim who died in the fire was a guy named Christopher Narcourt, who had apparently been reported missing for the last two years. Turns out that's because he was arrested by LEO. Just like Dasovic."

Natalie picked up the printed list of mage convicts from the table, and Jon saw that it was much more dog-eared than it had been when he had seen it the previous evening. Several names were highlighted now, and she pointed to the entry listing Christopher Narcourt.

Jon narrowed his eyes. "The arrest was a little over two years ago," he pointed out as he read the pertinent details off the list. "Charged with possession with intent to distribute. If that was a first offence, he might have served his time and had the Character Test. If so, there's no reason why he couldn't have been, ah, wherever that was."

"True," Natalie agreed. "But I've got a third one, and I'm seeing a pattern here. Take a look at this one." Natalie walked up to the spreadsheet hanging in mid-air and pointed to a particular line that was glowing a vivid purple. As soon as she touched it, the glowing square to the right changed to what looked like an ordinary Web page. In fact, Jon realized it displayed the logo of the *Vancouver Sun* newspaper. The headline said something about a car accident, but Jon was having a bit of difficulty looking away from Natalie's nicely shaped derriere in her snug jeans. Natalie made a gesture with her hand that was very similar to the way someone would do it on a touch screen, like an iPad, to make the image larger, and the page did, in fact, get larger so that it was legible from further away.

"So this is from early spring this year," Natalie said, pointing to the date on the floating window. "There was a Catholic cardinal from someplace else in Canada who was visiting Vancouver and died in a car accident while he was there. Here they name the woman driving the other car, who also died." She pointed to where she had highlighted a name. Then she picked up the hard copy of Jon's list from the table and tapped on the same name, which included information of an arrest date several months earlier.

With some difficulty, Jon focused his attention on the name Natalie was pointing to on the list, before glancing back up toward the enlarged newspaper article floating in the middle of the room. He briefly glanced over toward Jake, but the young man was still texting rapidly, apparently oblivious to his surroundings.

"This woman doesn't come up anywhere else on Google that I could find—not anywhere that looked relevant anyway," Natalie continued. "I assume she got arrested by LEO without having a mundane criminal record or anything. So once again, we've got someone who was arrested by LEO, out and about in Vancouver three months later. Your list says she was convicted, charged with theft over $5,000."

"That certainly wouldn't carry a sentence of only three months," Jon agreed, a frown creasing his forehead. "Not when there wasn't even any time served to factor in."

"So that makes three mage convicts who died, when they all should probably have still been in Neekonnisiwin. Or possibly one could have been out, but it's still kind of odd. What if this car accident wasn't an accident after all?"

"What are you saying? Vehicular homicide? Some kind of kamikaze wacko causes an accident that also kills him—uh, herself?"

"Yeah, maybe," Natalie said. "I know this sounds weird, but there's another similarity between these three situations. I looked up the Catholic guy's name, and it turns out he's just as vocally antimage as that MP. And there's no question the rapists were very antimage." She stabbed a finger at several of the links beside the *Vancouver Sun* story, and each new Web page opened up in mid-air beside the first. They seemed to be articles of some sort, though not newspaper reports.

Jake looked toward them, and Natalie broke off what she was saying.

"Um, can I use the bathroom, please?"

"Just down the hall at the end," Natalie said, pointing in the right direction.

Jake cocked his head, his expression puzzled.

"Oh, he can't hear me," Natalie murmured to Jon. Once he broke the spell, Natalie repeated her directions and Jake walked down the hall.

"Is there a balcony accessible down there?" Jon asked in a low voice.

"No, the only balcony is that one." She gestured toward the patio doors opening from her living room. "And we're 15 floors up, so unless he can fly, I don't think he's going anywhere."

"I'm pretty confident he can't fly," Jon said. "Although I was only 17 when I first turned into an animal, so I probably shouldn't make assumptions."

"My God, that's pretty advanced magic for someone just starting," Natalie commented.

"It was mostly an accident," Jon admitted. "I couldn't work out how to turn myself back for three days. My parents were furious. They thought

I'd just run off for three days, and how could I tell them I was in a tree in the garden the whole time?" He kept glancing toward the closed bathroom door to keep track of his prisoner.

Natalie laughed. "A tree? What kind of animal were you?"

"A squirrel," he admitted sheepishly. "No idea why. I suppose I was just looking at one and it happened. I was starving, too."

Natalie shook her head slowly as she contemplated that. "What a way to get into magic. Anyway, I realize this whole thing seems a bit far-fetched, but that's three situations that all fit a similar pattern. In each case there are two victims, except the Dasovic one, where the attempted murder was prevented. One of the victims is a mage who maybe shouldn't have been able to be where they were. And the other one is a non-mage who hates mages."

"'Once is happenstance; twice is coincidence; three times, it's enemy action,'" Jon quoted.

"Exactly."

"Are any of these convicts named in the investigation against your firm?"

"No, but I'm beginning to think there's something going on that's way bigger than the investigation against my firm."

"I'll report this at headquarters when I get there, and they can start an investigation," Jon said thoughtfully.

"Well, actually, I, uh, I've been wondering whether I should tell Seth about these anomalies. I'm not really sure."

Jon was completely taken aback. "Chief Turner? Why wouldn't you want to? Seth is the chief LEO of North America. This is totally his jurisdiction."

"Don't get me wrong; I don't have anything against Seth. I trust him. And yet …" She hesitated.

Jon raised a questioning eyebrow. "And yet?"

Natalie leaned against the back of couch and spoke slowly as if she were afraid of offending him with her opinion. "I appreciate that I've only found three anomalies, but I'd like to keep investigating and see if there's more. The thought that occurs to me is that, if I'm right, we may have had mage convicts going missing, perhaps for years, and absolutely nobody appears to have noticed. Have you been aware of anyone escaping from our prisons? Ever?"

"Well, no," he admitted. "And three convicts, or even ex-convicts, dying fairly soon after their release is a bit suspicious in any event."

"True. So I know I probably sound totally paranoid, but hear me out. I don't think it would be all that easy, if we had lots of inmates going missing, to keep that information under wraps. So who might have the ability to do something like that? Not likely the lowly jail guard or a cop on the beat, right?"

"Bloody hell, Natalie, are you suggesting that the chief LEO of North America is a serial killer?" Jon was clearly shocked at the implication.

Natalie sucked in a startled breath and was silent for a moment, her eyes wide. "Oh my God, I know this is going to sound stupid, but I actually hadn't thought *serial killer*," she admitted. "I was just thinking cover-up. But obviously, multiple deaths in a similar pattern ..." She was quiet for a moment, and then she raised her eyes again to meet Jon's and respond to his question.

"I most sincerely hope Chief Turner isn't involved in any way, but I also can't dismiss the possibility," Natalie said. "And more to the point, I am seriously afraid that it's got to be *someone* in the law enforcement or criminal justice system, someone high up who knows the system and knows how to obscure the records in such a way that the very people who run the jails are somehow unaware that there are inmates missing. Even if it's not Seth, the more white-collar LEOs who know about it, the more likely it is that our actual bad guy finds out someone's onto him. And I'm getting a strong feeling that he or she doesn't have an issue with getting rid of people who are inconvenient."

Jon was silent for a moment as he considered that. "You have significant and very valid reasons to believe there's a serial killer on the loose in Canada who has already committed at least five murders and maybe even more," Jon pointed out soberly. "There is no way in hell I can get away with not reporting that."

"Could you report it to your chief in London instead of to Seth?" Natalie suggested.

"Switzerland, actually. There's one chief for all of Europe. But it's not his jurisdiction," Jon objected. However, he was thinking about the possibility even as he made the objection. Natalie evidently guessed that was the case, as she remained silent. "But there could be valid precedent to deal with it that way," he acknowledged. "Sorcier-Havre is the mage capital, so to some extent, Chief Thibault is sort of the chief of the LEO chiefs since he reports directly to the Arch-Mage. At least until we can establish an alibi for Chief Turner."

Natalie smiled, and some of the nervous tension left her face. She made several gestures. Jon heard the sound of the printer in her office expelling several sheets of paper. She walked in there and shortly after handed him an envelope containing copies of several of the articles.

"Did you sleep at all last night? Seems like you must have been up half the night." Marvelling over her painstaking attention to detail, Jon was thinking Natalie would be a very valuable addition to LEO's chronically short-staffed team. He wondered whether she would be open to the idea, particularly if the investigation against her firm went against her.

"I'm addicted to coffee." She laughed. "Who needs sleep?"

"Maybe somebody who's under a killer amount of stress?" Jon suggested drily. "I experienced your memory stone yesterday, remember?"

"Yes, Mom." Natalie wrinkled her nose at him. "Anyway, you guys probably need to get going, huh?" she added, as Jake returned.

Jake paused on his way back to the couch, looking a bit nervous.

"Yeah. I'll see what I can find out about this stuff, and then I'll let you know," Jon promised.

Natalie picked up her silver pen from the kitchen countertop and twirled it between her fingers. Suddenly the pen was no longer a pen but a blue prism-shaped crystal. Jon saw Jake's eyes grow huge as the now-familiar glowing arch formed in the middle of the floor, pushing the giant spreadsheet aside as it increased in size. Jake almost dropped his empty coffee cup and did not resist as Jon took it from his hands.

"In we go," the police officer said calmly. He calculatedly shoved Jake off balance so that the young man stumbled through the arch.

Chapter 9

Natalie cursed under her breath as she attempted to pull her wheeled cart over some uneven paving stones. On one side, there was a low brick wall that formed the side of an exit from an underground parking garage. On the other was a temporary chain-link fence surrounding an area where some construction work was going on, which was likely the cause of the uneven paving stones. Plywood on the other side of the chain-link fence made the area into a narrow alleyway.

Bumping over the uneven pavement made her laptop begin to slide off the precariously loaded cart. The curse turned into a wordless snarl as her black court robe slid off her other arm and promptly got wrapped around the cart's wheel.

"Next time I'm taking a cab," she growled. "I don't care if it's only six blocks."

Raj chuckled as he set his own cart upright and bent down to help untangle the robe, while Natalie adjusted the bungie cord holding the boxes and the laptop to the foldable cart. At any other time, she would have put a subtle cantrip on the boxes and laptop to hold them together, making sure that their failure to fall was not obviously unnatural. But the vandalism and bomb threat of the previous week had been followed by the firm's Web site being hacked and replaced with threatening messages.

Between the College investigation and numerous threats from unidentified sources, Natalie was not willing to risk the slightest chance of being noticed doing anything magical or that even looked like it might be magical.

Twice since leaving the courthouse, she had thought there was someone following them but had told herself she was just being paranoid. There had been plenty of people around, until they had entered this temporarily narrow passage.

Natalie had just finished securing the bungie cord when she suddenly yelped as something hard struck one shoulder and she was knocked off balance. She staggered backward as she heard the clatter of a rock landing on the ground after it bounced off her shoulder. She caught the heel of her shoe in the gap between paving stones and knocked the poorly balanced cart over as she tried to regain her balance. Her purse flew off to one side, and the top box fell to the ground, where it burst open and spilled its contents. Natalie grabbed for the brick wall to her right and looked wildly around as she tottered on one leg, trying to figure out what had just happened. Her search quickly found its object.

"Witch! We don't need your kind around here!"

Shocked and speechless, Natalie tried to step backward and winced as she felt her ankle get wrenched as her shoe twisted sideways. Though she did not want to look down, it felt as though the heel of her shoe had been snapped off. Instead, she looked toward the voice and was startled to see that the person who had moved close enough to loom over her, his face obscured with the sun behind him, was a tall, clean-shaven man wearing a suit. If anything, she would have expected tattoos and piercings. Her surprise turned to alarm, though, as she saw that he had one large fist clenched as he glared at her. His muscles bunched, and a fist headed straight for her face. Natalie pushed a wave of force out from herself and ducked at the same time, but the magical protection had not moved far from her face when the man's fist connected with it. It was close enough that it still knocked her over, and she screamed as she fell to the ground. Her attacker might not even have been aware that it was not actually her face that he had connected with. She did not have time to protect the back of her head, which bounced off the brick wall hard enough to leave her seeing stars.

Natalie pushed herself to a sitting position, breathing rapidly as she looked up at her attacker, who loomed over her with a vicious sneer on his face. A second man stood slightly behind the first, his lip curled in disgust. He was a little less solidly built than his friend and had a slightly olive-toned complexion. He was in a shirt and tie but wore a blue windbreaker rather than a suit jacket.

"What the hell?" Raj demanded, whipping around to face the two. He let go of his cart and rushed back toward Natalie and her attacker.

"Take care of that, Don," the suit-clad man snarled as Raj went to step between him and Natalie. Don grabbed Raj's arm and spun him off balance, before punching him in the stomach hard enough to clearly knock the wind out of him.

A babble of voices penetrated Natalie's awareness. She looked up to see a shocked face peering over the construction fence, a red hard hat on his head.

"Call the police!" the partially visible construction worker yelled to some unseen people behind him. He appeared to wobble and then disappeared from sight, cursing. It seemed that he had fallen off whatever he had been standing on to see over the fence.

"Your kind are not welcome around here, asshole," Don growled, ignoring the construction worker. "Go back where you came from."

"I come from right here, dickhead," Raj snarled back, gasping for breath. "What the hell is 'your kind'?"

"Fucking mages!" Don's retort was cut off as his head snapped backward when Raj's fist connected with his chin. He staggered back and stumbled into his companion, who swore loudly and shoved him away.

The taller man lurched back around, his face contorted with anger and hatred. His focus remaining on Natalie, he drew back a large foot wearing hiking boots. But Natalie suspected that it was really a work boot kind of shoe with steel toes. A surge of fear effectively focused her mind, which previously had scattered in shock. She was better able to create a barrier of force this time, not far from her body, so that he still was not aware that it was not actually her side that he kicked. The barrier was pushed in under the force of the kick in any event, and the scream she emitted was only slightly exaggerated. She clutched her side and her eyes widened as she felt a jolt of pain when she sucked in a breath. She wondered if she had a broken rib or two. Evidently the barrier hadn't been far enough from her body.

As he went to reach down as if to jerk her to her feet, Natalie saw that Don's glare was locked on Raj, who still had his fists clenched and ready, a furious look on his face.

"Mike—" Don warned, as Raj rushed the larger man before he could grab Natalie. Raj shoved Mike hard into the wall, causing him to slide down to a sitting position, looking dazed.

"Leave those two alone!" Two construction workers appeared at the far end of the temporary passage, one carrying a short length of pipe, while the other was equipped with a two by four.

Natalie tried to get to her feet, pain stabbing into her side. She looked around Raj to see Don reach into the left side of his jacket with his right hand. When his hand came back into view, he was holding an oddly old-fashioned-looking handgun with a curved wooden handle.

The sight of the gun sent a surge of adrenaline through Natalie's veins. She needed her prism, but it lay in her purse, which had landed several feet away. Lacking her prism, she thrust out her hands and sent out a wave of force that knocked Don off his feet, unable to make the action subtle anymore. The two construction workers skidded to a halt, the one carrying the pipe dropping it with a clang, a shocked look on his face.

Natalie's wave of force caused Don to trip over Mike's legs. Mike snarled and thrust himself to his knees, one large hand pushing off the ground. Natalie lunged for her purse and pulled out the silver pen from the side pocket. It blurred into the large blue crystal abruptly as she swung her hand up toward Mike.

"No you don't, bitch!" yelled Don, raising his gun again toward her. She sent another wave of force toward him with her left hand while rapidly sketching the movements to immobilize both men with the prism in her right hand. She saw both men lurch to one side a split second before the gun went off with a sickening bang.

Raj grunted, and his legs collapsed under him as he fell backward over the toppled cart, a broad red stain rapidly spreading across his pristine white shirt.

All colour drained out of Natalie's face at the sight of the expanding bloodstain, though she finished the immobilization hex in sharp motions. The two construction workers remained in place, frozen by their own astonishment rather than by her magic.

Mike had a look of shock on his immobile face, but Don wore an expression of implacable hatred.

"Police! Oh my God, call the police! He's got a gun!" a person called from the direction opposite to where the construction workers had approached.

"And an ambulance!" came another yell.

As Natalie looked up to see several people running toward her, she saw a blonde girl stop suddenly and hold out an arm to stop the others.

"Shit, she's a mage!" the girl yelled. "Look at those guys. She turned them into statues!"

Natalie turned horrified eyes on the suddenly unsympathetic observers at both ends of the narrow alley. Then she looked back at Raj, who was unconscious, with his whole chest soaked in red. He was going to die of a bullet aimed at her and because of her.

She was momentarily undecided, her eyes flicking between the ominously spreading red stain and the hesitant faces of the people who were staying a safe distance away. One observer pulled out a cellphone and spoke briskly, clearly calling emergency services, but Natalie's eyes flicked to the street behind the caller, jammed with bumper-to-bumper traffic given that half the roadway was taken up with construction. What were the chances that an ambulance could actually get through and then that Raj's life could be saved, with a bullet having possibly pierced his heart?

A bullet intended for her.

With sudden decision, Natalie flicked the prism rapidly around and caused a thick black cloud to billow around the two of them, blinding the observers. Then she made another set of well-practiced gestures that built a glowing arch behind Raj. Ignoring the panicked babble of voices coming from beyond the impenetrable darkness, and taking a deep breath to steady her furiously beating heart, Natalie made another gesture that lifted Raj from the ground and propelled him through the arch. She was trying to jostle him as little as possible. Ignoring the fallen boxes, the carts, and their two laptop computers, Natalie screwed her eyes shut and jumped through the arch after Raj.

In the next second, she screamed as the whole world dissolved into a chaos of swirling colours, lurching reality, and stabbing sensations all over her body. She was vaguely aware of shouts of alarm as she passed into unconsciousness.

Chapter 10

Mikyla chewed nervously on one fingernail as she pushed open the door of the ambulance station. The uniformed paramedic behind the counter looked up as she entered.

"Is, um, Suzanne here?"

"Sue Timmons?"

"Yeah, I think that's her last name. Blonde, kind of small?"

"Yes, that's her. Hold on, I'm pretty sure she's in the back."

Mikyla felt a mix of relief and intense nervousness. She had thought about coming to see Suzanne a few times but had lost her nerve each time. She was relieved to find that the paramedic was actually there and that she wouldn't have to find the courage to come another time. Since her math teacher had been replaced with a substitute, and they were just doing review for exam prep, she had arbitrarily decided she wasn't going to class. So this seemed like a good time to try.

"Mikyla? Hey, great to see you. I thought you'd just call me."

"I'm kinda weird that way," Mikyla said sheepishly. "I dunno, I don't like talking to people on the phone. Or Facebook or Instagram or any of that."

"People person, huh?" Suzanne smiled. "We could do with more like you. It drives me insane when you see a group of friends together but they're all glued to their phones and ignoring each other. I have to wonder, how come the friends who aren't there are more important to you than the ones who are?"

Mikyla laughed. "Exactly! So, um ..." She took a deep breath and then unfocused her eyes and looked past Suzanne's head. Sure enough, she saw a steady glow that seemed to make Suzanne's light blonde hair glimmer with a subtle sparkle.

"Someone told you about that, huh?"

"I, well, I kind of figured it out." Mikyla suppressed a feeling of hurt as she thought about Jake and their mutual discovery of how to identify a mage. They had hung out frequently during the last month and gone out a few times. They had also been texting frequently, but she had heard nothing from him since Sunday morning, and he hadn't been in school the last three days. Even if he was sick, she would have thought he would have told her. Her texts to him had gone unanswered. Maybe he was sick *and* he'd lost his phone? Or maybe he'd decided he didn't want to hang out with someone two years younger than him.

"Great. Listen, I'm just restocking supplies in the ambulance. Wanna come along with me?"

"Sure." Mikyla looked around herself with interest as they went past the front desk and into a three-bay garage area that held two ambulances. The weather was beautiful, and the big doors were all open, letting a fresh breeze circulate. A third ambulance was parked out front, being hosed down by two paramedics who were almost as wet as the vehicle. One of them had a large blob of soap bubbles in his hair, which he didn't appear to be aware of.

"Clowns," Suzanne commented wryly. She pulled open the rear door of the ambulance in the middle and climbed into the vehicle. It was evident she had been partway through her task as some items were sitting out on a gurney strapped to one side of the ambulance, while a clipboard and a pen sat beside them. Two chairs that looked like airplane seats had the seats folded upward along the other side, leaving a narrow aisle. Several cupboards lined the edge of the vehicle, above the gurney, and a couple had their doors folded open. Mikyla saw that the supplies in those cupboards were all in containers that looked like a moulded part of the cupboard, and she assumed that was to prevent them from falling and getting all messed up while the ambulance was en route.

"So why don't you tell me what you've figured out so far, and I can sort of fill you in on whatever else you need to know."

"That could take a while." Mikyla laughed. "I need to know a *lot*."

"Unless that red light over there goes off, I'm all yours," Suzanne told her with a grin.

"So remember that guy I was with at the party?"

"Yeah, John? Josh?"

"Jake. I didn't know him before that night, but him and me went and had coffee and talked, and we figured out that we're both, um … mages." Mikyla's voice shook as she actually said that out loud, but Suzanne just smiled sympathetically at her.

"Bit of a shock, huh?"

"Huge," Mikyla admitted. "I don't know my dad, so I don't know if he might be one, but my mom definitely isn't. At least, I don't think so."

"She's not," Suzanne told her. "I checked after I realized you were that day."

"And does it run in families, or is it, like, totally random?"

"Mostly in families. But for some reasons nobody's ever figured out, non-magical families sometimes have a magical kid. It's quite rare, though. I'd guess it's more likely your dad might be one. Do you know his name?"

"No," Mikyla said. "My mom never talks about him, except to blame him for, you know, everything that ever went wrong with her life."

Suzanne laughed. "So, you figured out the glow. And told Jake?"

"Yeah. He can do a bunch of stuff I can't."

"Well, he's a couple of years older, isn't he? It usually starts when you're around 16."

"I'm 16."

"I thought you probably were."

"So, you remember that guy who beat up my mom? He escaped from jail about a month ago. And they're saying he's a mage too." Mikyla's stress and panic was evident as her voice turned into a squeak. "I mean, he hasn't showed up or anything, but …"

"You don't have to worry about him," Suzanne told her. "He got arrested by LEO."

"Leo?"

"Sorry, that's what we call them. Stands for law enforcement officer, or law enforcement organization. Magic cops, basically. I met one the other day, a friend of my sister's. He was the one who arrested your boy Lassiter, after he got out of the Don Jail. People might escape from the regular prisons, but you don't escape the magic ones."

Mikyla stared at her with her mouth open, then closed it with a conscious effort, aware of a feeling of profound relief. Pete wasn't going to come back and blame her for getting him arrested!

"That's awesome."

"I figured it wouldn't bother you that that guy won't be showing up."

Before Suzanne could finish, the red light she had pointed out earlier, a large beacon light mounted on the back wall of the garage, began flashing, and a loud siren went off at the same time.

A voice came over both the radio in the ambulance and the speaker system inside the garage, causing a slight echo distortion. "Shots fired at Nathan Phillips Square. Two victims, possible chest wound."

Suzanne gasped and grabbed the edge of the gurney. Mikyla saw that her fingers were tightly gripping the blanket while she breathed in sharp gasps. Mikyla froze, uncertain what to do. Why was a paramedic panicking about a medical emergency?

The driver's-side door opened, and one of the paramedics who had been washing the other vehicle jumped in, his dark blue T-shirt still soaked. Mikyla realized it was Suzanne's partner, whom she had seen twice before.

He grabbed the microphone attached to the radio at the front.

"Number 9264. We'll take this one." Turning around as he secured his seat belt, he did a double take when he saw Mikyla and his hyperventilating partner.

"Suzy? What the hell? What's wrong?"

"It's Natalie. She's the one at Nathan Phillips."

"What? How do you know?"

"I don't know, I just know! Go, go!" Lurching into motion, Suzanne ran to the back and slammed the doors shut, then came back and unfolded one of the seats, which she half fell into, visibly trying to gain control of herself. The other paramedic looked at both Suzanne and Mikyla uncertainly for a moment, then shrugged and fired up the engine.

Not sure what to do, Mikyla grabbed the remaining loose supplies and shoved them back in the cabinet. She buckled herself into the other seat as the ambulance roared into motion, the siren sounding seconds later.

Mikyla's heart hammered as she watched out the front window while Suzanne's partner skilfully drove the ambulance, slowing slightly at red lights and then roaring through as soon as it was evident the traffic was paying attention and yielding to the emergency vehicle. Sometimes he pulled over to the wrong side of the road, sounding a very loud, angry-sounding horn as he did so. It was bizarre seeing the other vehicles moving aside, though both Suzanne and her partner muttered curses at vehicles that failed do so. There were quite a few drivers who seemed to think that the other vehicles pulling over just gave them room to pass, as if they didn't even notice the large, extremely loud vehicle coming up behind them.

"Number 9264, do you copy?" Mikyla heard the slightly muffled words coming over the radio.

Dave pressed a button and acknowledged. "Number 9264. Dave here."

"Dave, it's some freaking magic shit. The victims have disappeared."

"Disappeared?!"

Suzanne's head jerked up and she stared at the radio, her eyebrows drawn in together in a worried frown, though from what she could see in the rear-view mirror, Mikyla thought that her partner looked more baffled than worried. Then she remembered that Suzanne had identified the victim, who seemed to be someone she knew. Also she recalled that Dave did not have the mage glow, though she looked again now to double-check.

"Witnesses say there was a male and female victim and two other men. Not sure if the two men were assailants," the voice over the radio clarified the report. "Contradictory reports about whether the male party was shot, but the female did some kind of magic that immobilized the other two. Then there was a load of black smoke with some kind of glowing light in the middle of it. When it dissipated, the other two weren't frozen anymore. The man and woman were gone, but they left some boxes and laptops and stuff spilled on the ground. Police are on the scene."

"They got there quick. We'll still go, in case we're needed," Dave replied. "Out."

He left the lights and sirens on, but it was evident to Mikyla that his driving was not quite so urgent now.

"Suggest anything to you?" Dave directed the question over his shoulder. Mikyla looked at Suzanne and was startled to see that she was, if possible, even more pale than she had been moments ago, clearly fighting down panic.

"She went through her own gateway," she said in a strangled squeak.

"What the fuck, Suzy? In English maybe?"

"Oh my God." Suzanne took a few deep breaths with her eyes closed. Then she opened them and looked between Mikyla and Dave.

"Natalie is my sister," she told Mikyla. "And, Dave, there's something I'm not really supposed to tell you about—in fact, it's against mage law to tell a non-mage—so please keep this confidential." She was looking at her partner as she spoke, and she paused as if debating with herself. Mikyla tried to hide her surprise. That sounded like Dave knew Suzanne was a mage and was comfortable with the knowledge.

"You need to know now," she said firmly, as if she were trying to persuade herself. "Nat's a gatemaker. That's a skill that not many mages have. She can make a sort of doorway that goes to another place. But she *can't* go through it herself. Gatemakers have died doing that. She can only transport other people."

"Shit. Where would she have gone, do you think?"

"A hospital, probably, if the guy with her got shot. I just don't know if it would be a local one or if she'd have gone to Neekonnisiwin."

"Are you serious? Isn't that place in the middle of the Rocky Mountains?" Dave demanded. "You're telling me she can transport people to the other side of the fucking country?"

"She's a First Circle. It's really rare. They're people who have one particular ability, way stronger than other mages. She's the most powerful gatemaker in the world."

"Well, does that mean she's more likely to survive going through it?"

"No," Suzanne answered with a sob in her voice. "It means she's more likely to die."

Dave punched the button beside the radio just as traffic became so congested that he could not squeeze by in spite of the best efforts of some of the other cars that attempted to make room. "Mary, check the local hospitals to see if the victims showed up there?" he asked the dispatcher.

"No reports of that," was the reply. "St. Mike's would be closest. I'll call."

Moments later, the ambulance finally pulled into the area where a row of fountains sprayed water toward three graceful stone arches looming over the pool. In fact, Dave pulled right onto the sidewalk. Just as he opened the door, the radio crackled back to life. "Nothing from St. Mike's, Dave."

"All right, thanks for checking. We're on-site now."

Dave and Suzanne strode over to where two police officers were talking to a small group of people.

Mikyla scrambled to follow and noticed that quite a few people were walking away in different directions, most of them looking as though they were trying to pretend they were not hurrying to leave the scene. She rolled her eyes. That was a sight she was all too accustomed to. In her neighbourhood, it was definitely not good for your long-term health to tell the cops what you had seen.

She was a little surprised to find the same would hold true here in the middle of the financial district of the city. The vintage façade of Old City Hall was reflected in the gleaming skyscraper that loomed behind it. The clean concrete arches that curved over the fountains in the centre of the square were unsullied by graffiti. Yet people were behaving the same way they did in the darkened alleys and on the cracked parking lots that were more familiar to her.

Mikyla kept her distance behind the paramedics since she wasn't a witness, so she didn't hear the exchange with the police. She did see Dave veer over toward a man in a blue windbreaker, sitting on a nearby bench with an angry expression on his face and a nasty-looking bruise on his chin. Suzanne followed, but Mikyla could tell that she was tense and not particularly enthusiastic about doing her job.

"It's okay, Suzanne. I've got this," Dave said loud enough for Mikyla to hear. "Don't you need to go see that guy at Scarborough General? We need those test results."

"Um, yeah," Suzanne said.

"Your friend going with you?" Dave's eyes flickered toward Mikyla. In spite of his casual tone, she got the impression that he was actually really worried about Suzanne for some reason and maybe did not want her to be alone.

"Sure," Mikyla answered for them both, not really sure what she was agreeing to.

"Okay, great. I'll call you when I'm done," Suzanne said. Gesturing Mikyla to join her, she trotted over to the other side of the square and flagged down a cab. Once inside, she gave the driver an address in Scarborough, on the eastern edge of Toronto.

"Um, where are we going?" Mikyla said quietly after a few minutes of tense silence.

Suzanne jumped as if she'd forgotten that Mikyla was there and then moved her hand to cover Mikyla's.

Mikyla frowned as she heard a voice in her head, though the sound was distorted like a radio with very poor reception. She could not make out very many words.

"Place ... Scarborough ... portals."

She frowned and shook her head. Suzanne took her hand away.

"Gotta pick something up in Scarborough," Suzanne said instead, in a deceptively casual tone. The look she gave Mikyla suggested that wasn't the case at all, but she figured she'd have to wait for an explanation. She might not have a clue what was going on, but it was way more interesting than exam prep with a substitute teacher. The last thing she wanted was to get dropped off to make her way home, cut off from the first real excitement that she'd felt since she stopped believing in Santa Claus.

They pulled up in front of a small commercial building. Suzanne led the way inside. She walked straight past the empty reception desk and waved her hand at the security sensor set beside a heavy steel door into the back. Mikyla was startled to see that the warehouse behind the door was completely empty. She followed Suzanne through another door into a passage that held a set of stairs leading down. Lights which Mikyla assumed were motion-sensor controlled turned on as they went through the doors. Suzanne ran down the stairs at a breakneck pace, and Mikyla hurried to keep up.

At the bottom of several flights of stairs, there was nothing but a tiny room with what appeared to be an old stone arch set into one wall. To Mikyla's confusion, Suzanne reached out and grabbed her hand, pulling her into the little nook. She put one hand on the side of the arch and said, "Sioux Lookout."

A bright flash of light happened too fast for Mikyla to close her eyes, so she blinked rapidly, trying to clear the coloured spots of light that were dancing in front of her eyes. Suzanne pulled her forward while she still couldn't see very well. Once her vision cleared, her jaw dropped.

They were someplace else. She glanced behind her to see another rough slab of rock with a stone arch bizarrely embedded into it, looking like it was half melted into the rock. For a second, she saw nothing unusual about the rock at all, but as she sharpened her gaze, she saw the archway again. There and not there. But as she swung her head back to the front, she saw that the terrain in front of the rock was no longer a room at the bottom of an industrial staircase.

Mikyla looked all around her and saw that she was in a thick forest, enclosed among trees far taller and thicker than any she had ever seen in Toronto. The ground was a thick padding of old leaves that seemed to muffle all sound. The wind rustling the leaves of the trees high above was the only sound she could hear over her own breathing, although she jumped a moment later when the call of some kind of bird broke the near silence.

Without giving her any explanation, Suzanne spun them both around to face the arch again and stepped into it, even though Mikyla's nose was almost pressed up against the rocky wall.

Suzanne put her hand on the side of the arch and said, "Swan River."

This time, Mikyla was prepared and shut her eyes before the flash of light, though she could still see the brilliance through her eyelids.

There was a small platform of rough rock in front of her, and as Mikyla stepped forward, she could see a river far below and buildings along the edge that looked like they might be a hydroelectric plant or something.

"Careful, this is just a tiny ledge," Suzanne told her, pulling her back.

"Where are we?"

"Swan River, Manitoba," Suzanne answered, breathing a little heavily. "These are like gateways, but they're stationary, a series of portals scattered across the country. Natalie can build a gateway to send people directly where she wants; the rest of us have to jump in phases."

"So you just say the name of where you want to be?"

"It's a bit more complicated than that," Suzanne said. "You have to know where the portals are that are linked to this particular one, and you sort of do something with your mind to make it happen. Plus part of it is actually strengthening the network as you go. For the networks that don't get used very often, people have to go and strengthen them intentionally to keep them active. It's kind of harder than it looks. Okay, ready for the next one?"

"Sure." Mikyla reached out for Suzanne's hand.

"Pinehouse."

"Fort Vermilion."

"Toad River."

"Atlin."

Each time, they emerged into different surroundings, usually in a forest or a wilderness area, always with a rocky wall behind them.

"Give me a minute," Suzanne told her, her voice sounding strained. Mikyla could tell the strain was just as much worry for her sister as fatigue from whatever these portals were taking out of her.

Once again, they turned back around to face the stone arch embedded in the rock wall, and this time Suzanne said, "Neekonnisiwin."

Mikyla did not know how many of these stops would be required, so she was expecting another vista similar to those before. Neekonnisiwin, however, was nothing like the ones before.

Rather than a rough rocky wall in a wilderness area, this archway opened onto a large courtyard in a checkerboard pattern of multicoloured squares. The colours were subtle pastel shades, but they glimmered slightly in the late morning sun. The air was cooler and less humid than had been the case back in Toronto.

The courtyard was surrounded by stores, each with an open front, making the square look something like an old-fashioned open-air market, and a lively hum of conversation filled the air. Nobody looked at all surprised to see two people step out of a doorway from nowhere. Mikyla glanced behind her to see that this time, it was not a stone arch embedded in a cliff, but a beautifully decorated series of white marble arches with a subtle pearlescent pattern that seemed to move. As she looked, another person stepped out of nowhere through one of the adjacent arches and strode purposefully away.

The courtyard was half full of people talking to others, browsing the goods on display at the stores, or simply passing through. Many of them were dressed in a variety of ordinary clothes, from business suits to shorts and T-shirts. A teenage guy hurried past, carrying a completely ordinary-looking skateboard. But intermingled in the crowd were several people with long braided black hair wearing traditional native outfits of beautifully tooled leather so covered in beads that in some cases the leather was barely visible.

Every single person she saw had a glow around their heads when she squinted, using her peripheral vision, though it was hard to see in the bright sunlight.

Placed at equal distances around the courtyard were a dozen tall totem poles, clearly carved from trees bigger than anything Mikyla had ever seen. Several of them were large enough that four people encircling them, hand in hand, would barely be able to reach around the poles' perimeters. Yet every inch of wood was carved with fantastic imagery. Many of them had wide wings jutting out from the sides, some of them so colourful they reminded Mikyla of some of the more elaborate figureheads she had seen during the dragon boat festival in Toronto.

Near some of the further totem poles, she saw a group of people about her own age wearing uniform gym outfits. A ball was in play, but with a start, Mikyla realized that nobody was actually touching it. It looked like they were playing dodge ball, but the ball would alter trajectory abruptly for no apparent reason. A groan went up from the group to one side as the ball narrowly missed one of the totem poles and clipped someone on the leg. Someone who looked like a teacher blew a whistle while the other team cheered. A guy slightly older than Mikyla stepped away and sat on the ground amid a small group of other participants who had evidently also been disqualified.

Mikyla thought her eyes were going to pop out of her head.

"Do you need transportation, Miss?"

"Yes, the hospital, please," Suzanne said in a tone that sounded full of gratitude. Mikyla couldn't figure out why she sounded so relieved. The man who had asked her the question was a perfectly ordinary-looking guy, forty or so, wearing jeans and a golf shirt. Mikyla looked around, but there was no vehicle, so how did he plan to offer transportation?

Moments later, she had the answer as he pulled a glittering purple stone with silver bits embedded in it from his pocket. He frowned in concentration and traced a pattern in the air with the stone. A vague shape began to form in the air, growing larger and appearing to push aside the view that used to be in front of him. The shape opened up like a doorway, and the view through it was of a building with broad windows nestled in the curve of a mountain. Mikyla looked around her and saw that there was a mountain over to her left, but it looked much closer through the doorway, which now looked like it was made out of strands of subtly shimmering light.

Suzanne pulled a $10 bill out of her purse, handed it to the man with a nod of thanks and then stepped through the glowing arch. Mikyla wasn't sure if she was supposed to follow, but she certainly didn't have $10 to give to the guy, so she just ran through anyway, her heart racing.

Well, she had wanted more of the crazy excitement, right? She didn't understand much of what was happening, but nobody could deny it was crazy and exciting.

Stepping through the glowing arch, Mikyla turned to look behind her. The strands of light faded and then seemed to draw in upon themselves and disappear. The buildings which had surrounded the checkerboard courtyard were still visible but were now a significant distance away, lower down in the foothills of the mountain. There was a quality to the air that was entirely alien to the city-bred girl, but it made her want to take deep breaths.

The sound of rapid footsteps fading with distance brought her back to the present as she saw Suzanne disappear into the wide glass doors of the building ahead of her. Two more totem poles, smaller than those in the town square, stood to either side of the door.

She hurried to catch up and went through the doors to see Suzanne speaking in an urgent voice to a silver-haired woman at an information desk. The inside of the building smelled of antiseptic and looked like any other hospital, with smooth polished walls and floor and generic institutional-type seating in the front. A gift shop with a variety of teddy bears and flowers stood to one side of the front lobby. A mop was moving about by itself in the middle of the floor, occasionally dipping itself into a nearby bucket of water and then wringing itself out. Mikyla noticed that the water in the bucket had a distinct pink tinge to it. She had the impression it looked more like blood than some kind of pink antiseptic cleaning solution.

"Yes, Dear, they arrived about an hour ago," the woman was telling Suzanne. "The young man is still in surgery. I'm not sure if the bullet pierced his heart. Your sister is still unconscious, I'm afraid. She is in room 362. You don't happen to know the young man's name, do you? Or his next of kin?"

"Uh, his name is Raj, but I can't remember his last name. He works at the same law firm as my sister. I don't know anything about his family, but he's not a mage, so probably they're not either."

"Oh! I didn't realize. Tori, what are you doing here? Aren't you supposed to be at work?" The woman on the desk was looking directly at Mikyla, who glanced around. There was nobody else in the lobby besides the three of them.

"Who's Tori?"

"Oh! I'm sorry. I mistook you for someone else. I must be losing my marbles! Never mind. Follow this to Ms. Benson's room." She gestured with one hand, and a shimmering line of sparkles appeared on the floor and disappeared around a corner.

Suzanne was already rushing down the hall, following the sparkles. Mikyla was uncertain whether she ought to follow, but she did so, glancing back at the silver-haired woman who still looked after her, a puzzled frown marring her forehead.

Mikyla ran along the hall behind Suzanne, passing doors with plates engraved with numbers on each side of the corridor. The sparkling path took her into an elevator and down several different corridors. When she reached the door through which Suzanne had disappeared, she hesitated and decided to give Suzanne some privacy with her sister. Instead of going in, she slid down the wall to sit on the floor outside the room and pulled her phone out of her pocket. Before she could do anything, her eyes almost popped out of her head again as a parade of brightly coloured dinner trays approached her, floating in mid-air without any apparent form of support. A man, perhaps in his early twenties, was walking beside the procession of trays, carrying a clipboard in one hand and a green crystal of some kind in the other. His dusky skin and thick black hair pulled back behind his head identified his First Nations heritage. The trays moved with military precision, each one peeling off, sometimes singly and sometimes in pairs, to enter patient rooms. The young man came to a stop near Mikyla, frowning at his clipboard, the line of trays coming to a halt.

"No lunch for 362?" he said aloud in a puzzled tone. "Oh, that's the gatemaker? Unbelievable. All the way from Toronto! … No kidding, right? Okay, thanks." Mikyla's eyes flicked around, wondering whom he was speaking to.

"Oh, sorry, I didn't see you there," he said as he suddenly focused on Mikyla. "Are you here to see the gatemaker?" He gestured toward room 362, making it clear he was talking about Natalie.

"Um, well, I came with her sister," Mikyla answered hesitantly.

"Ah. That was incredible. I never knew someone could build a gate over thousands of kilometres. I hope she'll be okay."

"I never knew about gates at all before today," Mikyla said with a nervous laugh, "or portals."

"Oh, it's all new to you, huh? Rough introduction! Good luck." The young man moved away, his remaining trays still keeping pace with him in a smooth flow.

Hoping to find free Wi-Fi, Mikyla found a network simply called Neekonnisiwin and selected it. She typed a text message to Tara, telling her that a friend's sister had been in a car accident and saying she was at the hospital with her. She did not specify which hospital.

Moments later, Mikyla's phone beeped, and she saw a reply message from Tara: "2bad. Hope shes okay. Check out msn. Crazy mage stuff @ City Hall."

With a sinking feeling, Mikyla called up MSN, surprised at how fast it came up. The hospital's Wi-Fi must be really good. The "crazy mage stuff" was apparent as soon as she reached the site.

"Oh shit!" she said to herself in dismay as she scrolled through the report, which described what had taken place but clearly put a different spin on it than she had experienced. The gunshot was described as a rumour, no gun or shell casing having been found. Witness accounts had been contradictory on whether a shot had been fired. Worse was the fact that Suzanne's sister was identified by name, and as a lawyer at a firm called Mason Sullivan. It went on to say some things about Mason Sullivan that did not make much sense to Mikyla.

"What is it?" Suzanne's voice sounded strained, and Mikyla looked up to see Suzanne, still inside the hospital room, her face pale. Mikyla hesitantly entered the room and held out her phone, staying away from the bed. Suzanne came closer.

"Take a look at this," Mikyla told her soberly.

She passed over the phone, and Suzanne rapidly read the article.

"Shit is right," she remarked in a dead-sounding voice, handing the phone back. She sighed as she looked toward the bed. Mikyla followed her gaze.

Lying motionless on the hospital bed was a woman whose face bore a slight resemblance to Suzanne's. Her hair was a darker blonde, and it looked like she was a bit taller. But her face was slack and absolutely expressionless, and her eyes were closed. Her skin was a horrible greyish colour, and her cheeks looked gaunt. Though there were no visible sensors attached to her, there were screens above the bed which Mikyla could tell were monitoring things like heart rate and possibly other vital functions. A woman in a lab coat sat beside Natalie, her own eyes closed, while she held Natalie's hand and frowned in what looked like concentration.

"How is she?" Mikyla whispered hesitantly.

Suzanne sighed. "It's really impossible to tell. She had some minor injuries, a cracked rib and some cuts and bruises, which they've fixed, but obviously the big thing is the impact of going through her gateway."

"Why can't she go through her own gateway?"

Suzanne shrugged and shook her head. "Nobody really knows. There's not a lot of records on it. It's called Boadicea's curse, and the theory is that the more distance involved, or the more powerful a gatemaker you are, the worse the effects of going through your own gateway are gonna be."

"And we're somewhere in the Rockies?" Mikyla's eyes widened as she remembered Dave's shock. The Rocky Mountains were between Alberta and British Columbia, over 3,000 kilometres from Toronto. Considering that it had taken Suzanne and Mikyla about six or seven of those portal things to get here, it was obvious that Suzanne's sister's power was incredible.

"Actually we're in the Yukon. I don't think these mountains are part of the Rockies," Suzanne said. "Further west. And north." She sounded as if only half her attention was on the question as she stared worriedly at the corpse-like figure of her sister.

"She's not dead, though," Mikyla pointed out hesitantly, knowing that Suzanne had feared that. Yet it seemed that her fear had not lessened much by discovering that her sister was alive.

"I don't even know what happens if the gatemaker doesn't die. But I'm guessing it's still not good. I mean, if you're holding open a gateway from point A to point B, and then you go through it yourself, all of a sudden point A is no longer where you are. I guess it's impossible to actually flip the starting point and the destination midway, so it's like the spell implodes, with you in the middle."

"Ms. Timmons, I assume you've previously had mental communication with your sister?" It was the doctor by the bed who spoke, sounding dispirited. "I'm Dr. Santos. I'm a psychiatrist, and pretty good at mental communication usually, but I can't sense a thing. But you know her, so maybe …?"

"I'll try. Nat and I don't tend to talk mentally all that much, but we used to a lot when we were younger." Suzanne took a deep breath and sat on the side of Natalie's bed, taking her sister's hand and clasping it in both of her own. In seconds she was visibly sweating. A deep frown creased her forehead.

Suddenly, Mikyla felt a wave of fear and dizziness so strong that she stumbled. Without stopping to think about what she was doing, she put her hand on the back of Suzanne's.

Darkness, spinning, flashes of colours and sudden lights, more spinning dizziness, and a feeling as though she were being inexorably sucked into a large drain, instantly assaulted her senses. Mikyla staggered at the onslaught of sensations and images.

In the next moment, all of her considerable stubbornness kicked in, and she dug in her figurative heels, trying to pull herself away from that sucking maelstrom, feeling the bright light that was Suzanne and the dim flickering light that was her sister. All three of them were sliding relentlessly into the darkness. Mikyla remembered a video she had seen on YouTube of a person who had fallen into icy water, and the way that a group of rescuers formed a human chain, lying down on the thin ice to disperse their weight and try to pull the victim free.

135

Mikyla was terrified. Suzanne was clearly helping her, helping all of them, to try to escape the hole, but her sister was a dead weight at the end of their chain. Suddenly some strength seemed to flow into Mikyla from somewhere outside herself. She was vaguely aware of other presences, as though more people had joined their chain. They stopped slipping toward the darkness, but there was nothing to grip, no way to pull themselves away from it. It was impossible to tell which direction to go to get away from it. Up and down had no meaning as reality flipped and spun around her.

Mikyla's eyes were squeezed tightly shut, but moments later, she felt a cool green touch, a sense of purpose and direction, entering into the equation. A fleeting thought wondering how strength could have a colour flickered through her mind, but she dismissed it, concentrating on pulling away from the engulfing nothingness, following the clear lead of the green glowing power. Rather than getting tired, more strength seemed to be flowing into her.

With agonizing slowness, they crept further away; as the suction weakened, their speed gradually increased. After far too long, a period in which Mikyla felt as though she had run a marathon, she suddenly felt as though they had flown through a door which slammed shut behind them, and the pulling sensation was gone. Though oddly pulsating blobs of coloured light still moved around her, leaving her feeling nauseous and dizzy, the spinning had reduced to almost nothing. Now she simply felt as if she were floating in a bizarre gravity-free nothingness. With an abruptness that was startling, Mikyla became aware that she was still standing in a hospital room, though she was breathing hard and was drenched with sweat. She let go of Suzanne's hand and clutched the rails of the hospital bed in front of her as her heart rate gradually slowed.

"What the hell was that?" Suzanne gasped, also breathing hard.

"The three of us pulled Ms. Benson back from the brink of … something," Dr. Santos said, her voice turning hesitant at the end. "Insanity or death. I'm not really sure. Young lady, yours is the strongest mind I have ever touched. Incredible! You most definitely provided the power to achieve whatever it was we just achieved."

"Uh, what?" Mikyla opened her eyes slowly, her chest heaving. Her unsettled stomach was gradually settling, and she could see that Suzanne and Dr. Santos both looked as dishevelled and sweaty as she felt.

"That was incredible!" Suzanne said.

Tears were trickling down her cheeks, and suddenly she engulfed Mikyla in a bear hug, crying and laughing at the same time.

"She's going to be okay?"

"Oh yes, I think we can be confident she's going to be okay. Look at her vitals."

Dr. Santos was pointing to a graph beside the machine that Mikyla thought looked like some kind of brain thing. She remembered seeing something like that in a movie. Before, that graph had been jerking and spiking in a bizarre and jagged pattern, but now it recorded smooth waves. The heart rate monitor, also, showed stronger and more regular spikes, and when Mikyla looked at the patient's face, she could clearly see a difference. Whereas before the woman's face had been slack and dead-looking, now she simply looked like she was sleeping.

"She's going to be okay." Suzanne's voice was trembling with emotion, but she also had a big smile on her face. "Mikyla, you've got to be First Circle, but I don't know what kind. That's nothing I've ever heard of or experienced."

"I'm a what?"

"She's a joiner." Mikyla turned to see another doctor entering the room. He was sitting in a wheelchair, wearing blue-green hospital scrubs under his white lab coat, but the name tag hanging off his pocket was too far away for Mikyla to read. His hair was the same colour as Mikyla's, dark brown with subtle hints of red, and he wore a neatly trimmed beard. As he came further into the room, Mikyla gasped.

The right side of his face was seamed with scars, and there was an area on that side of his head where the hair was missing, along with half an ear. His right eye was pulled into an odd shape by the scarring. She gasped as she also realized that he did not have a right arm. The wheelchair propelled itself forward with no visible means of control.

"It's one of the rarest … wait. Tori? What?!"

"Geez, that's the second time today someone's called me Tori. Who is she?"

"God, sorry, I'm an idiot," the doctor said. "The resemblance is incredible. It doesn't help that Tori changes her hair colour about as often as I change my underwear, so I kind of expect her to look different all the time. But you have the exact same face!"

"Enough about your whack job sister, Jimmy. What the hell is a joiner?"

Mikyla looked back and forth between the two doctors.

Jimmy frowned thoughtfully at Mikyla. "I'm trying to remember. I heard about it years ago. It's got to do with group magic, but it's one of the First Circle things. Let me ask you something. I know this is going to sound weird, but tell me what that lady standing behind you is feeling. Don't look at her."

"Who, Suzanne? Or the doctor?"

"Suzanne."

Mikyla was baffled, but she closed her eyes, trying to remember what Suzanne had looked like after they had done whatever it was.

"Relief," she said slowly. "Really strong relief. Like she was terrified her sister was going to die, and now she's not. And, um, surprised. And really confused. More focused on the confusion now. Which, you know, me too."

"That's what I thought," the wheelchair-bound doctor said, a note of glee in his voice. "You're empathic."

"I'm a what now?"

"You didn't just figure out Suzanne's feelings from her body language. You felt them."

Mikyla's mouth dropped open as she spun around to look at Suzanne and Dr. Santos. Suddenly she realized that she was aware of feelings of surprise and something like awe, and that in fact those feelings were coming from outside herself. It suddenly dawned on her that she had often been really good at figuring out what people were feeling, even when their words or actions suggested the exact opposite. There was no question it was suddenly much clearer now, though, and she wondered if what they had just done together might have had some kind of impact.

"People who are good at group magic are usually the ones who are good with non-verbal communication—emotions as well as reading body language and all that," Jimmy said. "Women are often better at it than men, though not always."

"Certainly not in my case," Dr. Santos noted. "And anyway, group magic requires, you know, a group of people who are all good at group magic. And I know I suck at it."

Jimmy nodded. "A joiner is a First Circle mage who can merge lots of people's minds, if they're willing, and combine all that power together. I don't think there's been one in about a hundred years, and it's totally scary shit. Imagine what could be done with power like that?"

"You've got to be kidding me," Mikyla said flatly. "I couldn't even move my keys off the park bench when I tried. I could barely hear Suzanne when she tried to talk to me mentally. All I can do is make fizzy drinks either go flat or explode, and I don't even know which it's going to be. No way I'm some kind of all-powerful anything."

"No immediate plans for world domination then? Glad to hear it." The doctor smiled. "I'm Dr. Sabourin." He held out his left hand, since he didn't have another, and Mikyla went to shake it, but she flushed as she realized she needed to switch hands to do so. The doctor just grinned, easing her embarrassment.

"Mikyla Burton."

"Suzanne Timmons." Suzanne also introduced herself and shook the doctor's hand. "What if Mikyla channelled the power and someone else controlled it?" she suggested. "Dr. Santos is probably the one who knew what to do, but couldn't connect and didn't have the power. I guess I could connect since Nat's my sister and we have communicated mentally before. And it seems Mikyla had the power or got it from someone."

"Lots of someones," Dr. Sabourin corrected her. "I felt a sort of yell for help, except it wasn't words. I was thinking it was a mental contact from the ER, hopefully not another gunshot wound to the heart! I'd only just come out of surgery and just thought, *Oh crap, now what?* But then the next second, I felt like I was part of this river of power that was coming from all around me and being directed into a tight funnel. That's the best I can describe it, anyway. And I sensed what I think you were all sensing, the disorientation and nausea, and the feeling that whatever was on the other side of that funnel was being pulled into a black hole. But that focused power was stopping that drag and then pulling everyone back to safety. It was an amazing feeling. I'm not sure if I have the energy to even light a candle right now, yet I feel great."

"This has been the weirdest day of my life," Mikyla commented.

"You should make a memory stone of that," Dr. Santos said. "I know I'm going to."

"Uh, memory stone?"

"It's where you can embed a memory, with all your feelings and stuff, in a stone, and other mages can experience it," Suzanne explained. "It's like a virtual reality movie, but better because of the emotions."

"The thing is, there could be some danger to Mikyla over this," Dr. Sabourin said thoughtfully.

"Danger? Why?" Suzanne asked, with a sharp look at the doctor.

Mikyla also stared at him. Not only did she not really understand what had just happened or his explanation, but now she could be in danger because of it? The day was changing from crazy and exciting to crazy and inexplicable, and now getting scary.

"We haven't had a joiner in over a century. It strikes me as a power that could easily be abused. If you want to make stones, go ahead, but don't make them publicly available just yet. We're going to need to figure out who can teach Mikyla how to use this. And how not to get sucked into other people's heads. I have a feeling the First Circle weakness of a joiner is something about losing a sense of self. I'll have to look it up; I don't remember the details."

"I need a coffee," Mikyla muttered.

"There's a coffee shop in the market square," Dr. Sabourin suggested. "Would you mind if I come see you there in a bit? I'll go look stuff up now."

Mikyla looked to Suzanne to decide.

"Do you know if Natalie is likely to wake up soon?"

"I don't really know," Dr. Santos said thoughtfully, "but we can certainly call you if she does."

"Look, I'll just go wait in the lobby," Mikyla told her, realizing that Suzanne was reluctant to leave her sister. "Take your time."

Mikyla wandered back toward the front of the hospital, her mind whirling with everything that had just happened.

Chapter 11

Dr. Sabourin propelled his wheelchair toward the information desk in the front lobby, where his mother volunteered three days a week. His hair was damp, and his scrubs were newly changed. In his mid-thirties, he did not much resemble his mother, even if you looked past the scars. He would have been tall if he had been able to stand, and he was fairly slender. His dark brown hair had a slight reddish tone and almost always looked a bit messy. In contrast, he wore a neatly trimmed beard and moustache.

"Hi, Mom. Wow, what a day. That was a really challenging surgery. He'll be fine, though, especially once Lilly Coetzer finishes with him. She's a wiz with scars." He frowned as he saw the expression on his mother's face. "Uh, what's wrong? You look like you saw a ghost."

He wondered if she had also been pulled in to Mikyla's joining effort but did not want to mention it in case she hadn't.

"You're not far off," Sylvia Sabourin replied. "It probably feels very similar."

Dr. Sabourin chuckled. "I'm not actually sure what would feel similar to seeing a ghost," he admitted. "But then I've never seen one, so what would I know? Have you seen many?"

His mother rolled her eyes at him. "It wasn't a ghost, it was a young lady who came in to visit a patient. She was the spitting image of Tori. It was uncanny."

"Oh, yes, I met her. She does look a lot like Tori. It's weird."

"Oh, I have a feeling I know exactly why she looks like your sister."

"Oh?" Dr. Sabourin was thinking about what he had read about joining and was only paying partial attention to his mother.

"She came and talked to me, so I asked where she's from and things. Her name is Mikyla Burton. She's 16. Her mother's name is Tina Burton. She goes to CWC in Toronto, and apparently her mother did too. Her mother became pregnant with her right near the end of Grade 12. And she doesn't know who her father is, other than that her mother told her he moved away right after school finished that year."

The doctor's attention sharpened at the long list of facts. He looked at his mother quizzically, one eyebrow raised. "That's a lot of personal information to get out of someone visiting a patient," he said. "What do you do, ask them to fill in a 15-page questionnaire before they can go in?"

Sylvia sighed. "You're not usually this slow on the uptake, Jimmy. The child is 16, which means she was conceived just short of 17 years ago. And 17 years ago, her mother, *Tina Burton*, was in Grade 12 at CWC."

Dr. Sabourin suddenly jerked upright. "You ... what—? You aren't suggesting—?"

"You tell me, Jimmy. Did you, or did you not, have sex with Tina Burton when you were in Grade 12? Unprotected sex, presumably?"

"Tina Burton is not that uncommon of a name!" he protested.

"I'll take that for a yes," his mother said drily. "How many Tina Burtons were there in Grade 12 at that school in that particular year? And how many of them do you suppose might have gotten pregnant and produced a child who not only looks the spitting image of your sister but also is, in fact, a mage? Which I'm quite sure Tina was not."

"Oh my God." The doctor had his hand buried in his hair, looking as though he were going to pull it out in chunks. "Oh my God."

"Congratulations, Jimmy boy. You appear to be the father of a 16-year-old girl."

"I need a drink."

Mikyla's eyes were everywhere as she and Suzanne walked slowly back down the sloping path toward the town centre.

"Aren't there any cars here?"

Suzanne took a few seconds before she answered. Mikyla could tell her mind was not on the question.

"No. They're really not needed. Everything is close enough to walk, and heavy deliveries are done by gatemakers."

"Huh." Mikyla thought about that for a moment, and then her attention was drawn to the circular formation of totem poles surrounding the town square. "Do they use magic to carve the huge totem poles?"

"I doubt it. Some of them are really old, and they use magic to preserve them, but there's a lot of tradition associated with totem poles. They probably wouldn't want to mess with that."

"There's lots of First Nations stuff here."

"Yeah, there's a lot of Canadian history that you won't learn in normal school. Natalie's the history buff. She loves memory stones, the older, the better. Most of what I know, she probably told me. I think that the earliest mages who came to North America, who were from Europe and from Asia, were able to integrate quite peaceably with the First Nations. It was only later, when more white people came, that relations broke down. A lot of those early mages were fleeing persecution. There was a terrible part of the Crusades that was focused on annihilating mages. We call it the Purge."

"Wait, I thought the Crusades were religious, something about Israel? And didn't white people bring disease and stuff that killed loads of the Indians?"

"Yes, to both. There's just a bunch more to history that has gotten lost. I think the early mages were able to avoid spreading the diseases, possibly due to magic, or maybe it was more that they had more success with cures if they did infect the natives. Parts of this community actually date all the way back to the 1600s. See that one?" Suzanne pointed to a fairly squat totem pole that was very weathered grey wood, with the carved features looking worn down. "Most of the totem poles are carved of western red cedar. That's a soft wood, so they don't tend to last, but that one is from 1730 or something like that. I'm pretty sure it's the oldest totem pole in the world."

"How do they know?"

"Probably a memory stone from someone who saw it carved, or the actual carver or something. The stones have allowed us to preserve history in a far more accurate way than the non-mages can do. You can't fictionalize a memory stone, even if you try. And you can't make a memory stone about something someone else has told you about. It's only possible when it's your own memory."

Mikyla kept looking all around as she walked through the town at Suzanne's side, her head on a swivel. "It's different, but I guess it's not crazy magical," she noted. "Mostly it's just all the native stuff. And there's no tall buildings."

Suzanne grinned. "Well, if you look over at the mountain when we pass this next street, you'll notice a ski hill, and there will probably be people skiing on it."

"There's snow here in June? But it's hot."

"I didn't say it was natural." Suzanne laughed. "But it's a lot of fun to go skiing in the summer. The magic isn't too obvious, but it's also not nearly as hidden as elsewhere. People don't have to hide what they are here. Actually, we're at such a high elevation, it wouldn't be possible to live here and be comfortable without the magic that makes the air breathable and keeps it from getting too crazy cold in the winter."

"So I guess the only way to get here is by those portals?"

"I mean, maybe you could climb the mountain," Suzanne speculated. "I don't actually know how high up we are, but I've been told that that one there is the highest mountain in Canada." She pointed to the next peak over, which was only slightly higher than the top of the one they were on. "No, come to think of it, I'm pretty sure the town is hidden from climbers. I've heard that if a plane flies over, we don't register on their instruments. I'm pretty sure the only non-mages who can ever come here are those who are brought here by mages and know all about us. Dave loves snowboarding in the summer."

"He comes here?"

"Yes. Well, he's my husband."

"Oh, I didn't realize."

They were silent until they reached the coffee shop and took seats in a pretty courtyard off to one side, where a vine-covered trellis provided some shade.

"This is all pretty weird for you, isn't it?"

"For sure." Mikyla grimaced. "I've travelled across the country in a few minutes, learned I'm some kind of weird thing that hasn't been seen in a century, and apparently done some kind of bizarre magic that I have no clue how I did it."

"Yeah, I can't help you with that one. I've never heard of a joiner. I hope that doctor can find the information he was looking for."

"Well, I was hoping it would be crazy and exciting when I came with you. Be careful what you wish for, right?" Mikyla laughed a little shakily. "What was that thing you said about not going through the gateway? Something about a curse?"

"Boadicea's curse. Boadicea was a queen in ancient Britain who fought the Romans, and she was a First Circle gatemaker," Suzanne explained. "If I remember it right, the Romans managed to outflank her and defeated her eventually. She saved what was left of her forces by building a gateway for them, but then either she jumped through herself or got pushed through it. Nobody really knows. The only memory stone was made by someone who watched her go through it. Next anyone knew, she was dead. Since then, what happens when a gatemaker goes through her own gateway was known as Boadicea's curse." She shuddered, and it was evident to Mikyla that she was remembering the corpse-like state of her sister when they had first arrived.

"What can I get for you ladies?"

A woman somewhat older than Suzanne had come over to their table, a small notebook in her hand.

"A large coffee for me, please," Suzanne said. "Black. Mikyla?"

"Do you have iced coffee?"

"Sure do. What size?"

"Oh, medium, please."

"Coming right up." The woman bustled away, disappearing back through the wide doorway, its lintels painted a brilliant yellow. A delightful smell of freshly roasted coffee beans was emanating from the interior.

Mikyla replayed Suzanne's explanation in her head, wondering how she could keep Suzanne's attention off of worrying about her sister.

"What's a First Circle? You've said that a few times."

"Most of us can do a lot of the same sorts of things. Some people are better at some things than others, of course, just like anything else. But then there are First Circles, who are very rare. Up until a couple of weeks ago, my sister was the only one I'd ever met. It's a person who has one particular magical ability that's way stronger than anyone else's. You know that guy who built a gateway for us to get from here up to the hospital?"

"Yeah?"

"So he's an ordinary gatemaker. He can probably build a gateway that takes you maybe somewhere between 10 and 50 kilometres. Most of them can't manage more than that."

"But your sister can do one that goes across the country."

"Yep."

"Um, Mikyla?"

Mikyla turned around, wondering who here would know her name. "Oh, hi, Dr. Sabourin." She laughed. "Your wheelchair doesn't make a single sound." She pulled a chair away from the table that she and Suzanne were sitting at to make room for his chair, then noticed that Suzanne was giving the doctor a strange look.

Looking more closely at him, she realized that his hair was awry and his eyes were wild looking.

"Oh God, what now?" she said. "You found out something really freaky when you looked up this joining thing?"

"Uh, no, it's not that. Didn't my mom tell you?"

"Your mom? Have I met your mom?"

"The lady on the information desk."

"Oh, I didn't know she was your mother. I was talking to her for quite a while. She's nice."

"Well, I'm glad you like her, since she's your grandmother."

"My what?!" Mikyla's voice disappeared in a squeak.

"I understand you told her that your mother's name is Tina Burton and that she got pregnant with you when she was in Grade 12."

Mikyla's eyebrows shot up. Why was this guy asking about her mother? She immediately started to feel wary.

"Yeah, so?"

"I had a girlfriend named Tina Burton when I was in Grade 12. I went to CWC in Toronto. I graduated 17 years ago."

Suzanne and Mikyla both had identical looks of shock on their faces. "You ... you're my ... uh—"

"Yeah, I think I am." He ran his hand through his hair, making it evident why it was all messed up already. He took a deep breath and looked back at Mikyla. "I'm your dad. I mean, we can do a DNA test or something if you want, but my mom was right, you look exactly like my sister. And, of course, there's the mage thing."

Mikyla looked down at the table and picked up a napkin that was sitting there, twisting it nervously between her fingers.

"I swear, I had no idea, not the slightest. I never would've, you know, not been around if I'd known." He pulled out a phone and was scrolling through pictures with his single hand, which was shaking slightly.

"From what I heard, you and your family disappeared like the cops were after you. What was that about if you had no idea my mom was pregnant?" Mikyla stuck her hands in the pockets of her hoodie to hide their trembling, not looking at him. It had always been her habit to go on the offensive when she was nervous, but she was kind of surprised that she could still do it with a mage. Finding out that she was one herself hadn't done much to erase her fear of them.

On the other hand, the wheelchair made him look far less threatening, and a thought did cross her mind that he looked like a half-decent kind of guy, nothing like any of her mother's other boyfriends. And he was a *doctor*, way better than the lowlifes her mother had frequently hooked up with. Her brothers' father was the only one of them who had actually lasted for more than a few months.

Jim looked away, a dull flush creeping into his face. "It wasn't because I knew she was pregnant," he told her. "I swear, I had no idea," he repeated. "Here, that's my sister."

Suzanne and Mikyla both looked skeptical at his claim, but Mikyla's expression turned to shock as she took the phone he was holding out to her and saw a picture of someone who could definitely be her in another few years. The young woman had bright pink hair, an eyebrow ring and several piercings in the ear visible in the photo, but there was no question there was an extremely strong resemblance.

"I remember my mom saying not a single one of your friends seemed to know how to get hold of you." Mikyla focused on the picture of her aunt, who didn't look that much older than she was herself, while she made the accusation in a slightly trembling voice.

Jim hesitated, then responded without looking up from his lap. "The truth is, I got arrested. I was a big idiot. The last day of school, my friends and I got drunk and high, and we decided it would be a great idea to rob a gas station."

Mikyla sighed. So much for thinking he wasn't a lowlife. That gave her two for two in the parent department.

"Didn't work, of course. We managed to get out of there and scattered, hoping they wouldn't be able to figure out who we were. LEO was on my doorstep by ten o'clock that night. My parents were livid. They refused to post bail, told me I could sit on my ass in jail and think about what a moron I was."

"LEO? Oh right, the mage police."

Jimmy took a deep breath and looked at Mikyla, the embarrassed flush still colouring his face.

"I was in jail here. This is where you get taken when you're arrested by LEO. My parents moved the whole family here since I wasn't allowed to leave. They let me go to university in Vancouver, but I had to commute from here. They wouldn't let me live in residence for the whole of my first year. And I had to check in with a parole officer. No cellphone, and no way would my folks let me call any of those friends I had in TO. I have a strong feeling my mother was constantly checking to see if I'd been drinking or doing drugs. I bet she'd have practically killed me if I had. My parents were way worse than the parole officer." The doctor took a deep breath.

"So it's actually true that none of my friends had any information on what happened to me. I swear I didn't know about you. But then, to be honest, if I had heard about it, I would've wondered about this guy Steve Moorhead."

"Who's he?"

"I kind of don't want to say too many bad things about your mom to you." Dr. Sabourin was clearly as uncomfortable as Mikyla was herself.

Mikyla snorted. "You won't be shattering any illusions, trust me," she told him.

After another slight hesitation, he sighed and explained. "I caught her with Steve in the back seat of his car after a school football game. You can guess the rest. We broke up. We were only together for, like, two months. To be honest, it was more my ego that was hurt than my feelings. She was, well, pretty popular back then. One of the hottest girls in school."

Mikyla choked on a laugh. "Those glory days are long gone." She thought of her mother as she had seen her yesterday. As usual, Tina had been drunk, unaware that her excessively applied eyeliner had smeared or that she had forgotten to brush her hair. Her eyes had large bags under them, her nose was a mass of broken capillaries, and her face was far too lined for a woman in her mid-thirties. It occurred to Mikyla that if her parents were in Grade 12 together, they were the same age. But the doctor looked far younger in spite of his scars.

The server came over and placed their drinks in front of them. Suzanne handed her some money, and she made change from an apron with deep pockets.

"Good afternoon, Doctor. Coffee?"

"Sure. Yes, please." She evidently knew how he took it since he didn't specify and she didn't ask. She nodded and went back inside.

There was silence for a few moments, and then Jimmy pulled a face. "This is really uncomfortable, isn't it?"

"Pretty weird," Mikyla agreed. "On top of a totally bizarre day."

"Look at it this way," Jim pointed out. "At least you knew you had a father, even if you thought he was a deadbeat jerk who never showed his face. I had no clue. I am *way* too young to have a 16-year-old daughter. I'm 35!"

"Imagine if Mikyla got pregnant." Suzanne smirked. "You could be a 35-year-old grandfather."

"Aargh!" Jimmy said, looking horrified. "That's a *horrible* thought. Please don't." He shuddered, but then grinned at Mikyla. "In fact, if you wouldn't mind waiting until you're, like, forty or so, that would great. Then I'd be a 58-year-old grandfather, which is way more reasonable."

"Forty it is," Mikyla agreed with a laugh that was still slightly higher pitched than normal. How strange that in less than an hour of acquaintance, she could have a better conversation with this guy than she could with her mom, whom she'd known her whole life. He seemed to have the same sense of humour that she did, which probably helped.

"So, you, um, you said you went to university?"

"Yeah, well, I'm a doctor, as you know. A surgeon actually. I operated on that guy who was shot, the one who came in with your friend's sister." His gaze swung to Suzanne.

"Is he okay?" Suzanne asked, her face worried. "There were conflicting stories about whether or not there was a gunshot."

"Oh, there was definitely a gunshot. He'll be fine. He was very lucky your sister was willing to risk her life for him. The bullet hit the top part of his heart and ruptured the main artery. If he hadn't been in surgery so quickly, I'm not sure even magic could've saved the guy. We can't fix everything." He scowled down at his own wheelchair-bound body.

"Magic." Mikyla sighed.

"I guess you haven't known for very long, huh?"

"Only like a month since I knew for sure. Maybe a couple more months of being freaked out by weird things going on before that. So, this joiner thing, are you sure?"

"Oh yes," Dr. Sabourin said. "I was sure when you merged so many of us together. I've never been all that good at group magic. To me it was always like, oh, how can I describe it? Do you remember those old 16-pin computer plugs? Probably before your time, before USBs came along. I remember trying to plug those things in but finding some of the pins were bent. Now try doing that while jumping out of a plane." He looked thoughtful for a second. "Throw in a tornado while you're jumping," he added. "That's group magic."

Suzanne laughed at the doctor's description.

"But it was effortless merging power with all those people. You're the one who caused it to be effortless."

Mikyla shifted uncomfortably in her chair. "I'm just getting used to the idea that I'm a mage. Now you're telling me I'm, like, something that nobody's heard of in a century?"

"I've never even heard of it at all," Suzanne said. "How does it work?"

"I looked up some information on it. It's a kind of projective empathy thing whereby you're just really good at combining the power of lots of people to do something together."

"So not all of that power actually came from Mikyla?" Suzanne asked.

"Maybe none of it," the doctor answered. "She might just be the person who merges everyone together and forms the power into a seamless whole."

"I've heard that all First Circles have a weakness, an Achilles heel," Suzanne said with a frown. "Gatemakers, obviously, can't go through their own gateways. Salt is apparently deadly to metamorphs. I have no idea what Constance Reeve's weakness is, although I'd love to find out."

Dr. Sabourin looked startled at the vindictive tone. "I wonder if anybody likes that woman?" he asked. "God knows why she's keeps getting elected. From what I read, there's a risk to Mikyla in merging with others, particularly if someone's a bit unbalanced or something." His gaze swung back to Mikyla. "You could end up with bits of other people's personalities, which could really mess with your mental state. What happened today could have gone seriously wrong. You could have been sucked into that black hole and stayed there, like an endless loop, even if you had been able to detach yourself from the patient. It was probably Dr. Santos who prevented that."

Mikyla turned pale and swallowed hard a few times.

"How does she learn how to do it if there aren't any joiners?" Suzanne asked grimly.

"And maybe even more important, how do I learn to *not* do it?" Mikyla asked fearfully. "It wasn't exactly intentional. Nothing I've done has been intentional." She thought again of her mother's beer fizzing over and the ginger ale going flat. Did magic ever make sense?

"You talk to some people who are good at group magic, for a start," her father told her. "There is a basic course for new mages, anyway, that you should take. They do it every summer. Is school finished yet for the summer? He picked up his phone and turned it back on, looking at the date.

"Another week and a half, and then exams," Mikyla told him.

"Okay, what's your phone number? I'll get you registered for the first course this summer. And I'll line up a group magic specialist."

"Um, I don't have a phone plan. And I'm guessing you might not want to call my mom's landline."

Dr. Sabourin grimaced. "God, I guess I owe her 16 years of child support, don't I?"

"I suppose." Mikyla shifted position uncomfortably. Given how often her mother complained about lack of child support payments, that was not something she wanted to talk about. "Do you have Facebook Messenger?" She pulled out her cracked phone.

"I thought you said you didn't have a phone?"

"I said I don't have a phone *plan*," Mikyla clarified. "This works fine as long as I'm in Wi-Fi. And it's free."

"Ah, I see. I can get the app. It goes by e-mail address, right? Even if you're not on Facebook?"

"Yeah."

Dr. Sabourin pulled a napkin toward him and held his hand over it. An e-mail address appeared on it in neatly typed font.

"Typing by magic?" Suzanne asked. "That's a good trick. I'd like to learn to do my reports that way."

"I never did manage to learn how to write legibly with my left hand," the doctor explained. "So I came up with a workaround."

"Um, how …?"

"Car accident," Dr. Sabourin answered the question before Mikyla actually asked it. "I got T-boned by a drunk driver. If there hadn't been a mage surgeon at Vancouver General, we wouldn't be having this conversation right now."

"If you don't mind my asking, how do you do surgery with one hand?" Suzanne asked.

Dr. Sabourin just grinned. Suddenly all of the items on the table did a coordinated little dance. His eyes flickered a little, but there was no other sign of any effort on his part.

Mikyla's attention was drawn away from the choreographed cups and napkins by two people who approached the service hatch of the coffee shop to her right.

"Good afternoon, Councillor. What can I get you?"

"Two medium black coffees, please, Anna. To go."

Mikyla glanced over to see a man in a black suit with a thin pinstripe addressing the waitress. Then her eyes widened as she saw the young man standing beside him, dressed in jeans and a plain white T-shirt, with a Chinese symbol tattoo clearly visible on the side of his neck. With the sun high overhead, neither of them cast a shadow in the bright courtyard.

The man in the suit and Jake swung around at the exact same time. Mikyla froze in hurt confusion as Jake's gaze met hers and swept over her as if she were a complete stranger.

"Afternoon Jimmy," the man greeted Dr. Sabourin in a jovial tone. "Ladies." He nodded at them. Jake said nothing but nodded as well, with no expression on his face.

"Hi, Doug. Going somewhere?"

"Yeah, meeting in Chicago with the US councillors."

"Constance doesn't go?" Jimmy asked, looking at Doug's companion curiously.

"She's not feeling good. Better get going. See you." The man did not offer any explanation for Jake's presence.

As the two walked away from the coffee shop, Mikyla noticed that they both flipped the plastic tabs on their coffee cups at the same time and took a drink. She stared after them as they moved out of sight.

"Mikyla? Hey, Mikyla, what's wrong?"

Mikyla jumped, realizing she had missed responding to a couple of questions already.

"He didn't even say anything to me. He acted like he didn't even recognize me."

"You know Councillor Hayes?" her father asked, surprised.

"Not him. Jake."

"Wait, was that Jake with him?" Suzanne said.

"You didn't recognize him?"

"I only met him once," Suzanne reminded her. "And I was kind of focused on the patient at the time."

"What's a councillor?"

"Government rep," Dr. Sabourin answered. "We've got two in Canada, members of the International Mage Council. So, you know the guy who was with the councillor?"

"He's the one who told me I'm a mage," Mikyla explained, a hitch in her voice. "We were talking and texting every day for like a month. But the last I heard from him was Sunday, and he wasn't at school at all this week."

Dr. Sabourin and Suzanne looked at each other, puzzled. Mikyla could feel that both of them were worried about her. But all of the strange experiences of the day were catching up to her now and starting to feel overwhelming.

Abruptly, she stood up. "Can we go home now?" Her eyes were sparkling with unshed tears.

"Of course," Suzanne replied, sympathy colouring her voice. "Goodbye, Dr. Sabourin. It was nice meeting you."

"And you," he replied absently.

Mikyla couldn't bring herself to say goodbye. She just rushed out of the coffee shop ahead of Suzanne and walked back to the gleaming arch on the other side of the courtyard.

As Suzanne took her hand and spoke the name of their first destination, Mikyla remembered that the last time she had seen Jake drinking coffee, the night it had almost spilled in the park, it was light coloured with cream.

"He doesn't drink his coffee black," she whispered to herself.

Chapter 12

"Back with us, are you?" a coolly amused male voice asked. Natalie couldn't quite tell where the voice was coming from, because she felt entirely disoriented.

"I'm not quite sure," Natalie muttered, keeping her eyes tightly closed. "The room is still spinning. How long have I been out?"

"Four days," the voice replied, the tone turning more concerned. "It's Sunday today. I didn't think it would go on for this long, actually. I'm Doctor Sabourin."

"Four days?! What about Raj?" Natalie asked, alarmed, her eyes flying open and attempting to focus on the nearby figure. Instantly, her vision filled with lurching blobs of colour, reminding her of a memory stone she had once experienced of a drug addict's near-fatal overdose of something with hallucinogenic properties. Her stomach heaved, and she shut her eyes quickly again, sucking in rapid breaths in an attempt to calm her stomach. Judging by the abused feeling of the stomach muscles, it was evident that she had vomited more than once since pulling herself and Raj through a gateway to the hospital in Neekonnisiwin. The brief glimpse was just enough to tell her that the doctor was wearing pale green scrubs and was very short.

"That would be the man you brought with you, right?" the doctor asked, a note in his voice that Natalie couldn't interpret. It might have been concern, but it sounded more like disapproval. Irritation pulsed through Natalie, and she opened her eyes again, keeping them to just a very narrow slit, this time able to control her stomach even though her vision still lurched and pulsed.

"Yes, my business colleague, who took a bullet meant for me," she said in a harsh tone. She was implying that he had voluntarily stepped in front of that bullet, which wasn't precisely true, but she was determined that he would not experience any lack of care at the magical hospital just because he was a non-mage.

As she hoped, the disapproving look disappeared from Dr. Sabourin's face. Although Natalie's vision was gradually becoming steadier, she could still see odd splotches of colour appearing around the doctor and then elongating, moving away and disappearing, like a lava lamp. The colours around the doctor were mostly of a pale green tone. Something seemed to be wrong with one side of his face, but as she attempted to focus on whatever it was, her stomach lurched again, so she hastily closed her eyes and pressed her fingers over them.

"He's going to be fine," the doctor told her, his tone suddenly professionally neutral. "It was extremely fortunate that you were able to get him here so quickly, though. Things would have been very different with more of a delay. We've been keeping him in an induced coma, partly to ensure the healing process and partly because we don't know what he saw or would remember. There's the possibility that waking up and seeing an obviously magical hospital might cause him stress that would—well— impede his progress."

Natalie raised a skeptical eyebrow, though she kept her fingers pressed over her eyelids. "And partly because the Council is up in arms because I brought a non-mage to Neekonnisiwin," she added drily to his words. Suzanne had told her she got a lot of flak whenever she brought Dave here. Her sister stubbornly ignored the disapproval, refusing to let anyone get away with treating Dave as if he were of lower status. Natalie was determined to follow that example.

"Well, yes," the doctor admitted, his tone clearly uncomfortable. "And apparently made a gateway in front of a whole crowd of non-magical observers. And since you left all your stuff there, the Toronto newspapers are all over it. Of course, they already knew who you were anyway. I gather there was already some scandal …?"

Natalie's eyes snapped open, though she narrowed them immediately. "I'll deal with the Council," she said tersely, ignoring the not-so-subtle query. "They've used me for years, and I've done as I was asked. Now they can do this one thing for me, or else they can do without my services. I figure I'm in a very good bargaining position." She took a deep breath. "Provided I can keep the contents of my stomach where they belong," she added in a disgruntled tone.

The doctor grinned, the expression transforming his careworn face. As Natalie's vision remained somewhat steadier, she was now able to focus and realized that what she had thought was just her eyes playing tricks had actually been accurate. There was something wrong with the side of the doctor's face. He was badly scarred and had only one arm. She had thought he was sitting in a chair beside her bed, but she now realized it was a wheelchair. The sharpened focus made her stomach flip over again, and she sucked in several hasty breaths and closed her eyes again.

"I look that bad, do I?" the doctor said in an amused voice.

Natalie flushed in consternation. "No! I—"

"Don't worry, I'm just teasing you," he interrupted. "You've been throwing up ever since you got here, and dry heaving when you had nothing to throw up. Makes me glad we can clean things up around here without actually having to touch them."

Natalie smiled weakly, once again trying to carefully crack her eyes open just a slit and taking deep breaths.

"I think I'll just stay out of your way for a little longer," he mused. "There are advantages to being a surgeon. I can pull rank."

"Oh God, don't make me laugh," Natalie begged, clutching her stomach when even her aborted chuckle made the abused muscles complain. "When am I likely to be able to get out of here?"

"Now that you've regained consciousness, I'd just like to run a few tests, and then I suspect the rest of your recovery will just be a matter of rest. You could do that just as easily at home. There's not a lot we can do for you anymore. We fixed the stuff we could. I wouldn't be surprised if you have a hard time even going to the bathroom by yourself just yet, though," he answered wryly. "So you'll have to stay put until you can at least navigate under your own power. At this point, it's just the classic Boadicea's curse. Nothing for it but time."

"Damn," she muttered. "How long does it usually last?" Now that she could finally keep her eyes open, she glanced around to take in her surroundings. She lay propped up in a typical hospital bed with rails along both sides and what looked like video monitors beside her, although they were floating, unsupported, in the air, with no visible connections. Beyond them was an empty bed and, past that, a wide window with a stunning view of a snow-topped mountain peak.

The doctor shrugged, a rueful expression on his face. "There's not a lot of clear records on that, because very few gatemakers ever want to endure it. But the speculation is that the more powerful of a gatemaker you are, the longer the effects last. I would assume that you must be one very powerful gatemaker since this is the first time you have even been able to manage coherent conversation. Besides, I've never heard of a gateway crossing thousands of kilometres."

Natalie grimaced. "And there's something else I don't want the Council speculating about." She took a few more deep breaths to settle her still-rebelling stomach. "You said you fixed the stuff you could. What stuff?"

"You had some very nasty bruising on your right cheekbone, a contusion on the back of your head and a cracked rib on the right side. Just a hairline fracture, but if we hadn't fixed it, you probably would have made it worse with the vomiting, since it's been quite violent. Oh, and there was some bruising there too that we got rid of. Even once the physical stuff was fixed, though, you were in a bad way. It took the combined skills of our most powerful mind healer, your sister, and a young First Circle mage she brought in to save you. We don't even know precisely what they did, or how, but it worked."

"My sister? And a First Circle mage? Who was the mind healer?"

"Dr. Santos. She's often able to deal with deep emotional trauma, particularly the kind that surrounds a severe injury. In your case, though, you were so deeply unconscious, she couldn't reach you. Your sister had the personal connection with you that made communication possible. The young girl she had with her provided the rather incredible amount of raw magical strength, and the mind healer provided the guidance."

"Who was the young girl?"

"Her name is Mikyla Burton. Do you know her?"

"Don't think so. I don't recognize the name."

"In any event, I definitely don't recommend you ever go through your own gateway again."

Natalie shuddered. "No chance of that. It was brutal. Thanks for looking after me. And Raj. Do you think he is capable of being awakened safely?" she asked. "Perhaps if I were there so that there's at least one familiar element? I'd probably need a wheelchair," she added drily.

"The Council is still debating his case," the doctor admitted.

"Debating what?" Natalie demanded, immediately defensive again.

"I don't precisely know," Dr. Sabourin said with a frown. "But we've been asked not to allow him to wake up until they give us permission."

Natalie's eyes narrowed. "Is there any possibility that keeping him in a coma might cause him harm?" she asked. With her mind focused on other matters, her stomach was starting to behave itself.

The doctor looked thoughtful. "Not yet." He shook his head, although he was frowning slightly.

"Are you sure about that?" Natalie asked sharply. "I am not willing to allow the slightest risk to my colleague to pander to the Council's prejudices."

"I would have argued the point much more strenuously if I thought the patient was at risk," Dr. Sabourin told her, shaking his head. "Frankly, I would not have considered waking him up just yet in any event, since right now the coma is helping him heal, especially with replacing all the blood he lost. But absent any other concerns, I'd rather see him awake within the next day or two."

"All right." Natalie accepted his verdict, her eyes still narrowed. "Will you keep me posted? Oh my God, did anyone contact his family?"

"Yes," the doctor assured her. "Your sister mentioned that he worked with you, so we contacted your firm and got them to advise his family that he was being cared for."

"You contacted the firm?"

"They already knew that you were a mage by that point, I'm afraid. There was no hiding it after the gateway and after your laptops and other things were recovered."

"That's right, you said it was in the papers already too." Natalie sighed. "My career is so over."

"I thought my career was over when I got T-boned by a drunk driver," Dr. Sabourin told her sharply. "There are always other options; you just need to open your mind to them."

Natalie looked at him again and was reminded of the extent of his disability. She nodded meekly, accepting the rebuke. "So, um, about Raj's condition?"

"We need to assess his cognitive functions to make sure there was no brain damage from any temporary loss of oxygen to the brain. I don't think there will be. The bullet did not actually pierce his heart; it just grazed the top of the left ventricle and ruptured the aorta. Oh, and it shattered a rib, both in the front where the bullet went in and where it got stuck in the bone at the back. Since we had him in the emergency department so quickly after the injury, we were able to maintain his body functions magically while we repaired those things. But to make sure there's no brain damage, we need him conscious, at least for a while."

"And how long after that is he likely to need to remain in hospital?"

"Probably not that long," the doctor said cheerfully. "At least as long as the tests are all okay. Everything's all sewn up so to speak. He's had multiple blood transfusions to replace what he lost, and all the tests that can be done on an unconscious patient show the heart function is fully restored. We even have a nurse who is amazing at minimizing scars. Fresh ones, that is," he added wryly. "Pity she was still in elementary school back when I had my accident. I don't know whether we'll be able to completely eliminate your colleague's scar, but it won't be a significant disfigurement. If you don't tell him he was shot in the heart, he need never know."

"I think I'm done keeping secrets from the people I'm closest to." Natalie shook her head. "I can't hide this from him."

The doctor nodded understandingly.

"So he needs to be awakened shortly. I know how slowly the Council operates. I need to speak to them," Natalie said with a sigh. "But there's no chance I can even light a candle right now, let alone do the dialogue cantrip. How can I contact someone? Preferably *not* Constance Reeve."

The doctor's eyes twinkled. "Do you have a cellphone?"

Natalie snorted. "Cell service totally sucks here; it always has," she objected.

"Not anymore. About six months ago, Councillor Hayes decided it was high time Neekonnisiwin caught up with the times. He put a cell tower up himself, right on the roof of the Convocation Chamber. Councillor Reeve persuaded him to move it to the peak of Mount Yakama the next day. After that, he organized excellent-quality high-speed Internet service throughout the whole town. Free Wi-Fi wherever you go."

"I like him already." Natalie grinned. "Did I bring my purse with me?"

"I think it may be in here." The doctor moved his wheelchair toward her bedside table and opened the drawer. "This it?" He pulled out a dust-smeared black leather purse.

"Yeah, thanks." She reached for the phone and powered it on. "Is it okay to use it in the hospital?"

"No problem," the doctor assured her. "That's an old rule anyway, even in ordinary hospitals. Cell signals don't interfere with delicate electronic machinery or anything anymore. And especially here, it's mages who perform those functions. I'll go find the councillor's number for you. And possibly some Gravol, although I understand it's likely to be only partially effective since the symptoms are more magical than physical."

"I'll take any help I can get," Natalie confessed. "I think I hate nausea worse than anything."

"Good afternoon, I'm Doug Hayes." The councillor looked to be in his late forties, though his light-coloured sandy-brown hair did not show much grey. He was wearing a golf shirt and suit pants and held two disposable coffee cups. "Coffee?"

"Oh my God, yes please!" Natalie took the cup and sipped the hot coffee with an expression of bliss on her face. "I'm Natalie Benson, as I guess you know. Sorry to drag you over here to see me."

The councillor chuckled. "My dear, it's obvious just by looking at you that you're not in any shape to go anywhere just yet. I recall doing the memory stone of someone who watched a gatemaker get shoved through his own gateway. Looking at you, I would say the effects haven't gotten any easier since whenever that was."

"It's way worse from the inside, trust me," Natalie said drily. She could still see the blobs of colour, though they were now strangely elongated, disappearing and reforming with no logical pattern. Those around the councillor were a bizarre mix of colours, most of them murky and unattractive shades of yellow and green, quite different from the ones that had surrounded the doctor. She firmly decided to ignore them.

"I've been wanting to meet you for a while," the politician said jovially. "Pressing charges against Connie was a brilliant move. That woman is far too impressed with herself. It'll do her a world of good to be disciplined by the Arch-Mage."

"As long as it is understood that I'm not changing my mind. She is not to contact me ever again. And I do mean ever."

"And the prisoner transfers?" The man's voice was a shade more wary now.

"I'm not doing those anymore either," Natalie said firmly. "In fact, I feel very strongly that LEO needs to open lines of communication with the non-magical law enforcement bureaus and work with them. It probably wouldn't be a great idea to reveal to them just how many police resources have been wasted over the years, but they should work together going forward." The councillor's face was getting darker as she spoke, and Natalie knew she had a significant uphill battle to fight if she ever wanted her newly formed opinions to effect change.

"My own recent experiences have made me realize that it's likely that loads of people, prison guards and such, have probably lost their jobs or suffered in other ways because of LEO's practice of taking criminals out of prisons and keeping the whole thing secret. You probably heard that the commissioner of Corrections Canada was asked to resign? That was only so the government can look like it's doing something, but the truth is, there is nothing they can do."

"Your own recent experiences?" It was clear now that the man's tone was getting less friendly. The splotches of colour appearing around him seemed to darken as he spoke.

"My firm is on the verge of bankruptcy, and if that happens, it will ruin the careers of a hundred or so perfectly innocent lawyers because we have been implicated in the disappearance of fugitives," Natalie told him, shutting her eyes as the disorienting lurching of her vision threatened to overwhelm her stomach again. "The public perception is that a huge majority of criminals are mages, and they're all getting away with it."

"How many of those lawyers are mages?" Douglas Hayes asked, his eyes narrowed.

"That is completely irrelevant," Natalie snapped. Her good opinion of this man was rapidly going downhill. Bringing her coffee and organizing free Wi-Fi was not sufficient to endear to her a politician with that kind of attitude. She recalled that she had voted for him last time around, though she couldn't remember what his platform had been like. Mostly she had voted for him because she did not want to vote for Constance. She decided the last platform didn't matter. It would be the next election that would count.

"None of them have anything whatsoever to do with missing fugitives. But all of our careers are going to be ruined regardless. Besides it's not even just the lawyers who will suffer. Anyone who has to put Mason Sullivan on their résumé is going to have a harder time finding a job than an equally qualified person who isn't associated with the firm. God knows what's going to happen to me when I go back."

"What? Why?!"

"Because people hate mages!" Natalie opened her eyes to yell at him. "How can you not know that? How can you represent mages if you don't have a clue what it's like out there?"

Suddenly, Natalie realized this was the main problem with the Council of Mages. Even those who had lived and worked in the outside world prior to election invariably moved to a mage community upon being elected and were then surrounded by mages virtually all the time. How could you truly represent the 90 percent or so of mages who did not live in exclusively magical communities if you lost touch with what that kind of life was like? Natalie narrowed her eyes and tried to calm her temper. It was vital that the Council become more aware of the growing hate and the increasing problems that it was causing for mages everywhere.

"Non-mages are terrified of us," she said in a calmer tone. "They are convinced that we manipulate and coerce our way through life, riding roughshod over anyone who gets in our way. Fear makes people lash out, and ignorance is the biggest cause of fear."

"We don't harm those who don't harm us," the politician replied stiffly.

"Oh, and it's okay to harm those who do harm us?" Natalie responded. "I beg to differ. I don't have the excuse of not knowing what it's like for them. And speaking of harm, the doctor tells me that my colleague Rajit Naresh must be allowed to wake up within the next 24 hours. Otherwise they cannot guarantee that the induced coma won't harm him. That is completely unacceptable." Natalie didn't care that she was exaggerating what the doctor had told her.

"How will he react to being in a magical hospital?" the councillor responded, one eyebrow raised.

"He'll have to deal with it," Natalie replied sharply. "I'm sure it will come as a shock, but I wasn't about to let him die of a bullet intended for me, and I'm sure as hell not going to allow him to be damaged by being kept in a coma because you're scared of how he will react. We can prevent him from doing anyone any harm, including to himself."

"He could be returned to Toronto without any awareness of what has happened," the councillor suggested.

Natalie ground her teeth and tried to hold onto her temper. She was liking this man less and less as the conversation continued. "He's not going to have forgotten being attacked, and if he has, he'll soon get the whole story. It was all over the news the day it happened. You people have been using my special skills for years, and now it's about to ruin not only my life but also numerous other lives. You now have an obligation. You can start with Raj. Give the doctors permission to wake him up as and when they think best for his medical condition. They need to run some tests, and he has to be conscious for that."

"Well, we will need to discuss—"

"No, forget it. The time for discussion is over." Natalie's tenuous hold on her temper snapped. "I've had enough of this crap. It is going to be done as soon as the doctors feel it should be done. If any harm has resulted from your fear about how he and others will react, you and this hospital can try explaining that to a judge when you are slapped with a multimillion-dollar lawsuit for medical malpractice, negligence and punitive damages! And that action will not be brought before a magical court." Fortunately,

Natalie's vision temporarily resolved itself enough to allow her to direct a ferocious glare at the politician.

"Ms. Benson is right, Councillor," Dr. Sabourin spoke from the doorway. "Mr. Naresh's condition could be irreparably harmed by any further delay. There is no justification for it. And I am certainly not prepared to try to defend that kind of lawsuit."

"Are you threatening to disobey the order of the Council, Doctor?" the councillor snapped.

"The Council hasn't made a decision yet," Dr. Sabourin retorted. "They have been debating this for four days and haven't come to a decision. I'm not willing to allow a patient to be harmed. Unless you get an order signed by the Arch-Mage himself in the next two hours, and the Council confirms in writing that it indemnifies me and this hospital for any and all liability that may result, I am waking Mr. Naresh up."

"We'll just see about that." The councillor stalked out of the door, his back rigid.

Chapter 13

The orderly who came into the room with Dr. Sabourin magically lifted Natalie into a wheelchair, telling her to close her eyes and let him move her. Although it had been nearly two days since she had regained consciousness, she still felt as weak as a newborn and was happy to obey. Even the thought of trying to work magic herself was enough to induce another wave of nausea, and she had a sickened fear of the possibility that the experience might have damaged or destroyed her magical abilities. It would be like suddenly losing her legs. She felt guilty for the thought while in the care of a surgeon who evidently had lost the use of his legs. She reminded herself again of his advice: be open to other options. It was an attitude she needed to adopt, given recent events.

She noticed that both the doctor's wheelchair and her own were the ordinary manually operated kind, but he was evidently propelling his by magic, whereas the orderly pushed hers, following the doctor. Dr. Sabourin led them into a room containing ten beds, about half of which were occupied with unconscious patients. One medical attendant sat in a comfortable chair at the far end of the room, her eyes closed, both hands grasping an unusual-looking green prism. The orderly stopped near the doorway, giving Natalie a good view of the room without getting in anyone's way. Dr. Sabourin rolled his chair forward and gently touched the attendant on the arm. Her eyes sprang open.

"We're going to take over with Mr. Naresh and move him out to a private room, okay?"

"Good, that will make things a lot easier. I never realized it would be so much more difficult with a non-mage," the attendant said, shaking her head. "It's like there's nothing to grab hold of. Well, not nothing, just, I don't know, like it's more slippery somehow." She extended her right hand, palm flat and facing him. Dr. Sabourin pulled a deep red-coloured prism out of his pocket and placed his left hand against the attendant's palm, with his prism held between their two hands. Natalie saw that he closed his eyes and moved his prism between their joined hands in a pattern that made Natalie's stomach lurch. She closed her eyes, not opening them until she felt herself moving again. Raj, still unconscious, was now floating horizontally beside her, supported on nothing. A blanket was wrapped tightly around him. She glanced behind to see that her chair was still being pushed by the orderly. However, she could tell, from the look of concentration on his face, that the orderly was responsible for Raj's transportation as well. The doctor's face showed no sign of strain, and she felt impressed with his magical skills. It took a lot of concentration to do different magics simultaneously. Yet apparently he was moving his own chair and also holding Raj in his magically induced coma at the same time, a spell that the attendant had indicated was quite a bit more difficult with a non-mage.

Once Raj was laid on a bed in a private room with a picture window looking out onto the same stunning view of the mountain that was visible from her room, the orderly left the room. Dr. Sabourin spoke to Natalie soberly.

"All right, when I wake him, he will have no awareness of the passage of time. So, he will probably think it's only seconds since whenever he was last conscious. What was happening just as he lost consciousness?"

"We were being attacked by a couple of vigilante antimagic types who thought we were both mages," Natalie explained. "Raj has no idea that I'm a mage. Well, he *had* no idea," she corrected herself, "but he had just seen me do something obviously unnatural and had given me a shocked look, so I'm pretty sure he had figured it out. Then he got shot." She paused and frowned thoughtfully as she reflected on the doctor's advice that Raj would have no awareness of the passage of time. "I would guess he might come up fighting. Watch his fists."

Dr. Sabourin nodded and moved his chair to a position further away from reach of a thrown punch. He pulled his red prism from the pocket of his white coat. Natalie was still seeing the odd blobs of colour, but she noticed that those around Raj's head were sort of flickering, as opposed to the smooth pulsing that she had seen with each of the mages who had so far come into her line of sight. Also, they were an unwholesome-looking yellow colour that looked oddly familiar. With a shock, she remembered the coercive magic Jon and his temporary partner had used against the prisoner in her condo a few weeks ago.

"Is that," she said, hesitating, "coercive magic? And is it flickering, or is that just me?"

"It is flickering," Dr. Sabourin confirmed. "That's because he's not a mage. It would be more stable when used on a mage, as well as brighter. And yes, it is coercive magic," he added. "One of the few legally permissible forms. We use magic to induce a coma, rather than drugs. Since that is persuading the body to do something unnatural, it is coercion of sorts. Not so much coercion of the conscious mind, but still. It's permitted because it's quite a bit safer for the patient since drugs can interact, sometimes with negative consequences, or there might be allergies or other reactions. We had no way of knowing anything of Mr. Naresh's medical history and whether he would be using any drugs, prescription or otherwise."

He began to move his prism around in a pattern that Natalie did not recognize. As soon as Raj's eyes began to flicker, the doctor immediately began speaking in a soothing tone of voice.

"You are in a hospital, Mr. Naresh. Your injuries have been treated, and you're fine now. You are in a hospital ..."

In spite of the words, Raj's body jerked, and he sat up quickly, both hands clenched into fists. As the doctor raised his hand in a soothing gesture, Raj pulled himself sharply out of reach and whipped around with a furious expression on his face. He then did an obvious double take upon seeing the doctor in his wheelchair, an easily recognizable white lab coat, and the other accoutrements of a hospital room nearby. Dr. Sabourin continued to speak soothingly in spite of the threatening posture of his patient while Raj's head whipped back and forth in confusion.

"You are in a hospital, Mr. Naresh. Your injuries have been treated, and you're fine now."

"Seriously, Raj, you're in a hospital," Natalie added, and his eyes flew to her. His tense posture still did not relax.

"You look like shit," he remarked, breathing heavily. His voice sounded a little odd, slightly higher pitched than usual. With a jolt, Natalie realized the doctor's voice was not quite as low as Raj's normal speaking voice. Was that the coercion still wearing off?

"Thanks," she replied drily. "I guess you've never seen me without makeup before. Behold, Natalie with a naked face."

Raj made a scornful noise in his throat, coughed slightly and then cleared his throat. "It's not lack of makeup," he said, his voice now sounding more normal. "You look green. And your eyes look like you're having a hard time focusing."

"Yeah." Natalie grimaced. "I am having a hard time focusing. And keeping my breakfast down."

"And me?" Raj asked hesitantly, turning his head to look at the doctor, who moved forward into his line of sight now that there seemed to be no danger of getting punched. Raj's posture was finally relaxing, though he still looked wary and confused.

"We've been keeping you in a medically induced coma," the doctor explained. "Sorry for the disorientation. I know you would have no awareness of the passage of time. Actually, you've been out for six days."

Raj swore and then took a deep breath with closed eyes as he adjusted his thinking. When he opened his eyes again, he looked around the room and frowned. "What kind of hospital is this? It looks like a hotel room," he exclaimed. Natalie glanced around and recognized some of the things that would seem odd to someone who had only ever seen a normal hospital. The bed he was in had a colourful comforter on top of crisp white sheets, rather than the more industrial-looking bedcovers usually found in a hospital. The floor was dark laminate that resembled wood, and there was a large mural featuring what looked like hand-painted First Nations artwork taking up most of the wall he was facing. "Uh, in the mountains?!" he added as he glanced toward the window, which featured a view of a snow-tipped peak in the distance. "Where the hell am I?"

"Yukon Territory," Natalie answered. "You got shot in the chest. You needed treatment that you weren't going to be able to get at Toronto General. At least not fast enough."

"Shot?! In the chest?!" He looked down at himself in alarm and pulled open the wraparound-style hospital gown that was covering his upper body. "No bandage? What? Wait, there's a hospital in the Yukon that's got better emergency services than Toronto General?" Raj asked in confusion, his eyebrows raised.

"Getting you to Toronto General was the difficulty," Natalie answered, not meeting his eyes. "Traffic was really heavy, and there was that crowd, most of them pretty hostile."

Raj's eyes widened suddenly as he remembered the events just before he had been shot.

"You—you're a—" He broke off, staring at her with mouth open.

"Yeah, I'm a mage," Natalie admitted, now looking him in the eyes with a solemn expression on her face. "I brought you here because you needed treatment fast, or you were going to die. I couldn't let that happen, not when we were attacked only because they thought we were both mages. And you're not."

"I have known you for seven years," Raj ground out accusingly. "*Seven years.* And you've kept this a secret? In spite of recent events?"

Natalie sighed. "We all keep it a secret," she told him. "We have to. The amount of prejudice and hatred is off the scale. You, yourself, have made plenty of antimage statements, particularly in the last few weeks. I can just imagine how you would have reacted if I'd told you. Not to mention how James and Phillip would have reacted. Will react," she corrected herself with a sigh, closing her eyes again as the thought of what awaited her return made her feel nauseous all over again.

"Will react?" Raj repeated ominously through clenched teeth.

"I didn't have time to grab our laptops or stuff from court. They know now who it was who disappeared from the middle of the city, in an obviously magical way," Natalie admitted. She started taking short quick breaths, keeping her eyes closed and bending forward in the wheelchair.

"I'm almost tempted to just not go back," she added when she could speak again. "It's going to be hellish."

"Why are you so sick?" he asked, diverted from his shock by her obvious physical distress.

"The transportation spell is supposed to be for short distances," she told him, having considered and discarded several other stories to explain away her gatemaking abilities. It was against mage law to reveal First Circle abilities to a non-mage, a law she had never before had any desire to break. Now that she was beginning to question some of the secretiveness, she was having second thoughts about that. But then, someone as intelligent as Raj would easily put knowledge of gatemaking together with magical prisoners disappearing and would likely jump to the worst conclusion. "But I had to get you here fast. I badly overextended myself. I've been unconscious almost the same length of time you have, except in my case it wasn't medically induced."

"Actually, Ms. Benson almost died," Dr. Sabourin told him bluntly. "Both of you were in a very bad way, for different reasons."

"I was in a coma?" Raj turned back to the doctor with a frown on his face.

"Medically induced. Essentially, you've been kept anaesthetized for six days," the doctor explained. "It was necessary on account of the nature of your injury, to give you the best possible chance of healing, because in some cases the body will perform radical triage by shutting off blood flow to damaged areas, and that would cause permanent damage. We had to operate on your heart. Non-magical hospitals do the same thing, they just use drugs."

"And you don't use drugs?"

"Not for an induced coma," the doctor explained. "We use a form of coercive magic. It's safer, with no possibility of drug interactions."

"Magic." Raj took a deep breath, visibly shuddering. He turned to Natalie. "You're a *mage*," he repeated, accusingly, clenching his fists again.

"Look this way, please, Mr. Naresh," Dr. Sabourin said firmly, ignoring the tense byplay. Obedience to the doctor's orders distracted Raj, and he looked toward a small pencil light the doctor was shining toward his eyes.

"Focus on my finger, please, and move your eyes without moving your head." He gripped the pencil light between his teeth and then held up a forefinger directly in front of Raj, moving it from side to side. "Good. Now I'd like to listen to your chest, if you don't mind?" He pulled out a stethoscope. Raj looked back down at his chest. There was a blanket covering him to the waist, and when he lifted a hand to the cotton hospital gown to pull it further apart, he saw a drawstring waistband that looked like the same kind of scrubs the doctor was wearing.

A thin pink line traced a slightly jagged path up the middle of his chest, faint stitches visible in a neat line. The edges of it looked inflamed, but it looked much more healed than one would expect only six days after major emergency surgery.

"Deep breaths," the doctor instructed, and he reached forward with the stethoscope and then mumbled a half-audible swear word as he realized he could not reach his patient's chest. "Sorry, I'm going to have to do this the other way," he said with a shrug, and the stethoscope left his hand and floated over to Raj's chest. Raj jerked backward in shock, but then he acquiesced, as the doctor moved the stethoscope to various positions on his chest without touching it.

"Now your back," the doctor said, and Raj pushed himself forward, eyeing the stethoscope with some trepidation as it floated around behind him. It disappeared under the back of the hospital gown and stopped in several positions on his back. "Excellent, everything sounds fine," the doctor told him. "It was indeed very lucky you were brought here so fast. We had you in surgery probably no more than 10 minutes after you were shot, and we had you magically stabilized before that."

"Why is there no bandage? The scar looks almost healed," Raj said in a baffled tone. "I was actually hit?"

"Oh yes, the bullet grazed the top of your heart and damaged the major artery," the doctor told him cheerfully. "Don't worry, you're fine," he added hurriedly as Raj's face paled in shock. "And the scar is faint because here in this hospital, we don't have to hide what we're doing from non-magical eyes; we can use our skills to the fullest extent. We have one particular nurse who is fantastic at minimizing scars. Any kind of blemishes, actually, but she prefers to use her talents where they're really needed, and not just for cosmetic work. She was also the one who dealt with your bruises, by the way," he added to Natalie, who nodded. "If you're willing to return for follow-up treatment, we may be able to remove the scar entirely."

"If you can save lives using magic," Raj began in an accusatory voice.

Dr. Sabourin held up his hand and shook his head. "I know where you're going with this. Trust me, there are mages in every hospital in the world, using their skills to the extent possible to save lives and reduce suffering wherever they can. The vast majority of mages do not live in isolationist magical communities like this one. I assure you, we do far more good in the greater world than harm. But how likely is it that someone like me would still be able to practise as a surgeon in the non-magical world? Out there, people see only the missing arm, the scarred face and the wheelchair. I can never be anything but a handicapped person there. Here, it is understood and accepted that I can move things with my mind just as easily as I could if I had two arms."

Raj's mouth dropped open as he turned around to look at the doctor and realized the extent of his disability.

"But we are hated and feared wherever we are known, and it's been that way for hundreds of years," the doctor continued sadly. "Or thousands, maybe. As Ms. Benson said, we have no choice but to hide what we are, even from our closest non-magical friends."

"I think I'm gonna throw up," Natalie suddenly said in a slightly panicked tone. Dr. Sabourin immediately went to her side and placed his fingertips on her temples.

"Oh, *oh!* Oh my God, that feels so much better," Natalie said in tones of relief within moments. "How did you do that?" she asked curiously. "You said before that I was throwing up a lot."

"It's sort of a combination of coercive magic and how ordinary analgesics work," the doctor explained. "Just persuading the brain to ignore the signals it's getting from pain sensors. Or in this case, the signals that are telling your brain to make your stomach throw up. It's not that different from how we knock people out for surgery, just more subtle. It is a little bit coercive, though, and nurses aren't allowed to do it. I hope you don't mind?" he asked Natalie.

"You're not getting any objection from me," Natalie said in relief. "Coerce away."

"And there's the other reason we are limited in what we can do in the outside world," Dr. Sabourin said with a sigh, now looking back at Raj, who was looking at both of them with an obvious expression of distaste on his face, his jaw clenched. "There's a huge ethical debate about using magic without a patient's awareness or consent. And how many non-mages actually would consent if they knew?"

"Not to mention, how many mages would lose their jobs if they admitted to what they were," Natalie added drily.

"I am having a really hard time dealing with this," Raj complained, looking between the two mages.

"Just remind yourself that she's still the same person you've known for years. She just happens to have an extra skill you didn't know about."

Natalie suddenly laughed. "I remember when I learned you can play a wicked game of basketball in a wheelchair. I was blown away."

"A wheelchair?" Dr. Sabourin asked in surprise.

"Yeah, Raj volunteers at the Y, playing wheelchair basketball with a group of mostly people who really are restricted to wheelchairs."

"Not the same thing," Raj muttered, his jaw still tense.

"Why not?" Natalie demanded. "I can't play basketball in a wheelchair. Actually, I can't play basketball, period."

"But you could probably get a basket without touching the ball," he accused, his eyes narrowing.

"That would be cheating," she retorted. "And since I actually have some ethics, I don't do that kind of thing." She took a deep breath and tried to shake off the flare of irritation. "Look, I need to lie down. And you could probably use some time to rest and get your head around this stuff. I'll come back later."

She attempted to move the wheels of the chair with her hands, but she couldn't figure out how to go backward and turn at the same time.

"Let me." Dr. Sabourin laughed. "I've had lots of practice. I'll leave you as well, Mr. Naresh. Please don't get out of bed just yet. I'd like to keep you in hospital for at least one more day. We'll bring you a proper meal in a bit and then get you up and walking. And in fact, after that, I recommend that you take it easy, preferably no stress, for at least 48 hours. You lost a lot of blood, and even though we gave you some transfusions, your body needs time to fully recover."

"Who pays for all this?" Raj asked suddenly.

Dr. Sabourin grinned. "The same national Medicare that operates in the rest of the country," he explained. "We merge our records with a hospital in Whitehorse, with the assistance of a mage working at the Medicare office."

"You guys manipulate everything, don't you?" Raj directed the snarky remark at Natalie, who just sighed and ignored it.

Natalie looked at the cellphone in her hands for a few minutes. She needed to call the office, but what was she going to say? Eventually she punched in the number rapidly, before she could change her mind.

"James Behrman's office."

"Hi, Wendy, it's Natalie Benson. Can I speak to James, please?"

There was the sound of a startled indrawn breath at the other end and then silence. Natalie sighed inwardly and waited. After a brief pause, Wendy spoke again, this time sounding like her heart rate had just tripled in speed.

"He, uh, he's not here. Can I—can I take a message?"

"Wendy, you've known me since I was a summer student. You've never been scared of me before, and I'm afraid I have always been a mage. I never harmed you before this, and I'm not going to harm you now, especially since I'm sitting in a wheelchair in a hospital far away from you. I'm not going to harm James, either. But I really need to speak to him."

"You're in hospital?!"

"Yeah. Long story. I'm in kind of rough shape, but I'll recover. Raj and I were attacked by these two jerks while we were coming back from court. One of them had a gun, and Raj got shot right in the chest. But he's just been brought out of his coma, and he's gonna be okay too."

"Oh my God." At least Wendy's voice sounded a bit warmer now, her shock at the news overriding her previous nervousness. "I ... I wasn't lying when I said James wasn't here, though. He's in hospital, too. He had a heart attack."

Natalie swore and then took a few deep breaths. A few tears leaked out the sides of her eyes. "I always had a feeling he was going to," she said in a shaky voice. "But I don't have any ability to tell the future."

"But you encouraged as many of us as possible to get trained in CPR," Wendy pointed out. "And you got the firm to buy a defibrillator machine. We used it on him, you know. The paramedic said it probably saved his life."

"Thank God for that," Natalie said.

"You get some credit, too," Wendy said. Natalie felt a few more tears gather in her eyes.

"Thanks, Wendy. I really appreciate you saying that. Is he going to be okay?"

"I think so. It might just be the wake-up call he badly needs. Maybe you should speak to Phillip Mastersen instead?"

"Yeah, I guess I should." Natalie sighed. "This won't be a fun conversation."

"If you really are a mage, is it, um, well …" She stumbled to a halt without properly finishing the sentence.

"The allegations are a load of crap," Natalie said firmly. "I have never helped any criminal evade justice, and I never will."

"Good to know. I'll put you through to Phillip."

"Thanks, Wendy."

Wendy transferred her to Phillip's office, but the warm feeling Natalie had received from Wendy instantly dissipated as the managing partner spoke.

"You are not welcome to return here, Natalie."

"Is that so? Well, in that case, I see two possible futures for us, Phillip. I say 'us' quite deliberately. Your future is as attached to mine right now as if we were joined at the hip."

"I refuse to be associated with people like you."

"Are you really that much of a bigot, Phillip Mastersen?"

"You are a mage." He said the word as if it were the filthiest epithet he could imagine.

"Yes, Phillip, I am. And you're a Jew. And Raj is an immigrant. And Susan Wildman is gay. So fucking what?"

"This firm is on the brink of disaster because of people like you."

"The firm is on the brink of disaster because of irrational prejudice and wildly illogical allegations based on the most circumstantial evidence imaginable," Natalie snapped. "You don't want me to come back? I'd be happy to stay where I am and never have to deal with the prejudice and hatred ever again. But guess what happens if I do that?"

There was silence on the other end of the line, but Natalie thought she heard the sound of grinding teeth. She answered her own question.

"The whole firm goes down the tubes. Bankruptcy, Phillip, and as an equity partner, guess what happens to your personal wealth? How would you like a job at McDonald's? Every one of the 129 lawyers at Mason Sullivan can kiss their legal careers goodbye. Everyone loses, Phillip."

"And whose fault is that?"

"It will be the fault of the narrow-minded, bigoted idiot who is too busy pointing fingers at the scapegoat to actually step up to the plate and do anything to help fix the problem," Natalie snapped. "I have been a mage my whole adult life, but I have never helped a fugitive to evade the criminal justice system."

She heard a sound of scornful disbelief but ignored it. "Solving this is going to require all of us to work together against a common enemy: blind prejudice and wild accusations that have no evidence or truth. If we do that, maybe we can salvage something out of this mess. But it's going to require co-operation. And I'm not prepared to tolerate being treated like a pariah while we do it."

"And what do you propose if we are able to clear our names?" Phillip's voice was still hostile, but at least he had said *we*.

"We can regroup and decide at that point. If you all still want me out, then I'll leave. But you'll have to give me proper severance. I don't deserve this crap any more than anyone else."

"I beg to differ."

"I deserve this crap just as much as your grandfather deserved to die in a Nazi concentration camp, Phillip Mastersen! Stop being such a fucking asshole. Raj and I will be back as soon as the doctors give us the go-ahead. Two or three more days. And just so you know, Raj is not a mage. Have a nice day," she added sarcastically and hung up the phone.

Then she dropped the cellphone on the bed and started to cry.

Chapter 14

Natalie knocked lightly on the door of Raj's hospital room and stepped hesitantly inside, unsure of her welcome. Raj was sitting in a chair by the window, still wearing the cotton hospital pants, although he was now shirtless. Natalie was surprised to see that his chest was very muscular though quite hairy. She had never seen him without a business shirt or the occasional loose golf shirt. He swung his head around to see who was at the door. His expression grew shuttered as he identified his visitor, and her heart sank. Clearly, he was still not happy with the revelation of her magical abilities.

"I just have one question that I have to have an honest answer to," he told her abruptly. "Is there any truth to any of the allegations?"

"Absolutely not," she answered immediately. She raised her right hand in the air as if she were swearing an oath in court. "I swear I have never had anything whatsoever to do with assisting fugitives to evade justice, so help me God."

"You've never been religious as far as I ever knew," Raj pointed out. "Of course, it turns out there's plenty I don't know about you." His gaze swung back to the expansive view from the window, which Natalie realized was one that it was hard to keep from looking at. She and her family had visited

Neekonnisiwin many, many times, but the grandeur of the snowcapped mountains never lost its appeal.

"Fine, then. I solemnly affirm and declare that I have never had anything whatsoever to do with assisting fugitives to evade justice," Natalie responded, trying hard to keep hold of her temper. The alternative wording was acceptable in court for those who did not want to swear an oath on any kind of holy book. "Anything else you'd like to know about me? My weight? Law school marks? Boyfriend history? I don't date empty-headed bimbos, and I've never played wheelchair basketball."

"That's different." Raj ground out the words, ignoring her dig about some of the women he had dated.

"Yeah, my secret is one that doesn't reveal that I'm a shallow, narrow-minded bigot," Natalie snapped.

"Are there other mages at Mason Sullivan?" Raj demanded through clenched teeth.

"One other," she confirmed, "but I'm not going to tell you who it is. Nonetheless, I absolutely guarantee 100 percent that that person isn't helping fugitives evade justice either. The truth is, there is a magical criminal justice system, and it's a lot harsher." She was still having difficulty holding in her irritation in the face of his obstinate hostility, but nevertheless she was trying to respond in a neutral tone.

"How harsh?"

"Well, I don't know what prison conditions are like, but I do know that even after you've done your time, you are required to stay living in a magical community like this one. It's over the top, really. They have an attitude of once a criminal, always a criminal."

"And they enforce that how?" Raj said in a voice that clearly expressed his lack of faith in the concept.

"Very simple, actually," she answered. "The Convict's Curse is a spell that can't be removed from the inside, and it just makes the person glow if they leave the magical community. It's put on as soon as a person is convicted, so even if it were possible to break out of one of our jails, it's already in place. Imagine how people would react to someone who glows when they walk down the street. You might not be able to see it in bright sunlight, but you'd definitely see it if there was any shadow, or indoors. It would even reflect in a window or shine off a mirror. I've seen it demonstrated."

Raj just looked skeptical. "How can you be sure the mage criminal can't break the spell him- or herself?"

"It's really difficult to undo any spell that someone else has set," Natalie told him. "Magic is mental, and nobody thinks in precisely the same way as someone else. There are certain formulas, and we trace a pattern in the air, sometimes with a jewel shaped like a prism, which sort of focuses the mental effort and makes it easier. But it's still, at root, a mental thing."

"Do you generally carry around a prism-shaped jewel?" he asked with a raised eyebrow.

Though he was still sounding unconvinced, at least he was no longer quite so hostile. As long as he was merely curious, Natalie was content to try to satisfy that curiosity. She firmly believed that the primary cause of the antimage prejudice was ignorance and fear, so more knowledge could only help.

"Well, I keep an illusion on it most of the time," she admitted, dropping her eyes. "You might recognize it." She pulled her silver pen out of her back pocket, held it on the palm of her hand and released the illusion, revealing the sapphire prism. Raj's mouth fell open.

"Your silver pen with your name engraved on it?!" he exclaimed. "You use that thing all the time. I've used it!"

"It's a very complete illusion," Natalie told him. "It looks like a pen, it works as a pen, it's the same weight as a pen. It produces the ink by magic if you write with it. Actually, it sucks the ink from a nearby pen, since it's really difficult to create something out of thin air. I try to always keep the same make of pen around at work so the ink doesn't change colour. Of course, if someone actually tried to open it up and put a new inside thingy in it, that wouldn't work so well. I can't make the illusion go that far."

Raj's jaw was tense, and he looked at the prism as though it were a live snake.

"Why are you here anyway? You're all fixed up. You don't have to wait around for me."

"Actually, you can't really leave town without a mage's assistance."

"So I'm a prisoner here, am I?"

"No, you're just an obstinate ass. You got shot in the heart, you lost tons of blood and you nearly died, and the only way to get back to the ordinary world without magic is if you can climb down a mountain and then hike about 250 kilometres to the nearest town. I think there's a tiny airport in Atlin. Possibly you could sort out flights from there, but getting there would be a problem. Good luck with that in your present condition."

Raj turned around to look out of the window, pointedly ignoring her. Natalie glared at his reflection in the window, but even there he would not meet her eyes. A silent battle of wills ensued, and Raj did not speak.

Finally Natalie turned to leave. "I am *so* done with this shit. Like I don't have enough crap going on." She stalked out of the door, before the tears springing to her eyes made it evident that she was more hurt than angry.

Natalie sat in the visitor's chair at the foot of her bed, which was now stripped of bedding. With the monitors gone and nothing on the bed, the room looked far more sterile and empty than its previous appearance. The flowers that had been sent to Natalie had been removed because the scents had made her upset stomach worse. Natalie reflected that it was mostly the colourful bed coverings and wall art that made the Neekonnisiwin hospital look more like a hotel, but it was a thin disguise. The room was too bare now. She got up to go stand by the window. At least that view remained as spectacular as ever.

How had her life spiralled out of control so quickly? It had been not quite two months since a wildly circumstantial newspaper article had suggested that someone at Mason Sullivan was helping people escape from jail. And here she sat in a hospital on the other side of the country, her career almost certainly in tatters, while the secret she had struggled so long to hide had been splashed across the front page of several major newspapers. A good friend and colleague was barely speaking to her, someone had shot a gun at her, almost certainly aiming to kill, and her managing partner had made it clear he considered associating with her to be similar to accidentally stepping in animal feces. The view did nothing to raise her spirits.

"You—you're okay!"

Natalie looked around in surprise to see Jon in her doorway, looking pale and stressed.

"Jon? I was expecting Suzanne to come and get me."

"I thought you were going to die. The newspaper said—" He walked toward her and put both hands on her arms as if needing to reassure himself that she was actually there.

Close up, the fear in his eyes was more obvious. A warm feeling began to disperse the depression Natalie had been feeling moments ago. Maybe not everything in her life was complete crap.

"Journalists are the bane of my existence just now," Natalie said tartly. "How would they know? All they know is I disappeared." She brought one hand up to cover one of his, which still gently gripped her upper arm. He shivered as she ran her fingers across the back of his hand.

"Not the ordinary ones. *Mageworld Today.*"

Natalie was startled. "*Mageworld Today* is reporting me dead? Or dying?"

"Well, yeah. A gatemaker going through her own gateway? Everybody knows that's really bad, and it's thought the more powerful you are, the worse the effects. You're the most powerful gatemaker in the world. What were you thinking?" Jon's voice shook, and his hands tightened on her arms.

Natalie moved her other hand up to cover his and squeezed gently. "I was thinking that Raj got shot in the heart because I deflected the bullet. I couldn't let him die."

"But you could let yourself die?"

"I didn't die," she pointed out, lifting one hand to lightly stroke his tense jaw, noticing that a shave was slightly overdue. "I admit I wasn't thinking very clearly. I could probably have just pushed Raj through and stayed put, but I wanted to get away from those assholes anyway. And I guess I was kind of thinking I'd have to tell the hospital about Raj and didn't really consider that I wouldn't be able to." She dropped her hands and wrinkled her nose as she confessed to her short-sightedness.

"So it was really bad, then? I mean, I don't know of anybody who actually has gone through their own gateway in hundreds of years, so it's just a theory—"

"Oh, it was bad. I did almost die, so I'm told. Apparently, there was some fairly spectacular magic involved in saving me." She saw Jon's jaw tense again at this information. "My sister is being kind of tight-lipped about what happened. I think she's afraid it will stress me out too much or something."

Jon started to speak, then appeared to change what he was going to say. "How is your colleague?"

"I don't really know," Natalie replied gloomily. "I tried to go see him, and he told me to get out. He's totally pissed off at me now that he knows I'm a mage and I never told him. I figured I'd better just give him some space. Medically, I think he's going to be okay. They just want to run some more tests, make sure his heart is fine and that his brain function wasn't damaged and stuff."

"Can I ask you something?"

"Sure."

"Is there anything between you and him?"

Natalie smiled and shook her head. "We're just friends. Well, we *were ...*"

"Or anybody else?"

She shook her head again. "No, but I'd kind of like there to be," she hinted with a smile.

"Thank God for that." Then he began kissing her like a starving man at a banquet.

Natalie parted her lips to deepen the kiss and heard a small groan as he pulled her closer. Her grip on his arms tightened as her knees suddenly seemed to lose strength.

Jon pulled just far enough apart to say, "I've been wanting to do that for a long time."

"Um, you only met me two months ago. Less."

"It's been a long two months."

Natalie's response was to pull Jon even closer by hooking her fingers in his belt loops. And then she took up where he had left off.

After sending Suzanne a text to let her sister know her whereabouts, Natalie discharged herself, and she and Jon left the hospital. Natalie was unburdened, carrying nothing other than her purse. Jon was holding a small bag of her personal items that Suzanne had brought to the hospital for her. He refused to let her carry it.

"Did you call your office yet?" he asked Natalie in a sombre tone as they exited the hospital and started down the slope toward the town square.

"Yeah," Natalie said with a sigh. "Turns out my department head had a heart attack when he learned what happened and got proof positive that at least one of the two of us is a mage. Fortunately, he didn't die, but he's in hospital too. So I spoke to the managing partner, who I'm beginning to realize is the biggest bigot on the planet. He started by telling me I'm not welcome to come back, and the conversation went downhill from there." She looked away from him, hoping to hide the wetness in her eyes as she replayed that conversation in her head.

"You're gonna get through this. *We* are going to get through this."

A smile showed briefly on Natalie's face as Jon squeezed the hand that he held in his own.

"You know, in some ways, I guess it's silly of me to be so wrapped up in my career, like that's all there is. My whole identity, in some ways, is wrapped up in being a lawyer, and it's like losing that will be losing everything," she admitted.

"I can understand where you're coming from, but you wouldn't be losing everything if you had to change careers," Jon said. "I kind of feel the same way about being a LEO, but I know there are other things I could do and still make a difference."

Natalie nodded without looking convinced. She sighed as she looked around at the stunning vista on all sides as the path from the hospital led downhill toward the town. Evergreens dotted the nearer slopes, but higher up only some kind of low-growing green groundcover was visible. And higher still, it was bare rock. A few of the highest peaks were clearly snow-covered, though cloud cover obscured some of them from sight.

"Do you think they're really all that likely to disbar you?"

"A week ago I would have said no chance. But I'm more pessimistic now. Having someone point a gun at me has totally shaken up my worldview."

She shuddered. "You see guns in the movies or TV all the time, but it's so different when you're at the wrong end."

"That, I can relate to," Jon agreed. "So getting the College investigation dismissed is priority one."

"Well, frankly, figuring out what's up with this possible serial killer has to be priority one, doesn't it? That's way more important than my career."

"All right, priority two. So, let's assume you don't get disbarred. Then what?"

"I suspect I won't be employed by Mason Sullivan for much longer regardless. We were already losing clients just based on the rumours of magery. The fact that I'm fully out of the closet now will make that worse, even if we can get the College Application dismissed. I just hope Raj doesn't lose his job as well."

"Would you consider working for LEO?"

Natalie made a face. "LEO's wanted me for years, but frankly, just transporting people here and there sounds like the most deadly dull boring job I can imagine. Worse than a job in a call centre." Natalie had a vision of working a job in a dreary cubicle in a large room filled with identical grey cubicles, where everyone felt like an automaton.

Jon laughed. "Yes, I can see that. But we're stretched thin as it is. After what you managed to put together on these anomalies, there's no way they're going to just ask you to build gates and nothing else."

Natalie smiled, but her face turned more serious as she went over the facts relating to missing mage convicts and multiple deaths that she had unearthed. Then she sighed.

"There's something else I'm concerned about," she said. "Let's go up to the lookout for a bit first." She waved her free hand toward a hill crowned with benches and a small gazebo, which boasted the best view of the mountains and the picturesque town among the foothills.

"The fact that I'm always travelling?" Jon asked worriedly. "I know it might be a bit …"

"No, it's not about us," Natalie said. "Besides, I can gate you from pretty much anywhere. You know that."

"Oh, right."

His tone sounded surprised as though he had not considered that, and she wondered how many previous relationships had failed because of his incredibly demanding schedule.

"Gives whole new meaning to 'booty call,'" she added with a grin, bumping him with her hip.

Jon's shoulders jerked backward in surprise, and then he started laughing. "Just so you know, I'm hoping for a bit more than a friends-with-benefits kind of scenario. Though I like where this conversation is going …"

Natalie laughed. "The conversation is going to take a sharp left turn, I'm afraid. I'm still wondering about whether or not to tell Seth about these anomalies."

"Ah," Jon said, nodding as he took a seat on a bench under the gazebo and stretching his long legs out in front of him. "Well, I think I can set your mind at rest on that. I did report your suspicions to my captain in London, and he reported it to Chief Thibault in Europe. LEO has been investigating this past week. Unfortunately, there was another event, last Wednesday, that looks like it has some similarity. But we know exactly when the death occurred, and if it was magically caused, that probably would have to have been within no more than a few hours before. Seth's got an alibi."

"Wait, what?" Natalie interrupted his story. "If they know exactly when the murder happened, why do you say it could have been caused several hours earlier?" She took a seat on the bench beside him, leaning toward him with a confused look on her face.

Jon hesitated, and Natalie's eyes hardened. "Don't even *think* about telling me I'm not LEO and you can't tell me about an ongoing investigation," she said fiercely. "I'm the one who started figuring this out."

Jon looked undecided, but then he nodded. "Just maybe if you could please not tell Seth that I told you about this one?" he asked. "It really is against protocol to discuss an open case with someone outside of LEO. And Seth is *very* strict about regulations."

Natalie rolled her eyes. "Yes, okay, I get it. Bureaucracy and rules. Blech. Worse than politics. Another reason I don't want to work for LEO."

"An organization like LEO wouldn't really function very well without a hierarchy and strict regulations," Jon pointed out. "So anyway, it happened in Washington."

"The state? Or DC?"

"Um, the one where the White House is. DC, right?"

"Yeah."

"There was an American congresswoman who collapsed and died in the middle of the street, with no visible attacker. They couldn't resuscitate her, but the cause of death appeared to be some kind of lower respiratory tract infection, like bronchitis or pneumonia or something. Her lungs were full of liquid, and a bunch of stuff in there was all swollen and infected when they did the autopsy. That's why we're thinking the magical cause could have been earlier. If it really was a magical attack."

"How would you create a lung infection and cause it to develop so rapidly with magic?" Natalie asked.

Jon spread his hands and shrugged. "I have no idea. I believe European LEO was consulting with several mage doctors who specialize in respiratory stuff, to see if they could figure that out. But the suspicious thing is that she had just had a really thorough physical examination one week earlier, and there was absolutely no sign of anything like this at that time. The mundane doctors are baffled. There's no way that that degree of swelling and infection wouldn't have been at least somewhat evident a week earlier. Nor would it have developed that rapidly without some very obvious symptoms, so I'm told."

"You said this was last Wednesday? That's the day I was attacked." Natalie stood up and moved toward one of the arched entryways to the gazebo, leaning against the pillar and looking toward the distant mountain peak, reliving her feelings of helplessness and terror when she looked down the barrel of a gun held by a man whose face was twisted with hatred for her and everything he thought he knew about her.

Though she dealt with fraud all the time in her job, it had always seemed like a rather bloodless crime. Not victimless, obviously, but lacking the heart-pounding drama of murder. She felt entirely out of her depth dealing with this situation and wished she was comfortable just handing it all over to LEO and staying out of it. It wasn't really clear, even to her, why she felt like she couldn't. When had she ever distrusted LEO? Although sometimes she felt the mage laws might be too harsh, and occasionally LEO's demands of her had been irritating, she had always believed that they would get the bad guys.

Thinking through the story Jon had just told her, she realized what was missing.

"And a mage victim?"

"We haven't found one," Jon admitted. "So that part of the pattern doesn't match up. But that congresswoman was also well-known to strongly dislike mages and to be in favour of proposed laws that would be problematic for mages in America. More significantly, as you may know, there's very tight security at portals in places like Washington, for obvious reasons. But although you can tell from the portal itself that at least two people arrived and then went through it again about 45 minutes later, which brackets the time of death, the security officer in charge of that portal has no memory of anybody arriving or leaving during that time. It was that officer himself who reported the anomaly, and his report came in very shortly after reports of the congresswoman's death started hitting social media."

Natalie's eyes narrowed suspiciously, but Jon held up a hand before she could interrupt.

"I know what you're thinking, and yes, of course we checked out the officer's story. The cameras show nothing, but the record is one hour too short. The missing footage is seamless. There is magical security on that camera that would set off an alarm immediately in Chi Wajiwan, in Colorado, if anybody disabled it or did anything, magically or physically. Nobody has access to the footage in Washington; it's only accessible in Chi Wajiwan, in a secure facility. So the security officer couldn't have done it himself."

"So you're saying somebody accessed the footage in Chi Wajiwan after the fact and seamlessly altered it?"

"Must have. And did so within an hour of the event."

"And Seth?"

"We know that he was here in Neekonnisiwin for the whole morning. He had a video conference with several local captains less than one hour earlier, and he was seen in footage in the public areas of headquarters less than 15 minutes after the murder happened. Even by portal, he couldn't have got back to Neekonnisiwin that fast. Not to mention, the footage in Chi Wajiwan was inspected less than two hours after the attack, so if it was altered, it would have been before then."

Natalie looked relieved. "Thank God for that. I hated the thought of not being able to tell Seth about this," she said. They got up and began walking slowly back down toward the town centre and the LEO headquarters.

"There was another one too," Jon told her with a worried expression on his face.

"Oh my God, what is this guy doing, murdering people every week?"

"This was two weeks ago, the day before my brother's party. In fact, it was on the news when I was at your condo."

Natalie replayed that evening's events over in her mind and sucked in a startled breath. "The rape victim and the preacher?" She swallowed hard. It certainly fit the pattern. A non-mage who clearly hated mages, and a mage whose presence where it happened did not seem very likely or predictable, albeit not impossible, as would be the case with a convict.

"Actually, it's a case of mistaken identity," Jon told her. "Serena Pryor is alive and well, still in Chi Wajiwan, and fortunately hadn't heard about the story. She avoids social media like the plague and doesn't watch live TV or read newspapers."

"Makes sense after what she went through," Natalie said. "That's a relief. So then, who was the girl? And why did they report it was Serena?"

Jon looked cynical. "I'm guessing that wasn't an innocent mistake. Taking the opportunity to slander a known mage probably sells more newspapers than having a completely unknown drug overdose victim."

Natalie's face registered her distaste as she thought about that, but she had to agree. "But do you know who she was?"

"Yeah, also a convict who shouldn't have been able to be where she was." He gave no further details and did not look at her, making it evident he wasn't going to further breach the regulations and give her additional information.

"That's at least eight murders," Natalie said quietly. "Nine if there actually was a mage victim with the American congresswoman. In just over a year. And there could easily be more."

Jon just nodded, his face grim.

Jon guided Natalie straight past the reception desk and toward the office of the chief LEO. He knocked courteously on the open door, and

Seth Turner looked up and beckoned them both in, though he did not smile. His eyes flickered briefly between Jon and Natalie with a slight frown between his eyes. The Chief was silver-haired but with a body as trim and fit as a man half his age. He wore a version of the uniform that Natalie had never yet seen Jon wear, and she spared a brief thought to wonder if Jon even had one. Considering he did so much undercover work, it seemed unlikely he would have much use for a uniform.

Seth's office was not particularly large and was cluttered with files and papers, with most of the wall space taken up by corkboards with various notes and charts pinned haphazardly in every available spot. A desktop computer with a fairly small monitor sat on a side table. The only concessions to the man's rank as chief LEO for North America was the comfortable-looking leather chair that he rose from as they entered and the view from a broad picture window behind the desk.

"Natalie, what a surprise. You are recovered, I hope?"

"Mostly," Natalie said with a grimace, shaking his hand. "I swear on a stack of Bibles, I will never, ever go through my own gateway again. Nothing is worth that!"

"Perhaps you might consider making a memory stone of it?" Seth Turner suggested. "There really aren't many records of that from the gatemaker's experience. Future gatemakers could benefit from knowing just how bad it is. Some of my gatemaking LEOs have been tempted, even though it's strictly against regulations."

"It's a very good thing it is against regulations," Natalie confirmed. "I certainly understand why it was so easy for the Romans to kill Boadicea after she went through her own gateway. She would have been as helpless as a newborn baby. In fact, death might have been a relief."

"Jon, I thought you were supposed to be in Texas?" The Chief's tone was slightly disapproving.

Natalie glanced sideways at him, hoping he wasn't interrupting his duties to play knight in shining armour to her.

"I took care of both assignments there," Jon replied. "Then I heard what Natalie had been through, and I wanted to come see if she was all right."

Seth raised an eyebrow but did not comment further.

"I was sorry to receive that e-mail from you three weeks ago," Seth told Natalie, "but I certainly understand. I apologize for evidently not explaining things clearly enough to the councillor. I had to show her the e-mail." Seth sat back down, waving his hand to indicate they should take the chairs sitting in front of his desk which were, surprisingly, free of the piles of paper that adorned every other surface.

"Nobody can apologize for Constance Reeve except for Constance Reeve," Natalie said in disgust. "And she's far too arrogant and inconsiderate to do that."

"I'm guessing you've got something else you want to discuss? You look kind of grim."

"I want to discuss the serial killer we appear to have in our midst."

Seth's expression immediately darkened, and he directed a ferocious glare at Jon.

"No, Jon didn't tell me about it," Natalie told him, causing his gaze to flick back to her.

"It was the other way round," Jon added drily. "Natalie's the one who actually started figuring this whole thing out."

"Indeed? Well then, perhaps both of you might be able to tell me why *I* didn't know anything about it until this morning?"

"Because we couldn't rule you out as a suspect," Natalie said bluntly, noticing that Jon winced as she spoke. As she glanced in his direction, she also noticed that Seth's office door was still open, and she waved a hand at it, causing it to swing shut.

A strangled noise was all that Seth was able to articulate. His face was turning an unattractive purple shade.

"Sorry, Seth, you know I would never want to think badly of you, but you know better than most that you can't let sentimentality get in the way of finding the facts. And the fact is, our suspect has to be someone high up in LEO, someone capable of covering up the fact that a number of mage convicts have gone missing from jail."

Natalie stayed silent while Seth digested that information, his expression turning thoughtful. When he eventually spoke, it was after he had cleared his throat a few times.

"Once I received the report this morning, I suppose I was more focused on the non-magical murder victims and a motive," he said. "I wasn't paying as much attention to the mage victim."

"Were you, by any chance, considering those mage victims to be less of an issue considering they were convicted criminals?" Natalie asked drily.

"I'm not a total asshole," Seth told her drily. "It's just that I do get a whole lot more flak from the politicians when magical crime impacts the non-mage world. It tends to increase the hatred, which certainly had a fair bit to do with the attack on you."

"Good point," Natalie agreed. "Still, the fact remains that we don't have the death penalty, so murdering convicts is just as unacceptable as murdering anyone else."

"I've only made a very cursory review of the matter so far," Seth said. "Why don't you tell me everything you know about it so that I can see if the official reports include everything you've got."

Natalie noticed him flicking an admonitory glance at Jon as he spoke, and she guessed that a non-verbal communication was probably taking place at the same time. It wasn't hard to guess that he was probably reminding Jon that she was not LEO and was not to be provided with information not available to the general public.

Recognizing that her irritation was probably not fully justified, she ignored it and began to describe the three pairs of murder victims or attempts on victims which she had discovered and how she had begun to put it all together.

Seth pulled a pad of paper toward himself and rapidly made notes as she spoke.

"And how did you know that Paul Dasovic, Christopher Narcourt and Elizabeth Chin were convicts?" he asked.

Natalie sighed inwardly. She had been hoping to avoid mentioning the list of convicts Jon had given her, but it didn't seem like that was going to be possible. She explained the details of the College Notice of Investigation and why she had asked for a list of which escapees really were arrested by LEO.

When Seth's face darkened, she said, "Isn't information on people who actually have been convicted in the public record? I'm pretty sure it is in the non-mage world."

"We are not the non-mage world," Seth said repressively, and did not elaborate.

When she had finished going through each of the deaths that appeared to fit the same pattern, by which point Seth had three pages of notes, the chief LEO for North America looked up at Natalie with an expressionless face.

"Thank you, Natalie, for noticing this pattern. Your assistance has been invaluable. We'll take it from here."

"What?!" The mild irritation Natalie had felt before suddenly exploded into full-fledged fury. He was stonewalling her? When she had figured this thing out in the first place?

"An active LEO investigation is not to be discussed with a member of the public, not even the one who reported it," Seth said repressively. "I trust you are familiar with the regulations on that point, LEO Forrester?"

"LEO did not even notice a string of murders that has been happening under our noses," Jon pointed out, his tone troubled. "Natalie did. For all we know this might have been going on for a lot longer than the ones unearthed so far. We haven't gone back further than three years yet."

"An active LEO investigation is not to be discussed with a member of the public. Is that clear?"

"Yes, sir," Jon said in a tight voice.

"Six years," Natalie said, her eyes widening as she suddenly put something else together.

"Excuse me?"

"Six years ago, there was a guy who escaped from a maximum-security psychiatric institution in northern Ontario. I'm guessing that's the kind of thing you were probably involved in," she said to Jon.

He did not answer, but a slight widening of his eyes confirmed her assumption.

"Let's see, I believe he had murdered the president of a Montreal newspaper," Natalie said slowly as she recalled the details that she, Raj and James had discussed the day the first newspaper article had started the whole downward spiral that had become her life. "If I were to look up that paper, I wonder how many antimage editorials I might find? So then that mage convict somehow ended up in a small town in BC, where he blew his brains out while surrounded by police. I wonder how he got away from LEO? Maybe twice, considering he already had a rap sheet a mile long *before* he committed the murder." She remembered that last detail from having looked it up after her meeting with Raj and James. Some of the details didn't make sense—no doubt she was missing some pertinent information—but the list Jon had given her only went back five years, which is why that man's name was not on it.

Jon stared at her, his jaw tense as he absorbed that information, but he looked away uncomfortably as she met his eyes. Seth just looked expressionless, although Natalie had seen him jotting another note at the bottom of his third page as she spoke. Neither of them said a word.

"There is a solution to this impasse," Chief Turner suggested mildly. "You know LEO has wanted to hire you for years. What you've done here makes it obvious how much we need you. Then you would be a member of LEO, and the regulation wouldn't be a problem."

"I will not be blackmailed into considering your job offer."

Natalie gave both of them a frigid glare, stood up and stalked from the room.

Chapter 15

Suzanne looked in the doorway of the room that had been her sister's and was startled to see that it was unoccupied. Even Natalie's bag was gone. She had not seen the text that Natalie had sent her, and she gave Dave a puzzled look and turned around, intending to go to the information desk and find out what had happened. But seeing a familiar figure approaching in a wheelchair, she went to meet the doctor instead.

"Morning, Doctor. Um, can you tell me what happened to my sister? I thought I was supposed to come help her check out, but she's gone."

"There was a man who came to get her instead," Dr. Sabourin replied. "Red hair, British accent? Boyfriend, I assume, based on what I saw from the doorway. I decided not to interrupt." He wiggled his eyebrows and smiled.

"Boyfriend?" Dave asked his wife in surprise. "I didn't know she had one."

A slow smile appeared on Suzanne's face. "Yeah, that's new. But I'm definitely glad to hear it. I met him. He seemed like a really nice guy. Are you allowed to tell me the status of her colleague?"

"Well, obviously not in any great detail," the doctor admitted apologetically. "Patient confidentiality and all that. But he's okay. I would just really like to be able to do some kind of tests of his heart function, preferably without actually stressing his heart."

Suzanne pursed her lips, thinking about an e-mail she had received from Natalie outlining her attempt to talk to her co-worker. "What about, ah, emotional stress?"

"You have something in mind?"

"I made a memory stone about saving Natalie's life. Since you were involved, you know how bad it was. If he experiences it, knowing that she did that to save his life, maybe it would achieve the effect you want?"

"And get through his obstinate antimage attitude while we're at it?" Dave guessed the unspoken part of her sentence.

Suzanne wrinkled her nose. "Yeah. Natalie's pretty upset about it. I'm more pissed off, though. She risked her life to save his, and he's being a total jerk. I don't know him at all, but I know they've worked together for years, and they're pretty good friends. Or were."

"Can a non-mage experience a memory stone?" the doctor asked.

"Yeah, I've done loads," Dave replied.

The doctor looked surprised. His eyes flicked to the side of Dave's head.

"There's some great extreme sports ones. All the adrenaline without actually having to get off the couch. What's not to like?"

Dr. Sabourin grinned at him, and they got into a discussion of their favourite extreme magical athletes while they made their way to Raj's room.

Before they got there, the doctor turned more serious and looked up at Suzanne.

"Have you, ah, heard anything from Mikyla?" he asked. "She hasn't contacted me, and you know, she didn't give me her number or e-mail address."

"Oh, she just took yours, didn't she?" Suzanne remembered. "Actually, I haven't, and I don't have her phone number either. She didn't phone me; she just came to the ambulance station. So I wouldn't even have her number in my phone."

The doctor frowned and turned his wheelchair toward a small sitting area off to the side of the main corridor. "I'm concerned about getting her that training as soon as possible. That's a dangerous skill to have with no ability to deal with it. As she put it herself, she doesn't know how *not* to do it. And, uh, I bought her an iPhone. With a plan. I hope she won't mind."

"I'm not sure any teenager would object to being given a free iPhone," Suzanne told him. "Other than the typical intro camp, did you figure out anything specific for her?"

"I talked to a psychiatrist who is really good at group magic. She thinks she may be able to work with Mikyla to figure out what she needs to know." The doctor sighed. "It was probably all way too much, especially in one day. What was the deal with that young man who didn't recognize her?"

Suzanne noticed that Dave was looking puzzled and realized he would have very little idea what they were talking about. She quickly filled him in on what had happened at the coffee shop, as well as the discovery that the doctor was the father of the young girl who had been in the ambulance that day.

"Who was she, anyway?"

"Remember that domestic a few months ago with the teenage daughter and the two little boys? She was the daughter."

"Domestic?" Dr. Sabourin repeated, his jaw tense. "As in, domestic assault?"

"Yeah," Suzanne admitted. "The mother had been beaten up by a boyfriend. He was being arrested as we arrived. She was in pretty rough shape."

The doctor looked at his feet for a few moments. "I know I'm going to sound like a total ass, but I don't really feel much for Tina. I mean, I feel sorry for anyone who goes through that, but it's like reading about a stranger in the newspaper. It was a short-lived relationship, and she cheated on me. Not to mention it was years ago. But I hate the idea that that's my daughter's home life."

"We ran into her a second time, about three weeks later." Suzanne explained the circumstances of the party. "She and this guy Jake were helping the patient. You know, she said they'd been talking and texting for a month after that, and then he had just stopped. I'm assuming she had a thing for him."

"Didn't really look like it at the coffee shop," the doctor replied. "At least not on his side."

"Well, exactly. I figured that's why she was so upset. Or wait a second, I think I saw something on the news …"

Suzanne tapped a query into her phone, and she sucked in her breath as she turned the phone around so that the two men could see the headline she had found:

"Please come home." Family of missing
Toronto youth makes emotional plea

The photograph looked to have been taken a year or so ago and was clearly a school photograph, but it was unmistakeably Jake. "It says he's been missing for almost two weeks now, since Sunday the third," she said.

"Wasn't it Wednesday that we saw him, last week?"

"Yeah." Suzanne was silent for a moment as she scrolled through the article. "Well, my first thought was that he told his family he was a mage and they wanted nothing to do with him, but judging by this, I think I'm way off base," she admitted. "The family sounds frantic."

"How old is he?"

"About eighteen I would think," Suzanne replied. "Just finishing Grade 12. And no, that's not too old for your 16-year-old daughter," she told the doctor with a grin.

"Not that I have any right to play the heavy in any event," he admitted.

"I know where she lives. I could go by, see if she's okay," Suzanne offered.

"I'd appreciate it. And could you give her the phone?"

"Sure. Would you be willing to come to Toronto, if she's okay with seeing you?" Suzanne asked. "Uh, I mean, you are able to, right?"

"I assume you're not asking about the wheelchair," the doctor said with a rueful look on his face. "Yes, I'm able to, on both counts. I had that Character Test. I assume you've heard of that?"

"A little bit."

"It was awful," he told her. "Like mental rape. If I'd known it would be like that, I don't think I'd have gone through with it. But back then, which was before my accident, I didn't want to work here. I had a job offer at a hospital in Vancouver."

The expression on Dave's face made it clear he had no idea what they were talking about, but this time Suzanne did not enlighten him, either about the doctor's minor criminal past or about the mage law that said a convict could never leave a magical community unless cleared by the test that Jon had described. She wasn't entirely sure how much she was permitted to tell her husband about the magical law enforcement system.

"I recall you saying something about Constance Reeve the other day," the doctor continued, looking at his knees. "I don't know what she's done to get on your bad side, but that's how she alienated me. She's the one who did it. I've always been very aware of patient dignity since then, even if they're unconscious. I know how I felt when my dignity was entirely stripped away."

Suzanne did not know what to say in reply to that.

"Would you mind waiting here?"

The doctor turned his wheelchair toward Raj's room.

Dr. Sabourin knocked on the door to announce his arrival. Suzanne and Dave were close enough to see that the doctor put the clipboard he had been holding between his knees as he used his single arm to operate the wheelchair. Suzanne had a strong suspicion that he was still using magic to propel the wheelchair since it would probably be fairly difficult to move it in a straight line and with any speed with only one arm. But at least that wasn't obvious. She thought it was considerate of him to try to reduce the appearance of things that clearly made his non-magical patient uncomfortable, not that Natalie's colleague deserved that level of consideration, in her opinion.

"Well, Mr. Naresh, if I didn't know you work in an office, I would never have been able to guess it. Without actually doing stress tests, I'd have to say you appear to be the most physically fit individual I have ever done heart function tests on," Suzanne heard him say. "Most of my heart patients are overweight, out of shape and have terrible nutrition."

Raj laughed. "Well, I can't promise you my nutrition is all that great, but I do exercise."

Suzanne and Dave couldn't hear the next part of the conversation, but it sounded like the doctor was going into somewhat more detail about his patient's present condition.

"So all the tests are okay, Doctor?" she heard Raj say.

"It would be useful if we could test heart function with the heart rate raised somewhat, but I don't really want to do a normal stress test. I'd like to raise the adrenaline in a non-physical way, and in fact Ms. Benson's sister offered to lend me a memory stone that would be ideal," the doctor said.

"A memory stone?"

The doctor explained what that was. There was silence in the room. Suzanne raised her eyebrows at Dave, who smiled ruefully. He had also been quite nervous the first time she had offered him the option.

"I don't think I like the idea of having someone else inside my head," Suzanne heard Raj say.

"I'm probably not explaining this all that well. Would you mind if Ms. Benson's sister and brother-in-law come in here?"

"Okay."

The doctor rolled out of the room and waved to Suzanne and Dave. They entered the room, and Suzanne saw that Raj's eyes were hostile as they flicked between the two of them, a sharp difference from when she had met him two weeks earlier.

"I guess you're both mages too, huh?" he said without a smile. "And that British guy who was at Natalie's condo that day?"

"My wife is a mage; I'm not," Dave replied, stepping slightly in front of Suzanne as he spoke. Suzanne's mouth twitched at his fairly obvious protective stance. Dave was a big guy, and kept himself in excellent physical shape since he often had to lift heavy patients. Since he also hid his prematurely receding hairline by shaving his entire head bald, it was very easy for him to look extremely intimidating.

Raj's eyes flicked quickly between Dave and Suzanne. Suzanne thought he still looked nervous, but somehow in a less hostile way as his gaze settled on Dave.

"So, do you know about these memory stone things?"

"Yeah, they're like 3-D movies, but all your senses are involved. Nobody's in your head. The person who made the stone basically recorded their memory in it so you can experience it. They can't tell who's watching it or anything."

"You've seen one?"

"Lots. They can be fun."

"Okay, I guess." He still looked reluctant, and he visibly swallowed hard after he gave his consent.

Suzanne pulled a milky-white piece of quartz from her pocket and walked up to Raj. "Hold out your hand," she instructed him.

She dropped it into his palm and folded his fingers around it, then traced a pattern in the air over his hand with her other hand, a small red prism on a key ring dangling from her fingers.

Raj's body language betrayed his nervousness as he drew his body further away from what she was doing with his hand, but within seconds, his eyes went blank as he stared at something only he could see, and shortly he started breathing in short gasps. Seeing the expression of anguished terror on his face and knowing those were her own emotions that he was feeling, Suzanne thought of what the doctor had said about stripping away dignity. She probably wouldn't want people who were almost total strangers watching her if their positions were reversed. Looking away from his face, she placed her fingers on his carotid artery and then nodded at the doctor.

"Heart rate is accelerated, Doctor."

Dr. Sabourin raised his eyebrows, then moved his wheelchair closer, no longer pretending to maneuver it with his single hand. Instead, he placed his hand on Raj's shoulder while several monitors suddenly appeared, floating in mid-air, displaying a heart rate graph that spiked rapidly and several other graphs that the two paramedics only vaguely recognized the purpose of. He watched them intently, nodding thoughtfully.

"What exactly is on that stone, Suzy?" Dave asked quietly.

"My memory from the time I walked into Natalie's hospital room and saw her looking like a corpse, through until the doctor, Mikyla and I did whatever it was we did that pulled her out of where she was."

"Where she was?" he repeated the phrase in confusion.

"She was caught in some kind of bizarre mental vortex trap. She was either going to die or go insane because of what she did to pull the two of them all the way here in one jump. *I* think this guy needs to know just what she did for him." She knew she sounded defensive, but somehow she couldn't admit that she was feeling guilty now, when earlier she had felt quite vindictively glad about what her sister's colleague was going to experience.

"I've only done fun ones, like heli-snowboarding. This is pretty different."

Suzanne shrugged. "He's getting a lot of emotion and fear right now. But it won't hurt him. As soon as he's out of it, he can separate himself from my feelings."

Dr. Sabourin took his hand off Raj's shoulder before Raj was finished with the stone. He smiled and gave Suzanne and Dave a thumbs up. "Perfect bill of health," he told them. "He can leave whenever he wants. It's a pity he can't take it easy for a few more days. I have a good idea of the kind of stress that's waiting for him back home."

Dave nodded. "They're both gonna have a tough time. But at least Natalie can come back here if she can't clear her name. What's this guy gonna do?"

"So much for innocent until proven guilty." Suzanne sighed.

"Oh my God." Raj looked shaken, and the earlier hostility was no longer in evidence, at least for the moment. "'Can be fun,' you said?!" He looked accusingly at Dave. Suzanne had a feeling he was still more comfortable talking to the only non-mage in the room, but she stepped up and held out her hand silently for the stone. Raj dropped it into her hand like he couldn't wait to get rid of it.

"Well, depends on the topic," Dave admitted. "The last one I did was made by a totally insane dude who was whitewater rafting near the Victoria Falls in Zimbabwe. I'm pretty sure that's the tallest waterfall in the world, and class 5 rapids downstream."

"Yeah, well, this one was just a bit different." Raj was still breathing hard as he turned a sombre gaze on Suzanne. "All that was because of this transportation thing that she did?"

"Yep," Suzanne said soberly.

"So how did you guys get here?"

"Through the portal network," Dave replied easily. "It's way cool, like *Star Trek*, except no pretty coloured lights and being broken up into atoms. You just step through this stone arch thing, and when you step out, you're in another place. They're scattered across the country. They don't work unless you're a mage, though, or in close physical contact with one." He smiled fondly at his wife.

Raj sighed. "I was a total asshole to her," he admitted. "And she risked her life to save mine. Did she know it was going to be like that?"

"Well, maybe not entirely," Suzanne admitted. "Nobody has transported themselves that kind of distance in, I dunno, hundreds of years. It's just well-known that you can't."

"Why didn't she take me to a local hospital then?"

Dave laughed. "Can you imagine how they'd react to two people popping into existence in the middle of the emergency department? I suspect everyone would be so freaked out and panicked that they probably wouldn't have gotten you into surgery fast enough to save you. Not to mention whether they would have been able to, in any event. You got shot in the heart, dude. That doesn't have a great prognosis usually."

Raj was silent as he contemplated the fact the both he and Natalie had come very close to dying in recent days. Suzanne suspected that death was not something he had ever thought much about before, at least not as it applied to himself.

Raj walked slowly downhill toward the cluster of buildings nestled in the valley below. He breathed deeply, startled at the invigorating clear air. To his left a mountain peak rose above the panorama. He had been told it was Mount Logan, the highest elevation in Canada and only slightly smaller than one in Alaska. It wasn't too much higher than where he presently stood, though, yet the air did not appear to be unusually thin or hard to breathe. He wondered if that was not a natural phenomenon and pushed the uncomfortable thought away.

All of the people he had seen in the hospital, and the few he had seen during his walk so far, seemed perfectly normal. The most unusual sight was a woman whose clothing and hair betrayed her First Nations background, and she was only different looking because her black silver-threaded braid reached almost to her feet and she was dressed in an exotic outfit of beaded leather. With one notable exception, everyone seemed friendly, nodding or saying hello though he was clearly a stranger. There was a small-town feel to the receptive atmosphere, which made sense once he saw the very small group of buildings that apparently comprised the town centre. Houses dotted the slopes above the town, most of them with plenty of property separating them from their neighbours.

The exception was a man who had come to speak to him after Natalie's sister and her husband had left. The interaction had been sharply antagonistic, and he had felt rather like a witness being cross-examined. It had felt a lot like the interview with the College representative a few weeks ago, except that he had actually understood the motivation of the College rep. This man's questions seemed to jump from topic to topic with no unifying theme and had left Raj feeling oddly on edge. On the other hand, the man's attempts to trip him up by asking the same question in different ways had been pathetically obvious. Raj's willingness to be polite had been stretched to the limit, and he had only resisted the urge to tell the man where to go because of the presence of the wheelchair-bound doctor who had evidently saved his life. Even the doctor had given the other man some strange looks at some of the questions, and in fact it was the doctor who had eventually hustled the guy out.

It had been a startling realization that just as the College rep had clearly had strong biases against mages, so this other man seemed to have the same kind of prejudice toward non-mages. Raj had experienced racist attitudes before, but it seemed decidedly odd to be on the receiving end of mage-related prejudice, from a mage. It had left him thinking about his own actions and how much irrational bias he might be guilty of without ever really thinking about it.

He stopped abruptly as he rounded a corner and saw past a thick cluster of trees that had previously obscured his view. Another mountain slope rose to his right, fairly well populated with people skiing and snowboarding. Even from this distance it was clear that most of them wore shorts and T-shirts. The temperature was warm but not humid, and there was a pleasant breeze. It clearly wasn't cold enough for a snow base deep enough for skiing to be maintained on the nearby slope.

Swallowing hard, Raj averted his gaze and started walking toward the town, hoping he would be able to find the coffee shop he had been told about. He would have preferred something stronger, but the doctor had told him to avoid alcohol for a while, and even said to go easy on caffeine, since he had lost a lot of blood.

Prior to leaving the hospital, he had started and then deleted half a dozen text messages to Natalie, before finally deciding to just keep it simple: "I'm sorry, I was a jerk. I'm over myself now. Friends?"

It was just a moment or two before her reply popped up: "You're forgiven. I think I need all the friends I can get right now. Meet you at the coffee shop?"

Reminded of the hurt evident on her face when he had been a jerk to her, he stopped and forced himself to turn and look back at the skiers.

Get a grip, he told himself. *What is really bothering you here? They are evidently controlling the weather, making this high elevation livable, and while they're at it, they've made it so you can go snowboarding in the summer. That looks like a lot of fun.*

He shook his head, mocking his own discomfort. *They're not harming anyone. And they saved my life. I need to get over myself, like I told Natalie I already did.*

As he entered the town square, he saw that it was paved in subtly varicoloured pastel checkerboard paving stones which had a slight shimmer in the bright sunlight. The stores placed around the square all had large open-front windows, with wares displayed on slanted boards. The effect was rather like an old-fashioned market. Seeing a men's clothing store, he altered direction and went toward it. The shirt he had been wearing the day of the shooting had been completely destroyed, so although the hospital had been able to clean his suit pants, he was wearing a plain white T-shirt that he had been given, and he felt a bit self-conscious in the mismatched attire. Uncertain whether these people actually used ordinary money, he loitered near the open-front window and was relieved to see not only a cash transaction using normal Canadian money, but also even someone paying by tapping a debit card on a completely ordinary-looking POS machine.

Once clad in a collared golf shirt that did not look so odd with suit pants, Raj made his way to the coffee shop. He hadn't really needed the proprietor of the clothing store to direct him; the smell of coffee was easily detected in the clear air.

He saw a red-haired man enter the coffee shop ahead of him and recognized him as the man who had been at Natalie's condo on Saturday night. He reminded himself that that was actually the previous Saturday night, almost two weeks ago.

As he entered the coffee shop, inhaling the fragrance of roasted beans with delight, he saw the red-haired man join Natalie at a table where she sat with her sister and brother-in-law. She raised a hand toward Raj in greeting and gave him a half smile, though he saw her expression had been somewhat unfriendly as she said something to the British guy. He seemed to look a bit shamefaced. What was his name again? And what was that about? They had certainly seemed pretty cozy the last time he had seen them together.

A waitress was just placing a large mug of coffee in front of the lone empty seat as Raj approached.

"Hi, Raj. You remember Jon, right? And my sister Suzanne? This is my brother-in-law, Dave."

"Yeah, we met actually, at the hospital," Raj said, nodding at them as he sat down. "Um, how did she know …?" he asked, looking at the coffee in surprise. He liked his coffee with just a tiny amount of cream, barely enough to lighten the black liquid, but with three teaspoons of sugar.

"Ma-a-agic," Natalie said in a spooky voice. "And it's not quite the stuff you're used to; it's actually made with powdered bat wings. Hope you don't mind."

"Purple ones," her sister put in. "You have to use purple bat wings for decent coffee."

"Yeah, yeah, okay," Raj said, knowing he was being teased as he looked behind the counter to see a row of perfectly ordinary coffee machines and a bean grinder. A roaster sitting in the far corner was clearly the source of the aroma that advertised the shop's wares so effectively.

"I saw you coming," Natalie told him. "And I've known how you like your coffee for, what, seven years?"

"I liked the other version better," Suzanne complained.

"You've terrorized the poor guy enough for one day, Wife," Dave told her, digging an elbow into her ribs.

"Oh?" Natalie asked, looking sharply at her sister, who gave her a patently false look of innocence.

"What did she do to you, Raj?"

"Ah, she showed me a whatchamacallit, a memory stone."

Natalie's eyes narrowed. "And what was on this memory stone?"

"You. Looking like you'd been dead for three days," Raj told her with a shudder. "After that, frankly, I don't understand a quarter of what I saw. It was freakishly terrifying, that's all I know. I have some idea why you looked so sick when I first saw you."

Natalie raised an eyebrow and held out a hand wordlessly to her sister.

"I'm not sure if you should—"

"Hand it over, Suzy. It's my medical history after all. I seem to be the only person who *doesn't* know."

With a sigh, Suzanne fished the innocuous-looking off-white stone out of her pocket and dropped it in her sister's hand. Raj swallowed hard at the sight and looked down at his coffee as he saw Natalie pull a blue prism from her own pocket.

"May I?"

Raj glanced up to see Jon, who had not spoken since Raj had entered, hovering his hand over Natalie's.

"I dunno," she said, making a face at him. "Private and personal medical information and all that. Since you're sooo fond of regulations."

Raj had no idea what that interchange was about, but Jon sighed.

"He's my commanding officer. What am I supposed to do? He's already threatening disciplinary action."

"What, for giving me the list?!"

"Yeah."

"You weren't kidding. He's quite the authoritarian, isn't he?"

Raj saw Suzanne and Dave exchange a puzzled look, so at least he wasn't the only one who didn't understand whatever they were talking about.

Natalie loosened her fingers a little, and Jon placed his hand on top of the stone, threading his fingers through hers to clasp it between their joined hands.

Natalie traced a pattern using her blue prism, and their faces went blank for a moment. Raj felt as though he were watching something too intimate, as their faces then simultaneously began to mirror the emotions he remembered all too well. He looked back at his coffee and took a large drink.

"Dear God," Natalie said in a shaken tone moments later.

"Bloody hell," Jon replied.

"Who was the young girl?"

"Oh, that's a bizarre story," Suzanne replied. She explained how she had met Mikyla and also how she had turned out to be the surgeon's daughter.

"She must be a joiner."

Raj had no idea what Jon was talking about, but both women looked sharply at him, Natalie looking surprised.

"That's what Dr. Sabourin said, but I'd never heard of it," Suzanne said.

"What is that, Jon? And is she First Circle? It felt that way to me."

"I would think so." He had an uncomfortable-looking frown on his face, and his eyes flickered briefly toward Raj and away. Raj wondered what that was about, feeling a surge of irritation at how much of the interaction seemed to be going over his head. He was not accustomed to not knowing what was going on around him. "It's got to do with group magic, being really good at merging people together. It's usually super difficult to do group stuff, yeah? But it felt like there were a lot of people in that merge."

Raj swallowed hard, really not wanting to be part of this conversation. He had already learned far more about the mage world than he was comfortable with. Group magic was something he didn't even want to think about.

"It gets easier," Dave told him with a smile.

Raj shifted uncomfortably. "I know I'm being a jerk—"

"Nah, I was terrified when I figured out my partner was a mage."

"You guys were together when you didn't know?"

"Not together as a couple; we work together. We're paramedics, and we've been a team for five years now."

"I can't believe you were scared of me," Suzanne told him. "You could crush me with one hand."

Looking at her petite frame, in comparison to her very solidly built husband, Raj had to agree.

"Oh really? I'm pretty sure you could do something magically if I tried that."

"Well, okay, yeah, I guess."

"How did you, um, get past it?" Raj asked curiously.

"It was one night when we were dealing with a motorcycle accident. The kid was only about eighteen, and from what the witnesses said, he wasn't being an idiot. Someone just cut him off, and he couldn't get out of the way in time."

"That was one of the worst," Suzanne put in, a haunted expression on her face. "He was so young, and I kept thinking of his family. Even the driver who had cut him off was a mess. She had a teenage son herself."

"I think usually Suzy tried to be subtle about her use of magic," Dave said, smiling down at her fondly, "although I'd started to suspect already by then. But she was just desperate to save that kid, and when she couldn't, she totally fell apart. That's when I realized it's just a skill, one I don't happen to have, but it's not all-powerful. And she was only using it to save lives and reduce pain. What's the point of getting worked up about that?"

Raj's attention was diverted as Jon's phone rang and he sighed as he looked at the caller ID.

"LEO Forrester," he answered formally.

Raj was puzzled. He was never great at remembering people's names, but he could have sworn the guy's name was Jon. Wasn't that what Natalie had just said? But nobody else was looking confused.

"All right, is there a team assembled? Yeah … okay … all right, I'll be there as soon as I can." He ended the call and looked at Natalie apologetically.

"Duty calls?" she asked. "Don't worry about it, I'm fine."

"I smell a bit of a rat," Jon said sourly. "Trying to make sure I don't have a chance to disobey that order, maybe?"

Natalie made an irritated noise in her throat and clenched her fists.

"Can you handle portalling?" he asked in a concerned voice.

"I should think so, and Suzanne can give me a hand if I have a problem."

"All right, I'm off." He tilted Natalie's face up with two fingers and kissed her. Then, leaving his half-drunk coffee on the table, he strode away. Moments later, the waitress came to remove his coffee cup. The waitress happened to glance at Raj and suddenly gasped, her face draining of colour.

"What—ah, is that—?"

"Induced coma," Suzanne told her in a completely relaxed tone. "Dr. Sabourin or someone at the hospital did it."

"Oh, that's okay then. Do you know, I thought I saw it two weeks ago as well, but when I looked again, I thought I must have been mistaken. But twice in a month, well, that's something you don't see too often!" She hurried off.

Raj raised a questioning eyebrow at Suzanne.

"Okay, what was that about?" Dave asked, when all his wife did was to exchange troubled glances with Natalie.

Natalie sighed. "Do you remember the doctor mentioned that they use coercive magic for an induced coma instead of drugs?" She directed the question to Raj.

"Yeah," Raj said slowly. "I didn't really know what he meant, though. Just that it was magic instead of drugs."

"There's a few things we're not allowed, by law, to tell non-mages, and I'm pretty sure the existence of coercive magic is one of them. Still, Jon's gone, and the cat's out of the bag anyway. Coercive magic, making someone do something that bypasses their free will, is one of the most highly restricted forms of magic there is. Totally illegal for most of us. Only police officers and doctors are allowed, and even then, there's specific rules."

Raj's eyebrows shot up. "What other kind is restricted?"

"Anything that could be seen as combative or as some kind of attack, unless it's in self-defence," Natalie answered. "Particularly if used against a non-mage."

"Magical interference with sporting or athletic events or competitions of any kind," Suzanne added. "Or any kind of test, examination or election. Or to affect the outcome of any military action."

"Huh." Raj pondered that for a minute, deciding that the mage laws made sense, which made him feel a lot more comfortable. The thought of mages altering elections or even the outcome of the basketball season would have angered him deeply.

"And she could see that this coercion thing had been done to me?"

"Yes. Remember I told you about the Convict's Curse, where the person visibly glows? That one is visible to non-mages, but what you've got is only visible to mages. Problem is, it's yellow, and it's unique to coercive magic. So she was pretty freaked out, thinking something highly illegal might have happened."

"She thought she saw it two weeks ago, too," Suzanne noted with a frown. "It's pretty obvious. How can you be unsure about something like that?"

"Maybe if it was bright sunlight?" Natalie suggested. "It's a bit hard to see outside. Anyway, that reminds me of something. When I suddenly felt really sick in Raj's room and the doctor fixed it, he said he was using something a little bit coercive, which nurses aren't allowed to do. But you did something to Jon that time. Was that coercion?"

"God, no," Suzanne said, horrified. "I like my freedom, thanks. No way would I do coercive magic on a LEO. Or anyone else. He was sick specifically because he had, well, um ..." Suzanne's voice trailed off, sounding uncomfortable, but Natalie finished her sentence for her with a chuckle.

"Been drinking too much. It's okay; you can say it. It was a party, and he was off duty. He's allowed."

"Right, well, all I did was manipulate his liver to speed up the natural process of dealing with those toxins. No coercion involved. The doctor must have been doing something involving persuading your brain not to react to the mixed signals it was getting from the rest of your body. That would be coercive."

"LEO?" Raj repeated.

"It's an acronym. It's short for law enforcement officer," Natalie told him.

"He's a cop?"

"Yeah."

"Like, a cop in the magical law enforcement agency, or a mage who happens to be an ordinary cop?"

"The first one."

"You know about that?" Suzanne asked, in surprise. "Aren't we not supposed to talk about that either?"

Natalie sighed. "I've had it up to here with the secrecy. Raj deserves to know the truth, and considering that it could have some impact on our College thing, he *needs* to know the truth."

"How does it impact the College investigation?" Raj asked with narrowed eyes.

"Some of those missing fugitives really are mages who are criminals, but they're not going missing; they're getting arrested by LEO. And once you're in jail here, you're not getting out anytime soon. Like I said before, our system is quite a bit harsher than the ordinary one."

"How many of the escapees would that be?"

Natalie shrugged. "Not all of them. Remember the statistic in the first article about more than half of them being re-apprehended? Those would not be magical criminals. I don't really know how many of the others are."

Before he could respond, Raj's phone beeped a split second after Natalie's did. The sound effect indicated a work e-mail, so he pulled his phone out of his pocket to check it.

Natalie started swearing as soon as she read the e-mail on her own phone.

Suzanne glanced between her sister and Raj, and since Natalie was still muttering curses, she raised her eyebrows questioningly at him instead.

"It seems the College served a Request to Admit on the firm, and they accepted service on behalf of everyone," Raj said, biting out the words angrily. "Due date to respond was today, and since Natalie and I did not respond, we are deemed to have admitted whatever was in this thing. Do you have any idea what it is we're supposed to have admitted?"

"No," Natalie snarled. "And what's more, I talked to Phillip two days ago and he never mentioned this. What do you want to bet the firm is hanging us out to dry as scapegoats in order to save their own necks?"

"Duck and cover," Suzanne said, her tone more satisfied than cautionary. "Natalie's back on the warpath. About time."

Chapter 16

Almost all of the partners of Mason Sullivan were in the biggest boardroom, sitting around the very long, highly polished boardroom table. Several of the partners were staring out of the plate glass windows, their tense body language betraying their level of discomfort.

"Excuse me?!" Natalie's voice was icy as she glared at Boris Tarmenek.

"You know that when a Request to Admit is ignored, it's a deemed admission," Boris replied, though his tone suggested he was not convinced himself of what he was saying.

Susan Wildman, sitting to Boris's right, gave him a disgusted look.

"We did not ignore it," Raj snapped. "You failed to inform us that you had accepted service on our behalf, and you failed to inform the College that you had not been able to bring it to our attention."

"You disappeared," Phillip Mastersen said coldly.

"I got *shot*," Raj fired back. "In the heart. So sorry I wasn't able to pick a more convenient time that worked for you."

"You look remarkably healthy for someone who got shot in the heart," another partner said snidely.

"Turns out mages can be extremely useful members of society, if only we'd let them," Raj replied. "I've had my eyes opened a lot in the last couple of days."

"And are you also claiming to have been shot?" the managing partner asked Natalie.

"No, but I did almost die as well. I told you that when we spoke on Monday," she said coldly. "And you had every opportunity during that conversation to tell me about this Request to Admit, which you failed to do. Nor did you ask for an extension on our behalf once you were aware of our situation."

"I hardly see the point," Phillip replied scornfully. "It is a Request to Admit that you're a mage. You are a mage. What difference does it make that you have been deemed to admit it?"

"I am a mage," Natalie agreed. "But Raj is not, yet he has apparently been deemed to admit that he is one, too. In fact, you knew where we were before that call. The hospital called the firm to get contact information for Raj's family. Regardless, you had an ethical obligation to let me know about this."

"You had an ethical obligation to disclose to this firm that you are a mage, especially once these allegations started causing us issues," Phillip snapped back.

"That's a load of crap," Raj replied rudely. "If someone made wild accusations against Jewish people and implicated this firm on completely circumstantial evidence, that doesn't cause us any ethical obligation to disclose who's Jewish. Natalie is just as entitled to her personal privacy as the rest of us. The question is whether she assisted any mages to escape from jail or helped any to avoid being arrested, or whether she has done anything else that specifically contravenes the Rules of Professional Ethics. She hasn't."

"And we're just to take her word for that?" Phillip said. "She can't prove that she had nothing to do with any of these disappearances."

Natalie directed a withering look at him. "That's true, Phillip. I probably can't prove that. But you might have heard of the concept of innocent until proven guilty. The onus is not on me to prove I'm innocent; it's on them to prove I'm guilty. Like it or not, the fact that I'm a mage does not make me a criminal."

"I can prove that you had information relevant to these allegations that you failed to share with this firm," Phillip announced in a ringing voice.

"Do tell," Natalie said drily. "Clearly you've been trying to work out how to make this announcement in the most dramatic way possible."

An almost inaudible chuckle came from one corner of the room, and Phillip's shoulders stiffened in reaction, but he did not turn around to see who had laughed. Natalie thought it sounded like a woman.

"After what happened last week, the College of Legalists stepped up its investigation. Both of your laptops were subjected to a forensic examination at their request," the managing partner stated. "There was nothing untoward discovered about Raj's computer, except perhaps a little too much surfing on the TSN Web site during business hours." He directed a fierce frown at Raj, who made a disgusted noise in the back of his throat.

"I put in over 2,400 billable hours in the last year, Phillip," he retorted. "I am not going to apologize for doing a little personal Web surfing now and then."

"Twenty-four hundred? And you call me a workaholic," Natalie commented.

"On your computer, however, there is a spreadsheet created the day after the Notice of Investigation was received by this firm," the managing partner went on, now directing his glare at Natalie, and ignoring Raj's comments. "Over the course of the next three days, you did a series of Google searches relating to prison escapes. Several times during that same period, our network records show, you logged in remotely to the accounting database and searched the same names which are listed on the spreadsheet. How did you have those names? And why did you not inform us of your findings?"

"I told James about it the following Monday," Natalie said. "I guess he didn't mention it to you before he landed in the hospital himself. And if you had taken a look at the text of those Google searches, the answer would be perfectly obvious. I was attempting to figure out the names of all escapees in the Toronto area within the last year and then see if there was any relation between any of them and the firm. I would suggest that's a fairly obvious approach to figuring out how to defend the firm against the allegations."

"How did you know the text of the Google searches would be there?" the managing partner asked with narrowed eyes.

"I've used computer forensics many times in my practice. I've certainly seen several Internet history reports."

"Natalie gave me a printout of that spreadsheet," Raj added. "I think it was last Saturday. No, the Saturday before last. It included about over 150 names, if I recall correctly, and only 15 people are mentioned in the Notice of Investigation. Goes to show, if you're actually being objective about this, how ridiculous the allegations are. The firm has a purely circumstantial connection to a fraction of the Toronto-area escapes."

"Just out of curiosity, Phillip, what have you done to try to clear the firm's name?" Natalie asked. "Besides looking for a scapegoat?"

"You have a smart response for everything, don't you?" Phillip was practically grinding his teeth as he spat the words at her.

"I'm certainly trying," Natalie agreed, her fists clenched at her sides. "I have the most personal incentive for clearing this firm of these allegations. Now if you would be willing to put as much effort into achieving that as I am, instead of doing your level best to try to blame me for something I didn't do, maybe there would be hope for this firm."

"Fidelity Insurance is taking steps to remove all of their active files from the firm," Phillip said. "They are one of our biggest clients. The best thing you can do for this firm is to resign."

Before Natalie could respond, there was a knock on the boardroom door, which was then opened by one of the firm's receptionists. She did not meet anyone's eyes as she stepped into the room, followed by two very burly police officers.

"Which one is Natalie Benson? I assume you're Rajit Naresh?" The police officer was looking at Raj after glancing at a piece of paper in his hand.

Raj raised an eyebrow. "I am," he confirmed.

"I'm Natalie," she identified herself.

"You are both under arrest, on charges of assault and battery causing grievous bodily harm," one of the police officers stated, while they both moved to seize the two of them.

"What?!" Both of them spoke simultaneously.

The first officer grabbed Raj's arm, spun him around and put handcuffs on both wrists, but the second met with an invisible barrier as he attempted to do the same to Natalie.

"You are now resisting arrest, Ms. Benson," he stated.

"I'm entitled to defend myself," she told him in a clipped voice. "Last time I was in Toronto, I was attacked by two vigilantes who kicked and punched at both of us," she said, indicating Raj with a wave of her hand. "Raj got shot in the chest. I already phoned the police and reported it. Who, exactly, are we supposed to have assaulted? And what grievous bodily harm did either of us inflict?"

"The details can be discussed at the police station," the police officer replied. "Are you going to come voluntarily, or do I add a charge of resisting arrest?"

"I will come, but I'm not being marched out of here like a criminal," she told him frostily. She picked up her purse and stalked out the boardroom, her back rigid with anger.

Nobody else said a word as the two of them left, but Natalie heard a babble of raised voices behind her as she strode toward the elevators, not looking at any of the people sitting in the reception area.

Natalie handed over her purse without protest when they reached the police station, but she still did not release her shield, making it impossible to put handcuffs on her or touch her directly. The shield extended out about three inches from her body. Although the police officer was attempting to hold onto her arm as he led her into the station, in fact his hand was wrapped around an empty space in the vicinity of her arm.

Natalie waited while an officer went through the contents of her purse and noted down personal information from her ID, asking her to confirm that the information was current and accurate. She was also asked to remove her watch and a necklace, which she handed over, along with her iPhone.

Raj arrived while this was taking place and was also asked to hand over his wallet and cellphone. Both of them then had mug shots taken. Since Natalie was angry enough to be petty, she made the sign bearing her identification details float in front of her instead of holding it, to the obvious discomfort of the police photographer.

She and Raj were taken to separate interrogation rooms. She noticed that one police officer entered the room with Raj, whereas three came into the room with her, two of them particularly large men, while the third was a female officer, who also looked very athletic. At least that suggested that they might have believed her when she told them that Raj was not a mage. They had driven them both here in two separate police cars, however.

"All right, we're here," she said, as she took a seat on the far side of the small metal table that was bolted to the floor in the middle of the room, in response to the police officer's gesture. "So, who am I supposed to have assaulted, and when?"

"We will be asking the questions," said the same burly officer who had attempted to put handcuffs on her in the boardroom of her law firm. His name tag read "J. Thompson."

Natalie raised one eyebrow. "Yeah, sorry to disappoint you, but I am a lawyer and I do know my rights," she said. "I have the right to know the nature of the charges being pressed against me in all particulars, and in fact *you* should have told *me* that. Of course, you were also supposed to tell me that I have the right to retain a lawyer. Even though I am one, I'm actually not a criminal lawyer, and even if I was, I would *still* have the right to hire one and to speak to him or her before being interrogated. I'm willing to co-operate with you up to a point, but it is not acceptable for you to stomp all over my legal rights just because I'm a mage." She took a deep breath, trying to keep control of her temper, and closed her eyes for a moment. "I am prepared to waive the right to hire a lawyer, at least for now. But I do require that you tell me about this alleged assault."

Natalie noticed that the female officer nodded very slightly to the one who had spoken, her eyes narrowed.

"We are informed that the assault took place on the afternoon of Wednesday, June 6, at approximately 12:30 p.m., in Nathan Phillips Square. It was in a walkway beside one of the entrances to the City Hall underground parking lot," Constable Thompson said, his jaw tense. It seemed likely that he was not happy to have been corrected by her or by his fellow officer. "The victim identifies himself as Michael Stanton."

Natalie's nostrils flared in annoyance at hearing her attacker characterized as the victim, but she did not speak.

"He alleges that he was walking past you in the opposite direction, that he stumbled into you unintentionally, and that even before he could apologize, you or Mr. Naresh had used magic to throw him to the ground, where he struck his head hard, and where he was then magically immobilized, unable to speak or move." Constable Thompson consulted a printed sheet in front of him before he continued. "He states that a large black cloud appeared and that there was a glowing light within the cloud. When that dissipated, the two of you were gone. Several witnesses have corroborated the story."

"I see," Natalie said gravely. "Well, the best way to lie is, in fact, to mix it with the truth. I did knock two men off their feet, after I had been knocked off my own by a large rock that had struck my shoulder. I was punched and kicked. Raj was punched at least once, and he did hit back. I did immobilize them with magic, but that was at the very end. I knocked them off their feet after I'd had a rib cracked by being kicked. I immobilized them after knocking them down, when Stanton was getting up clearly intending to do more damage. And yes, I did cause a large black cloud to appear, and I did initiate a transportation spell to remove myself and Mr. Naresh from the scene, which would have caused the glowing light that he refers to. I admit that I am a mage, and as I already told you, Raj is not. But I never prevented anyone from speaking, and in fact their verbal abuse toward me continued while they were immobilized. I take it my attacker did not mention that there was another man with him? My colleague and I were attacked by two men, not one."

"Only one man has pressed charges against you," Constable Thompson responded tersely, although Natalie noticed that he did not actually confirm or deny that there were two involved. Her eyes narrowed at the obvious omission.

"I'm guessing the one with the gun didn't press charges," she said drily.

"There is no mention of any gun in any of the witness statements, including that of your accuser." It was the female police officer who spoke, and Natalie's attention switched to her. Her name tag identified her as C. Caruso. None of the three police officers had shown even the slightest surprise at the mention of a gun, which Natalie thought was interesting. No matter their training, if the idea that a gun had been involved was completely unknown information, it was unlikely that none of them would react in any way. So evidently there was no "official" evidence of a gun.

Natalie snorted her disbelief. "Personally, I never heard a gun fired before, outside of a movie or on TV," she noted. "I had no idea how loud they were. Not the kind of thing you can fail to notice or forget to include in a statement, I would have thought. Particularly if you saw my colleague with a large scarlet stain spreading across his chest."

"You allege that your colleague was shot in the chest? One week ago?" Natalie's primary questioner's tone was clearly disbelieving. She flicked her gaze back to him.

"That is the only reason I performed obvious magic in front of a hostile crowd," she confirmed. "I had to save his life. I knew perfectly well that getting outed as a mage was going to cause me a large number of problems, but letting him die was not an option. Particularly not when we were attacked only because those two jerks thought we were both mages."

"You continue to allege that you were the victim, not the assailant," Constable Caruso noted in a neutral tone of voice.

"We absolutely were the victims," Natalie confirmed. She kept her gaze on the officer facing her across the table, rather than on Constable Caruso at the back of the room, though her eyes flicked briefly to the woman as she spoke. It seemed likely the two were playing the well-known "good cop, bad cop" roles, which Natalie hoped she would not be influenced by.

Instead, she looked Constable Thompson directly in the eyes and tried, for the most part, to speak in the same kind of calm, measured tone she would customarily use while appearing in court on behalf of one of her clients. She was aware that some of her anger was evident, however.

Natalie launched into a detailed description of the events of the attack, including physical descriptions of their attackers. She saw expressions of skepticism when she described injuries that were now nowhere in evidence, but continued her story without acknowledging that. The officer who had not yet spoken was taking notes, although there was also a recording device with a microphone between Natalie and Constable Thompson. She described the initial stages of the fight succinctly, confirming that Raj had thrown several punches, although only after he had been punched himself at least once.

"After shoving the second guy, I think Stanton called him Dan or Don, out of the way, Raj came to my defence. Raj rushed Stanton and knocked him down. It's possible Stanton might have hit his head on the wall, I don't know. That's when Dan pulled a gun.

"They weren't immobilized at that point, and they certainly weren't prevented from speaking, at any time. I made a kind of strong wind that I aimed at Dan. I was intending to knock the gun out of his hand, but actually I knocked him off his feet. He tripped over Stanton, who started to come at me again. That's when I immobilized both of them. Dan fired off a shot before it took. He was aiming at me, but my spell unintentionally deflected his aim. The bullet hit Raj in the chest. They were definitely both sitting at that point, so if anyone struck his head, it was before I immobilized them. Then I made the smoke, activated the transportation spell and took the two of us to a hospital with mages on staff so that Raj had the best possible chance of being saved."

"You were both gone for a week. Where were you?"

"In an isolated magical community which you won't find on any map," she told him. "We were both in hospital." She described what Dr. Sabourin had told her of Raj's injuries in some detail. "We returned to Toronto late this afternoon, and we have been at the offices of Mason Sullivan since we got back. I phoned the police about pressing charges against our attackers on Tuesday, after I regained consciousness. And speaking of the assault charge, even if the other guy's story was accurate, does striking one's head and being immobilized really count as grievous bodily harm? I would have thought that charge would be reserved for serious injury, something of a life-threatening nature, no?"

"That will be up to a judge to decide," the officer answered tersely. "Your version of events is extremely different from all the other evidence."

"I noticed," Natalie said. "May I have some water, please?" All three police officers had plastic bottles of water, but none had been offered to her. There was a very bright light which seemed to be aimed mostly at her seat, but it had small metal vanes inside it, hidden underneath the Plexiglas covering, and she had altered their angle slightly so that the light would not bother her eyes. Her seat was a flat metal sheet, whereas she noticed the one on the other side was the more normal moulded plastic. As it began to get uncomfortable, however, she just altered the nature of her personal barrier slightly to provide a cushioning effect. She felt sorry for Raj, who would not have the ability to alter any of the subtle discomforts of an interrogation room. There was a noticeable hesitation, but then the second male officer left the room and shortly returned with a plastic water bottle, from which he had already removed the cap.

"Thanks." Natalie lifted it to her lips and immediately found that it was very warm. She sighed, held it away from her and rolled her eyes. "Really?" she said sarcastically, and then lifted her other hand over the bottle. Almost in unison, all three officers pulled their firearms and aimed them at her. She raised an imperious eyebrow and continued with her gesture over the bottle, showing no sign of alarm. In fact, she was not entirely certain whether her passive barrier could stop a bullet, but then she hoped it was unlikely that they would actually shoot. Though her heart rate had immediately sped up, she strove to keep her face or body from expressing any nervousness. The effect of her gesture was immediately apparent, as condensation instantly formed on the outside of the bottle. She was almost certain she heard the sound of grinding teeth from Constable Thompson as she tipped back her head and drank almost half of the now cold water in one go. She also tried to keep her hand from shaking, but in fact she was getting very tired from the various magics she had been doing, including the barrier that she had, as she had told the officer, been holding over herself since they had arrived back in Toronto. It did not help that her prism, in its customary disguise as a silver pen, remained in her purse and out of her reach.

The firearms were slowly lowered, but only the officer questioning her actually put his back in its holster.

"You are going to be taken to a holding cell," he said abruptly, a slight tremor in his voice betraying the fact that she was not the only nervous person in the room. "There will be a bail hearing in the morning."

Natalie's jaw tightened angrily, but she did not respond. She merely stood up and nodded. She was fairly certain that people charged with assault generally did not get held overnight, particularly where there was no particular danger of ongoing violence, even if there had been any validity to the charges against her. But it was equally obvious that she was not going to be treated as a normal prisoner.

Constable Thompson once again tried to grasp her arm, and she felt the barrier constrict a little as he evidently attempted to force his fingers closer to her arm. She did not visibly react in any way but merely moved forward when he began to pull her in that direction. As they passed the door to the interrogation room she had seen Raj being led into, she saw that it was closed. There was no one-way window as she had sometimes seen on TV, so she could not tell whether he was still inside, but it seemed likely. She did not speak as she was led into an elevator and then taken into an area which contained about ten barred cells, two of them occupied by women. Both of those women directed dirty looks at the officers, particularly the men, and Natalie wondered if male officers were allowed in an area containing holding cells for women or whether they would have given dirty looks to any police officer. She still did not say anything, however, and did not resist as one officer unlocked a cell as far away from the occupied ones as possible and Constable Thompson pushed her inside. The cell contained a single bed with a thin mattress and a grey blanket. The bed was fixed to the wall. A stainless steel toilet and a stainless steel sink were the only other items in the cell, and she noticed that there was no soap, although a small roll of toilet paper was sitting on the floor beside the toilet. With a sigh, she lay down on the bed, kicked off her shoes and put her hands under her head, finally releasing her barrier with a sigh of relief.

After she heard the sound of the officers leaving and the echoing slam of a heavy metal door, one of the other women spoke.

"Well, you don't look like the usual type," she commented drily. "What're you in for?"

"Holy shit, that's the mage!" the other one answered for her. "I seen her picture in the paper. She's that one that froze those two guys and disappeared."

Natalie sat up. "The fact that there were two of them was in the paper? Those officers wouldn't acknowledge that there were two."

Neither woman responded, and she saw that both of them had moved to sit on the far ends of their respective beds and were watching her warily. She sighed.

"I'm not about to hurt either of you," she told them. "You've got nothing to fear from me." As she spoke, she noticed that in addition to a circular camera that was affixed to the ceiling, there were two more cameras, both with glowing red lights, standing on tripods and aimed at her cell. She rolled her eyes at the sight. "Overkill much?" she muttered.

Since neither of the women had responded, she shrugged, drank the rest of her water and then lay back down, closing her eyes.

Sometime later, she realized that she needed to use a bathroom, and she opened her eyes to look with disgust at the stainless steel toilet, which had a moulded seat as part of the main structure instead of a hinged separate piece. Then she glanced at the cameras, which still had red lights glowing on top of each. Standing up, she directed a mocking look at the cameras and then raised both hands, drawing a pattern in the air with ostentatious gestures. A glowing, mostly opaque wall appeared in front of the toilet, and just in case there was a hidden camera as well as the obvious ones, another wall appeared on the other side, enclosing her in a smaller, private space. They would be able to see her moving shape, and it would be apparent what she was doing, but it would be only as a vague shadowy image.

It took about 30 seconds before she heard the big metal door being unlocked. Thoughtfully, she altered the lock on her own cell slightly so that it would not be possible to unlock it.

"Come out of there with your hands up!" a female voice demanded.

Natalie snorted. "I'm busy right now," she replied. She flushed the toilet and adjusted her clothing before letting the walls melt away and dissipate as mist. She barely glanced at the officer as she washed her hands, rinsing off obviously visible though inexplicable soap bubbles, and went back to her bed and lay down. "I am prepared to co-operate with you, up to a point, on these ludicrous charges. But that point does not extend to indignities. I am not going to pee while who knows how many people are watching me on a security monitor. Your fast response makes it obvious you've got people staring at those screens. You should go catch some real criminals and stop wasting taxpayers' money."

She heard a muffled laugh coming from one of the other cells. She closed her eyes and counted to 60 before she heard the sound of the metal door being closed and locked again, but she was still too angry to smile at her small victory.

Chapter 17

Natalie came awake suddenly, to find that the lights had been switched off, plunging the area with the holding cells into darkness, except for two glowing circles of what looked like red LED lights where she knew the cameras were. She ground her teeth in irritation at the evidence of night vision technology, wondering what had awakened her.

The next moment, she heard a mental voice whisper her name.

Jon? she responded the same way, almost certain that the voice had been his.

Yeah, I'm under your bed, he replied. *Don't look. You won't see anything but smoke anyway.*

You know there's at least two night vision cameras on me, don't you? she pointed out. *As well as the ordinary one on the ceiling?*

I noticed, he said, his mental voice betraying his disgust. *Don't worry about that. I've had a lot of practice at this. They won't have seen a thing. Ready to get out of here?*

They'll see that, she pointed out, a smirk crossing her face as she remembered the fast response when she had built an opaque barrier around the toilet. *Thanks, but no. I could have resisted being arrested in the first place if I wanted to, but that wouldn't have done me any favours, and it won't do me or Raj any good if I disappear now.*

You're willing to stay here?!

It's only one night. It won't kill me. Strikes me that as long as I can prove Raj and I really were injured, we've got a perfectly good case. Surely we can get records from Neekonnisiwin. Let's see what happens at the bail hearing. How did you find out?

I tried calling you, and it just kept going straight to voice mail. So then I got hold of your sister, and she called your office.

I'm surprised they told her the truth.

They wouldn't at first. Then she started freaking out about you being missing, saying that you'd only just gotten out of hospital after a head injury. She was very persuasive.

Natalie smothered a grin, unsure how much detail the night vision cameras could pick up. *She always was good at melodrama when she wanted to be,* she said. *It didn't occur to me, but they didn't offer me my one phone call. I'm pretty sure you're supposed to get one. Are you sure there's no salt in here? I don't want you losing any more fingers because of me.*

Oh, trust me, I scan every surface for salt now before I go anywhere. I alter my vision and sense of smell to be particularly sensitive to it. I figured out that trick after I lost my fingers.

How do you do that when you have no eyes or nose?

He chuckled. *Don't ask me to explain that, because I can't. You sure you want to stay put then?*

Yes, but thanks. I really appreciate you coming. Hey, I just remembered you got called away somewhere this afternoon. Was that just Seth trying to keep us apart?

No, it was legit. Well, he might have been, but the situation was valid. It was in Brazil.

You went from Yukon Territory, to Brazil, and back to Ontario today?

It doesn't take that long through the portals since I've got special security privileges, Jon pointed out. *No delay for me at border crossings. I was in Brazil in under an hour.*

And it's what time now?

About 3:30.

You rarely get enough sleep, do you?

I'm used to it.

I'm sorry about telling Seth about the list, Natalie said with a sigh. *I couldn't think of any other way I could have answered that question. Are you really in trouble?*

I think he might let it slide with the warning, but only because he thinks it was nothing more than a list of names. Please do me a favour and don't let him know how much information I actually gave you? I suspect I'd get suspended for sure if he knew that. And probably bumped down a rank.

He's being totally unreasonable, Natalie said angrily.

I don't disagree with you, but I'm between a rock and a hard place.

Yeah. Do you think you could find out if Raj is being held too? I assume there must be another holding area for men.

All right, I'll give it a go.

Natalie opened her eyes and watched the floor in front of the cell. She thought perhaps she saw a slight ripple but could not even be sure if she had seen it. Shrugging, she lay back. Then she noticed movement near an air vent on the ceiling, where the night vision LED lights reflected slightly off the metallic grill. She smiled slightly as she saw a swirl of smoke disappear into the vent.

Thinking about Jon was a pleasant change from the near constant irritation, or even outright anger, that had been plaguing her lately, and she pictured what it must look like as his body dissolved into smoke. It was more enjoyable to picture the opposite, as she envisioned his body emerging from smoke instead. Good thing he couldn't actually read her mind when she wasn't thinking actual words and intending to communicate them.

She kept her eyes on the vent, and it was no longer than about five minutes before the smoke reappeared. She couldn't see much of it, but she got the impression he was slightly further away when she heard his voice in her head again. Perhaps he was just staying in the vicinity of the vent to avoid having to sneak around the cameras again. While he was not moving, she couldn't see anything anyway, so she looked away. There was no point triggering any kind of alarm with those who were probably still watching the cameras' footage on security monitors.

Yeah, he's there. He's asleep. I didn't wake him. No night vision cameras on him, just the ordinary ceiling one.

Well, that's a good thing. I'm fairly sure they believe that he's not a mage. They know for sure you're one, then?

Oh yes, everyone does now, she told him glumly. *It's been all over the news, apparently—my name and even my photo. One of those women over there recognized me. I am completely, 100 percent out of the closet.*

Did they ask about your gate?

Not in any detail. They were more focused on allegations that I was the aggressor.

You were what? How was that supposed to work?

They're charging me with assault, she said in a disgusted tone. *Or both me and Raj. Supposedly the guy just stumbled into me, it was an insignificant accident, and I immediately overreacted like a crazy woman, knocked him down, immobilized him, prevented him from speaking and then disappeared.*

And witness statements don't contradict any of this?

Apparently not. Even though I could swear I heard someone say, "Oh my God, he's got a gun." And I know someone called an ambulance. Seems they've misplaced those witness statements.

I did a bit of snooping before I came down here, Jon told her. *I heard them discussing the fact that you claimed there was a gunshot and they were saying they hadn't been told about that. I was wondering if they might admit among themselves that that wasn't true, but they didn't.*

Natalie thought about the attack again, remembering her feeling of shocked panic at the sight of the blood soaking through Raj's shirt. She frowned as another thought occurred to her.

I don't know much about guns, but I thought there was something about a part of the bullet that falls to the ground, and they can sometimes use that to identify which gun it was fired from? Or something like that?

Yes, the shell casing. But it's possible that someone picked it up or kicked it down the drain. Or, to be fair, the gun might have been a revolver.

What difference would it make what kind of gun it was?

Revolvers hold the casings inside the cylinder; they're the only kind of gun that doesn't drop the casing.

Natalie sighed. *Great. I did tell them we were in a hospital in a magical community, but I didn't actually specify where. I really want to stop lying about everything, though. Even lying by omission.*

I'm not fond of the lies myself, but there's not a lot of options, Jon said with a sigh.

I'm not so sure that's as true as I always used to think, Natalie replied. She stared at a barely visible crack on the ceiling above her head as she voiced her growing issues with the secrecy that dominated mage interactions with non-mages. *I mean, I agree about keeping First Circle stuff quiet. But I have begun to realize that a lot of the other stuff we keep secret is stupid and is causing mages everywhere a lot of problems.*

How so?

Natalie rolled over onto her stomach and propped her chin in her hands.

The general public believes that we're all criminals and we are always getting away with our crimes. Also, most of the fear comes from a belief that we can actually do way more than we really can. Dave said the reason he got over his fear of Suzanne was that she was trying to save a life and actually couldn't, and she fell apart over it. Realizing she wasn't all-powerful was the key.

All the more reason not to let them know about First Circles.

Yeah, I agree on that part.

There is no way we can tell the nons about our law enforcement system either, Jon said firmly.

I already did, she said flatly. *I told Raj and Dave about it.*

What?! Natalie, I'm pretty sure you've just broken several laws.

Natalie tried not to grind her teeth, but her jaw was tense as she replied, trying to keep her mental tone from sounding snappish.

The woman at the coffee shop in Neekonnisiwin saw the coercion taint on Raj and freaked out a little bit. As she should. I hope that anyone who saw that would report it. So then obviously we had to explain to them both what she was talking about.

Neither spoke for a few moments as he thought that through. *You still didn't need to tell them about LEO,* he pointed out. *Raj's coercion taint was a magically induced coma, wasn't it? You could have just told them about the medical application.*

I suppose, but anyway, too late. So tell me why, in your opinion, it's so terribly important that we keep it a secret that we have our own law enforcement system and that they can't know we have anticoercion laws.

She remembered, with a feeling of dismay, that it was also illegal to discuss with non-mages the types of magic that were forbidden or restricted, but in fact she had told both Raj and Dave about coercion and about the prohibition against offensive magic. It would probably not be a great idea to tell Jon that she had done that, too.

I've been in a lot of jails. All around the world. This one is palatial luxury compared to plenty that I've seen, Jon began slowly.

Yeah, what's your point?

In many parts of the world, just being a mage is a crime. They don't even bother coming up with a trumped-up charge. If magical law enforcement became public knowledge in this part of the world, the knowledge wouldn't stay here. Soon every country would be aware of it. And once that was the case, those mages would get executed instantly, to avoid magical law enforcement taking over. We wouldn't be able to hear about it and get there fast enough to prevent it. We're short-staffed as it is.

Maybe mages should move out of those countries, Natalie suggested.

That's their choice. We don't have the right to tell people where they can live.

Then it's also their choice to take that risk. It's a situation that's causing lots of problems in many countries of the world. I don't accept that we should allow those problems to continue because some countries would react badly. Those countries already react badly.

And what about those young mages who are born to non-magical families? It's hard enough finding out that you're a mage in that situation without also learning that you'd be better off leaving the country and everything that's ever been familiar. There was a hint of raw pain in his mental voice. *There needs to be a good population of mages around, particularly in the industries that are likely to come across those young mages, to help them. If it wasn't for a certain football coach, my life might have turned out very differently.*

Suzanne had once told Natalie that substance abuse among young mages was one of the things that had made her decide to become a paramedic. Natalie realized with a jolt that the football coach Jon mentioned might have been someone who had deliberately chosen that career for a similar reason.

I don't want to fight with you, Natalie said with a sigh. *Seems like I'm fighting with everybody these days. Constance, the Council, Seth, Raj, Phillip. It's just, something has to give.*

Where's this bail hearing, then?

She told him where the City Hall court was located. *I don't know what time, but I'm guessing probably around ten o'clock,* she told him.

What happens if they don't permit you to post bail?

Then we'll revisit the option of you getting me out of here, Natalie replied grimly. *I am not sitting around in jail for this nonsense. Besides, I can't. I have that hearing of my Complaint against Constance next Thursday.*

I'll be there, he promised. *You might not see me, but I'll be there in one form or another.*

Thanks, Jon.

No worries. See you tomorrow.

Then his presence was gone from her mind.

Entirely awake now, Natalie contemplated the four hearings she now had to face: a bail hearing in the morning; her charges against Constance; the College hearing at some point; and eventually there would be a criminal trial where she would be the accused. And all of this was just distracting her from the far more significant issue of trying to figure out if there was, in fact, a pattern between the various deaths she had discovered and a controlling mind behind them all. What if more people died while she was tied up with stupid, pointless allegations, circumstantial evidence and falsified witness accounts?

Some vague memory swirled at the back of her mind, something someone had said recently, perhaps even today. She had a vague idea it was significant, that it might actually provide a much clearer direction to investigate. But try as she might, she could not bring the elusive thought to the forefront of her mind.

She rolled over again, trying to find a comfortable spot on the thin mattress. The best thing she could do right at this moment was simply to try to get some sleep.

Chapter 18

Natalie put the last pin into her hair, securing it into a deliberately unflattering tight updo, then shrugged into the jacket of a sober black suit. She picked up her oversized purse, put her tablet into it and went downstairs to wait for Suzanne in the lobby.

When her sister's car pulled up, it was a plump, red-haired woman who hurried out of the building and climbed into the passenger seat.

"It's me," Natalie said to Suzanne.

"Um, why the disguise?"

"Hey, if I can get shot at just because I work at a law firm suspected of having a mage involved in prison breaks, how much more likely am I to get attacked now that people know my name and what I look like? I'd kind of like to stay safe in my own home." As the car merged with traffic, the illusion melted away to show her true appearance.

"So even as you, you look kind of tired. Are you all right?"

Natalie grinned. "I'm engaging in a bit of theatrics," she admitted. "I know stark black and white doesn't do me any favours, and I am quite deliberately not wearing any makeup. I want to look like the overstressed assault victim."

Suzanne chuckled. "Will Jon be there?"

"I doubt it. Remember he got called away yet again before the bail hearing started? I saw him on Monday night, but I had to gate him to me and then send him back. I had him to myself for all of an hour. Something about a war between some drug lords in Colombia."

"Yikes."

They didn't speak again until they were on the highway heading out to the Scarborough commercial building that housed Toronto's portal.

"So how did they react when you went back into work?" Suzanne asked. "You haven't said a word about it."

"Well, I resigned."

"You *what*?!" Suzanne's voice disappeared in a squeak, and she swerved partway into the next lane before course correcting. Natalie yelped and looked over her shoulder. Fortunately, there was nobody in that lane.

"Hey, I've already been in hospital once this week—well, okay, last week. Could we *not* get into a car accident please?"

"Don't throw me a curveball like that when I'm driving!" Suzanne retorted. "What the hell?"

Natalie sighed. "More like a leave of absence, actually. The College temporarily suspended me. I heard about that the Monday after the bail hearing. But I negotiated a deal with the firm, and I got it in writing. I promised to assist with the College hearing, which technically is against the whole firm, not just me. If the College dismisses the Application, I get a proper severance package. If they don't, I resign. I don't think I had a choice, really. The managing partner was right, in spite of the fact that he was a total jerk to say it: the best thing I could do for the firm was to resign."

"That's completely unfair," Suzanne protested. "It's wrong. That investigation is not just about you, and it's not only your responsibility to fix it."

"Life isn't fair." Natalie sighed. "But what would be wrong would be for me to let a couple of hundred people suffer because I wanted to stick to my stubborn guns. By resigning and making that resignation open and public, I'm hoping the firm's biggest client will change their minds. The firm can stay in business; nobody else's legal career has to end. There's no question that, since it became publicly known that I'm a mage, and since

---

the College is stupidly thinking that Raj is one too, they're only focusing on the two of us."

"I can't believe you're just giving in to a bunch of bigots!"

"I'm not giving in. The College investigation is still absolutely lacking in evidence, and I still intend to make them accept that and kill the investigation. I'm not suggesting that I'm going to meekly take the blame for something I never did. I will certainly fight tooth and nail if they try to disbar me."

"But what will you do?"

"Probably work for LEO, at least for a while, until I figure out if I've got some other options."

"LEO?"

"They've wanted me to work for them for years. I just hope I can do more than constantly transport people around, though. Boring!"

She thought again of Seth's intransigent position on not discussing the investigation with her and then of the e-mail she had received from him on Friday. Without actually apologizing, it had been somewhat conciliatory in tone and had included a formal offer of employment with a generous compensation package. He had pointed out that while he had made it clear for years that he would love to hire her, he had never actually given her a formal offer, so he was rectifying that now. Natalie was still of two minds, however, on whether she could work in an environment that was so militaristic. Red tape had always made her want to bite someone.

"Why don't you take a vacation for a while first?" Suzanne suggested. "I don't think you've had an actual vacation in years. Even when we rented that cottage last summer, you spent the whole time cuddled up to your precious laptop, bemoaning the slow Internet connection."

Natalie laughed. "Yeah, maybe I will." She was surprised at how little concern she now had for the work priorities that had dominated her life for years. Doubtless the fact that so many fellow employees and clients had turned hostile toward her had completely reversed her previous workaholic need to attend to all of her clients' urgent demands. Remembering Wendy's kind words, however, she reminded herself again not to take the same bigoted attitude so many people around her were taking. If she assumed all non-mages were jerks, she was no better than those who lumped all mages into one category.

"Anyway, there's something else I'm going to be focusing on. Remember the day when you cured Jon's hangover?"

"Yeah."

Natalie reminded her sister of their discussion about the attempted murder of the MP who was widely disliked by virtually all mages, among others, and the various other situations that had begun to show a pattern.

"Why haven't you gone to LEO?" Suzanne demanded, horrified. "Has Jon reported it?"

"Yes, but LEO is horribly short-staffed, and I feel like I want to keep investigating myself. I dunno, I can't just hand this over to someone else and forget about it. Besides, I'm afraid our bad guy is someone high up in LEO himself." She explained to her sister the same reasoning she had given Jon, although she did not say anything about Chief Turner specifically.

"Hence why you look like you didn't get much sleep," Suzanne noted with a sigh. "But I don't get it. Even though I see that there's a similarity in all these deaths, how exactly do you figure this possible serial killer is making it happen?"

"It's coercion. It's got to be."

"Oh my God," Suzanne said as she also realized what Natalie had put together. "You're thinking he's taking these convicts, coercing them into killing the other person and then coercing them to kill themselves?!"

Natalie nodded slowly.

"If there's another way for him to be doing it, I'd love to hear about it," Natalie said grimly, looking out of the window without really seeing what was there. "You said it's impossible to tell if a dead person was a mage, right? The glow disappears?"

"That's right," Suzanne confirmed.

"So I'm guessing you wouldn't be able to see the yellow taint either as soon as they're dead, right?"

"Probably not."

"The perfect crime. The apparent murderer is dead, so case closed."

"And no evidence linking him to the mastermind."

Natalie was struck by Suzanne's use of the word *mastermind* instead of the phrase *serial killer*. Somehow the former was a much more comfortable word to use.

"So, either he's coercing the mage to kill him- or herself, or our mastermind is killing them himself and making it look like suicide or something that's not foul play. Remember, Dasovic died of an aneurysm. I doubt that could be self-inflicted. Could it be externally inflicted?"

Suzanne thought about that for a moment.

"I guess if you can magically suture a wound together, it should be equally possible to magically burst a blood vessel."

"Of course, your average LEO probably wouldn't have a clue how to do that," Natalie noted.

"No, but a doctor would, and doctors also have some practice with coercion, because it's the other permissible application."

"Oh God, I never thought about doctors."

"But then, a doctor wouldn't have access to mess with the prison records."

"That's true." Natalie thought about this hole in her theory for a moment. "Well, the reality is, just because it's only LEOs and doctors who legally *can* use coercion, that doesn't mean they're the only people who are actually able to do it. They're just the only ones who have legitimate practice and experience."

"This is insane, Natalie. You are *not* qualified to try to investigate a serial killer. Nor am I."

"Don't worry, I have no intention of trying to pretend I'm Sherlock Holmes. I'm not leaving LEO out of this; I'm just seeing if I can help. Besides, I'm going to need a job. I don't know if I want to be an actual police officer. But investigating behind the scenes is sort of like legal research. I can at least figure out if I'm any good at it and if I enjoy it. No matter what happens, I think it'll be a long time before anyone's going to let me practise law again." She sighed.

As the two women stepped out of the archway into the town square in Neekonnisiwin, they both sensed the vibration that said someone else was coming through, and they looked to one side to see that the next archway in the row of six was active. Natalie wondered briefly what would happen if more than six people were arriving via the portal network at once, but she dismissed the thought.

"Jon!" Natalie exclaimed as the portal revealed its traveller. He looked as tired as he had the first time she had met him, though his face lit up when he saw her. He carried a small, rather battered-looking gym bag and was dressed in jeans and another rumpled T-shirt, this one bearing the faded logo of a brand of beer that Natalie had never heard of.

"Natalie. My timing is perfect. At least I hope so. You're just arriving?"

"Yes, just got here. You look exhausted. What happened yesterday after you got called away?" Natalie reached up a hand to stroke what looked like two days' growth of beard. Though Jon had, as promised, been in the courtroom for Natalie's bail hearing, he had received an urgent phone call and had to leave before proceedings began.

"Hostage situation," he said. "Colombia. Strictly speaking it wasn't a LEO thing, since there were no mages involved. But a mage with the local police called us in to assist since there were a large number of innocent potential victims. Drug cartel situation."

Natalie looked surprised but pleased. "I didn't realize LEO got involved in things that involve no mages. It's good to know."

"We do all sorts," he told her. "I quite like the investigative stuff, and obviously rescuing a crowd of terrified hostages is a nice feeling." His mouth curved in a satisfied smile.

Natalie kissed him, and he pulled her closer when she would have made it brief.

"Break it up, lovebirds. We gotta go," Suzanne told them, though she was smiling.

Jon kept hold of Natalie's hand, and Suzanne kept pace beside them.

"And what happened to you after I had to leave?" he asked. "I'm really sorry about that, by the way."

"Don't worry about it. I'm getting the idea that that happens a lot?"

"Yeah. I usually have no idea where I'm going to be from one day to the next. You're changing the subject. Spill."

Natalie wrinkled her nose. "They set my bail at $100,000."

Her arm was jerked backward as Jon stopped abruptly, his mouth falling open. "A hundred thousand dollars? For a BS assault charge? And what was Raj's bail?"

"He got released on his own recognisance."

Jon swore very loudly, to the annoyance of a passing woman with three small children, who gave him a fierce glare. He apologized contritely to her.

Natalie's first exposure to the criminal justice system had been a series of shocks. The occasional similarity to the courts she was used to only served to highlight the differences. Being treated as not merely a criminal but in fact a particularly hated type of criminal had depressed her more than she had anticipated. However, the actual hearing had been short and abrupt, something that had evidently annoyed many of the people in the room, who had quite obviously been reporters. The judge had not given much insight into the reasons for his decision. The entire experience had left Natalie feeling off balance.

She decided not to mention to Jon that Meredith Baxter, the College investigator, had also been in attendance, her narrow face disapproving as she jotted notes in a book during the hearing.

Natalie shrugged. "Since I have every intention of showing up for my court date, it's not an issue. And, in fact, I'd say it's good news that Raj didn't have to post bail. It shows that they've accepted that he's not a mage, which bodes well for his ongoing legal career. And it suggests that the judge might not have been all that certain we really were the aggressors. Or at least that Raj wasn't."

Jon still looked thunderous, but he did not resist as Natalie tugged him toward the imposing building that housed the Council chamber, the offices of the two Canadian Council members, and the courtroom that was their destination.

As they entered the courtroom, Natalie left the other two as she stepped forward into the section in front of a low railing reserved for the parties and their lawyers, if any. As she took her seat, she glanced back and saw that Jon was sitting almost directly behind her, within clear view of the camera trained on Natalie, which would broadcast the courtroom scene to the councillors not from this continent, who would participate remotely. Given his globetrotting activities, she wondered how many of those councillors might recognize Jon on sight and whether his positioning was a deliberate gesture of support. She was warmed by the thought.

"Jon, I wasn't expecting to see you here."

Natalie looked back to see LEO Chief Seth Turner approaching the front row where Jon and Suzanne both sat. "Natalie, good morning."

Natalie nodded at him without smiling, still annoyed about their last interaction.

"Good work in Colombia," Seth said to Jon. "I heard from the South American chief that there were no casualties. Very impressive."

"Thanks, Chief. I don't know if you know Ms. Timmons? She's Natalie's sister. Suzanne, this is Seth Turner, Chief LEO of North America."

"I don't think we've met. How are you?" Seth reached past Jon and shook Suzanne's hand.

"Not too bad, thanks. Jon, I remembered I wanted to ask you something. You know that Character Test, the one that convicts have to take if they want to be able to leave town?"

"Yes."

"Aren't there supposed to be two examiners?"

"Absolutely," Jon replied. "Why do you ask?"

"Because I was speaking to someone a little while ago who had the Character Test, which was administered by Constance Reeve and nobody else, and who described it as mental rape."

Both Jon and the Chief looked shocked.

"Constance Reeve and nobody else?" Seth repeated. "Even if it was ever acceptable for only one person to do it, Constance Reeve would be the last person I'd trust to do it alone. Do you know the name of the person?"

"Um, yes, it was Dr. Sabourin, a surgeon at the hospital."

Both Seth and Natalie showed surprise at Suzanne's response, though for different reasons. Natalie was surprised to find that the surgeon had a criminal past. Seth's eyes immediately narrowed and he was silent for a moment, a frown on his face.

"Excuse me, would you? I'd like to go check into something."

After Seth had left the room, Jon winked conspiratorially at Natalie. "I have a feeling Councillor Reeve is gonna be having a bad day," he said in a stage whisper.

"You think he's going to look into that now?"

"You can bank on it," he said. "As you've already been made aware, Chief Turner does *not* approve of people disobeying regulations."

Natalie's lips twitched. "I suppose it's totally hypocritical of me to like that when it's in my favour," she admitted.

At that moment, a door in the front of the courtroom opened, and several councillors entered the room. Constance Reeve split from the main group and came to sit at the table not far from Natalie's, though she pointedly did not make eye contact. The others went to sit in an area set up like a jury box. At the same time, a large monitor to one side of the judge's seat came to life and revealed a larger group of councillors taking their seats in a similar arrangement in a distant courtroom. Natalie knew that it was in the courtroom at Sorcier-Havre. The magical community located in the mountains of Switzerland was considered the capital of the magical world, as it was the site where the mages who had escaped the Purge had formed the first exclusively magical community.

A second monitor flicked on, showing the empty high seat which would shortly be occupied by the Arch-Mage. This position, which was held for a five-year term and was voted upon by the other members of the Council, was currently held by the European councillor Sylvain LePierre, who had, in fact, held the position for three consecutive terms thus far.

"All rise." The voice which spoke was presumably that of a court official in Sorcier-Havre, but that person was not visible on the monitor.

As the councillors in Sorcier-Havre rose to their feet, the attendees and councillors in Neekonnisiwin followed suit. Almost immediately, the Arch-Mage stepped into the area captured by the camera and was seen on the monitor. He was a middle-aged man with olive-toned skin and piercing black eyes. His mostly grey hair still showed some streaks of black on the sides, and he wore a red judicial robe with a lacy white collar spilling out the front.

The unseen court clerk spoke again. "This court is now in session. You may be seated." All of the gathered mages in the remote courtroom took their seats, and those in Neekonnisiwin followed suit.

"Good afternoon, Ms. Benson. Or rather, good morning, yes?" Arch-Mage LePierre spoke with a French accent, but he was not difficult to understand.

"It is morning here, yes, Your Lordship," Natalie replied solemnly. "Good afternoon to you all."

"I had understood that your original intention was to attend in Sorcier-Havre in person. Was I mistaken in that information?" the Arch-Mage asked.

"I had considered doing so, but I am not permitted to leave the country at the moment," Natalie explained. She described the attack against her and Raj and their subsequent arrest. "I was obliged to post bail to be freed until my own trial. One of the bail conditions is that I may not leave the country. Actually, I'm not even supposed to leave the province of Ontario. However, since the nons cannot track the use of the portal network, my departure from the province will be unnoticed."

"I am given to understand that you created a gateway in front of numerous non-magical witnesses," one of the other councillors interjected. She was not one whom Natalie recognized, but her pinch-faced expression of disapproval was obvious. She was an older woman with lines graven deeply into her cheeks and wispy hair caught halfway between mouse-brown and grey. Her mouth formed words that did not match the sounds Natalie heard, and she realized that the woman was speaking in her own native language, which was being magically translated to English for Natalie's benefit or, presumably, to other languages for those councillors whose native language was something other than English.

"I felt that I had no choice," Natalie confirmed with a nod. "However, I obscured what I was doing with a large cloud of black smoke, and in explaining things since, I have been slightly less than honest. I have not given out any information about First Circle abilities to any non-mage."

The pinch-faced councillor, still looking disapproving, opened her mouth to continue her harangue, but the Arch-Mage held up a hand to stop her. "Councillor Potawicz, this hearing is not concerned with the actions of Ms. Benson on the day of her assault at the hands of non-mages, but rather with another charge of assault, in which Ms. Benson was also allegedly victimized by Councillor Constance Reeve. We will proceed with the matter at hand. Have all councillors experienced the memory stone submitted by Ms. Benson?" There were no denials, so the Arch-Mage continued. "Are there further details you wish to add to the events captured on the memory stone, Ms. Benson, that are pertinent to your Complaint?"

Natalie rose to her feet and succinctly described the events of the day in question, beginning with her attendance in court and a brief description of the nature of her professional role. She touched briefly on her e-mail to Chief Turner in which she indicated that she would not be able to provide gating services to LEO until after her College investigation was over.

"A copy of that e-mail has also been submitted with my Complaint," she noted. "I clearly explained why I need to withdraw my services. It is because I, and other members of my law firm, have been implicated in the growing numbers of what are perceived as prison escapes. If my firm can't fight these allegations, several lawyers may be disbarred, including me, and the firm will likely go bankrupt."

Since the memory stone included the repeated attempts to breach her mental barrier, she did not describe those. Her narrative concluded with the telephone call which had occurred several days later, as well as the several additional attempted phone calls.

"I concur that Ms. Benson's description of events does not contradict the memory stone which each of us has experienced," the Arch-Mage said solemnly. "Does any councillor wish to register a dissent?"

Constance Reeve raised her hand with a stubborn expression on her face.

"Councillor Reeve, you are excluded from this vote," the Arch-Mage told her with a snap of impatience in his voice. "You are well aware of this fact. As the accused, you may not participate in the jury process. You will have your opportunity to present your defence. Regardless, the vote is not about an opinion as to what was said or done; it is merely confirmation or denial that Ms. Benson's verbal account is consistent with her memory stone. Any other dissenters?" He looked around the room, saw no other raised hands, and struck his gavel on the stand in front of him. "The accuser's statement is confirmed as factual as perceived by her. Has every councillor experienced Councillor Reeve's memory stone?"

Again, there were no denials. "Councillor Reeve, you may now present any additional facts, if necessary, and thereafter your defence of your actions."

Constance Reeve rose to her feet. She was dressed impeccably, as was her usual custom, although her style of dress was not as businesslike as the suit Natalie wore. She looked rather like a wealthy woman at a midday semiformal social event. Her brilliantly white hair was piled on top of her head like a coronet, and she stood ramrod straight as she spoke. If it were not for the white hair and the liver-spotted hands, Natalie thought, one would never guess the woman was past seventy.

"My memory stone includes all of the pertinent events," she stated. Natalie squashed a feeling of irritation at the implication that her own memory stone was deficient as she had needed to provide additional information.

Councillor Reeve proceeded to give her defence. "The e-mail which Ms. Benson refers to was forwarded to me but did not come to my attention until very early on the morning of the events in question," she said in the abrupt manner, which was customary for her. She had an unusually low, gravelly voice for a woman. Natalie had often wondered if perhaps she had been a heavy smoker in her youth. "I was and am gravely concerned about her refusal to do her duty. She has a clear obligation to make her extraordinary abilities available to magical law enforcement."

Natalie's irritation increased at the woman's untenable position. She clenched her fists underneath the table.

"Her refusal to do so will hinder the justice process and cause irreparable harm. I cannot comprehend why she is not in the employ of LEO in any event. If she were, there wouldn't be any issue with this College investigation. It is irrelevant. Law enforcement is of far greater importance. I sought an explanation, and she refused to provide any such explanation in even the most cursory detail. She merely blocked me out. I found her behaviour intransigent, disrespectful and unacceptable. I therefore continued to attempt to gain the necessary information." She sat down abruptly, her mouth pursed in a prim expression of disapproval.

Natalie gripped the edge of her table as her temper threatened to overwhelm her. Irrelevant? The College investigation could ruin several hundred careers, but to the isolationist mage who had no interest in or concern for the non-magical world, it simply did not matter.

"I concur that Councillor Reeve's statement does not contradict her memory stone," the Arch-Mage said in the same neutral tone he had used in confirming the accuracy of Natalie's stone as compared to her verbal testimony. "Prior to proceeding to the defence, does any councillor wish to register a dissent with respect to the factual record?"

No hands were raised.

"Very well. The court confirms there is no issue of fact to be debated here, but only an issue of the appropriateness of actions taken in the circumstances. Does any councillor wish to speak to the matter before a vote is taken on the charges presented?"

Natalie stood up and raised her hand. The Arch-Mage frowned.

"You have already presented your case, Ms. Benson," he said in a disapproving tone.

"With respect, Your Lordship, I disagree," Natalie said in a firm voice. "I have only explained the facts of the matter. I request the opportunity to respond to the allegations made by Councillor Reeve."

Several of the councillors looked irritated, and the Arch-Mage's frown did not waver. He took a moment to think about the request and then shrugged.

"Very well, Ms. Benson. Kindly be concise. This is not a non-magical court proceeding in which all parties must present numerous witnesses to establish the facts; the facts are inarguable."

"Yes, Your Lordship. The allegation I wished to address was Councillor Reeve's statement that I have a moral obligation to make my abilities available to magical law enforcement and that I ought to be an employee of LEO instead of a lawyer. I have, in fact, made my services available, with absolutely no compensation, for over ten years. It has never been the practice of the magical community to force any mage into a specific career, and to do so is certainly not acceptable under the laws of Canada, where Councillor Reeve and I both reside. Even those countries that have mandatory military service do not require a lifelong commitment. I strenuously object to any suggestion that I am obligated to be a LEO employee when it is not the career of my choice. And since that is not a mage law, I submit that it should not be a factor in determining whether Councillor Reeve's actions were appropriate or not."

Natalie resumed her seat.

The Arch-Mage raised one eyebrow but did not comment. "Does any councillor now wish to speak to the matter?"

Several councillors raised their hands. The Arch-Mage granted each an opportunity to speak, providing their name and their country of origin as he did so, presumably for Natalie's benefit.

The pinch-faced Councillor Potawicz was the first to address the gathered Council members. She pointedly did not look in Natalie's direction as she spoke. Natalie fought to keep her face neutral, with limited success, as the councillor from Poland spoke in support of Councillor Reeve's actions.

"I concur with Councillor Reeve. Magical law enforcement *must* take priority over a petty scandal involving only one business in one country," she pronounced in a tone that might have sounded regal if it were not for the nasal quality of her voice. "It is entirely irrelevant whether the scandal has any basis in fact or fairness. If we as a society fail to contain magically talented criminals, the consequences could be staggering. The impact on all mages would be extremely negative. Naturally the impact on non-mages victimized by criminally minded mages would be significant also. It is the duty of all mages to contribute when and where they are able to the greater good. A mage with such an extraordinary ability as that possessed by Ms. Benson has an even greater obligation to contribute. Furthermore, as Ms. Benson's gate from Toronto to Neekonnisiwin demonstrates, she is capable of far greater range than she has been utilizing in assisting LEO. An allegation that she has been shortchanged in remuneration for her efforts is questionable when it is apparent she has been shortchanging LEO with those efforts."

Natalie was so astonished by this attack that she could barely even formulate all the arguments that clearly contradicted it. Nonetheless, her vision was becoming tinged in red. What had she ever done to deserve all of the vitriol that she was receiving from every side?

Upon being recognized by the Arch-Mage, an American councillor rose and moved toward the microphone so that his words could be heard in Sorcier-Havre. Councillor Alexander Roberts was a heavy-set man whose accent clearly betrayed his Deep South origins. Natalie had met him on a few occasions and thought he was an excellent councillor. Though he cultivated a folksy, approachable demeanour, he was a very highly educated man and one for whom she had a lot of respect.

"The greater good," he repeated thoughtfully, "is a concept that has been used throughout history by mage and non-mage alike in defence of their actions. Those actions are often seen very differently by history than they were by the ones who felt that they were acting for the so-called greater good. We cannot place the well-being of one person ahead of the well-being of many, but then it is neither just nor reasonable to place the well-being of many ahead of a reasonable degree of personal freedom and individual rights."

Natalie was conscious of a feeling of relief. She had been feeling for the last several weeks as though she were fighting with everybody. Each of the individuals who had been supportive stood out like beacons of light and warmth.

"The Council is a body representing mages worldwide, the vast majority of whom live and work in the non-magical world," Councillor Roberts continued. "If we are to fairly represent all of our constituents, including Ms. Benson, it is only right and fair that we accept that issues which affect her employer, her business and her personal life are clearly very high in her priorities, and that is absolutely the way it should be. Furthermore, it should be clearly understood that Ms. Benson does not perform a menial or inconsequential job. She is an attorney. A barrister. For those who are unaware, this is an extremely demanding and highly respectable career. I cannot fathom a single reason why she ought to exhaust herself gating LEOs and prisoners to the maximum extent of her range when they are perfectly capable of using the portal network and when *she has never been remunerated for her efforts.*"

Natalie ducked her head, feeling tears gathering in her eyes at the emphatic support from the American councillor.

She turned her head as she heard a slight disturbance at the back of the room. A uniformed LEO slipped inside, bowed toward the Arch-Mage and moved toward Chief Turner, who had entered the courtroom at some point without Natalie's awareness. As she swung her gaze back to the front, she caught the expression of absolute fury on Jon's face. She noticed that he appeared to be trembling, one long-fingered hand gripping the rail in front of him in a white-knuckled grip, while the other was clenched in a fist.

On the monitor, another councillor rose to his feet and was acknowledged by the Arch-Mage. Natalie did not recognize him, but as soon as he began to speak, a strong British accent was immediately evident.

"Ms. Benson is correct to say that we do not have a law requiring anybody to serve as a LEO, or as a councillor, or in any other capacity. People who hold those jobs choose them freely. We have been a democratic society since the founding of the Mage Council in the Middle Ages, before most of the non-magical world had even considered democracy as an appropriate form of government. Are we now going to move backward?" the British councillor demanded. Though he mostly looked toward the Arch-Mage as he spoke, Natalie noticed his eyes flick toward the camera partway through his speech. She suspected he was actually looking at Jon.

"If Councillor Reeve or any other mage were to contact me mentally at a time when I was interacting with non-mages and could not receive the communication, I would certainly expect her to respect that, especially if I indicated a more convenient time, as Ms. Benson did. The issue of whether or not Ms. Benson ought to assist LEO is completely irrelevant to the charges. Councillor Reeve mentally attacked Ms. Benson numerous times. Ms. Benson did nothing more than defend herself. That is the issue before this court this afternoon."

A babble of voices arose, and the Arch-Mage was obliged to strike his gavel several times to restore order. After his stern demand for appropriate conduct in the court, several more councillors spoke in support of or against Councillor Reeve's actions.

"The matter will now be put to the vote," the Arch-Mage stated when the last councillor who wished to speak had done so. "I remind all councillors that the question being voted upon is whether or not Councillor Reeve is guilty of mental assault and battery. Each councillor who wishes to vote for a guilty charge, kindly so indicate with a red flare above your head. Each councillor who wishes to vote that the charges be dismissed, produce a green flare. If any councillor feels that a guilty verdict on a lesser charge would be appropriate, then a blue flare should be displayed. No councillor may abstain from this vote, with the exception of Councillor Reeve, who may not participate." The Arch-Mage struck his gavel.

Within moments, the room was lit with various coloured flares. Three blue flares were visible, but the remainder were a jumble of green and red, making it hard to determine the final vote.

"Given that only a small minority vote for a guilty verdict on a lesser charge, those votes are overridden," the Arch-Mage declared. "Those councillors may, if they choose, alter their vote to green or red. No other councillors may alter their vote."

The three blue flares disappeared, replaced with two reds and one green.

The Arch-Mage raised his right hand, in which he held a topaz-coloured prism, and made a series of gestures with it. The flares in Sorcier-Havre immediately moved in front of the gathered councillors, while those in Neekonnisiwin disappeared and reappeared in the distant courtroom. They lined themselves up in two rows, one red and one green. There were two more green flares than red.

"May I be permitted to address the Council?"

Natalie swung around in her seat, startled, at the sound of Jon's request. Though his words were courteous, the tone was anything but.

Natalie looked back toward the monitor to see the British councillor hurry forward and murmur something inaudible to the Arch-Mage.

"This is most irregular, sir. Do you wish to provide information that is pertinent to the matter at hand?"

"Yes, my lord."

"Very well. Please come closer to the microphone," the Arch-Mage said in what sounded like a determinedly neutral tone, ignoring the twitter of clearly outraged comments from the councillors in Sorcier-Havre.

Jon pushed through the small swing gate in the low railing that separated the front area of the courtroom from the spectators' seats, looking neither at Natalie nor at Councillor Reeve as he strode to the microphone. Natalie's eyes flicked sideways to see that Councillor Reeve looked livid at the interruption.

"I am LEO Jon Forrester, First Circle metamorph," Jon introduced himself. "I have been an employee of LEO for 12 years. I *was* under the impression that that had been a choice that I made of my own free will. I now wonder if that is true. Am I, in fact, a slave? If I were to hand in my resignation, would I be subjected to having a mental steel spike driven through the base of my skull until I stepped into line like a good little boy?"

Natalie's eyes were wide with shock. She glanced back to see Chief Turner with a very troubled expression on his face. There was a murmur from both groups of councillors, the ones physically in attendance in the same room with her and those visible on the monitor. She clearly overheard one comment about "unacceptable interruption, clearly inappropriate."

Arch-Mage LePierre banged his gavel. "Silence, please," he sternly admonished the councillors. He gestured for Jon to continue.

Jon took a deep breath and appeared to make a visible effort to calm himself. "I am a LEO. Of course I believe that law enforcement is very important. But it is *not* the be-all and end-all. The level of antimage prejudice across the world is at or very near to the levels experienced just before the Purge. I assume I need not remind anybody here of the events of the worst massacre in our history? Suicide and substance abuse among mages aged 18 to 25 are at an all-time high. I fail to understand why the Council has taken absolutely no steps whatsoever to attempt to address these issues when there is an immediate danger to mages everywhere. And I absolutely will not meekly condone forced labour or violent abuse of a private citizen by a government that *supposedly* exists to protect our collective interests. That is all."

There was silence as Jon resumed his seat, his posture still one of intense anger. Natalie looked back to the monitor in time to see a uniformed LEO enter the remote courtroom, bow to the Arch-Mage, and place a piece of paper on the bench in front of him.

Arch-Mage LePierre picked it up and began to read, a fierce frown gathering on his face as he progressed through it. Finally, he sighed and rubbed his temples with both hands as though the proceedings were giving him a headache.

"New information has been brought to my attention which has bearing on this matter. Court is adjourned for a brief period. I would ask that the courtroom in Neekonnisiwin be vacated while the Council is apprised of this new information. Councillor Reeve is also to be excluded from this discussion."

Natalie rose to her feet and bowed, as protocol dictated, and then moved toward the railing to where the spectators' seats were. Seth, Jon and Suzanne had also risen to their feet.

Natalie, looking back around as she heard the sharp tap of heels, saw Councillor Reeve disappearing through the door at the front, from which the councillors had arrived initially. She turned back and strode out of the courtroom, followed in silence by Seth, Jon and Suzanne.

Chapter 19

Natalie caught hold of Jon's hand as the courtroom door swung closed behind them.

"I didn't know that suicide and substance abuse are at an all-time high," she said quietly.

"I did," Suzanne told her. "How many young people really want to be mages when they know they've got to keep it secret from every non-magical friend they've got? I don't recall being too thrilled with the idea myself, and I always knew."

"It's a lot harder when you don't know," Jon said soberly. "At first, you think maybe you're going crazy, which is terrifying, and which is equally something you don't want to confide in anyone."

"And lots of mentally ill people turn to substance abuse too," Suzanne put in.

Jon nodded agreement. "Then if you don't go off the rails because of the drugs and alcohol, you figure out what you are and have to deal with the hate."

Natalie looked down at the hand that she held in her own and suddenly sucked in a startled breath as she turned his hand around. A jagged horizontal scar snaked across the inside of his wrist.

Jon grimaced as he realized what she had just figured out. "Just as well I didn't know the proper way to slit my wrists," he said quietly.

"Oh my God."

"And now I find out that the government that I trusted, that I dedicated my life to serving, considers me their personal property, a slave." His jaw was tense as he turned his gaze on Chief Turner, who sighed.

"That shocked me too," Seth said, a defeated slump to his shoulders. Natalie thought he suddenly looked about 10 years older than when he had entered the courtroom, as if what had just happened had been a personal betrayal. "I will fully understand if you feel you have to resign, Jon. And I will fight on all fronts for your right to do so. But I cannot help but tell you that I really hope you don't. I don't know what we would do without you."

"Do you know what they're talking about now?" Jon asked, not directly responding to what the Chief had said.

Seth's lips twitched slightly. "As a matter of fact, I do," he admitted.

"You're not really going to keep us in the dark, are you?" Natalie said.

"I probably shouldn't say—" He was grinning now, so that clearly told Natalie that he was teasing her this time.

"Seth!"

"Okay, well, I asked one of my staff to look into this business of Councillor Reeve conducting the Character Test by herself." He sobered as he explained. "Frankly, I would prefer she wasn't authorized to do it at all, even with a second examiner present, but the thought of her doing it alone is horrifying."

"What did they find?"

"She's done it six times in the last 10 years," Seth said grimly. "Always alone, and the stamp that indicates the date the report was filed is always significantly after the actual examination. My guess would be that they were handed into the Records Office and filed directly specifically so that they would not come to my attention. I faxed the reports with an explanatory note to the European chief, who is in Sorcier-Havre, along with the information that a hearing on a matter of abuse of a private citizen was currently in session."

"And Chief Thibault decided it needed immediate attention," Jon guessed the rest with a vindictive smile. "The Council is overdue for a reality check. Since they're so over the top about law enforcement, it's about time they recognized that the law applies to them just as much as to the rest of us."

"You know, an ironic thought occurs to me," Suzanne remarked quietly. "Many of the more isolationist members of the Council think that anything outside the mage world is irrelevant. But the reality is, most mages who live in the real world think the Council is largely irrelevant. That's why there's such low voter turnout."

"True, but then we shoot ourselves in the foot because then the same old sticks keep getting voted in by the small percentage of mages who do actually vote," Natalie said.

"How do you figure they're irrelevant?" Seth said in surprise.

"The regular government takes care of things that we need a government for, from national security to education to health care to road maintenance," Natalie pointed out. "The Council sticks their nose into law enforcement and takes days debating completely pointless questions like whether or not my non-mage colleague was to be awakened from his magically induced coma while he was still in Neekonnisiwin. They debated that decision for *four days*, and they still couldn't come to a consensus. And for people who achieve very little, they have far too much power."

"The Council exists to manage interactions between the mage world and the non-magical people, to minimize friction and danger to mages," Seth protested.

"That's what they're *supposed* to do," Natalie said with heavy skepticism. "But do they really? What have they done along those lines in the last 25 years? Passed a law that LEO should take mage criminals out of the justice system and should not reveal its activities, and then flatly ignored all of the consequences of that decision. It seems to me that, more and more, they are focusing on petty internal matters in order to avoid the much more significant issues that urgently need to be addressed." She stroked the scar on the inside of Jon's wrist with her thumb, her expression deeply troubled.

"I must admit, I have severe doubts about the appropriateness of elected politicians acting as judges, as well," Jon added. "Most of them are not qualified for that role. Arch-Mage LePierre has a legal background, but Constance Reeve? What did she do before being a councillor?"

"I'm not sure. She's been a councillor for about 25 years, so I was a kid before that," Natalie said. "I definitely wasn't paying attention to politicians back then."

"She was a teacher," Seth said. "And then a principal for years."

"But that was the high school here, wasn't it?" Suzanne asked. "I don't know if she ever lived out in the real world."

"Doug Hayes was a doctor before he became a councillor, wasn't he?" Natalie asked.

"Yeah. But I'm pretty sure he's lived in Neekonnisiwin forever, too."

Natalie frowned as she thought about the two Canadian representatives of the Mage Council. "It's funny. Non-magical politics are split along party lines; magical politics are split between isolationists and inclusivists. And the isolationists have held power for far too long."

"What will you do if they let her off?" Suzanne asked fearfully.

"Move as far away as possible," Natalie replied. "Maybe southwestern Australia might be far enough. Enough so that I could block her out successfully. I will *not* tolerate that kind of abuse, no matter what the Council decides."

"And you, Jon?" Seth asked, his tone wary.

Jon frowned and did not respond for a minute, then he sighed. "Frankly, I don't really want to resign," he admitted. "But I do want to discuss my working conditions. There are situations where I'm called in for no better reason than that it's just more convenient, exactly the same as when that idiotic councillor suggested Natalie ought to gate people all the way to their final destination just because she can. The result is I work 70 or 80 hours a week, often for several weeks without a day off. It's not remotely unusual for me not to see my own home for weeks or months at a time, even when I'm on the same continent and ought to be able to portal home."

"There are some situations where your unique skills are the best solution, perhaps even the only solution that can minimize casualties, like what just happened in Colombia," Seth pointed out.

"True," Jon agreed without false modesty. "And I'm not objecting to irregular hours or being called on for stuff like that. But I have just found a reason to want to have a bit more of a personal life," he said, smiling at Natalie. "And I think I've paid my dues; I'm entitled to ask for better working conditions. I may not have been working for free all these years, but the truth is that I have been putting up with unnecessary abuse the same as Natalie has. And now I see that the more abuse we put up with, the more the Council thinks they're entitled to heap it onto people like us."

"Sadly, I'm forced to agree," Seth replied. Then he grinned as he added, "Though I'll confess to being quite glad First Circle abilities don't breed true. I'd be terrified of the kids you two might produce otherwise!"

Jon burst out laughing, while Natalie turned bright red.

"This court is back in session. You may be seated," Arch-Mage LePierre said as Natalie and her party re-entered the courtroom, before they even had time to get to their seats. Startled, they hurried to resume their places.

Natalie, surprised to see that Constance was already in the room, assumed the councillor must have been invited to return before she herself had been advised that the *in camera* portion of the proceedings was concluded. She was momentarily irritated at being treated differently, until she looked more closely at the elderly councillor. Constance's former ramrod-straight posture and prim disapproval were no longer in evidence. In fact, she was now looking every year of her age, and she kept her eyes fixed on the table in front of her. Many of the other councillors were also looking chastened.

"As the duly appointed Arch-Mage of the Mage Council, and in accordance with the Judiciary Conclave Statute of 1592, I have elected to exercise my right to overrule the vote of the councillors in this matter," Arch-Mage LePierre spoke in a stern tone of voice. "Let it be heard and recorded that the decision of this court is as follows: Ms. Constance Reeve is hereby found guilty of mental assault and battery against Ms. Natalie Benson in respect of her actions taken on May 22 of this year."

Natalie's mouth fell open in shock. For the Arch-Mage to override a majority vote, even a close one, was virtually unheard of. It was a decision which would likely have a severe impact on his chances of being voted to the high position in future given that it was the other councillors who voted on that role. At the same time, a rising tide of relief filled her at the knowledge that no extraordinary measures would be needed to protect herself from the councillor's continued abuse. But the Arch-Mage was not finished.

"Ms. Reeve is also found guilty of a breach of the regulations surrounding the Character Test on six occasions over the last 10 years. Those regulations are part of the Statute of the International Magical Law Enforcement Organization. There are two reasons for the requirement for two independent, unbiased examiners. One is so that both can independently verify that the person should have the Convict's Curse removed, and the second is so that the test is conducted with due regard for the person's privacy and dignity. After all, it is never administered unless the person has served their sentence, as well as any probation.

"Let it be heard and recorded that no member of the Council is above the law. Indeed, a councillor has a higher obligation than most to uphold the law. Abuse of private citizens is intolerable."

Natalie sneaked a glance backward toward where Jon sat. She saw an expression of pleased surprise on his face.

The Arch-Mage banged his gavel on his desk, and Natalie jerked back around to face the front, embarrassed at her breach of courtroom etiquette.

"The judgment of this court is as follows: Ms. Natalie Benson is granted judgment in an amount to represent twice the appropriate level of financial compensation for the services rendered to the International Magical Law Enforcement Organization over the last 10 years."

Natalie was startled yet again. Although Jon had included a demand for compensation in the Complaint that he had drafted for her, she hadn't really given that much thought. It wasn't the money that she was concerned about; it was the abuse—and then the principle of forced labour once it had become apparent that the majority of councillors seemed to believe she was obligated to provide her services. Still, she reflected, the money would be useful to pay for the bail bond that she had been obliged to purchase. If it weren't for the Council's actions, chances are she would not have had to spend a night in jail or post bail to be released.

"The assistance of North American Chief LEO Seth Turner is requested in calculating what the appropriate compensation would be," the Arch-Mage continued. "Chief Turner, I would be obliged if you could arrange to have the calculation delivered to my office within seven days."

"Yes, Your Lordship," Seth said, rising to his feet and bowing.

"One quarter of that amount is to be paid by Councillor Constance Reeve personally, within 90 days from the amount being finalized. The remainder will be paid by the Mage Council. Councillor Reeve is also required to pay restitution in the sum of $10,000 in Canadian funds to each of the six persons to whom she administered the Character Test without due regard for regulations and procedure and is also required to personally apologize to each of those persons. Court is dismissed."

Natalie was so startled at the unexpected finale of the hearing that she was late in rising to her feet as the Arch-Mage banged his gavel again, rose, and turned to leave the distant courtroom. Constance Reeve was also rather slow to get to her feet, and in fact, she took her seat again as soon as the Arch-Mage had left. She neither moved nor looked at anyone as the other councillors, Natalie, and her three companions left the courtroom.

In spite of feeling entirely satisfied with the result of the hearing, Natalie also suddenly felt a bit of sympathy for the autocratic woman, who had likely just suffered the worst humiliation of her life.

"What did Councillor Hayes want?"

Jon, Suzanne and Seth were waiting when Natalie walked out of the Convocation Hall.

"I'm not really sure. It was quite an odd conversation." Natalie frowned as she thought about it. "Which is actually not that different from the last time I had a conversation with that guy. He was asking me about the College investigation and the bail hearing."

"Mild curiosity? Or an actual intention to do something about it?" Seth wondered.

"Like what?" Natalie said skeptically. "This is the same guy who wanted to ship Raj back to Toronto before he was awakened so that he wouldn't know he'd been treated in a mage hospital."

Seth just looked troubled.

"I kind of don't want to get my hopes up, but I definitely like that Arch-Mage," Natalie said. "Of course, there's a fair bit of self-interest there."

Seth chuckled.

"Jon, unless some terrible emergency that involves thousands of potential casualties arises, you're off until at least Monday," Seth told him. "Go get some sleep. I suspect you're well overdue. Ladies, good day."

As Seth strode away and Suzanne started walking toward the portal, Jon tugged on Natalie's hand.

"Do you really have to go back to Toronto right away?" he asked. "I'm sick of these brief snatched moments. I want to actually see you for more than half an hour here and there."

Natalie smiled. "I am unemployed and free to do what I please. Technically, I'm already in breach of my bail conditions, but since that whole thing is utterly ridiculous, I don't really care. The only way they'd find out is if a mage here in town were to report me. Of course, Constance and the other councillors are aware that I'm in breach …"

"I'd say the odds of any of them reporting you to the Ontario police are fairly slim." Jon grinned. "Do you snowboard by any chance?"

"I never got very good at boarding. I ski, though it's been a few years."

"Don't let her fool you for one second." Suzanne laughed. "She was a competitive skier in her teens, and she's a very competitive person."

"Bring it." Jon grinned. "You have met your match, Ms. Benson."

"Oh, really? And just when did a boy from London who grew up dirt-poor learn to ski?"

"Snowboarding, not skiing. And it was after said poor boy started travelling the world and also learned how to fly away from an impending crash before he could break numerous bones."

"That's cheating."

"Hey, I wasn't competing." Jon laughed. "I was just saving my ass."

"I'll see you later then," Suzanne told her sister with a wave, and strode off toward the portal arch.

Jon hitched his gym bag further up on his shoulder, and Natalie looked at it curiously. "Is that seriously all of your stuff?"

"Yep. I learned how to travel light a long time ago."

"That gives whole new meaning to travelling light! Didn't you say you're on this continent for three months?"

"Yeah, but really I only need the same kind of clothes over and over. A couple of pairs of jeans, four or five shirts, underwear, socks and toiletries. It's easier to wear the same pair of shoes every day and have to replace them after four months than to carry three pairs around with me. I need a bigger bag in the winter, but summer stuff packs down small."

"That's incredible. What if you have to be formal for something?"

"I keep a uniform at the LEO office in Colorado and at the one in London. And shoes, since these things wouldn't do." He held out a long foot encased in a ragged running shoe that had definitely seen better days. "I can usually either get to one of those or have someone bring it to me. I was planning to change for this morning, but I ran out of time."

"I wondered if you ever wore a uniform."

"Not very often."

They spent an enjoyable few hours on the ski hill. True to his word, Jon was an excellent boarder and frequently pulled stunts on the terrain park that Natalie wouldn't have dared try. She reflected that being able to shape-shift out of danger if a jump started to go wrong would certainly make it easier to take crazy risks. Her own gatemaking ability was starting to seem very tame and boring in comparison.

During the rides back up to the top on the lift, she learned that Jon was the youngest of seven children, having three half-siblings from his mother's first marriage, two half-siblings from his father's first marriage and only one full-blooded sister. Two of his siblings were also police officers, and one was a firefighter. His father had also been a police officer before his retirement. Jon was the only mage.

Though her own childhood growing up in a small town in northern Ontario was quite different, there were also a lot of similarities. The closeness of the siblings was one, though Jon was shocked that she had not confided her recent troubles to her parents until after the attack had put her on the front page.

When he started yawning and could no longer hide his flagging energy, Jon admitted that he had only had about four hours' sleep the previous night, and Natalie called a halt to their faux-winter fun.

"Don't worry about it," she overrode his protests. "I don't have to leave if you don't want me to. I need to do some work to prepare for my College hearing anyway, which I can do just as easily here as back at home. You can sleep. How about Verenelli's for dinner?"

"Why didn't I meet you 10 years ago?"

"Oh, I'm not so sure you would've wanted to. Ten years ago, I was an overly perfectionistic university student. I dated a few guys back then, but none of them lasted for very long. I have a strong suspicion that was more my fault than theirs."

They checked in and were shown to a spacious room boasting a sitting room and a separate bedroom, with an excellent view of the ski hill they had just left.

"I need to scrub off two days' worth of grime," Jon admitted. He frowned as he scratched at his ragged chin.

"I need to go buy some more clothes," Natalie said. "I think a four-day break sounds like just what the doctor ordered, but I didn't bring any clean underwear with me!"

Natalie kissed him and left to go visit the stores in the town square. From time to time, her mind wandered away from her shopping as she thought about Jon. As she had told him, none of her previous relationships had lasted for long, other than a high school romance that had lasted for almost three years. That guy had been a non-mage, and the revelation of her magical abilities had been the demise of that relationship. It was quite bizarre that a man from another country could be a better match for her than anyone she had ever met on her native soil. But he was protective without being smothering, clearly highly intelligent, and fully prepared to admire intelligence in others. He was someone she could respect and admire, without any evidence of arrogance as far as she had been able to tell. He was incredibly interesting, as well as very funny, particularly when he exercised his skill for mimicry. And what she had seen of his body definitely made her want to see more.

When she quietly re-entered the room laden with shopping bags, she was dismayed to see that Jon was sitting on the couch, though he had fallen asleep with his head resting on the back in an awkward position.

She put her bags down and shook him awake.

"You're going to have a horrible stiff neck sleeping like that," she told him. "There's a perfectly good bed in the other room. Why aren't you in it?"

"Mm," he mumbled incoherently. "I was hoping you'd join me in it."

Natalie grinned. "Let's hold that thought until after you get some sleep. You're going to need some energy, you know."

Jon smiled with some self-mockery. "You promise you won't disappear? Or go through your own gateway? Or have somebody shoot at you?"

"Or get arrested," she added to his list with a laugh. "I'll do my best to avoid needing to be rescued for the whole rest of the day," she told him. "Not that I anticipated any of those things, so you know, no promises."

She kissed him, refused to let him extend the kiss, and pushed him toward the bedroom.

Natalie stretched, looking at the spreadsheet floating in the air in front of her. It actually resided on her tablet, but that was even smaller and more difficult to work with than her laptop.

Though she had told Jon that she was going to be working to prepare for the College hearing, the information on the spreadsheet was entirely about the murders and not the allegations in the College's Notice. While she had reluctantly accepted that Jon could not disobey regulations and discuss the investigation with her, she had never agreed or promised to stop investigating herself.

She had spent some time looking up all of the information she could find on the man who had killed the Montreal newspaper president, been sentenced to a maximum-security psychiatric facility, and then "escaped" and ended up committing suicide in a small town in British Columbia. It definitely appeared to fit the pattern, although there were some missing facts that Natalie knew would be impossible to source from the Internet.

Then she had created a timeline using another type of design software, putting together the murders and noting which ones would have required a border crossing, regardless of whether the mastermind was a Canadian who sometimes went to the States or an American who was sometimes in Canada.

She had brought Jon's list with her, disguised as a small makeup compact, and after ensuring that he was deeply asleep, she had expanded that in mid-air as well. Then she had searched for any names that she did not already have linked to a murder. She had not really expected to find any, but to her surprise, one more became apparent, and she spent some time looking into everything she could find about that situation. Now, how would she tell LEO about this?

She wished she could think of a way to find similar information outside of Canada, but without LEO's information on convicted criminals, her hands were tied.

Realizing her neck muscles had been tensed for long enough to start causing a headache, she decided that she had done as much as she could think of for now on the murder investigation. She dismissed the airborne versions of her documents and shut down her tablet, returning the hard copy list to its disguise as a makeup container. Then she stood and walked toward the doorway that separated the spacious sitting room of the guest house's premier suite from the bed.

She caught her breath as she looked down at Jon sprawled across two-thirds of the king-size bed. The light blanket was tangled around his legs, leaving his chest bare. Clad only in boxers, he lay on his back with one arm tucked behind his head. The abs she had caught a brief glimpse of a few weeks ago were on full display, and even in his relaxed state, it was apparent he had a full six-pack. His chest and the arm tucked behind his head were equally muscular. A very fine sprinkling of reddish-brown hair decorated his chest, and a thin line of hair below his belly button disappeared into the waistband of his boxers.

With sudden decision, Natalie decided a hot shower would help relax her tense neck, and she was quite confident Jon wouldn't mind helping her relax further when he awoke.

Natalie awoke to the feeling of a hand stroking her side and continuing down her hip, the featherlight touch incredibly arousing.

"I reckon I'm still asleep." She heard the husky murmur from behind her. "I'm having a lovely dream where a beautiful woman has climbed into my bed, and she's not wearing very many clothes."

Natalie chuckled. "I figured I'd better take my chance while I could get it, considering how often you get called away. And that you probably wouldn't mind."

"Oh, I *definitely* don't mind."

Natalie rolled over and propped herself up on her elbow to face him. Her eyes travelled over his hard stomach appreciatively.

"I'm curious about something." She ran a finger lightly across his stomach, and he sucked in a sharp breath and shivered in reaction. "If you work 70 or 80 hours a week, how on earth do you find time to work out as much as these stomach muscles suggest you do?"

A grin appeared. "Are you checking me out, Ms. Benson?"

"Why, yes, Mr. Forrester." Natalie laughed. "Definitely. And I like what I'm seeing."

The grin broadened, and his eyes lingered on her matching lacy bra and panties. "You and me both," he said.

"So? How do you do it?"

"Do what? Oh, right. Well, I don't exactly need a gym, you know."

"Why not?"

"It's mostly because I fly. Almost every day. God, I love flying. It's the best stress relief there is. I like being something like an eagle that can go crazy high, where the air is thin. It doesn't bother the eagle. The air is so clear up there, and the view is spectacular, given how good an eagle's eyesight is. It's brilliant. And great upper-body exercise."

"I'm jealous." Natalie sighed as she pictured that. "You can't turn someone else into a bird, can you?"

"Unfortunately, no. I could make you a memory stone if you like. But in any event, just at the moment, I would really, really like for you to stay you."

They did not make it to Verenelli's after all.

Chapter 20

The following evening, Jon and Natalie were enjoying their postponed Verenelli's dinner, when their tête-à-tête was interrupted.

"I'm really sorry to do this to you …"

They both looked up to see Chief Turner standing by their table, looking worried.

"I thought you said something about 'unless there's a risk of thousands of casualties,'" Jon said with a sigh.

"And there aren't thousands, but I got a call from Chief Thibault. Chief el-Dawabi contacted him, hoping to find you. There's a young lady in Pakistan who was imprisoned yesterday on suspicions of magery but who possibly isn't actually a mage at all. You know how badly suspected mages are treated in Middle Eastern prisons. The poor girl is only 15. We've got people moving into place to see if they can do something about it, but there's no question you'd be the most effective."

Jon sighed.

"Also, we'd like to do something before the Council can pass an order. That obnoxious councillor from the Middle Eastern quadrant will probably say if the girl's not a mage, it's not our problem and order us to leave it alone." Seth looked nauseous as he said this.

"You're manipulating me."

"Wait, what?!" Natalie said.

"The councillor from the Middle East gives a whole new meaning to *isolationist*," Jon said sourly. "You think Constance Reeve is bad? Abdul-Aziz Qutuz is 10 times worse. The fact that the victim is a girl is probably also likely to make him consider it not worth our time and effort."

"I was hoping we might be able to get you on a flight tonight," Seth said.

"How long is that flight?" Natalie asked thoughtfully.

"About 20 hours." Jon sighed. "And that's assuming I can get a one-stop."

"Could you use the portal network to get to Pakistan from England? Or, better yet, from Switzerland?"

Jon's face brightened. "Yes."

Seth's mouth had dropped open. "You're not suggesting you can build a gateway to Switzerland, are you?"

"Well, I've never tried further than England, but that was okay, wasn't it, Jon?"

"No worries at all."

"Right, well, I know what the courtroom in Sorcier-Havre looks like now. Can I have him to myself for a bit longer if I cut that much time off his travel?"

Seth was still looking like a stranded fish.

"And by the way, that's top secret information," Natalie added sternly. "Absolutely no member of the Council gets to know about that."

"Deal," Seth agreed, his eyes still looking wild. "I'll leave you to your dinner."

Natalie grinned conspiratorially at Jon as Seth turned and walked away.

"I'm sorry about this," Jon told her with a sigh.

"Don't worry about it. Frankly, if something happened to that poor girl, I'd have that on my conscience as well, now that I know. Besides, I like thinking of you as the knight in shining armour who goes charging off to rescue damsels in distress. As long as I'm not the damsel," she added, wrinkling her nose. "I hate feeling helpless."

"I wouldn't mind rescuing you, though. Not that you seem to want to let me," he grumbled.

"Sucks when the damsel rescues herself, huh?"

"I'll keep trying. I like a challenge." He grinned, and Natalie laughed.

"Let's pay our bill and leave. We could go back to Toronto by portal first, at least shave a few thousand kilometres off the gateway."

As they left the restaurant, she checked to ensure that nobody was within easy listening distance. "So, I know you can't tell me anything about the murder investigation, but am I allowed to tell you if I figure anything out?"

"Sure. But just so you know, I know nothing more about it," Jon said ruefully. "I'm not sure Seth really trusts me to keep my word now that he knows we're together, so he's keeping me out of it. Atlin," he said, as they stepped into the portal entrance in Neekonnisiwin.

"So what happens next?"

He kept hold of her hand and spoke the name of their next destination: "Toad River."

High on a forested hill, Jon frowned thoughtfully as he looked down at the fast-running river. "All I know is that Chief Thibault is dispatching some investigators to look into some of the situations in the U.S. more closely."

"Why the U.S. and not Canada?"

Turning back into the archway etched shallowly into a rock face, Jon said, "Fort Vermilion."

The portal in Alberta was actually some distance from the town of the same name, on the other side of the Peace River.

"Seth is concentrating on Canada. It's a bit delicate, two chiefs operating in the same jurisdiction, with their people on two different chains of command. So they split it geographically. Also they're trying to track the timeline, putting it together with the ones you already found in Canada. And that is literally all I can tell you. That's probably already breaking the rules."

Natalie thought of her timeline, which was probably redundant now. She wanted to ask him about checking security records for border crossings but realized he couldn't discuss that. Besides, surely that was a fairly obvious investigative step. Maybe she should do as Suzanne had said and stay out of it. It wasn't her area of expertise, and clearly Seth was not going to assist her with the information she needed to expand on what she knew.

Jon pulled Natalie back into the archway they had just emerged from. "Pinehouse."

"Jon, had you thought about how this person, the mastermind, is doing this? Can we speculate about that if we're not actually discussing what LEO is doing?"

Jon looked at Natalie soberly. "It would pretty much have to be coercion, wouldn't it?"

"That's the conclusion I had come to," Natalie said with a sigh. "I was hoping you might have had a different idea."

"I can't see what else it could be. The mage victim, usually a convict, is coerced to kill the non-mage victim and then coerced to kill themselves." Jon looked slightly nauseous as he said this.

"Or the mastermind kills the mage victim himself," Natalie suggested. "I'm thinking of Dasovic, who tried to kill the MP and then died of an aneurysm. Suzanne and I were talking about that one, and she wondered if our mastermind might actually be a doctor."

"Why a doctor?"

"Because it's the only other situation where it's legal to perform coercion, which means a doctor would also have legitimate experience at it. And I imagine a LEO wouldn't have a clue how to make an aneurysm happen."

"Uh, no," Jon agreed. "I certainly wouldn't. So Suzanne knows about it too, huh?" Tugging Natalie's hand as he turned back into the portal archway, he said, "Swan River."

"Yeah." Natalie continued the conversation as if it had not been interrupted by a distance jump of over 700 kilometres. "She told me the mage glow disappears when you die, and I'm guessing the yellow coercion tint would too."

Jon nodded.

"But anyway, just because only LEOs and doctors can legally do it doesn't mean other mages aren't capable of it."

"Sioux Lookout." Jon frowned as they emerged into the forest in northern Ontario. "Technically any mage might be able to do it," he agreed. "It just requires a fairly strong degree of concentration and ability to multitask. But then I know quite a few LEOs who can't, so I reckon it's harder for some. Toronto."

As they emerged from the cellar of the building disguised as an ordinary warehouse which housed the Toronto portal, Natalie opened up the Uber app on her phone and called for a cab. As the industrial area was all but empty at this very late hour, she assumed it would take a while before it would arrive.

They sat in the reception area of the empty warehouse, where they could see the lights of the cab when it arrived. Natalie saw from Jon's face that he was thinking hard about something, and she waited until he broke the silence.

"You know, I'm thinking about the one with the Catholic priest and the car accident. Putting that with our coercion theory, I'm really struggling to think how that could be done," Jon said with a frown. "Bearing in mind you've got to be within about 100 feet or so of your coercion victim, that would mean our mastermind would have had to be in a car behind the convict, controlling her as she drove, while also driving his own car *and* somehow knowing exactly where and when they'd pass that cardinal and recognize the car, in enough time to make the accident happen. That's a lot of balls to juggle at once."

"Are you sure you have to be that close to do coercion?" Natalie asked sombrely.

"Actually, yes. That's been pretty thoroughly tested by LEO," Jon told her. "It would be handy if we could get coercion on someone a bit sooner in some situations, like if you're catching them in the act, but it doesn't work until you're close by."

"Do they have to meet your eyes or anything like that?"

Jon shifted in his chair, looking away, and Natalie realized he was uncomfortable discussing how coercion would work with someone not authorized to practise it. He was still skirting the prohibition on discussing an active investigation, but as long as he wasn't actually telling her about what LEO was currently doing, hopefully he was staying just on the right side of the line.

"No," he admitted. "It's easier if I can see their eyes, but it's not absolutely necessary. I've even done it from a hidden position when the person wasn't aware I was there."

"I saw something in one of these stories. What was it …?" Natalie used her phone to do some Google searches, but the cab arrived before she found her answer.

"That's the thing I was trying to remember." Natalie scrolled through the article and passed her phone over to Jon, pointing to the last paragraph, after she had given the driver her address. She had also taken the precaution of altering her appearance again, before they had entered the cab.

Local police routinely conduct a mechanical inspection of any vehicle involved in a fatal accident. The examination of the car in which the Cardinal was riding revealed a device of unknown origin attached to the inside front bumper. Though the device was too severely damaged to positively identify it, it appeared to be some kind of GPS tracking mechanism. The chauffeuring company which owns and operates the fleet of cars stated that while their cars do have trackers on them, this device was not the type they use.

She changed to mental communication, closing her eyes as if she were tired. *It doesn't seem as if they ever pursued that, or if they did, I didn't find any further mention of it. But if our mastermind was tracking the Cardinal's car, then the only mystery is how he was close enough to coerce the other driver but keep himself safe.*

Suddenly she remembered what Jon had said about learning to do crazy snowboard tricks because of his ability to transform himself into a bird to evade an imminent crash. Most mages, however, could not turn themselves into an animal, other than by illusion. Even if it were possible, it was believed that they would immediately become limited to the mental capacity of that animal and be unable to turn themselves back. Regardless, you could not turn yourself into anything that was significantly different from your own size. Jon was clearly a very unique exception to that rule. But then her own gates were also an exception to the rule, and gatemakers were much more common than metamorphs, albeit not with her range.

I wonder if it's possible to transport yourself a very short distance? Natalie speculated. *What if our mastermind was in the car and transported himself to the side of the road just as the car began to cross the median? Even if he lost control of the coercion, it would probably have been too late for the driver to correct, given the speed.*

I've never heard of anyone having the ability to transport themselves short distances, except for gateways. And you'd know better than me how much concentration those take, Jon responded the same way.

Hmm, lots, Natalie admitted. *It would be incredibly difficult to build a gateway and do some other kind of complicated magic at the same time. Besides, no witness account mentioned any kind of super-bright light in the car. Well, even if I can't figure out how it was done, that doesn't mean I'm going to throw this one out.*

Jon scrolled up and read the whole article before passing Natalie's phone back. They did not resume the conversation until they got back to her condo.

"So, I found another one."

"Oh?"

"Did you hear about the death of the lead singer of Ace's King? I think it was about three years ago."

"Vaguely. Some kind of explosion, wasn't it? Stage effects gone wrong?"

"Allegedly. But that guy was all over social media bashing mages, so he fits our profile as well. And two other people died. One was a stagehand who evidently tried to contain the fire, and the other was a security guard whose death was reported as completely bizarre because he seemed to run into the worst part of the inferno for no apparent reason."

"And let me guess, the security guard is on my list of convicts too?"

"Bingo. That was in the regular news, too, because he was also a prison escapee and there were questions about how someone with a prison record could have been hired as a security guard."

"Maybe I'll just tell Chief Thibault about this one," Jon suggested with a grimace. "Seth will overreact, I'm sure. Hey, wait, didn't that happen in the U.S.?"

"Yes, which also begs the question of how a convicted criminal got across the border. Convicted in their system and ours."

Jon thought about that for a while.

"I'm confused about something else, but if you can't answer, I won't give you a hard time. It's about that one with the Montreal newspaper president and the murderer who was in the mental hospital. It seems that guy had a rap sheet a mile long *before* he committed the murder. He'd been in and out of prison for about twenty years. Non-magical prison."

"Twenty years?"

"Does LEO get involved if a mage is committing crimes but not using magic to do it?"

"If we know about it, yes. It's still a criminally minded mage, and we want to contain those. But I suppose we might not have become aware of it," Jon admitted. "We're spread pretty thin."

"Well, from my Google searches, I learned that he had gone missing for about three years before the murder and was wanted for breach of probation. Evidence came up during the trial that he had been in and out of some mental hospitals in the States during that time, which they figured explained his disappearance."

"So, you're wondering if the evidence about American mental hospitals was falsified?"

"Yeah. The murder would fit the pattern if his absence for three years was really because he was already a convict in our system before," Natalie said. "I doubt LEO would have put him in an American mental hospital if they'd arrested him in Canada, would they?"

"Probably not," Jon said.

Natalie noticed, however, that he carefully did not confirm or deny her assumption about an initial arrest.

"And he allegedly committed suicide in a small town in BC *after* he, um, escaped from the mental hospital." She made air quotes with her fingers as she said *escaped*, and Jon's lips twitched.

"Which suggests that he was taken out of LEO's hands twice," Natalie added. Jon's face sobered. He was silent for a moment.

"Our mastermind has a vivid imagination, that's for sure," Jon commented with a sigh. "All of these deaths are so different, no wonder nobody saw a pattern. Several of them don't even look like foul play."

Natalie was suddenly struck by a horrible thought which she ruthlessly suppressed, suggesting airily that it was time to get Jon on his way to Switzerland. Judging by the look of surprise and disappointment that flashed briefly across his face, it was evident that he had expected to spend the night and go overseas in the morning, but he didn't say anything. Natalie pretended not to notice and concentrated on building the gateway to a destination further than she had ever previously tried. She felt the drain on her magical energies as the gateway sought its end point, and she closed her eyes to concentrate. Once it latched on to the correct location, it became easier to build the rest of the structure. She smiled as she opened her eyes and saw the familiar courtroom, though it was now shrouded in shadow.

"I did it!"

"You didn't know if you could?"

"Well, I've never gone that far before."

"You're sure it's safe?"

"If it was beyond my reach, it wouldn't even have opened. Why don't you throw your bag across first if you're worried?"

With a shrug, Jon tossed his gym bag through the gateway and watched it skid across the highly polished floor, until it was stopped by the front of the raised platform where the Arch-Mage had sat.

Jon put his hands on both sides of Natalie's face and kissed her deeply. She felt her concentration waver and had to end the kiss.

"I'll see you soon, Sir Galahad."

Jon laughed at the reference and stepped through the gateway, waving jauntily at her from the other side as he went to collect his bag. Natalie blew him a kiss and collapsed the gateway.

Then she sank into her armchair. The smile slid off her face as she contemplated the thought that had popped into her head moments ago.

Jon had described the mastermind as having a vivid imagination, and his choice of words recalled his description of his own abilities when she had first met him: "I can be anything I can visualize. And I've got a vivid imagination."

What if …?

While she wanted to just immediately reject the awful possibility, she couldn't help but reflect that Jon might quite possibly have more practice at coercive magic than anyone else in the world, given that he likely used it on virtually every prison break that he did, as well as potentially other times during the course of his duties. Though he had clearly been desperately short on sleep when she had first met him, he had easily re-established the coercion when the prisoner did not want to go through the gateway, making it look effortless.

When she had initially felt reluctant to tell Chief Turner about her suspicions, since the mastermind clearly had the ability to alter prison records to cover up the missing fugitives, she had assumed that an ordinary LEO would not have access to those records. But how hard would it be, really, for someone who could turn into absolutely anything, including smoke or a fly on the wall, to get someone else's password and get into the system anonymously?

Had she, in fact, revealed her suspicions to the most dangerous person of all? The fragile new relationship had seemed like the first good thing to happen in her life for some time. What if it turned out that he was worming his way into her life in order to figure out how to get rid of her in a way that did not raise suspicions?

Chapter 21

Natalie and Raj got out of a cab near a side entrance to the elegant building that housed the offices of the College of Legalists as well as some courtrooms for the use of the provincial appeals court. Several police officers were standing in front of the doorway. They asked for identification as the two approached.

"What? Why are we being asked for identification?" Natalie demanded.

"Oh, you're the m—um, the lawyer for the hearing, right?" one of the officers said. "The College of Legalists has asked that the public be excluded from the hearing. It's a bit of a media circus." She tilted her head to one side, wordlessly indicating the wrought iron fence that started a few yards away from them, separating the sidewalk from the front of the building and also enclosing a front grass-covered area. Natalie's mouth dropped open as she saw a large crowd of people near the fancy gate with its ornate curlicues that opened onto the pathway leading to the grand front entrance. Several were holding placards, though she could not read the slogans from this distance. It was clear, though, that the line of police officers at that gate had to remain vigilant to keep the crowd away from the building.

"Oh my God," Natalie muttered. "Yes, we're the two members for the hearing." Without further ado, she pulled out her driver's license, but the officer barely glanced at it as she waved the two of them through.

"I don't believe this. Any of it," she muttered to Raj. "When did my life turn into such an insane spectacle? Do you realize the first newspaper article came out two and a half months ago? Less than three months for my whole life to be shot to hell."

"No kidding," he agreed, looking sideways at her. It was impossible not to notice that her face was pale and there were dark shadows under her eyes, visible in spite of her makeup. He knew that she had been to the office only twice since their attack, once for the meeting interrupted by their arrest and a second time when she had negotiated her provisional resignation. But the time off clearly had not been spent relaxing; she was probably more stressed than he was.

Raj was cautiously optimistic that the College hearing would be thrown out and that the assault charge against them would also be dismissed. If that happened, there was a good chance his career would be salvaged. But Natalie had no such assurance. Even if all of this went away, it was beyond obvious that her career at Mason Sullivan was over, and the odds that she would be able to get a job elsewhere as a lawyer were slim. He had thought he had experienced prejudice as a young non-white lawyer, but it was nothing compared to the vitriol he had heard directed at Natalie. He was deeply ashamed of his own thoughtless antimage comments of the past.

He had felt even guiltier after he had experienced Natalie's memory stone of the attack on them and had come to understand how guilty she had felt at having accidentally deflected the bullet that had hit him. He certainly didn't blame her for that. It was clear that she knew full well what the consequences would be to becoming publicly known as a mage, and she had done it anyway to save his life.

On Monday, he had been personally served at home with a Notice stating that the College of Legalists hearing was to be held on Friday. Furious at the repeated shortening of appropriate deadlines, Raj had spent several days with Natalie at her condo preparing for the hearing. Natalie had clearly been pleasantly surprised when Raj had arrived with Susan Wildman in tow on the second day.

Susan had informed her bluntly that she was going to be representing both of them and that she wasn't taking no for an answer. Natalie had tried to argue anyway, which did not surprise Raj in the slightest. He had long ago realized that while Natalie was a great friend and an excellent person to work with, she was incredibly stubborn and totally unwilling to rely on anyone, ever. He wondered how that would work out with the new guy she was dating. None of the men she had dated before had seemed to last very long, as far as he was aware, which was a good part of the reason he had never asked her out himself, though he had sometimes thought about it.

The cop seemed like a decent guy, although it had been obvious there were some things he didn't want to talk about in front of the non-mages in the group. Initially, Raj had found that irritating, but he hadn't been too comfortable once Natalie and her sister had started explaining some more things about the mage world. He had reflected that perhaps it was just as well that Jon had not been very forthcoming.

He had been startled when Susan had asked to experience Natalie's memory stone of the attack after Natalie had mentioned that she had made one, and an explanation had ensued about how memory stones worked. Raj had screwed up his courage to request the same, even though his first experience with a memory stone had been terrifying. Natalie's stone had also been alarming, particularly when the gun appeared, but somehow it was not quite as emotional, perhaps because Natalie had practically been in a state of shock. That had made the experience slightly easier to take, and it had certainly felt peculiar seeing the same events he had personally experienced from a different perspective. On the other hand, it felt incredibly intrusive, feeling his colleague's raw emotions.

"There's Susan," he pointed out, seeing the senior lawyer standing in the shadow of an interior archway and waiting for them.

"I still can't believe you're risking your career for me," Natalie told Susan as they came within hearing distance.

"Not this again," Susan responded, rolling her eyes. "I told you, those morons are not seeing the bigger picture here." She nodded toward a small group of senior partners of Mason Sullivan approaching the courtroom from the opposite direction. Those who caught sight of their small group looked away rather than meet their eyes. "It's like being back in elementary school, isn't it?"

Raj sighed at the blatant hostility he had seen repeatedly since their return to Toronto.

"Remind me again of the bigger picture?" Natalie asked drily.

"The Notice of Application was filed against Mason Sullivan, the whole firm," Susan pointed out. "Just because they're focusing on you two now, since you were deemed to have admitted that you're both mages, doesn't mean the Notice doesn't still name the whole firm. The Notice of Investigation alleges that the firm, or someone within it, was assisting people to escape from jail. If they think they can pin it all on you as a scapegoat and walk away without consequences, they're completely blind. I happen to know that permission has been granted to reporters from several major media outlets to be in attendance today."

"What?"

"No cameras," she clarified. "The public is excluded from this hearing, except for the media people and witnesses. The rest of the room is exclusively reserved for College members, and not just from Mason Sullivan. But this story is front page news. Whatever happens here today is going to be widely discussed, and it's in my best interests, in the best interests of the whole firm, to show that the allegations are purely circumstantial, that the haste and changes to procedure have compromised the neutrality of the process, and that it's all a load of prejudicial bullshit. Hanging you out to dry is *not* going to achieve that."

"There is that," Natalie agreed. "But you're a member of the firm too, and a partner even."

"It is what it is." Susan shrugged. "I do actually intend to try to show that Mason Sullivan has done its best to step up and respond in spite of the short deadlines. This way, we shift the negative publicity to the College and off us. Whether or not that works is probably going to depend entirely on if Phillip Mastersen can manage to hide his true colours as a total bigot."

"Yeah, good luck with that," Raj said. "I'm not all that confident he's even gonna try."

"Whatever happens today, I want you to know that I am grateful for your support," Natalie said quietly. "Both of you. It means a lot."

"You were right from the beginning," Raj said grimly. "If everyone had worked together instead of trying to defend themselves by pointing fingers at everyone else, we would be in a way better position right now."

Raising her chin, Natalie ignored the hostile glares from some of those already seated as she walked into the courtroom with Raj on one side and Susan on the other.

She recognized several of the people present as lawyers from other firms. There was also a contingent of strangers with notepads or tablets in the third and fourth rows whom she suspected were the media representatives. Natalie felt a pang of disappointment as she looked around the room, realizing that she had hoped Jon might be present.

It had apparently taken him until Tuesday to do whatever he had done in Pakistan. She knew he had been successful, but she had not asked for details, in light of the official warning he had already received.

When he had texted her, she had had to tell him that she couldn't manage to build a gate to Pakistan; it seemed that Switzerland was her absolute limit. She had had a strange kind of headache after sending him that far and had felt unable to do even very minor magic until the following day.

In fact, since both Susan and Raj were at her condo, it might be many hours before she could gate him back at all. He had told her not to worry about it, and she hadn't heard from him again that day, to her chagrin. Her texts to him later had not received a response, but the following morning, he had apologized for his silence, telling her that he had actually hopped on a flight from London instead, after getting to London by portal. He had been on the plane with his phone turned off when she had sent her texts. When she had told him the hearing had been bumped up to Friday, he had sworn colourfully, but then told her there were some things he needed to take care of. He had promised to be there if he possibly could. Of course, there was a chance he was present. She sent out a mental call just in case. Her heart sank when there was no response.

Though she had kept wondering, ever since he left, about the possibility of Jon being her suspect, she had finally told herself that if he were, it was already too late: she had told him everything she knew. And really, what were the odds that he was? Just as with the evidence in this College hearing, the reality was not that she had any solid reason to suspect him. It was only that she didn't have certain proof of an alibi. She had firmly told herself to stop stressing about it. She had enough real stress to deal with without manufacturing more.

Natalie strode up the centre aisle to take her place at the table at the front of the room for the member being tried by the tribunal. Susan and Raj had preceded her and were standing by the two chairs at the defence table. Susan signalled to a court staff member standing nearby and asked if a third chair could be brought in. She placed a notepad and two pens on the table in front of her, together with the 14-page document outlining the allegations being made against Mason Sullivan, as the man left by a door at the front of the courtroom in search of a chair. He was back almost immediately, having evidently found one just outside. Raj grinned as he directed the man to place the chair at the short edge of the table.

"Why don't you sit there?" Raj suggested to Natalie. "Then you have a perfectly valid reason to sit at the end of the table, where you can watch Mastersen turn purple every time Susan makes the point that the Notice of Investigation names the whole firm and has never been revised to name just you and me," he pointed out. "Plus with you off to one side, we're making it clear we are not treating you as the primary accused."

Natalie's lips twitched in amusement as she pulled the spare chair up to the side of the defence table.

Two College investigators entered and went to the prosecutor's table. Natalie saw that one of the prosecuting investigators was Meredith Baxter, the woman who had interviewed her at her office, though she did not recognize the other.

The court clerk asked everyone to stand, and then he held open the door at the front of the courtroom. Three people filed in and took their places at the judge's elevated dais. Natalie knew that the arbiters of the hearing were from among the lawyers elected by all Ontario lawyers to the governing board of the legal profession, known as benchers.

Yesterday, Susan had told them who the three benchers would be, and they had studied their bios. All three were known to be highly conservative. Presumably they would not have stood for election as benchers if they did not feel strongly about ensuring the integrity and respect of the profession. But if they disliked mages as much as Meredith Baxter evidently did, it was unclear whether their opinion on ethics would support the investigators' position or would be helpful to the defence in light of the way that procedure had been compromised and timelines compressed at several points.

The position of chair, in the centre of the head table, was taken by Sarah Morrison, a retired judge before whom Natalie had once appeared. On that occasion, Natalie had found her to be a fair but intimidating moderator, absolutely intolerant of any improper conduct, including ringing cellphones or the slightly snide comment her opponent had made to her. Natalie rechecked her phone to ensure that it was powered completely off. Even a vibrating sound would elicit a negative reaction from the former judge if it was audible.

To Ms. Morrison's left was the youngest of the three benchers, a woman in her late thirties who had only recently been admitted to partnership at another large Toronto firm. She worked in the area of family law for the most part and had a good track record of getting combative ex-spouses to mediate.

The man on the right was older than the judge. Thomas Merrifield was a sole practitioner for whom there was little information beyond what he had submitted for his election as a bencher.

Once the three benchers were in position, Ms. Morrison, in the centre of the head table, nodded at the investigators and the three lawyers at the defence table, who each took their seats.

"Today's proceeding is a disciplinary hearing concerning Natalie Ann Benson and Rajit Hardeep Naresh, barristers and solicitors of the Province of Ontario and members of the College of Legalists. You are Ms. Benson, I presume?" Ms. Morrison spoke directly to Natalie.

"I am," she replied, standing up.

"And evidently you are Mr. Naresh?" She nodded at Raj. "Your representative is Ms. Wildman?"

"Yes, Your Honour," Susan responded, standing to do so. "I am Susan Wildman, also of Mason Sullivan, and I am representing both Ms. Benson and Mr. Naresh. As you are presumably aware, we were given permission yesterday to conduct the hearings for these two members, which have been prioritized over the investigation of the rest of the firm, simultaneously, given that they are identical allegations based on exactly the same evidence, so far as we have been informed."

There was a flurry of low-voiced commentary from the audience, which subsided as the Chair swept a frowning glance across the crowd.

"That is correct, Ms. Wildman," the retired judge said. "However, although I was a judge, for today's proceeding, it is appropriate to address me as Madam Chair."

"Thank you, Madam Chair."

Ms. Morrison next addressed the two people seated at the prosecutor's table.

"Ms. Baxter, Mr. Carmichael. You may make your opening statement."

Meredith Baxter stood up. Natalie reflected that she looked even more prim and disapproving than she had the day of the interview at her office. She was wearing a high-necked white blouse with a prissy lace collar. She perched her thick black-rimmed glasses on the end of her nose as she picked up a sheet of paper. Natalie reflected that if she just updated her hairstyle and wardrobe, she would probably look 20 years younger.

"This hearing concerns allegations that certain persons within the firm of Mason Sullivan are believed to have assisted criminals from evading arrest or escaping jail. Evidence has narrowed those suspicions to these two members in particular. The request to hold their two hearings simultaneously, received late yesterday, was made on the basis that this matter has proceeded with undue haste. The College wishes to note that the expedited process was authorized as a result of the two members' failure to co-operate with the investigation. Ms. Benson refused to answer questions during her first interview and abruptly terminated it, and both members had disappeared at the time of the second."

Natalie sighed inwardly at that summary. It did look bad that she had stormed out of that first interview, and a migraine headache was not much use as an excuse. But then Meredith Baxter knew that she had been in court all morning and would not have had a chance to actually see the Notice of Application even if she had been aware, at that point, that one had been served. It would be hard to prove that her questions had been deliberately misleading, but Natalie had genuinely believed she had been asking solely about the two newspaper articles.

"Nobody at Mason Sullivan was aware of their whereabouts, and nobody had received any contact from them," Meredith Baxter continued in a prim tone. Natalie felt a slow burn of anger in her stomach at that comment. She knew that the hospital had contacted the firm one day after the attack, looking for Raj's family's contact information, so clearly someone at the firm had had knowledge of their situation.

"Such behaviour is not likely to provide reassurance of ethical and respectable practice. Furthermore, both of these two members were arrested late last week, charged with assault causing grievous bodily harm. Having persons charged with such serious crimes practising law is detrimental to the whole profession. Where the public is deemed to be at risk, the College has an ethical obligation to proceed more expeditiously. Though the members allege that they were victims rather than attackers, the judge did not dismiss the charges and, in fact, set Ms. Benson's bail at $100,000. I have here a copy of the arrest warrant for the two members, which outlines the charges, and a copy of the judge's reasons at the bail hearing, which includes a summary of the allegations made by the plaintiff. I wish to mark these documents as exhibits 1 and 2."

The court clerk stamped the documents to mark their entry into the record and passed them up to the judge's bench for the three benchers to peruse. A second copy was handed to Susan.

Natalie bent her head, hoping to hide the fury that was probably clearly displayed on her face. She had been attacked, punched and kicked, and had had someone attempt to shoot her, and yet *she* was being described as a person who put the public at risk? Her career was going to crash and burn on the basis of prejudice and outright lies, and it seemed like there wasn't a thing she could do about it. Furthermore, the trial on the bogus assault charges had not yet taken place, but because she had had to post bail, the College investigator was essentially suggesting that she was guilty until proven innocent.

"The College of Legalists regulates the entire legal profession," Meredith continued. "Our aim is to maintain those in the profession in a position of high regard and respect by policing ethical violations. When our members land on the front page of every major newspaper in the city, having clearly been involved in significant violence, this is detrimental to every lawyer in the province. I would like to mark articles dated June 7 from the *Toronto Sun*, the *National Post* and the *Globe and Mail* as exhibits 3, 4 and 5."

Natalie leaned forward as copies of the newspaper articles were placed in front of Susan, and Susan pushed them toward her. Natalie's mouth fell open as she saw that the first one showed a picture of her attacker sprawled on the ground, a pool of blood on the pavement beside him. Natalie instantly realized that the blood was, in fact, Raj's and that this picture was likely taken shortly after she and Raj had disappeared. Her attacker must have posed for maximum effect. The headline read, "Violent Magical Attack at City Hall." She had read the articles from the other papers but had not previously seen this picture.

The other two were not quite so graphic, but both showed her attacker looking like he had been the victim, as he was alleging. Naturally, none of the photos actually showed any wound that would account for the large quantity of blood. Interestingly, the second attacker was visible in one of the pictures, which Natalie pointed out to Raj, but no gun was visible. The man simply appeared to be one of the crowd of onlookers.

The Chair next invited Susan to make her own opening statement.

Susan strode to the front of the room and turned so that she could be seen by the audience and the three benchers. Natalie reflected that there was a sharp difference between the two representatives. Susan was dressed in a designer suit with impeccably coiffed hair and polished nails. The position she had taken made her easily visible to the whole room, and her demeanour exuded confidence. She did not consult any notes as she presented her summary in a measured tone, easy for the whole room to hear.

"The Notice of Investigation prepared by the College references 15 lawsuits or files in which Mason Sullivan has been involved and which also involve a missing fugitive. In all but one case, the fugitive was on the other side; there was only one in which the fugitive was the party being represented by Mason Sullivan.

"The 15 matters represent virtually every different area of law practised within Mason Sullivan, including corporate, family law, estate administration, litigation and real estate. Only two were matters of commercial fraud litigation, which is the area of law in which both Ms. Benson and Mr. Naresh practise.

"The facts linking Mason Sullivan to the missing fugitives are circumstantial and vague. There is no particular reason to focus on the two fraud matters or on these two members in particular, beyond the fact that it has become known that Ms. Benson is a mage. That became public knowledge as a result of a violent attack that took place on June 6. It is true that one of the two men who attacked Ms. Benson and Mr. Naresh has alleged that he was the victim and not the attacker. We will be presenting evidence that contradicts that position.

"The justice system which we all strive to work for has always operated on the principle of innocent until proven guilty. These members have not been found guilty. I submit that suspending them on the basis of unproven allegations was inappropriate and unethical. Using those unproven allegations to speed up the process and give them even less time to organize their defence is even more so.

"The Notice makes no specific allegations about magery; it is merely a speculation put forward by the media that mages are involved with the missing fugitives, or that those fugitives are mages themselves. Thus, the fact that Ms. Benson is a mage is entirely irrelevant. Mr. Naresh is not a mage but was not given an opportunity to respond to the Request to Admit. His failure to respond resulted in a deemed admission that he is a mage, which is not true."

Susan went on to summarize the timeline of the College's investigation, pointing out the shortened deadlines and changes to standard procedures at several points. As she had planned, she referenced it being an investigation of the entire firm many times, having nothing to do with magery, and Natalie noticed Phillip Mastersen's face getting darker each time she did so. She questioned the propriety of a Request to Admit being a mage, referencing the language in the Charter of Rights and Freedoms forbidding discrimination on a variety of grounds.

"Finally, I would like to advise the court of some statistics I obtained from the Royal Canadian Mounted Police." At this point Susan did step across to the table and pick up a bound report bearing the crest of the federal police organization as she continued. "There are currently over 700 wanted persons in Canada, and 180 of these are from the area within approximately a one-hour drive of Toronto, namely, Hamilton to Oshawa. A total of 147 of those fugitives are not prison escapees but people who have not been arrested, being both those who have not been found and also some parolees who have missed appointments with their probation officers. Clearly there is no particular need for an accomplice, magical or otherwise, to miss a parole appointment. Of the 15 people mentioned in the College's Notice of Investigation, *three* escaped from prison, and one of those was two years ago, so the allegation about public safety is, on two grounds, highly questionable. I wish to have this report marked as an exhibit to these proceedings." She handed two more copies to the court clerk.

Natalie felt like cheering. Susan had managed to sum up all of the weaknesses of the College's case very succinctly. She was struck by the realization that the firm's partner had presented a much better opening statement than she likely would have been able to. She was forced to recognize the validity of Raj's accusation that she never wanted to rely on anyone but herself. That stubbornness was clearly a weakness.

Meredith Baxter called Natalie to the witness stand first. She wore an expression of obvious skepticism as Natalie took an oath to answer all questions truthfully.

Natalie was unsurprised when Meredith immediately launched into questions about Natalie being a mage and alleging that she had denied it during her interview.

"I did not deny it," Natalie responded, keeping her voice neutral. "I stated that it was an inappropriate question, much the same as asking about my religion or my sexual orientation." She remembered that she had also made a snide remark about her bra size, but it was probably best not to bring that up.

"You can, in fact, transport yourself and another person to another location by magic. Is that correct?"

"To some extent, yes."

"To some extent?"

"I did that to save my colleague's life after he was shot. But in fact, I overstressed my abilities to such an extent that I myself was unconscious in hospital for several days."

"What hospital was that?"

"One located in an isolated magical community that is inaccessible to non-mages," Natalie replied.

"A hospital that none of the rest of us can get to, in a town whose very existence is impossible to prove, from which you emerged looking none the worse for wear? Are there records of this alleged hospital stay?"

Before Natalie could respond, Susan stood up.

"Madam Chair, those records have been requisitioned, and we asked that the request be expedited when the date of today's hearing was put forward. We hope to be able to present them later today."

Meredith raised an eyebrow.

"Well, we will have to wait to see if such records are forthcoming," she said in a tone which clearly indicated her disbelief. No doubt she would seek to establish distrust of their genuineness if they did arrive. Natalie wanted to kick herself for not getting copies while she had been in Neekonnisiwin. There was no question she had had plenty of things on her mind, but it would not have been difficult for her to get them. Instead, she had indulged herself with skiing and a romantic weekend.

"The ability to transport people away from the scene could easily be used to assist criminals from getting out of jail," Meredith suggested.

"I doubt it. That spell creates a very bright light, one that's impossible to hide. And even if it were possible, I have never assisted any criminal to get out of jail."

"Does all magic create a visible light?"

"No."

"Ah, just this one then."

Natalie ground her teeth at the obvious inference but did not respond since it was not a question.

"You claim you have never assisted any criminal to escape from jail or evade arrest?"

"That is correct."

"Have you ever used magic in the context of practising law?"

"Not unless you count getting a legal textbook off a high shelf without going looking for a stepladder," Natalie said.

Meredith Baxter then launched into a series of questions about the matters referenced in the Notice of Investigation. Natalie confirmed that after obtaining an Anton Piller order, she had personally attended at the home of the accused in one case and at a business in the other.

"So you met both of those two people in person, prior to their arrest and prior to their respective escapes."

"I met Ms. Johannsen, who escaped from the Niagara Detention Centre, two years ago," Natalie confirmed. "I understand her escape took place four months after I met her. I did not meet Mr. Basman, who escaped from the Maplehurst Correctional Centre this past January. For that APO, I attended at the business address."

"The third escapee involves a matter of mortgage fraud. The fugitive is one Robert Belaccio. Where did you attend law school, Ms. Benson?"

Natalie was taken aback by the peculiar question.

"At the University of Western Ontario."

"In what years?"

"From 2008 to 2011."

"I would like to mark as exhibit 6 a copy of the transcript of Mr. Robert Belaccio, who also attended law school at UWO and also commenced his studies in 2008." Meredith handed another document to the court clerk and a copy to Susan.

Natalie's eyes widened as she suddenly realized what was happening here. She had received information relating to the evidence that the College would be presenting, as was required, but it had only said that the College had information that she or Raj had personally met each of the 15 fugitives at least once. Was she supposed to have known this man who apparently might have been in some of her first-year law school classes in 2008?

"Did you attend the client pre-Christmas event hosted by Mason Sullivan in 2016?"

"Yes."

"Mr. William Goldstein, a client of Mason Sullivan who was later found guilty of mislabelling health food products, was in attendance at that event." Meredith submitted a list of guests and had it marked as an exhibit. Natalie tried to keep her face expressionless as she reflected that that list could only have been sourced from the firm itself. Of course, virtually every partner in the firm and plenty of the other associates would also have been present, so it was ludicrous to suggest that this was more evidence against her, as distinct from anyone else at Mason Sullivan.

"Paragraph 9 of the Notice describes an estate trustee who disappeared, taking with him several million dollars from the estate. The trustee, Geoffrey

Chong, was an employee of Magnetawan Loan and Trust. I understand, Ms. Benson, that your father is also an employee of Magnetawan Loan and Trust?"

"Yes. In their *North Bay* office," Natalie responded. Susan had cautioned her not to add commentary to her answers but to stick to yes and no answers, yet it was hard to do so when such nonsensical allegations were made. Magnetawan was a company with six offices across Ontario, employing hundreds of people.

"Ms. Alicia Thornton was involved in a car accident that also involved a client of Mason Sullivan in 2015. Ms. Thornton was found to have falsified records to exaggerate her injuries and was charged with insurance fraud in 2016. I have here a copy of a transcript of Ms. Thornton's examination for discovery." She handed Natalie a Cerlox-bound transcript, opened to the third page. "It states on page three that you were present, assisting at that examination, Ms. Benson. Is that correct?"

"Yes."

Meredith continued down the list of fugitives mentioned in the Notice. In each case, she had managed to come up with some connection that Natalie had with each person or some indication that they had likely met on at least one occasion. Although some of them were very questionable connections, Natalie nonetheless felt her spirits plummeting as the list continued. She saw the three benchers making notes and carefully scrutinizing documents that Meredith submitted as exhibits. By the time she came to the end of the list, Natalie was beginning to feel like a wrung-out sponge.

She hoped that the ordeal was nearly over when Meredith finished with the last name, alleging that the man who had created fake bank cards by stealing information from an ATM was a member of the same gym that Natalie attended.

"A Request to Admit was served on your office on June 7, which you failed to respond to."

"I was *unconscious*." Natalie bit her lip on the other accusations she wanted to make, knowing that Susan would raise them, but it was hard, particularly in light of the obviously skeptical expression on Meredith's face.

"So we have been told. No further questions."

Meredith turned away from Natalie with an air that suggested that it was a relief to be able to cease interacting with her.

Natalie felt as though she had been attacked all over again, though this time the weapon was words. She remembered the emotions of the New York rape victim from her memory stone, which had made it clear that the trial was almost worse than the attack that had preceded it.

She suspected she would have a hard time cross-examining witnesses in the future, knowing as she now did what it was like to be on the receiving end. But then it seemed extremely unlikely that she would ever again get the opportunity.

Chapter 22

As defence lawyer, Susan had the right to cross-examine Natalie. She began by progressing chronologically from the time of the first newspaper article back at the beginning of May all the way through to the day before the attack at City Hall had taken place.

Since it was standard procedure for all lawyers to enter dockets into the accounting system detailing every billable hour worked with a description of what was done, she had more than adequate documentary evidence showing Natalie's intense work schedule.

She then presented Natalie's time records from the firm's accounting system, which showed that she had either been in court or had docketed hours indicating extremely long days on each of the dates when the three escapees had disappeared from their respective correctional institutions. Since those prisons were in, respectively, Milton, Niagara and Hamilton, all some distance from Toronto, it would have been virtually impossible for Natalie to have been there and also do the work reflected in her accounting records.

The questioning next turned to the interview Natalie had had with Meredith Baxter.

"Did Ms. Baxter provide you with a copy of the Notice of Investigation at that interview?"

"No."

"Did you know that one had been served on the firm?"

"No, not at that point."

"Why did you think Ms. Baxter was there?"

"She told me the College had received a complaint and they were investigating. She went on to ask me about the two newspaper articles. Then she suggested I ought to voluntarily cease practice while the investigation was under way."

"Did Ms. Baxter ask questions about the specific cases referenced in the Notice?"

"No. She never even mentioned a Notice. She asked about the newspaper articles only, specifically the two Anton Pillers that were mentioned in the first one. She speculated that magic might have been used to influence the judge in each case. I offered to provide her with copies of the materials filed in court for each of them, which are voluminous."

"Tell me what happened on June 6 as you were coming back to the office from court."

Natalie described the events of the attack at City Hall, detailing each kick and punch. Her voice shook at several points, particularly as she described her feelings upon seeing Raj on the ground with blood soaking his shirt.

Susan held up the newspaper photograph showing their attacker beside the pool of blood. Having just refreshed her memory of how powerless she had felt that day, Natalie ground her teeth at the sight.

"Could you describe this photo, please?"

"That is one of our two attackers, posing beside Raj's blood, presumably with the intent of making it look like it is his own," she said with a tense jaw.

"Mr. Naresh's blood? How do you know it is his blood?"

Natalie was reminded that the formality of the proceedings required that she refer to people by their surname, and she strove to suppress her anger at the false evidence being used against her.

"The man in the photo might have struck the back of his head when Mr. Naresh shoved him into the wall. Maybe he might have cut his head, I don't know. But I know beyond a sliver of a doubt that if he did cut his head, it wasn't anywhere remotely close to a large enough wound to produce that amount of blood. I also know that Mr. Naresh had to have several blood transfusions to replace all of the blood that he had lost."

Susan asked Natalie about her phone call with Phillip Mastersen and then about the meeting she and Raj had both attended with all the partners upon their return, which had been terminated when both of them had been arrested. On several occasions, the prosecution attempted to object to this line of questioning as being irrelevant, but Susan made it very clear she was establishing how the investigation had proceeded with undue haste, giving neither Natalie nor Raj adequate time to properly respond or defend themselves, in contravention of the procedural rules which applied.

"Ms. Baxter provided evidence suggesting that you might have had an opportunity to meet each of the fugitives named in the Notice of Application. How many do you actually recall meeting?"

"The woman from one of the Anton Pillers and the woman at the examination for discovery that I was assisting at," Natalie said. "I might have met the CEO of the health food company at the Christmas function, but I don't specifically recall."

"None of the others?"

"No."

"Ms. Baxter mentioned that the estate trustee who disappeared with a lot of money from an estate works at the same company as your father. Where does your father work?"

"In North Bay," Natalie replied. Presumably most people in the room knew that North Bay was over 300 kilometres away.

"Does he come to Toronto often?"

"I don't think he's been here in the last 20 years. He hates cities, and his job does not require him to visit the other offices of Magnetawan."

"Could you please tell the court what this document is?"

Natalie looked at the letter Susan handed her, and her mouth fell open as she read it. "It's a letter to Phillip Mastersen from the president of Magnetawan advising that the full amount of the stolen money was sent to them by way of a bank draft shortly after the disappearance of the trustee. It says that the name of the person who drew the bank draft was illegible, and efforts to trace it had led to an anonymous numbered company, which was a dead end."

While Susan marked the letter as an exhibit, Natalie wondered whether LEO was responsible for returning the proceeds of the crime. She also wondered what possible reason there was for Phillip not to have advised the College that that money had been recovered.

"I understand you have a membership at Goodlife Fitness?"

"Yes."

"How often do you work out?"

"Not nearly as often as I should."

"Ms. Baxter produced evidence that Mr. el-Kerawi, the man with the fake bank cards, is a regular member at Goodlife. Had you previously seen this document that Ms. Baxter marked as an exhibit?" Susan held up the exhibit, but it was too far away for Natalie to see clearly.

"I don't think so. I don't know what it is."

"If you do go to the gym, which location do you go to, and when do you tend to go?"

"I always go to the one by Union Station, and usually late at night. Rarely before 9:00 p.m."

"Members check in at Goodlife facilities using a card or key tag with a magnetic strip," Susan explained to the benchers. "This document produced by Ms. Baxter is a computerized record of Mr. el-Kerawi's attendances at the gym in the three-month period prior to his disappearance. Could you please advise the court of what this record shows, Ms. Benson?" She handed Natalie the exhibit, and Natalie's jaw tensed in anger as she read the information which did absolutely nothing to link her to this man.

"It seems this man worked out regularly, on Mondays, Wednesdays and Fridays, at 5:30 in the morning, at the St. Clair and Eglinton facility," Natalie said in a flat voice, reading the information from the printout.

"Contrary to appropriate procedure, the prosecution did not provide the defence with copies of this evidence in advance of today's proceeding," Susan told the benchers in a tight voice. "We were merely informed that they have evidence that either Ms. Benson or Mr. Naresh had opportunities to personally meet each of the fugitives. It would appear that that evidence is flimsy in the extreme. Even if it were not, it does nothing to prove either of these members, or anyone at Mason Sullivan, had anything to do with their disappearance.

"Ms. Baxter mentioned a person who attended law school at UWO, beginning in 2008, the same year that Ms. Benson began law school. Could you please describe this document for the court, Ms. Benson?" She handed Natalie the exhibit submitted by Meredith related to that person, another document that Natalie had not previously seen.

"It is a transcript of marks from his first semester. It looks like he failed three classes and barely scraped a pass mark in two more," Natalie read, her forehead furrowed, not sure where Susan was going with this.

"While I cannot say for sure, not having been given an opportunity to look into it, I would suggest it's a reasonable guess that this man did not finish law school and may, in fact, have dropped out after that first semester. I suspect I would have if my marks were that abysmal," Susan pointed out. "A quick Google search has also told me that there are over 28,000 students at the University of Western Ontario. It is entirely possible that Ms. Benson never even met this man, let alone had an acquaintance with him."

"Could you please describe this document to the court?"

Natalie felt on firmer ground now, having seen this document before. "It is a letter from Mr. James Matheson of the Royal Canadian Mounted Police task force formed to investigate the prison escapes. In it, he states that Ms. Alicia Thornton missed two appointments in a row but has attended her appointments since that date and is no longer considered a missing person."

"Ms. Thornton was the person charged with insurance fraud at whose examination for discovery Ms. Benson assisted. I wish to point out for the court that 12 of the 15 persons named in the College's Notice disappeared or failed to attend parole hearings. They were either out on day passes, or free on bail or on parole. None of these disappearances requires an accomplice. Of the three who actually did escape from jail, Ms. Benson once met one of them, and in fact it was the evidence located by Ms. Benson during the execution of that Anton Piller which resulted in Ms. Johannsen's arrest.

"I have no further questions for Ms. Benson."

Though Susan's examination had been far easier to deal with than Meredith's, Natalie was nonetheless profoundly relieved to be able to leave the stand.

Raj was examined next by the prosecution. It was Mr. Carmichael who conducted his questioning, and it appeared that Susan's masterly handling of the evidence against Natalie had completely undermined Carmichael's confidence. His questioning of Raj was shorter, and Natalie noticed Meredith glowering at her colleague.

Raj admitted to having met the other Anton Piller defendant. He also recalled having met the pro golfer who had been found to have been accepting bribes to lose certain matches, at a firm-sponsored golf tournament, and suspected he might also have met the CEO at the same pre-Christmas event Meredith had mentioned. He had no knowledge of ever having met the other 12 fugitives.

To his visible astonishment, the prosecution produced evidence that the store clerk who had allegedly disappeared with a winning lottery ticket had worked in a convenience store located on the ground floor of the condo building where Raj lived prior to his disappearance. Another car insurance fraudster who had disappeared had rented a condo in the same building as well. A third missing fugitive was known to have regularly attended the mosque at which Raj's older brother was the imam.

Raj had an ability to gaze at a person in a way that managed to make him look like a very old schoolmaster peering disapprovingly over his glasses, even though he didn't wear glasses. Natalie knew from experience how effective it was, and she had to suppress her amusement when she saw the prosecutor reacting to it in exactly the same way as she had on the rare occasions when he had used it on her, when she had overlooked something.

The prosecutor moved on quickly to questions related to the facts of the two cases Raj and Natalie actually had been involved with, and to the attack and the meeting with the firm after their return. Raj's answers were almost exactly the same as Natalie's, except for the point after he had been shot, at which time he had no personal knowledge of the events. He reiterated several times that he was not a mage.

Susan's cross-examination focused mostly on the attack at City Hall, the meeting with the partners and the bail hearing from Raj's perspective. However, she also produced evidence that no claim had ever been made for the grand prize in the particular lottery draw from which the alleged stolen ticket had originated. Since the plaintiff had no proof that she had ever possessed a winning ticket and none had been claimed, no charges had been pressed against the absentee store clerk. Although the police had sought his presence for questioning, he could not technically be called a fugitive in the absence of charges.

Raj acknowledged that he sometimes shopped in the convenience store at the base of his building but said that he did not know the names of its employees. He advised the court that he was not a practising Muslim and did not attend mosque, which fact had caused some dissension within his family.

During the lunch break, Susan disappeared, returning just before it was time to resume the proceedings, giving no explanation for her absence. Her expression was somewhat smug, however, as one of the benchers addressed the room before the proceedings continued.

"Due to an urgent personal appointment, the court has agreed to alter the usual order of the witnesses at this time," Mr. Merrifield said in a low, gravelly voice. Natalie looked over at the prosecution's table curiously and saw that Meredith's face was thunderous. Then she looked back as she saw movement at the back of the room, and her eyes widened as she saw Dr. Sabourin rolling up the aisle. His wheelchair appeared to be moving entirely under its own power, which caused a flurry of murmurs among those close enough to see it. It was even more obvious when the wheelchair hopped up the step to the raised witness podium. Evidently the doctor had decided he was not going to make any effort to hide his magical abilities.

As he was a defence witness, Susan began the questioning.

"Please state your name and describe your background for the court," Susan requested of Dr. Sabourin, after the court clerk had taken his oath to testify truthfully.

"Dr. James Edward Sabourin, medical surgeon, and member of the College of Physicians and Surgeons of British Columbia. I graduated from the Faculty of Medicine, University of British Columbia, in 2008. I interned at the Vancouver General Hospital and then worked there as a critical care physician for six years, until 2015."

Then the doctor's face turned grim. "In 2015 I was involved in a serious car accident in which I lost my arm, broke my spine and ended up in this chair. After my recovery, I wanted to go back to critical care but felt I could better achieve this within a magical community where there would be no bar to my using magic to compensate for my physical disabilities. I have worked at the Neekonnisiwin General Hospital since that time."

"Could you please describe for the court what happened from the time that Mr. Naresh and Ms. Benson arrived at the hospital on June 6?"

"I was not primarily involved in Ms. Benson's initial care, though I became the attending physician later on. Mr. Naresh had clearly experienced ballistic trauma, with a projectile having pierced his upper left ventricle. He was extremely fortunate that the exit wound had not damaged the spine. However, he had lost significant amounts of blood and was going into hypovolemic shock, a condition characterized by inadequate delivery of oxygen to vital organs. I have some photographs here. May I display these?"

"Certainly."

Dr. Sabourin pulled out a photograph of Raj lying on the floor of the emergency department with a widespread bloodstain covering most of his chest and a clear gaping wound. With a casual gesture, the doctor created an enlarged image of the photograph, hanging in mid-air and visible from both sides. A shocked-sounding wave of murmurs swept the audience, although it was unclear how much of the shock was due to the graphic nature of the photograph and how much to the casual display of magic. Natalie glanced at Raj and noticed a distinct pallor had spread over his face as he saw for himself the extent of his injury.

As Dr. Sabourin gave a brief explanation of Raj's treatment and surgery, he produced more pictures, including several of the surgery and one of Raj lying in a hospital bed, hooked up to various monitors and clearly unconscious. All of the photographs looked as though they were taken from the perspective of the surgeon himself, as the doctor could not actually be seen in any of them.

Once Susan confirmed she had finished questioning the doctor, the prosecutor had the opportunity to pose questions to him. If Meredith was flustered by the weakening of her attack on Raj's credibility, it was not evident.

"Is it the practice in your hospital to maintain a medical chart of a patient's progress?"

"I have Mr. Naresh's and Ms. Benson's charts right here," the doctor confirmed, holding up two manila file folders. "However, this is confidential personal medical information. It would be up to Mr. Naresh and Ms. Benson whether they are prepared to allow me to hand over these files."

Susan looked at Raj, who frowned slightly. He stood up to respond, directing his response to the three benchers. "I would prefer that it not be in the public record, but I'm content to have it marked as an exhibit as long as it's kept confidential."

"I feel the same way," Natalie confirmed.

Upon examination, it was evident that the records were kept as meticulously as any non-magical hospital would have done. The prosecutor looked at them only briefly before evidently realizing there was not much to attack there.

Instead, she turned to Raj's surgery. "How can you perform that sort of intricate surgery when you have only one arm and restricted mobility?"

Dr. Sabourin rolled his eyes. "Clearly you are another person who can't see past the wheelchair," he remarked scathingly. "That was my issue with the non-magical medical establishment after my accident. Even without magic, I could have taught. I could have worked in any number of capacities in the hospital, but they just expected me to sit in my chair and rot, as if the loss of an arm made it impossible for me to be a contributing member of society."

Then he made the pens and water glasses on the defence table perform an elaborate dance, which he directed like an orchestra conductor with his one arm. Natalie was shaking with laughter while Raj grinned broadly at the sight. Almost everyone else in the room was visibly tense at the sight.

"How can we be certain those photographs are not Photoshopped?" Meredith snapped.

"Does this look fake to you?" Raj stood up and yanked his shirt up, revealing a pink scar in a neat line, with a ragged line angled toward the upper left where the bullet had entered his chest. Though the scar was faded, it was evident that most of the hair on his chest had been shaved, so the scar was clearly visible. "Why don't you provide proof that the evidence is faked instead of asking us to prove that it's real? In fact, here's a bright idea: How about you provide proof of *any* of your allegations?"

Meredith's face turned pale and then red as she gaped at his chest. Raj spun around so that the benchers saw the scar as well, before tucking his shirt back in and taking a seat.

"Your theatrics are inappropriate, Mr. Naresh," Chairperson Morrison said in a disapproving voice. "However, your point is taken. Unless you can provide any evidence that the photographs are falsified, Ms. Baxter, they are admitted as evidence."

The prosecutor's voice was higher than usual as she squeaked, "No further questions," and collapsed in her seat looking pale. Dr. Sabourin nodded at the occupants of the defence table with a smile as he propelled himself out of the room.

And ... challenge accomplished! Natalie stiffened in shock as she heard the voice in her head.

Jon? What? Are you here?

Yep. Been here all along.

Where? And what challenge are you talking about?

You're sitting on me, he said in a self-satisfied tone. *And since the damsel likes to rescue herself, it's really, really difficult for me to actually help. But I did it.*

Natalie half choked and managed to turn it into a cough, as she reached forward for a glass and the pitcher of water sitting in front of her. Surreptitiously, she dug her fingernails into the leather of the chair she sat on, which was absolutely identical to the chair Raj was using, and was also identical to those for the prosecution.

Ouch, Jon said in a voice filled with laughter.

What did you do?

Well, it's not actually standard practice to take photographs of patients during surgery, or when a critically injured person is bleeding all over the hospital's lobby.

I did think that was a bit odd. Please don't tell me they're faked after all?

Not faked per se.

Jon ...!

I have a friend at the Boston PD who's a visual communicator, an artist and an amateur photographer, Jon said smugly. *He works as a police artist, and he's in high demand because his sketches match the witnesses' recollections incredibly well. Quite some time ago, he perfected the ability to take pictures from a memory stone and convert them to photographs.*

You manufactured *evidence?* Natalie sputtered. She kept her head down since she had a feeling she was not being very successful at keeping her face expressionless during the silent conversation.

Of course not. I just put evidence that would have been acceptable to a magical court into a form that would be acceptable to a non-magical court. You know as well as I do that the doctor's memory stone could not have been fictionalized, he pointed out. *But I rather doubt you could have got those people to experience his memories.*

But …!

You know, Natalie, there's nothing wrong with using your abilities in the course of your work, he pointed out. *There's nothing inherently bad about having magical abilities. It depends how you use them, which is a question of ethics. It's not unethical to convert perfectly viable evidence into another form, as long as you can be absolutely certain you're not altering the facts. I experienced the doctor's memory stone myself. I promise you, that's exactly how Raj looked.*

Well, yes, but—

Look at it this way: If Raj had been treated in a non-magical hospital, there wouldn't have been any doubt cast on his credibility, largely because he'd probably still be there, assuming he hadn't died, Jon pointed out. *The situation only arose because he was treated magically.*

But … Natalie couldn't actually think of an objection; it just seemed somehow wrong.

But nothing. The most persuasive thing that prosecutor pulled out was the idea that you are a violent offender and therefore should not be practising law. The rest of her evidence was about as solid as ice cream on a hot day. Besides, how likely are your attackers to be able to successfully allege that you attacked them when that court sees these photos?

Natalie struggled to reconcile this with her previously unanalyzed opinion that using magic in any way would be completely inappropriate in conducting a trial. Was Jon right? And if not, should she be angry that he had taken these steps without telling her in advance how those photos were created?

Natalie, realizing that she had been zoned out for a while, looked up in surprise as she heard a familiar voice taking the standard oath of truthfulness. Her brother-in-law was on the stand. Dave did not look at her, and when she glanced at Raj questioningly, he shrugged, evidently not having known of this part of the plan either. It occurred to Natalie that if Susan had simply contacted Toronto EMS to ascertain who attended after the shooting, she might very well not even realize that her witness was Natalie's brother-in-law. Natalie struggled with the question of whether or not she ought to reveal this potential conflict of interest.

"I understand that you responded to the 9-1-1 call on June 6 about a possible shooting at City Hall?"

"That is correct."

"Could you please describe the nature of the injuries that you saw?"

"There were two people who claimed to have been attacked, a Mr. Michael Stanton and a Mr. Donald van Maaris. Mr. Stanton had a small contusion on the back of his head which was not bleeding. Mr. van Maaris had a large bruise on his chin and some abrasions on one elbow. The sleeve of his jacket on that arm was torn, as well. I cleaned up the elbow, but there really wasn't much that needed treatment."

"Did you see this picture in the newspaper the following day?" Susan held up the newspaper photo showing Stanton with the pool of blood. Dave snorted.

"Yeah, I saw it. That was not his blood. I don't know where it came from, but it definitely wasn't his."

"Did you see the blood when you were there?"

"Sure, you couldn't miss it. There was loads."

"It looked fresh?"

"I didn't examine it closely, but it looked pretty fresh to me."

"Can you suggest what kind of injury might result in that quantity of blood?"

The prosecution immediately objected to the nature of the question, which called for speculation, and Susan rephrased.

"Would that kind of puddle of blood be consistent with a gunshot wound?"

"Potentially, yes," Dave said. "Or maybe a multiple stabbing or something."

Meredith declined to pose any questions to the witness, and Dave was dismissed. He did not look at Natalie and gave no indication that he knew either of the defendants.

As Meredith called Phillip Mastersen to the stand, Natalie leaned over to Susan and said, "Did you know that was my brother-in-law?"

Susan's look of astonishment was priceless. "Who, the EMS guy?"

"Yeah."

"I had no idea. I wonder if I should disclose it."

"Considering the BS nature of half the College's evidence, and the fact that they didn't properly disclose lots of it to us? I'd say don't bother," Raj suggested. "You genuinely didn't know, and Natalie and I didn't know you were going to be calling him. Good job getting the doctor, by the way."

"He contacted me during the lunch break, believe it or not," Susan remarked. "Apparently he's got a daughter here and was already in Toronto for a visit. Otherwise, no way would he have been able to get here so fast."

Natalie did not meet Raj's eye as Susan said that, knowing full well that Dr. Sabourin could easily have travelled to Toronto in a very short time period. Raj was now aware of that fact too, but he didn't enlighten Susan either.

Was that your doing too? she asked silently of her chair.

I might have had something to do with it, Jon admitted.

As a result of this exchange, Natalie had failed to pay attention to the beginning of the prosecution's examination of Phillip Mastersen. Natalie only heard him admit that he had accepted service of the Request to Admit on behalf of the whole firm and had called a meeting of all the people named in the Notice to inform them of it. He was asked whether Natalie or Raj had been at that meeting, and he confirmed that they were not. She was unsurprised that both question and answer were phrased as if to imply that they had chosen not to bother attending.

It suddenly occurred to her that she had not even had an e-mail on her phone telling her about that meeting, which she ought to have had if the invitation had, in fact, been properly sent out to all the people named in the Notice. She scribbled a note to Susan, who smirked and handed her a hard copy of an e-mail from a folder of documents she was planning to enter into evidence. It was the invitation to the meeting, dated June 7, and it clearly was not sent to either Natalie or Raj. Once again, Natalie had reason to be grateful that Susan had volunteered to manage the defence.

It was the other investigator, Justin Carmichael, who was questioning Phillip at this point, and his questioning was brief. Once again, Natalie noticed Meredith glowering at her fellow investigator as he terminated the questioning. Presumably she felt that the managing partner was a better source of evidence than Mr. Carmichael had.

Susan began her cross-examination.

"Did you receive a phone call from Ms. Benson on Tuesday, June 12?"

"I did."

"During that telephone call, did you inform her of the Request to Admit that had been served on the firm, naming both her and Mr. Naresh, among others, the previous Thursday?"

"I don't recall."

"Did you inform her of the deadline to respond prior to the time when that deadline had expired? Or that all the others named, including yourself, had put in a response already?"

"I don't recall."

"Do you happen to recall taking an oath to tell the whole truth and nothing else?" Susan asked snidely.

Natalie definitely heard a few smothered snickers at that question among the audience, and she struggled to keep her own face straight.

"Of course I do. I don't precisely recall that whole telephone conversation."

"But you cannot say for sure that you did tell her about the Request to Admit or about the deadline to respond?"

"No."

"I have here a copy of an e-mail sent by you. Could you please read that aloud?"

Phillip read the e-mail inviting the recipients to a meeting to discuss the Request to Admit, scheduled for June 8.

"Are either Ms. Benson or Mr. Naresh on the list of recipients of that e-mail?"

Phillip was silent for a moment as he read the names, and then he frowned.

"Mr. Mastersen?"

"It appears that they were missed."

"So they were not invited to a meeting to discuss responding to a document that named them, nor advised that you had accepted service on their behalf?"

Phillip struggled with that for a moment before saying, "No, it appears not," in a barely audible voice.

"Did you inform the College of Legalists once you became aware that both Ms. Benson and Mr. Naresh were in hospital? Or instruct anybody else to do so?"

"No."

"Did you inform the College that they had not been made aware of the Request to Admit?"

"No."

Phillip's face was clearly registering his annoyance with the line of questioning, but he snapped his mouth shut after his one-word answer.

"Did you inform Ms. Benson that the best thing she could do for Mason Sullivan would be to resign?"

"During that call? No."

A clear mutter arose from the audience at that point, prompting the lead bencher to bang her gavel again and give a warning look.

"At any time after that call?" Susan amended her question drily.

"Fine, yes, I did say that, and it is just as true now as it was then."

"Why is that?"

"Because she is a mage." Phillip's tone was acidic.

"Is it against the law to be a mage?"

"It is unethical not to disclose that to her partners."

Natalie suppressed the urge to smirk. Clearly, she was not the only one who forgot to stick to yes and no answers under pressure. She always advised witnesses to ensure they answered only the question and did not volunteer additional information, but people almost always started volunteering info after a while. It rarely benefitted the witness's side.

"Is that written in the Rules of Professional Conduct?"

"No."

"Is there any requirement in the Rules of Professional Conduct to disclose personal information including race, religion, sexual orientation or magical ability?"

"No."

Susan turned to the table and picked up several papers from the folder she had prepared of documents to be introduced as evidence.

"I have here four performance reviews written by James Behrman, the partner to whom Ms. Benson reports, for each of the last four years. Is it the practice of the Management Committee to review performance reviews of all associates and initial them?"

"Yes."

"As managing partner, you are in fact head of the Management Committee?"

"Yes."

"How long have you held that position?"

"Four years."

"Are these your initials?"

Susan laid the four papers in a row on the podium in front of Phillip. His eyes flicked as if he were attempting to quickly read the reviews, which Natalie knew were almost uniformly glowing.

"Yes."

"Did you ever raise any issue with these reviews, either with Mr. Behrman or with Ms. Benson herself?"

"I don't recall any. I don't think so."

Susan presented four more reviews, for Raj, and Phillip confirmed having seen and initialled those also.

"I wish to submit these performance reviews as exhibits," Susan spoke to the benchers. "You may review them at your leisure, but I can assure you that they are highly positive reviews." The papers were stamped with identification marks listing them as exhibits and added to the folder with the photographs, the medical records and the docket entries. Reflecting on the nature of the exhibits, Natalie had the sudden thought that the defence's exhibits were all far more substantive than the prosecution's documents.

"Have you ever been aware, prior to receipt of this Notice of Investigation, of any issue of unethical practice on Ms. Benson's part?"

"I was never aware prior to this that she was a mage."

"That was not my question. Were you ever aware of any unethical practice?"

"I was not aware of any."

"Have you ever been aware, prior to—"

Susan's question cut off as a loud disturbance was heard in the hallway at the back of the room. Suddenly the door burst inward and a dishevelled man came running into the room, two police officers in pursuit.

One of the officers had a visible head wound, though he was ignoring the blood leaving a scarlet trail down the side of his face. Natalie noticed that the holster at his side was empty.

The other officer had her gun drawn and was pointing it at the man in front of her. Natalie gasped as she realized that the dishevelled man also held a gun, and he was aiming it directly at Phillip Mastersen.

Phillip dove to the floor. Natalie heard screams and belatedly realized that she was one of the ones screaming. What kind of insanity had taken over her life that she should see a loaded gun twice in less than a month?

Suddenly her scream died in her throat as she realized that the man whose face was twisted with fury had a bright yellow glow around his head, pulsing like a heartbeat. The sight froze her incipient panic, and her mind shot into high gear.

She jumped to her feet, suspecting that Jon might need to change form, though even as she thought of that, she spared a thought for how the benchers and others in the room would react if her chair were to suddenly turn into a person.

Her arm shot upward, fingers splayed, and the gun sailed out of the man's hand and up to the ceiling. This time, she was very careful to ensure that the business end was pointing away from any person.

Even as it sailed upward, however, the gun went off with a deafening bang, and the screams were renewed as the ornate chandelier that hung from the centre of the ceiling exploded in a shower of crystals. People cowered, covering their heads as shards rained down on them. Even in the midst of her panic, Natalie noticed that the sound of the gunshot was far louder in the enclosed room than the other one had been in the open air of Nathan Phillips Square. Her ears were ringing.

People scrambled to protect themselves, some climbing over the backs of the benches, and a shouting mass of people crammed the doorway, trying to get out. Two of the benchers had also fallen to the floor, though the retired judge still sat in her chair, her face furious at the panic that had erupted in the room.

Natalie, I need your help. She heard the terse command in her head. *I need to block the coercion and block his own magic, but I can't get a grip.*
What do you want me to do?

With one hand still above her head, holding the gun out of reach, she grabbed her silver pen off the table and released the illusion, revealing the deep blue prism. She heard Susan gasp, but she ignored that as she held the stone out toward the man in the aisle, who appeared to be partly frozen into immobility but also was evidently successfully struggling against the spell.

Remember that time you built a wall around your mind to keep Constance out? Jon said. *See if you can do that around his mind.*

Not sure if it would even be possible to do that with someone else, Natalie nonetheless concentrated as hard as she could on visualizing a brick wall, starting at the man's feet and rapidly building upward.

With a gasp, Natalie realized that she recognized the shooter. He was the same man who had been in her condo, having just been taken from the Don Jail, by Jon and his partner the first day she had met Jon. Lassiter was the name that came to mind after a few moments.

Lassiter's slight degree of movement was now halted, and he was standing in a strange position as if frozen, his hands still positioned as if he were holding the gun. Natalie felt a wave of exhaustion threatening, but she gritted her teeth and concentrated on completing the wall.

The police officer closest to Lassiter had just bounced off an invisible barrier that surrounded him and was yelling something that could not be heard over the din of the room. Natalie almost lost control of the magic at that point, not having previously realized her wall would actually represent a solid, albeit invisible, barrier.

"*Everybody be silent!*" The retired judge rose to her feet and shouted with more volume than Natalie would have thought the older woman capable of. There was a reduction in the noise level, though many people were still scrambling to get out and clearly too panicked to register anything.

Natalie repeated words that Jon dictated to her. "Officers, the suspect is contained, but there is some outside interference going on. The barrier is blocking that."

Abruptly, just as her invisible wall reached to the top of Lassiter's head, the bright yellow glow stopped pulsing and dimmed down to the same murky yellow taint that Natalie had seen after Jon had released his coercive spell in her condo several weeks earlier. She had been sensing intense struggle from Jon, which now eased.

With startling abruptness, Lassiter collapsed, his eyes rolling up into his head.

Can I drop the wall now? she asked Jon. She was breathing heavily and felt sweat soaking her hair.

I think so. I've got a grip on him now, Jon responded. *His magic is blocked, so even if he comes to, there's not much our mastermind can do.*

The room was in shambles. Broken glass littered the floor in the centre of the room. Lassiter lay unconscious, partly on top of the pile, and would doubtless have sustained cuts. Phillip still crouched behind the witness podium, his usually florid face pale and his breathing harsh.

Natalie felt a wave of weakness wash over her even as she allowed the invisible wall to disappear. She kept the gun high up in the air, however, just to be safe.

A few of the people who had scrambled to leave the room were still in the hallway. Natalie saw one of the senior partners peering around the door but keeping the solid wood between himself and possible danger. Several more people, who had not left the room, began to get shakily to their feet. Nobody spoke.

"It was her!" The sudden shriek caused Natalie to jump. Meredith Baxter had clambered to her feet, her hair coming out of its pins and her glasses askew on her nose. "She staged this whole thing to scare us all into dropping the investigation!"

"Be silent, Ms. Baxter," the lead bencher snapped.

Meredith completely ignored the retired judge, continuing to shriek increasingly incoherent accusations at Natalie.

Natalie ignored her, but she saw the judge gesture from the corner of her eye. A massively built security guard wearing a courthouse security pass strode up to Meredith, grasped her arm and led her out of the room.

The police officer with the bleeding head wound moved toward the unconscious prisoner, careful not to block the aim of his partner, who still had her gun trained on the suspect. The first officer rolled the man over and secured his wrists with handcuffs.

"I apologize for the disturbance, Your Honour," he spoke to the judge, raising one hand to wipe the dripping blood off his head before it obscured his vision.

"Is that your gun?" the judge asked, looking upward at the weapon still floating up near the remains of the chandelier.

"Yes, Your Honour. May I have it back?"

He looked at Natalie, a clear expression of discomfort on his face.

"Yes, just a second." Natalie lowered the gun, still carefully ensuring that it was not pointing at anybody. "I, um, don't know how to put the safety on."

The officer reached out and plucked the gun from mid-air as it came near him, snapping a switch of some sort on the side, which Natalie assumed was the safety, before putting it back into the empty holster at his side.

At that moment, Lassiter stirred groggily and said, "What the fuck ...?"

Although none of the other observers would realize, Natalie understood, with a sense of rueful sympathy, that Lassiter would have no idea where he was, how he got there or what he had been doing. She glanced toward her chair, wondering what would happen next.

However, her eyebrows shot upward as she realized that there were only two chairs sitting near the defence table. Raj was standing behind one; Susan was still on her knees near the witness stand.

Natalie tensed as she suddenly noticed that there was, once again, a pulsing yellow glow around Lassiter's head.

Don't worry, it's me doing it this time, she heard Jon say.

Where are you now? What are you now?

I'm an extra button on his shirt, Jon responded. *I'll be able to keep the block on him while they take him down to the station.*

How did you get there?

I was a fly.

Natalie almost choked at that. Although she knew he could take any form, it was staggering to realize that he literally meant *any* form, even something as small as a fly.

Could you text Seth?

Ah, okay. Natalie wasn't quite sure when she was going to be able to do that, since she knew the retired judge would not look favourably upon her pulling out her phone at this point.

As the two officers led the silent and unresisting prisoner out of the courtroom, Natalie raised a hand to wipe her sweaty forehead.

The lead bencher had remained on her feet since she had shouted for silence. She banged her gavel now to recapture the attention of everyone still in the room, and everyone turned to face her, though virtually everyone was standing.

"This has been, without exception, the most appalling circus I have seen in my entire career," Ms. Morrison stated crisply.

"Even ignoring this astonishing finale, this matter was a spectacle and an embarrassment to the profession and the College, which is supposed to maintain those in the profession in a position of high regard and respect." She directed a fierce glare at the sole remaining investigator as she said this, and Natalie realized she was paraphrasing from Meredith's opening statement.

"The prosecution has put forward absolutely no viable evidence that anybody from Mason Sullivan has ever had a single thing to do with any fugitive going missing. The evidence concerning either of these two members having even met them is ludicrously insubstantial, and even if it weren't, it *still* doesn't prove that they had anything to do with their disappearance."

Natalie felt a growing surge of hope as the judge continued her summary. The room was silent enough to hear the slight sound of a piece of broken chandelier rolling down the side of a pile of shards.

"The evidence concerning the assault relied heavily on an assumption of guilty until proven innocent, in complete contradiction of everything this profession stands for. The haste and alteration of standard procedure has been entirely unjustified. The defendants and their counsel are to be commended for their work in responding to unsubstantiated allegations in spite of being blindsided with evidence that ought to have been disclosed in advance. This hearing is dismissed in all particulars. The suspension of these two members is cancelled. Court dismissed."

Without waiting for anyone to say anything, the judge swept from the room, followed by the other two benchers. It occurred to Natalie that the other two had had no say in the decision, but it did not look as though Madam Justice Morrison was going to accept a dissenting vote in any event.

Natalie sat down in one of the two vacant chairs, her head whirling. Though the abrupt improvement of her personal circumstances was incredible, there was also the undeniable evidence that the one she had been calling the mastermind had attempted to strike again. Given that the target appeared to be Phillip Mastersen, the antimage attitude that marked one of the mastermind's targets was clearly limited to her own personal situation. Even she had never before been aware that Phillip hated mages that much. That made it still more likely that the mastermind was someone she knew.

Lassiter had clearly been under coercion, and the only mages in the room were her and Jon. But then Jon had also acted decisively to prevent him from doing the harm he had clearly been intending to do. The coercion had clearly been terminated just as her barrier had reached head height, which was when Lassiter had collapsed.

Jon had been clear that one needed to be within 100 feet of a person to effect coercion. But Constance could communicate over hundreds of kilometres with ease. There was simply no guarantee that there wasn't another kind of First Circle mage, previously unknown, who had perfected an ability to effect coercion over a longer distance. After all, she had never heard of a joiner before she had been told about Mikyla.

What other part of her world was about to disappear from under her feet?

Chapter 23

Suzanne was leaning against the side of the ambulance, watching the people near the main stage, which was set up not far from the entrance to the legislature building. Given the crowds expected at the annual Queen's Park Canada Day festivities, several crews of paramedics were on-site as a precautionary measure.

Her view of the stage was partially blocked by someone standing just in front of it, speaking into a microphone and smiling into a TV camera emblazoned with the CBC logo. A group of people were approaching from the building where the provincial government operated, and Suzanne recognized the Ontario Premier among the group. She grimaced slightly as the politicians came closer when she recognized MP Daniel Baxter walking beside several Ontario ministers. As the federal representative for a Toronto riding, it made sense that he would be at the provincial capital's function.

The Premier and the other politicians came closer and started shaking hands and making conversation with the people gathered near the stage, keeping a polite distance from the CBC reporter.

With no sound and no warning, Daniel Baxter suddenly gasped in a half-choking way, grabbed his chest and collapsed at the feet of a woman he had just been shaking hands with. The woman screamed, and all the

MPPs turned to see their federal colleague sliding to the ground bonelessly, his eyes fluttering shut.

There were several people shouting conflicting instructions at each other, but Dave did not hesitate as he rushed to the side of the collapsed politician. Suzanne glanced quickly around and thought she saw a fairly tall brown-haired person walking against the flow of the crowd, who were all pressing in to see what the fuss was about, but she could not spare any attention to identify that person when she had a patient in need of urgent medical attention. She pulled the wheeled gurney out of the ambulance and grabbed the defibrillator and some other equipment before asking people loudly to let her through. The crowd rapidly closed ranks after she got by, eager to watch what was going on. Suzanne collapsed the gurney to its lowest position and knelt on the other side of the unconscious man. Dave was already doing CPR, and Suzanne felt for a heartbeat. Finding none, she half closed her eyes as she quickly did some artificial respiration.

"Patient has no pulse, and he's not breathing," Dave said. He removed the patient's tie and pulled open his shirt. The MP's chest was nearly hairless, and he had very little excess weight. The fact that he was known to be an advocate of fitness and healthy eating was the subject of a flurry of shocked comments from his nearby colleagues.

"He's the last person I'd expect to have a heart attack!" Suzanne heard someone say.

"Blocked artery," she muttered to Dave. "Let's get him on the gurney." They did so with the smoothness of much practice working together. Then Suzanne took over the chest compressions while Dave set up the defibrillator. Suzanne's eyes remained half closed as she sank her awareness into her patient's body and identified the artery that was the problem. There was a piece of plaque that had blocked an entire smaller artery, but the sense of magic around that area clearly suggested that it had not broken off and lodged itself there on its own. Gritting her teeth, Suzanne tried to move it, but it was being pushed further against the narrow opening by the backed-up blood that was attempting to get through. Instead, she tried to break it up into smaller pieces that could be pushed through, and hopefully it would not then block a smaller vein.

"Clear the area, please."

Some police officers who had been on security detail around the politicians responded to Dave's request by asking the gathered crowd to move back. Suzanne did not look up, but she knew that her forehead was shiny with sweat. She struggled to hide the strength of the efforts she was making.

Dave placed the pads of the defibrillator and then glanced at Suzanne, who nodded, taking her hands off the patient.

"Clear!"

The MP's entire body jerked as the electrical current jolted through his heart. As he held the apparatus away, Suzanne reached forward and felt for the MP's carotid artery. She shook her head as she felt no pulse, then did some more artificial respiration while the defibrillator pads powered up again. Dave brought them back into position.

"Clear!"

"Still nothing," Dave said grimly. Suzanne knelt by the patient's head, her forehead furrowed as she stared at the MP's bared chest. Her jaw was tense, and she was breathing hard.

"Clear!"

For the third time, Suzanne removed her hands from the patient and watched anxiously as his body jerked again with the application of electrical current.

Dave felt for the pulse again and shook his head.

"Damn it," Suzanne muttered.

She held a hand up, clenched into a fist. She made a sudden pushing motion, splaying her fingers and shaking her hand, attempting to make it look as if she had just been shaking out a feeling of numbness in her fingers. One finger remained curled around a key chain hidden in her palm, which was actually her prism.

Suddenly the MP's body jerked again, although there had not been any further application of electrical current. He coughed a half-choking cough and sucked in a tortured-sounding breath.

"Pulse restored. Patient is breathing on his own," Dave said in relief. Half the watching crowd cheered. But the other half were staring at Suzanne with naked shock and fear showing on their faces, and several of them were drawing away from the scene.

"What the hell was that? And who are you?" one of the police officers demanded, glaring at Suzanne.

"He's alive, isn't he?" she answered in a gruff voice. She had momentarily considered trying to pretend that she had not used magic, but the expressions on the nearby faces suggested her actions had been a bit too obvious for that. She was still on her knees, breathing heavily, now not looking at anybody, although she had glanced up long enough to see the reactions of the nearby people.

"Yeah, and why did he collapse in the first place?" the officer demanded, clenching his fists.

"We don't have time for this, man," Dave said sternly. "He may be breathing, but he still needs medical care. We need to get him to the hospital." He was fitting an oxygen mask over the patient's face as he spoke. He shot a concerned glance at Suzanne, who struggled shakily to her feet but then swayed and almost fell, taking a staggering step backward. Dave reached out one long arm to give her some support as her legs buckled.

"Whoa, head rush!" she muttered.

"All right, who are you two?" The police officer now came forward and frowned menacingly at Dave and Suzanne.

"Toronto EMS. The patient needs to get to the hospital. Follow the ambulance if you have a problem with us, but we're leaving. Now."

Suzanne, grateful for Dave's authoritative handling of the suspicious policeman, managed to firm up her legs, though she avoided meeting anybody's eyes. She just hoped that the CBC cameraman had not got her face on film. Of course, with cellphone cameras and social media, the odds that nobody had caught an image of her face were not that good.

Dave took the bulk of the weight as he pushed the gurney with the half-aware patient on it toward the ambulance.

Natalie and Jon were enjoying a leisurely late breakfast when the text from her sister shattered her peaceful lassitude.

"Shit!" she exclaimed. At Jon's questioning look, she explained, "Baxter was attacked at Queen's Park. Suzanne says it was made to look like a heart attack, but it definitely wasn't. That suggests the secondary victim is nearby, assuming this is more of the same."

"Bloody hell, this bloke doesn't even take a break," Jon muttered. "Right, where's Queen's Park? That's the government buildings, right?"

"Yeah. We'd better take a cab. It would be brutal trying to find parking; it's Canada Day."

"This isn't your responsibility, Natalie. You don't have to get involved."

"I'm already involved, like it or not. I can't send you in there on your own."

"I won't be entirely alone," Jon said, pulling out his phone. "I've got at least one colleague in Toronto. He was looking into some stuff in Chicago, but he came up to Toronto yesterday after what happened at your hearing." He typed a rapid text into his phone as he spoke. "I'll send Seth a text as well."

"Good. But still, it'll take time for Seth's people to get here. I might not be a LEO, but I'm not useless."

"You're definitely not useless," Jon agreed. "I just hate putting you in danger."

"Ditto. Even if it *is* your job. I'm calling a cab."

"Point me in the right direction. I'll fly. It'll be faster."

"Good idea," Natalie said in a worried tone. "The secondary victim usually gets killed really quickly after the first one."

Jimmy Sabourin moved his wheelchair through the crowd at Queen's Park, his daughter striding beside him. He rode in a chair much more robust than the one he usually used at home. This one had heavy-duty wheels to handle rough ground and was equipped with a motor and controls that he could operate with his single hand. Jim's head swivelled frequently to take in all of the people, stalls and wandering performers. Mikyla, on the other hand, seemed tense and distracted. Given the newness of their relationship, Jimmy was reluctant to ask what was bothering her, hoping that she might confide in him eventually.

Mikyla gasped. Jimmy saw her head whip around as they started walking past some food vendors set up in a row with a number of trailers in the area behind them.

"I could swear that was Jake!" she said. "I'll be back in a sec."

She dashed off between two of the vendors' stalls. Jimmy turned his chair to follow, belatedly remembering that Jake was the name of the young man who had failed to recognize his daughter that day at the coffee shop, the same one who Suzanne had told him had been reported missing a few days later.

The food vendors' stalls were set fairly close together, making it evident that the attendees were not really supposed to go into the area behind them, where a large number of trailers were parked. Presumably these belonged to the vendors and to the companies that had provided the stages, temporary fencing and other features currently dotting the grounds of Queen's Park.

As he guided his chair past one vendor's stall, Jimmy saw a swarthy-skinned security guard hold out an arm to intercept Mikyla and say something to her.

"Get out of my *way*," he heard her screech as she darted around him, making a "move aside" gesture as she passed. To Jimmy's surprise, the security guard staggered and fell, though Mikyla hadn't actually touched him. Jimmy's mouth fell open in the next second as the man's dark skin paled and his black hair started to turn a very light colour as he got to all fours and then stood up, a fierce frown on his face. In the next second, his appearance shifted back to the South Asian visage he had sported moments earlier. Jimmy's heart rate sped up as he realized it was an illusion. Why was there a mage wearing a false face here, and why was he now starting in Mikyla's direction with a menacing expression on his face?

"Hey!" Jimmy yelled, magically propelling his chair forward faster than the electric motor could manage it.

The disguised mage turned his head to look back toward Jimmy, but in the next second, he suddenly disappeared. Jimmy was startled. That was not an ability he had ever seen or heard of before. Furthermore, Mikyla had also disappeared from view, and a young man was just stepping away from a trailer, carrying a large box and wearing an apron liberally splattered with what looked like barbecue sauce.

"Mister? Are you okay?" The young man shifted his box in his arms, sending a concerned look in Jimmy's direction.

Jimmy shook himself. *What just happened?*

"Yes, yeah, I'm, uh, I'm fine, thanks. Did you see a girl here just now? Teenager, pink T-shirt?"

"Uh, I think a saw a girl run by, that way, a couple of minutes ago." He indicated the same direction Mikyla had been heading with his chin since his arms were occupied. "Pretty sure she was wearing a pink T-shirt."

"Thanks," Jimmy said. "My daughter. She's, um, a bit more mobile than I am."

"Yeah." The aproned man laughed. He moved off toward the back of one of the food vendors' trailers. As he passed into a shadowed area, Jimmy quickly unfocused and looked at his head, wondering if perhaps the dark-skinned security guard was now wearing another face. But there was no glow.

Filled with concern for whatever was going on with Mikyla, Jimmy pretended to use his electric controls while he really used the faster magical method to propel his wheelchair in the direction she had gone.

As Mikyla ran past a gap between two trailers, she caught sight of a tall figure facing sideways, but with his face turned away from her, and she caught herself on the corner of the trailer, halting her motion forward and lurching back around and between the trailers, toward where she had seen Jake. The tattoo on the side of his neck was clearly visible.

"Jake!" she yelled, but he did not react in any way.

Instead he reached into his pocket and pulled out a thin rectangular metal object. Then his other hand came into sight, holding a gun, and he slid the rectangular thing up inside the handle of the gun with an ominous click.

"No!" Mikyla screamed. In her panic, it seemed like she was trying to run through thick mud as she tried to get her legs to dash toward him, heedless of the danger to herself. She tried to will the gun to fall from his hand and fly away from him, but as with each time that she had tried to consciously move something, nothing happened. It seemed she only ever managed to do magic when it was unintentional.

She desperately wished that the gun would not work, focusing on that and trying not to think about whether Jake had been intending to murder somebody or turn the gun on himself.

Suddenly a large German shepherd dashed around the corner from the opposite direction and launched itself at Jake. Jake went sprawling, and the gun flew out of his hand. But in the same second, Mikyla sensed the presence of other minds, as she had in the hospital with Suzanne's sister. She watched as the gun soared further away from Jake than the jolt from the dog would have caused. As she focused on it in mid-air, imagining it becoming incapable of harming anyone, it seemed like it actually might have changed shape. It flew in Mikyla's direction, falling halfway between her and Jake.

Mikyla raced toward Jake and stopped a few feet away from the huge dog, which stood with its two large front paws on Jake's chest, vicious teeth visible as it panted with its mouth open. The gun was behind her, and she hoped to be able to prevent any attempt on Jake's part to pick it up or carry through with whatever he had been planning on doing.

Her attention was fixed on Jake's face, which had abruptly changed. Where moments before he had worn a determined, almost angry expression, now he shook his head and looked shocked, his mouth falling open as his eyes darted all around, but quickly returned to focus on the dog still holding him down.

"What the fuck—?" he gasped out.

Suddenly remembering to look for the glow, Mikyla unfocused and sucked in a breath as she saw a dull, murky yellow tint around Jake's head, though it was hard to see in the bright sunlight. It was only slightly visible on one side, where he lay in the shadow of a trailer. She frowned, looking at the yellow tone to the glow, certain that none of the mage auras she had previously seen had appeared yellow.

Mikyla's head whipped around as a figure appeared at the far end of the trailers. It was a stocky brown-haired man wearing the uniform of a Toronto police officer and holding a dog's leash. She was momentarily aware of a peculiarly oppressive pressure in the air, but it dissipated moments later. And since she felt no ill effects from it, she hoped she could safely ignore it. There seemed to be something subtly wrong with the uniform worn by the policeman, but she dismissed it, turning back toward Jake, hoping that a police officer was no threat. She reached out a foot to kick the gun further away, but she stopped before touching it, goggling at it in amazement. The gun was lying on the ground, its barrel twisted into a pretzel shape with part of the handle completely melted.

"Did I do that?" she asked.

"More or less," the police officer answered her as he strode closer. "You merged a few of us and showed us what you were seeing. I think there were perhaps three or four of us, and we threw the gun and disabled it." He spoke with a strong British accent, but his grin was friendly. Though he stood in sunlight, making it impossible to see any glow, it was evident from his words that he was a mage. Mikyla realized that, once again, she was sensing something from the stranger, some evidence of his emotions. She had come to realize over the last few weeks that that awareness was very useful, like a built-in lie detector. She sensed no animosity from the police officer, but rather a calm and organized sense of purpose. He *felt* like a cop, in the sense of being trustworthy and someone you could rely on to take care of things.

"I think we pulverized it," Mikyla said, realizing that, once again, she had done that joining thing that she had inadvertently done at the hospital. Now thinking about it, she thought one of the minds had seemed a bit familiar. Possibly it was her dad, whom she belatedly remembered had also joined with her at the hospital. Remembering Jim's warning that she could be sucked into something, or lose part of her mind in someone else's, she shuddered. How was she supposed to stop doing something that she did without even being aware of it?

"Where the hell am I? Mikyla?" Jake asked in a baffled tone of voice. Mikyla's eyes swung back to see Jake's face looking shocked and confused as his gaze flicked between Mikyla and the dog that was still restraining him.

"Uh, Mister, can you call off your dog?" she asked the police officer.

"I'm LEO Gerry Benham," the officer introduced himself. "Don't worry about the dog. He's protecting your friend, not attacking him." As if in confirmation, the dog stepped back, releasing Jake, but remained beside him. He turned to face away from Jake, moving his head from side to side and sniffing the air around him.

"You're at Queen's—" Mikyla began answering Jake's question, but the police officer held up a hand in a "stop" gesture. She belatedly remembered that a LEO was a mage police officer, so evidently the Toronto police uniform was a disguise.

"Wait, before she tells you, could you please tell me what you remember having happened?"

"Since when?" Jake answered, pushing himself to a sitting position as he spoke. "Everything has been totally fucked up ever since I met that red-haired guy."

"What red-haired guy? And do you know when that was? It's quite important that you tell me as clearly as you can. Start with telling me your name, please."

Jake frowned. Mikyla sensed that he was both confused and somewhat irritated with the questions. "I'm Jake. Jacob Conrad. So, um, it was Sunday. Uh, the third? I think? I was in this fight. I was just trying to defend myself, but this red-haired guy, he said he was a mage cop, and he said a judge would have to decide if it was self-defence or not. He was, um, tall, and he talked like you. British accent."

Mikyla saw that Gerry's eyes flicked to the dog and back at Jake. "I think I might know who you mean. All right, go on."

"So then he took me to this lady's condo. She had this big spreadsheet floating around in the air, it was weird. Then she made a doorway that was really bright in the middle of the room, and we went through it and we were someplace else. We went to a police station, I guess. After the red-haired guy left, they took me to a courtroom. I could have sworn the judge said it was okay, I didn't do anything wrong, but the next thing I remember is being in a locked room with a tiny window, like in a basement, and it was night, which was weird because it should've been, like, early morning. After that, it kept changing from day to night really quickly, and the judge was always wearing different clothes every time. Then next thing I know, I'm here, and Mikyla looked like she saw a ghost, and then the dog knocked me over. That's it."

"Do you know what coercive magic is?" Gerry asked.

"No."

"It's when somebody is using mind control magic on you," the police officer explained. "And it's totally illegal, except in some very limited circumstances. I believe you've been a victim of coercive magic, mate, on and off for nearly a month. When you're under coercion, you're not aware of the passage of time. It's actually July first."

"No way!"

"It's true," Mikyla put in. "It's Canada Day. You're at Queen's Park, and you've been missing for weeks. Your parents are freaking out, and you missed all your exams."

"Shit!"

Jake's shocked face turned wary as another figure appeared at the end of the aisle between two parked trailers.

Mikyla looked over her shoulder and stiffened. An elderly woman was approaching with quick small steps. "Who's she?"

Gerry spun around and looked at the woman.

Her brilliantly white hair was fastened up on the top of her head, and she wore a silk dress with a matching purse and shoes, and several strands of pearls. A filmy scarf was looped around her neck. As she came closer, it was evident that her face looked angry and that her glare was directed straight at Jake.

"Councillor Constance Reeve, I am LEO Gerry Benham. Please state your intentions," Gerry said loudly, pointing the dog leash at her. It blurred and turned into an orange-coloured stone in his hand. The woman completely ignored him, almost as if she had not even been aware that he had spoken.

The dog jumped up and placed himself between Jake and Constance, baring his teeth at her.

Seeing more movement just behind the old woman, who had not even paused in spite of the police officer's threatening stance and words, Mikyla bent slightly to the side to see past her. She was relieved to recognize the figure in a wheelchair, approaching silently from behind the woman Gerry had called Constance. Dr. Sabourin looked worried, and his eyes met Mikyla's immediately. She felt a surge of relief to see him there. She flicked her eyes left as she saw more movement there, and was even more relieved to see Suzanne and Dave approaching, both wearing their paramedic uniforms. Another blonde woman was right behind them. Mikyla belatedly recognized Suzanne's sister.

Before she could say anything about the additions to their party, however, the old woman had flung her hands out in a pushing gesture toward the front and then toward each side of her body, and instantly all of the mages other than the old woman flinched back. The humans clapped hands over their ears and screwed their eyes shut, expressions of intense pain on their faces, most of them sinking to their knees. The dog yelped and cringed down, his ears flat on his head.

Mikyla breathed in short gasps, trying to shield her ears from what seemed like a million decibels of high-pitched noise. Plugging her ears with her fingers did not appear to make the slightest difference in the volume. Attempting to crack her eyes open enough to get some idea of what was going on, she thought it looked like Dave was unaffected. Suzanne had fallen to her knees beside her husband, her eyes streaming with tears. Gerry did not have his ears covered, but he looked like he was struggling to get to his feet, his face a rictus of pain. Mikyla thought she saw his mouth move as he appeared to shout something at the old woman, but she could not hear the words over the noise battering her ears. The hand that held the orange stone was held up in front of him, but if he was doing anything with it, Mikyla could not tell if it was making any difference.

Mikyla saw Dave focus his attention on the savage expression on the face of the woman whose hands were still extended outward. He launched himself forward, yelling, and in the next second, the ear-splitting noise was cut off. But before Mikyla could feel any sense of relief, she realized, with horror, that Dave had checked his lunge toward the elderly woman and was now turning to face her, or possibly Jake, with a look of violent fury on his face that exactly mirrored the expression the old woman wore.

Several of the group were swearing as they got back to their feet.

"Constance Reeve, you are under arrest," Gerry stated loudly. "You are charged with at least six counts of first-degree murder and numerous counts of the illegal use of magical coercion."

"Dave, what the hell are you doing?" Mikyla heard Suzanne yell, as Dave ran toward Jake, his large hands extended. Swiftly, the dog leaped toward Dave, meeting him halfway to where Jake was still sitting on the ground. Dave did not fall, but he staggered backward as the huge dog hit him. He swung a fist at the dog's head, and Mikyla heard a yelp as Dave's fist connected with the dog's skull. Dave pushed the dog aside and continued his advance toward Jake. Mikyla screamed, wondering if she could make this joining thing work again to do something to protect Jake. She had no idea what was going on, but it was clear Dave was acting in an unnatural way.

Gerry leaped forward, his hands sketching a pattern as his gaze focused on Dave.

Suddenly, Dave staggered, his face abruptly changing, the fury draining off it precipitously, to be replaced by confusion. Gerry looked just as confused, however, as though what had just happened did not match whatever it was he had been intending to do.

Mikyla jumped in front of Jake, just in case Dave was still a threat, but as she did so, she caught sight of her father, who had moved his wheelchair close behind the old woman. He had his hand out toward Constance, and there was a look of intense concentration on his face. The elderly woman was falling backward, her eyes fluttering shut. Her fall slowed, and in the next moment, she appeared to be floating on her back in mid-air. She was then lowered carefully to the ground, clearly unconscious.

"What the hell just happened?" Jake and Dave spoke almost simultaneously.

"Don't ask me," Mikyla muttered as she sank down to sit beside Jake, bringing her knees up to hug her chest. "I haven't got a fucking clue what's going on."

"Sir, you are also under arrest!" Gerry said firmly. Mikyla was shocked to see he was addressing her father, his tone one of shock. "You are not authorized to use coercive magic."

"Fine, you take over the coercion, then, and I'll be happy to co-operate," Dr. Sabourin snapped. "I don't see where I had much choice. You were all incapacitated. Probably the only reason that noise spell didn't hit me too hard was she didn't know I was behind her. Then she was about to make Mr. Timmons attack my daughter."

"Me? Attack who?" Dave asked. He was just helping Suzanne to her feet, but he froze, a look of shock on his face.

"Hold on," Gerry said loudly. "Sir, at what point did you start attempting to coerce the councillor?"

"When she was doing the noise thing," Dr. Sabourin replied. "For some reason, it was really hard to get it to work. Way harder than normal. I was going to stop trying when the noise cut off, but then Mikyla screamed."

"What do you mean by 'harder than normal'?"

"I'm a surgeon," he explained. "James Sabourin. I use coercive magic instead of anaesthetic during surgery, and sometimes afterward if there's a need to keep a patient in a coma. I don't know how to do any other kind, but I have practice at that kind. It's not that hard, but this time it was like I couldn't get hold of anything for a while. I don't know how else to describe it."

"I see," Gerry said. "I'm afraid I'm still going to have to press charges. It's not my place to decide whether the circumstances justify your use of coercive magic outside of the medical application. I will take over the coercion."

"Fine." The doctor held out his hand, clasping a red prism in his palm with his thumb on top of the stone. Gerry stepped around Constance's prone body and approached the doctor.

Then he stopped and turned around to look back. Mikyla realized that the LEO was staring at the dog and frowning. "You could be right, mate," he said to somebody. Mikyla exchanged glances with Jake at the odd comment. Who was right, about what? Gerry turned back toward Mikyla's father. "I'm going to authorize you to continue to keep the councillor unconscious for now."

Dr. Sabourin looked startled but did not ask why the officer had changed his mind. He lowered the hand he had raised toward Gerry.

"What's this about me attacking Mikyla?" Dave asked Suzanne.

"She coerced you, Dave," Suzanne said. "You were about to do something, either to Mikyla or maybe to Jake, I'm not sure."

"No way," Dave gasped. He looked at his outstretched hands as if they belonged to a stranger, and then he looked toward Mikyla's white face. "I'm sorry, Mikyla. I didn't know."

"I think you were going for Jake, actually," Mikyla said, nerves making her voice higher-pitched than usual.

"The old lady was doing something to all of you, though, a second ago," Dave said. "What was that about?"

"It was like nails scratching down a blackboard, but deafeningly loud," Suzanne told him with a shudder. "God, my head! Then it cut off, but that's when she started controlling you. The dog tried to stop you, but you hit him."

"I hit the dog?" Dave said. "Geez, buddy, I'm sorry," he said to the dog.

The dog shook his head and whined softly, then swung around to stare at Gerry, who was looking back at him. Gerry nodded slightly. Mikyla suddenly realized that Dave had been unaffected by the noise spell, but the dog had appeared to suffer the same pain as the rest of the group. Would a mage's police dog be more sensitive to magic than a non-mage? Or were animals, in general, sensitive to magic?

As she looked back and forth between the dog and the police officer, Mikyla realized that Gerry's clothing had changed. It was no longer the uniform of the Toronto police that she was familiar with. Instead, he was clad in ordinary-looking jeans and a golf shirt.

"I'm going to need to know how it comes about that each of you came to be here," Gerry said. His gaze fixed on Mikyla, to her intense discomfort. "I'd like to start with you, Miss, please. Your name?"

"Uh, Mikyla Burton. I was here with my dad. We just came for the Canada Day thing." She waved a hand toward Dr. Sabourin as she spoke, indicating whom she was talking about. "But then I saw Jake. I, um, know him from school. And, you know, he's been missing for a month. It's been in the news and everything. So I wanted to ask him where he's been."

"You are her father?" Gerry turned to Dr. Sabourin.

"Yes," Jim answered. "Mikyla and I saw Jake one other time, too, after he had apparently gone missing. He was in Neekonnisiwin, with Councillor Hayes, but on that occasion he didn't seem to recognize Mikyla. I didn't look for any yellow aura."

"Councillor who?" Jake asked Mikyla in a low voice. "When was that? And didn't you tell me you didn't know who your dad was?"

Suzanne sucked in a startled breath, and Gerry's gaze turned to her. "I was there that day, too," she said. "But Jake and the councillor were in bright sunlight. I guess that makes it really difficult to see it. I didn't notice any either."

"That was just a few days after you disappeared," Mikyla answered Jake's question. "That was the actually the same day I found out who my dad was. It was a seriously crazy day." Her attention was only half on the questions, though. Both her father and Suzanne had mentioned a yellow aura, just like the one she had seen around Jake's head. What did it mean when it was yellow?

"I remember seeing you Friday at lunch, but that seems like it was about three days ago to me."

"Hayes," Gerry repeated thoughtfully. "Jake, you mentioned a judge. That wasn't this woman?" He pointed to the unconscious woman lying on the ground, her peaceful face a significant contrast to the expression she had worn minutes earlier.

"No, it was a guy. I don't think I heard his name. Everyone just called him 'Your Honour,'" Jake said.

"Can you describe him?"

"Um, about forty or forty-five maybe, with light-coloured hair. I'm not sure if it was really light brown or maybe a sort of dark blond. I can't remember. Maybe a little bit grey, but not much. He was wearing a suit the first day, but after that sometimes more casual clothes."

Gerry made a gesture, and a picture started forming in the air. Mikyla thought it looked like the man she had seen Jake with at the coffee shop, but before it finished forming, the dog suddenly stiffened and a fierce snarl came from his mouth. The half-formed picture disappeared, and Mikyla's attention was jerked back to the German shepherd. He almost flipped over, he'd turned around so fast, and hurled himself toward Jake, his mouth open and all of his vicious-looking teeth in view.

Mikyla screamed again as the dog leaped toward the young man still on the ground.

Jake pushed his hands outward with a gasp, and suddenly the dog was hurtling in the opposite direction. His head smacked against the side of the trailer. He yelped as he fell to the ground, where he lay motionless. Jake made the pushing gesture again, causing the dog to slide underneath the trailer and out of sight. Jake was trembling as he did so and breathing hard.

Mikyla looked wildly around, searching for an explanation of the dog's bizarre behaviour. Surely it was the old woman who had been using that mind control thing on Dave, and she was still unconscious. Mikyla thought she saw a hint of movement at the other end of the aisle between the trailers, on the side away from where Suzanne, Dave and Natalie had appeared. But when she turned her head that way, there was nobody there. Maybe she was seeing things. This whole thing was certainly messed up enough for that.

Gerry strode forward to stand between Jake and the others. Perhaps he intended to protect Jake from any further attacks. But Mikyla wondered, *What if the mind control magic got turned against the police officer next? He or any one of the people here could turn into an attacker without warning.* She moved back to sink down beside Jake, trembling uncontrollably, wishing she could consciously control her magic.

Chapter 24

Natalie moved forward from between the trailers into the open area, where the rest of the group stood, and glanced toward where she had heard the dog yelp. The dog was not in sight, though an unfamiliar man whom she had heard identify himself as a LEO stood in front of two young people sitting on the ground.

Catching sight of Mikyla's white face, Natalie realized it would not go over well if she appeared to have more concern for a vicious dog than for its victims. Not everyone here knew the dog wasn't actually a dog.

"Did the dog hurt either of you?" she asked the two, belatedly realizing that she recognized the young man. He was the one Jon had arrested and brought to her condo the day after she had gated him back from England. She had sent them both to Neekonnisiwin. She didn't know why he was there, but then she was equally surprised to see Mikyla and Dr. Sabourin. She recognized Mikyla from Suzanne's memory stone and knew this was the young girl who had saved her life. She assumed that the unknown LEO was likely the colleague Jon had mentioned.

"N—no, we're okay," Mikyla answered for both of them, though the tremble in her voice indicated that *okay* only meant that the dog hadn't physically hurt them.

"Please identify yourself, madam," the LEO said.

"Natalie Benson," she replied. "Jon might have mentioned me?"

"Ah yes. Thank you."

"I'd like to gate these two young people to someplace safe. They're not experienced mages, and Mikyla is underage. Any objections?" Natalie directed the question to the whole group but looked at the LEO.

"Where?" Dr. Sabourin asked. She swung around to look at him.

"How about LEO headquarters in Neekonnisiwin?"

"Good. Yes, please."

"I've no objections," the police officer said. He was evidently as unsurprised as Dr. Sabourin, so he presumably knew about Natalie's range.

Mikyla and Jake made no objection either. Natalie pulled her blue prism from her pocket and sketched a pattern in the air. The gateway shimmered brightly, even in the sun. If there were any non-mages in the area of the vendors' trailers, the gate would inevitably be seen, but there was no way to avoid it. Natalie thought she heard a yell, but she could not spare any attention for the source.

As the gateway firmed, she gestured to Mikyla and Jake.

"Go through, please. That's the police station in Neekonnisiwin. You'll be safe there."

Jake got to his feet and pulled Mikyla up beside him. "I sure hope you're right, lady," he told her grimly. But as he walked toward the gateway, Natalie suddenly gasped, and the gateway wavered and collapsed. Jake jumped back in alarm, looking back at Natalie.

Natalie struggled not to scream as intense pain flung agonizing bands around her whole body. She felt as though she were bleeding from a thousand wounds which were also being burned at the same time. Since there were no visible injuries, it was obvious that the pain wasn't real. Gritting her teeth, she concentrated on building a shield around her mind the same way she had done the day Constance had kept attempting to demand answers. As she visualized the brick wall, she saw that the LEO was making some gestures too. The pain lessened slightly, though she was unsure whether that was through her own efforts or the result of something Gerry was doing. In any event, she was able to focus on the people in front of her. It was immediately evident that the coercion victim this time was Suzanne. Her face clearly showed anger and frustration. Natalie had the flippant thought that their real bad guy had a very expressive face, whoever he was, since it appeared that his victims mirrored his expressions.

Thinking of the conversation she has listened to just before Jon had apparently tried to attack Jake, she considered the shocking possibility that Councillor Hayes might be their suspect. He might fit the profile. As a councillor, perhaps he had access to records and the ability to alter them. Of course, the same was true of Constance, and Natalie wasn't entirely willing to accept that she was innocent. For that matter, she had to wonder about Dr. Sabourin, who had just demonstrated his own ability to easily impose coercion on another mage, a skill she had already seen him practise before.

Natalie could still feel some pain from the spell her sister was being forced to throw at her, but it was no longer debilitating. However, she exaggerated her reaction, pretending that it was still as bad as it had been at first.

Carefully, she built a gateway just behind Suzanne, feeling sweat breaking out on her forehead as she tried to perform two complicated magics simultaneously without the use of her prism. Feeling her control waver, she was forced to bring her prism up to finish making the gateway.

"Oh no you don't," Suzanne snapped, but it was clear it wasn't her voice. It was much lower than her usual voice. That certainly suggested the person coercing her was a man, although Natalie recalled that Constance's voice was unusually low for a woman. But then Constance was supposedly unconscious. Unable to spare attention to analyze who might be coercing her sister, Natalie concentrated on moving the gateway forward too rapidly for Suzanne to avoid. Usually a gateway remained stationary and the people had to go through it, but Natalie had begun to wonder if a lot of what she thought she knew about magic was just assumptions.

Even as Suzanne moved closer to her, Natalie managed to make the gateway move and engulf her sister. As soon as she saw Suzanne stumble on the ceramic tile floor of LEO headquarters, she collapsed the gateway. The residual pain immediately cut off, but she maintained the mental barrier anyway, since doubtless the attacker would shortly try to latch onto another victim. She also hoped the shield might prevent that next coercion victim from being her.

Then she quickly crouched down to look under the trailer, wincing at the sight of the smear of blood near the bottom. In the deep shadow of the underside of the trailer, the yellow glow around Jon's head was obvious. He looked as though he was just starting to stir, and she looked back toward the other LEO with a grim expression on her face.

"He was coerced. That's why he attacked Jake," she said. "But that means either Constance is pretending to be unconscious or we've got another attacker somewhere nearby."

Dave crouched down beside Constance, who still lay unmoving on the ground, and pulled back one of her eyelids.

"She's definitely not pretending," he confirmed.

"Right, I know about your involvement, Ms. Benson," Gerry said. "So, lastly, you, sir? Am I correct to think you're not a mage? Could you please tell me how you came to be involved?"

"That's right, I'm not a mage," Dave confirmed. "I'm married to Suzanne, whom Natalie just sent somewhere. LEO headquarters?" At Natalie's nod, he continued. "Suzanne is Natalie's sister, and I'm aware of Natalie's theory about what's been going on. Suzanne and I were on duty here. We're paramedics. There was an attack on an MP that was made to look like a heart attack. But Suzanne said it was a magical attack. When we came back from taking the MP to the hospital, Suzanne felt something from Mikyla, and that's why we came over here."

What did I miss? Jon's voice sounded slightly slurred, even though the communication was telepathic.

Natalie told him what had happened, including the fact that he had been coerced, and sensed his shock.

Remember when I kept Constance out by visualizing a brick wall around my head? she reminded him. *We all need to do that.*

If I visualize a brick wall, I'll probably become a brick wall, Jon grumbled. *I'll give it a try, though.*

Gerry, I'm going to go up above and see if I can see our mastermind. There was a slight echo to the words that made it evident to Natalie that she wasn't the only one hearing the comment.

Though Natalie did not hear Gerry's response, she saw him nod slightly. In the next moment, she noticed a very faint plume of grey smoke ooze up the side of the trailer. She did not look up to see what form Jon would take next, not wanting to draw anyone's attention to him.

"I'd like to get Councillor Reeve away from here," Gerry said. "Ms. Benson, would you be able to build another gateway?"

Natalie frowned. "I don't know how many more I can do. The more people I send and the further away, the harder it gets." She did not want to say aloud that she was also concerned about losing her ability to protect her mind if her magical abilities were depleted. "Are we just sending her through alone?"

"Perhaps the doctor could take her."

"I'm not leaving my daughter here," Dr. Sabourin objected. "But I'm happy to push Councillor Reeve through. It shouldn't matter that the coercion is released once she's there."

"What about Suzanne?" Natalie objected.

"Your sister is at LEO headquarters," Gerry pointed out. "The councillor won't attack her in front of a bunch of LEOs. And I have to wonder if she might be just as much a victim as anyone."

"Constance? A victim?"

"*Somebody* coerced Dave, then Jon, and then Suzanne, all while Constance was unconscious, Ms. Benson. And nobody can coerce more than one person at a time."

Natalie suddenly remembered when she and the doctor had gone to get Raj, just prior to waking him up. He had been in a room with several other unconscious patients, and the other doctor had been keeping all of them unconscious.

The doctor at the hospital had a bunch of people unconscious at once. She sent the thought out to Jon, hoping he could clarify.

Yeah, but that's different from making people do different things at once, Jon explained. *I've got reason to be confident the doc's not our bad guy, Natalie. I'll explain later.*

Natalie was relieved to hear it and realized she had better not distract him with further questions.

Free to use her prism this time, she rapidly built another gateway, this one just in front of Constance. She felt an odd tickle in her mind and firmed up her brick wall, wondering if the unknown mastermind was now attempting to coerce her.

Before the doctor could propel Constance through, however, Natalie yelled as pain exploded in her ankle. She fell, tears coming from her eyes, but managed to maintain the gateway long enough for Dr. Sabourin to push Constance through, even though it wavered slightly.

The source of the pain was evidently a large rock that had come to rest not far from her ankle, now splattered with some of her blood. She grabbed her ankle and looked to where the rock had come from.

Dave was once again wearing an expression of savage anger, but this time he was on the ground, evidently having been put there by Gerry, whose arm was just finishing some kind of pattern with his prism in Dave's direction.

Gritting her teeth, Natalie pulled the gateway forward rapidly and placed it in front of Dave just as he got to his feet and made a rush for Jake. Jake had jumped backward, away from Dave's rush in his direction. The gateway abruptly disappeared after Dave unintentionally ran through it.

The group had now shrunk to Natalie, Jake, Mikyla, Gerry and Dr. Sabourin, while Jon had gone out to scout around.

Gerry, having evidently seen something behind Dave, moved in that direction, his prism held out in front of him. Natalie looked down at her ankle, which was starting to swell and develop some purple discolouration.

"All right, this has gone far enough!"

Natalie's head jerked up to see that it was Gerry who spoke, although his British accent seemed to have disappeared. An Asian man in the uniform of a security guard appeared behind him, but as he turned his head, it was apparent that only half of his hair was black. The other half was sandy brown, and that was spreading to engulf his whole head. His swarthy skin went splotchy with pale patches.

"Mikyla!" Natalie hissed, beckoning to the girl to come closer. Warily, Mikyla did so. Natalie held out a hand toward her. "Do you think you can try to do that joining thing, but only invite me, Jake and your dad?"

"I'll try," Mikyla said, taking Natalie's hand and then holding out a hand toward Jake, who took it, though his expression was puzzled. Mikyla closed her eyes in concentration, and shortly Natalie felt the presence of other minds. Though she was accustomed to mental communication with people she knew, this felt very different. Mental communication was simply hearing voices without any emotional flavour. This was more emotional flavour without any voices. Quickly, she began building her brick wall around Gerry's mind, clearly visualizing what she had in mind. As she had found with Lassiter in the courtroom yesterday, it was much harder doing it to another person than when she had shielded her own mind. It didn't help that she was already feeling very drained from the magic she had been doing. She could feel the cold tentacles of coercion trying to keep a grip on the LEO. The extra power of three more mages gave her far more strength than she was accustomed to, though, particularly once they began to comprehend her intention. Nonetheless, she felt light-headed with exhaustion as the barrier was built up to head height.

With a roar of anger, Gerry suddenly stiffened and threw his shoulders back, turning around to face the oddly piebald security guard, and made a gesture at him. Instantly, the security guard turned into a completely white man, wearing light-coloured jeans and a pale-blue-collared golf shirt rather than the security guard uniform he had worn moments earlier.

"Douglas Hayes, you are under arrest," Gerry spoke clearly, his accent back in place. "You are charged with extensive use of illegal coercive magic and first-degree murder several times over. Drop your prism immediately."

The councillor did not speak but raised a hand containing a large black prism, his face twisted with a vicious expression of frustration and anger. Before he could do more than start to move the prism, however, an enormous snake reared up behind him, wrapped its huge coils around his upper body and started to squeeze. The black prism fell from his hand as his face turned bright red. The snake whipped its head around and pinned its murderous yellow eyes on those of the councillor. Immediately, Doug Hayes' eyes rolled up and closed, and the snake let the slack body down to lie on the ground. Releasing his coils from the prone man, he turned his head to look at Gerry.

The snake blurred and turned into Jon, who had a trickle of blood coming from one temple and a spreading bruise across the other. Natalie assumed the injuries were from Jake slamming him against the trailer and Dave hitting him. She heard a few gasps, presumably from those who knew nothing of Jon's abilities.

"I can't gate anyone else to Neekonnisiwin, Jon," Natalie whispered. "I'm completely done."

"Let me do something about your ankle," Dr. Sabourin said, propelling his wheelchair forward.

"After that, do you think you might be able to manage a gateway to the nearest portal maybe?" Jon suggested. "They can certainly go the rest of the way themselves, and then I can take care of you."

"Yes, I can probably do that," Natalie agreed. First, however, Dr. Sabourin held out his deep red prism over her abused ankle, and the trickle of blood immediately dried up. Natalie was looking at the jagged-looking cut and actually saw the skin pulling together to form a whole.

"Brace yourself," Dr. Sabourin warned. "One of the little bones is broken. This will hurt a bit."

Natalie nodded and closed her eyes. She felt a sharp pain as something moved in her ankle, but almost immediately the pain reduced to less than it had been before the doctor had set the bone. She breathed a sigh of relief.

"Try to keep that as immobile as possible," Dr. Sabourin said. His head turned to one side, and a light scarf that had been lying on the ground wafted toward him. "It's set, but it's not fused together. I hope you don't mind using Constance's scarf as a bandage?" he asked with a grin.

"Not at all," Natalie replied. Without apparent effort, the scarf wrapped itself tightly around her ankle, and one end tucked under the wrapping to hold the ankle so that she could not bend it. The support reduced the pain to a minor discomfort.

"Thanks, Doctor."

"You're very welcome."

As the doctor began to move his wheelchair back, he stopped abruptly and looked down at Councillor Hayes' prone body on the ground, then directed a shocked look up at Jon, who raised an eyebrow questioningly.

"This man is dead."

"What? No, I just coerced him into unconsciousness as you did with Constance."

"No, sir, I'm afraid you're mistaken. Douglas Hayes is dead."

Natalie looked down at the councillor, who looked nothing like one would picture for a man directly responsible for numerous murders. He was entirely ordinary in appearance, aside from being motionless. His sandy hair was awry, and there was a smudge of dirt on his pale blue shirt. His eyes were closed, and he looked like he was sleeping. But as she looked closer, she realized that his skin had turned grey, and his stillness went beyond that of a sleeper.

The doctor reached down his hand and felt for the artery in the neck with two fingers. Even Natalie knew that was the one that gave the strongest pulse. Dr. Sabourin shook his head and took his hand away.

"Release your coercion. He won't wake up," he said grimly.

Jon made a gesture with his prism, but the doctor was right. The councillor did not react in any way to the removal of the magic that had stopped him mid-attack.

"Fucking hell, Jon. What happened? Did you strangle him?" Gerry's voice clearly showed his shock at this turn of events.

"No! I didn't touch his neck, only his chest and arms. I squeezed enough that it would have been a bit difficult to breathe, but as soon as I could get my head around to coerce him, I released the pressure!"

Dr. Sabourin held out a hand over the corpse and frowned as he moved it up and down across the length of the councillor's chest.

"There are no broken ribs and no bruising on the neck," he noted. "I don't think strangulation was the cause of death."

"Then what was?!"

"I don't know."

In the distance, raised voices sounded like they were coming closer.

"We're going to have to sort this out in Neekonnisiwin," Gerry said firmly. He waved his prism at Doug Hayes' unmoving body, which immediately floated off the ground and draped itself over Gerry's shoulder. "If you please, Ms. Benson?"

Natalie took a deep breath and frowned in concentration. The gateway formed more slowly this time, and the glowing strands were not nearly as bright as her usual efforts. Gerry gestured for the others to precede him. Mikyla looked back through the gateway, her face white and drawn once she was across. Natalie gave her a small wave, and the gateway rapidly folded in on itself.

"Don't move! Put your hands up where I can see them."

"Oh, for the love of God," Natalie whispered, half turning to see two uniformed police officers running toward her and Jon, guns drawn and pointing in their direction. Suddenly a thick cloud of black smoke erupted between the two of them and the approaching policemen.

Alarmed shouts could be heard through the obscuring smoke.

"Don't panic; let me take control of things," Jon told Natalie. She nodded, suspecting what was going to happen next. She was exhausted, mentally and emotionally, which actually made it easier to let her mind go blank, in spite of the yells of the converging officers. The next second, it felt as though her body were melting. She squeezed her eyes shut and concentrated on not panicking, which was becoming harder. The deafening sound of a gunshot made her panic worse, but she forced her mind to completely surrender itself to Jon's control.

Minutes passed. The sound of shouting voices got briefly louder, sounding as though the people were underneath them, and then faded into the distance.

"All right, you can open your eyes now," Jon said in an amused voice.

Natalie opened her eyes to find herself in a completely different location, on the other side of the vendors' stalls, behind some kind of tent. Nobody was in sight except for the completely unfamiliar man standing beside her, holding her arm. He was a heavy-featured Asian man with a thick beard. Before she could begin to panic, he winked at her. Jon's voice came out of his mouth.

"You don't look like yourself either," he noted as he took in her look of astonishment at his appearance. "Can you walk?"

Natalie tried to put weight on her injured ankle and had to grab for Jon's arm for support as it failed to hold her weight. "I think that would be a no," she admitted shakily. Tears gathered in her eyes, although they were not entirely because of the pain in her ankle. She hated the appearance of weakness, but she was unable to keep from staggering. Suddenly a long black braid swung in front of one shoulder. She noticed that the hand that was gripped in Jon's was deep brown in tone. Several gold bracelets provided a nice contrast on her wrist, and she looked down to see the ankle-length skirt of a beautifully patterned sari taking the place of her jeans.

"It's all over now," Jon told her in a reassuring tone. "You did it. Now would you *please* let me look after you for a change? How about an electric mobility scooter?" Moments later, instead of leaning on the arm of the bearded Asian man, Natalie was leaning on the handlebars of a motorized scooter of the sort used by disabled people. A jaunty Union Jack flag was attached to the flexible pole behind the seat. With a shaky laugh, Natalie sat on the seat and used her hands to pull her injured leg into place.

Just guide the front tire in the right direction, and I'll take care of the actual propulsion, Jon said in her mind. *Let me know if I should brake.*

Just as well we're doing it this way, Natalie replied wryly. *Even if I could walk, I suspect I'd trip over this outlandish outfit you've put me in.* Although Jon had changed form, the flowing sari still hung in folds around Natalie's legs.

Jon chuckled. *It's just an illusion. I can't turn another person into something, unless it's smoke or water and I'm sort of wrapped around them. The sari isn't really there. Shall we just head down to the street and see if we can find a disabled taxi to drive us to the portal?*

You're very good at illusions, then, Natalie noted, turning the handlebars in the right direction. *I can even feel the bracelets.*

I have a lot of practice at visualizing different forms. I just take it a step further when I change.

As Natalie got into a cab on the street to the side of Queen's Park, she heard the sounds of multiple sirens approaching. She felt like a fugitive fleeing a crime scene, her heart hammering wildly, but the cab driver did not appear to notice anything amiss as he lifted the scooter into the cargo area of his van.

Chapter 25

The Neekonnisiwin courtroom was exactly the same as it had been for the hearing of Natalie's charges against Constance, yet everything seemed different in light of the completely different circumstances. A very subdued and mixed group waited silently for the Arch-Mage's arrival. To Natalie's right, her sister and brother-in-law talked quietly together. Dave wore a shirt and tie, something Natalie rarely saw him in. To her left, Jon was silent and unfamiliar-looking in his formal LEO uniform. Gerry sat beside him, dressed in the same uniform.

Dr. Sabourin sat in his wheelchair in the aisle between the two sets of benches. The empty arm of his suit jacket was pinned against his chest. Beyond him, Constance sat in isolation in the other front row. Her hair was styled in a simple knot at her neck, much different from her usual elaborate arrangement. Her face showed her grief and strain. Seth had told Natalie that Doug Hayes had been the closest friend of Constance's son, and after her son's death, Doug had become almost like a replacement son to her. She was taking his death hard. Natalie was concerned about how badly the revelation of all the facts would impact the elderly woman.

Several more uniformed LEOs, most of them unknown to Natalie, were in attendance. Mikyla and Jake sat near the back, looking uncomfortable. Seth sat two rows behind Constance, his face bearing the same neutral, unsmiling expression he had worn ever since he had learned that the serial killer he had been hunting had been right under his nose all this time. Beside him sat another man in the same kind of formal LEO uniform. Both had the extra insignia on their shoulders that indicated a top-ranked officer. Jon had identified the other man as European Chief LEO Francois Thibault.

The jury box was filled with councillors, many more of them than had been physically present during the previous hearing. The large monitor that displayed the courtroom in Sorcier-Havre contained a much shrunken group of councillors, as most of them had made the trip to Canada. The total numbers were the same, other than the fact that Constance was, once again, not sitting with her colleagues and that Douglas Hayes was markedly absent.

They all stood as the Arch-Mage entered the room, wearing the same judicial robe he had worn for Natalie's hearing.

"This court is now in session. You may be seated." This time, the Arch-Mage himself gave the direction usually provided by a registrar. He then directed a bland gaze at Councillor Reeve. "Well, Councillor, we find ourselves in a remarkably similar circumstance again. But this time, Councillor Douglas Hayes is dead."

Constance's jaw tensed as she got to her feet with some apparent difficulty. "So I've heard, my lord. But I have yet to hear how it happened or what I am accused of, if anything. I hope it's not being suggested that *I* murdered Doug?"

"As to that, I believe I will have to request Ms. Benson's assistance. I'm afraid you've made a liar of me, Ms. Benson."

Natalie was startled. "How so, my lord?"

"When we last spoke, I said to you that a magical court had no need of numerous witnesses to establish fact, that the facts would always be clear and inarguable because of memory stone evidence. But I have experienced the memory stones of everybody involved in Sunday's events, and I find myself utterly confused." The Arch-Mage indicated a row of a dozen memory stones of various colours and sizes set along the edge of his podium. "Are you able to suggest how best to proceed, Ms. Benson?"

"Yes, my lord. I believe I should start by explaining how I began to believe that we might have a serial killer at large who had perhaps been killing people for a very long time and had remained entirely undiscovered."

Natalie looked sideways at Dr. Sabourin and Constance and was unsurprised to see that both of them looked horrified. Most of the rest of the room's occupants were familiar with at least part of the later events, so this statement did not come as quite such a shock.

Natalie stepped up to front part of the courtroom. Glancing briefly at the gathered councillors, she faced forward and directed her remarks toward the Arch-Mage, using her well-practiced skills of courtroom oratory so as to be clearly heard by all present. As with most courtrooms, the chamber was panelled in polished wood for good acoustics. She also ensured that she spoke into the microphone in order to be heard by the remote participants in Sorcier-Havre.

Succinctly, she explained how she began to come across the situations she had been referring to as anomalies while investigating the allegations against her firm, and how she had told Jon almost immediately. She touched as briefly as possible on the events in her personal life that had intervened, including her hospital stay, and went on to explain why she had been initially reluctant to disclose her suspicions to Chief LEO Turner. She saw a few councillors glance toward the Chief, but she did not look in his direction.

"LEO Forrester pointed out to me that it would not be acceptable not to report my suspicions to *somebody*, given the pattern that was clearly developing, so he reported it first to his sergeant at the London LEO bureau, and it was then later reported to the European chief LEO. Chief Thibault is present, so I would next like to ask him to come up to the witness stand, to present the next part of the sequence."

"S'il vous plaît, Monsieur Thibault?" The Arch-Mage waved toward the witness stand. The European chief stood and paced to the witness stand, where he took the seat and adjusted the microphone at the small desk set to the left, slightly lower than the Arch-Mage's desk.

At Natalie's prompting, Chief Thibault explained the next stage of events, a strong French accent apparent in his words, though his English was faultless.

"Preliminary investigation identified several more of these anomalies, all in Canada and America, mostly in the northern part of the USA, and a few down the West Coast. I dispatched LEO officers to several locations to investigate locally. I was uncomfortable with stepping into my colleague's jurisdiction, but I concurred with the reasoning that had been presented to me and did not inform Chief Turner."

He went on to explain the circumstances of the American congresswoman's death and the fact that Seth had had a clear alibi on that occasion.

Chief Thibault went on to explain LEO Gerry Benham's presence in Chicago and the reason he had come up to Toronto on June 30, after the events at Natalie's College hearing.

"I am not familiar with the events of July 1," the European chief continued. "We had planned to consult with all of the investigators today to devise a plan of action. But it seems everything came to a head on Sunday."

The next witness called by Natalie was her sister, who described the attack on MP Daniel Baxter at Queen's Park and mentioned how she had known that it was not a heart attack. Natalie also touched on the previous attempt on Baxter's life a few months earlier and pointed out the similarity between an apparent heart attack and an alleged brain aneurysm. It was evident that the intelligence behind both attacks possessed medical knowledge.

"It was because of the attack on Baxter, and our fear that whomever had been used to effect the attack was now in imminent danger, that LEO Forrester and I went to Queen's Park. LEO Forrester also asked LEO Benham to attend. My sister and her husband got back as fast as they could after delivering the MP to the hospital, and though it had nothing to do with these events, Dr. James Sabourin and his daughter had also arranged to attend the Canada Day festivities, and ended up embroiled in what happened."

Natalie glanced at Jake, who sat with Mikyla near the back of the room, looking very nervous. She had debated whether to include him in the roster of people explaining the sequence of events, but really, his memory stone was perhaps the clearest of all in its very lack of information and obvious long gaps.

"As you know, my lord, Mr. Jacob Conrad was the coercion victim used in the attempt against Mr. Baxter, and he was in the process of being coerced to commit suicide when Ms. Burton was able to intervene and prevent that from happening." Natalie smiled slightly as she saw Jake kiss Mikyla on the cheek and observed how Mikyla smiled shyly in response.

"I would like to go out of sequence a little now and ask Councillor Constance Reeve to take the stand."

Trepidation showed briefly on Constance's face, but she complied, walking slowly up to take the seat behind the witness stand.

Natalie felt strange questioning witnesses who were not asked to swear the usual oath, but this was standard procedure in a magical court where memory stones were an essential part of the evidence, as they had long since been proven impossible to fictionalize.

"You are aware, I believe, Councillor Reeve, that there was a long period of time on Sunday when you had no memory of what happened, but you were aware that you had, in fact, lost a passage of time?" she asked in a neutral tone, holding up a pale pink quartz memory stone to demonstrate the source of her knowledge.

To Natalie's surprise, a deep flush crept up Constance Reeve's face. Constance dropped her eyes and did not meet anyone's gaze.

"I am, yes," she admitted, almost inaudibly.

The Arch-Mage raised one eyebrow, presumably just as puzzled by the councillor's reaction as Natalie was.

"It would appear that those periods of unawareness were because you were also a victim of magical coercion."

Constance's head jerked up and her jaw dropped as she stared at Natalie.

"C-coercion?" She gasped. "But there was no yellow aura. Was there? Nobody ever said ... No, I couldn't have been."

"LEO has figured something out in that regard. Before we get to that, would you mind telling us what you believed had happened?" Natalie asked. This was a part of the story that she had not been able to figure out, in spite of having been granted the opportunity to experience the memory stones of all the other participants. Constance's stone, of course, had simply stopped shortly after her arrival at Queen's Park with Douglas Hayes, and resumed upon her arrival at LEO headquarters, somewhat the worse for wear. As far as she was aware, Doug thoroughly enjoyed non-magical fireworks, and he had simply decided to attend the Canada Day events at Queen's Park on a whim. She had accepted his invitation to join him for a day out.

"I—I have had episodes like that for years," Constance whispered, though she directed her answer toward the Arch-Mage. "I thought I had Alzheimer's. I was taking medication. In fact, it was Doug who prescribed it for me, before he ever became a councillor. He was my doctor. I—I didn't want anyone to know. He agreed to keep it confidential, and he kept my prescription current even after he was no longer practising medicine."

"How many years?" the Arch-Mage asked in a steely voice.

"I—uh—I think maybe, um, five or six." Constance's voice was barely audible.

"Five or six years," the Arch-Mage repeated ominously. "For five or six years, you have been acting in the role of a member of the Council of Mages, in spite of numerous periods of being unaware of your actions. You believed yourself to be subject to a debilitating condition of dementia, and yet you hid this information from the Council?" the Arch-Mage rephrased the information in a biting tone.

"I—I … Yes, Your Lordship," Constance admitted, dropping her gaze to the marble floor in front of her.

"As far as I am aware, dementia is progressive; there is no medication that could halt its progress for five or six years," the Arch-Mage spoke in a stern voice. He looked toward Dr. Sabourin. "I understand, sir, that you are a doctor. Do you know whether I am correct in this?"

Natalie picked up the microphone from the desk in front of her and held it so that the doctor could speak into it.

"Dementia isn't my specialty, Your Lordship, but I believe that's true," Dr. Sabourin confirmed. "Further, Alzheimer's patients don't suddenly regain awareness and know that they have just lost a block of time. Their memory comes and goes, but when they are remembering properly, they don't usually realize that five minutes ago they couldn't remember their children's names."

Constance flicked a glance at the doctor as he answered, but looked back at the floor in front of the witness stand almost immediately.

"May I see the prescription bottle?" Dr. Sabourin asked.

"Councillor?" The Arch-Mage's tone left no doubt that he expected her to comply.

With visible reluctance, Constance reached into her purse and pulled out an ordinary-looking pill bottle. Natalie took it and handed it to the doctor.

Dr. Sabourin turned the bottle so that he could read the printed label. He frowned.

"Councillor, Your Lordship, this is a mild sedative. It's a kind that's often prescribed to people who have an anxiety disorder. All it does is help calm the person enough so that they can function. I'm pretty sure this drug has absolutely nothing to do with Alzheimer's treatment. Except maybe a situation where such a patient is violent."

Constance's mouth had dropped open, and she was looking at Dr. Sabourin in baffled confusion.

"But I— I— I don't understand," she stammered.

The Arch-Mage sighed. "Regardless of the outcome of this proceeding, Councillor, your actions in this regard demonstrate extremely poor judgment. The role of a member of the Council of Mages is an extremely serious duty. You have failed in that duty."

Constance nodded jerkily, saying nothing.

"Councillor," Natalie said, taking up her narrative at the Arch-Mage's gesture, "we have reason to believe that Councillor Hayes was the instigator of the anomalies that I described earlier. Essentially, we suspect that he was coercing you and others, and causing various victims, perhaps including you, to commit a number of very serious crimes, including multiple murders, many of which have never even been suspected, let alone solved."

Constance gasped and refocused her gaze on Natalie. Her face went several shades paler.

"He then coerced many of those victims to kill themselves, or else he killed them himself, often making it appear to be an accident or a natural medical situation. It now occurs to me that the reason he was able to achieve such a strong degree of control may, in fact, have been because he was coercing you, and thereby using your First Circle abilities as a communicator to effect the coercion on others. He may have been able to achieve a much higher than usual degree of mental contact, even with multiple victims simultaneously and over a greater distance than is usually possible. To some extent, though, I am guessing on this point," she admitted.

"It is my understanding that coercion renders the victim simply a puppet," the Arch-Mage objected. "The coercer is pulling the strings. I had not been aware that it was possible to use a victim's magical abilities."

"Some information has come to light in that regard, my lord," Natalie said. "Thank you, Councillor Reeve. You may return to your seat."

Constance's face was very nearly as white as her hair as she pulled herself to her feet using the edges of the witness stand for support. She walked with halting steps back toward the seat she had occupied earlier, among the spectator's benches.

"Dr. Sabourin, I wonder if you would come up to the witness stand next, please."

The doctor's wheelchair moved smoothly forward without visible control. The witness stand was actually raised up one step, but the wheelchair hopped up the step, and the chair that was already there floated aside. As before, Natalie was watching the doctor's face closely and was impressed by how little effort was evident as he juggled many moving parts simultaneously.

"Doctor, could you please describe the events that took place when you first entered the area where your daughter and the others were?"

The doctor laid out the events from the time of his arrival immediately after Constance appeared. Although these events were on the memory stone, Natalie, aware that Constance had no knowledge of what she had done, wanted to use the doctor's testimony to assist the Arch-Mage and the other councillors with the full sequence of events. She saw Constance's face take on a look of shock as the doctor described the noise attack that she had instigated. When the doctor described how the noise attack ceased but it then became evident that Dave had been coerced, she buried her face in her hands.

"What did you do once Mr. Timmons was acting in an unnatural manner?"

The doctor sighed and glanced uncomfortably toward the Arch-Mage. "Actually I was attempting to impose coercion on the councillor before Mr. Timmons began to behave strangely. I saw that everyone present, including the LEO, was incapacitated. I think the only reason I wasn't as badly affected by the noise attack was because Councillor Reeve did not realize that I was behind her. I had no idea what was going on, but I figured I had no choice but to do what I could to help the LEO be able to take control of the situation again. It wasn't working, at first, which I found strange because I use coercion to anaesthetize surgery patients all the time. It was almost like my attempt to gain control was sliding off a glossy surface. I was going to stop when the noise stopped, but then when Mr. Timmons launched himself toward my daughter, I was afraid for her safety, and somehow I managed to make the coercion grab hold. I made sure that Councillor Reeve did not fall; I floated her down to the ground gently."

"You are aware, Doctor, that your use of coercion in this context is not within the permitted parameters of your profession?" the Arch-Mage said sternly.

"Yes, my lord. But I didn't feel I had a choice, and I still think I did the right thing."

In spite of his words, he still looked very nervous. Several of the councillors had disapproving looks on their faces. The Arch-Mage simply nodded, and gestured to Natalie to proceed.

"When did you release the coercion on Councillor Reeve, Doctor?"

"Not until after I moved her through your gateway," Dr. Sabourin responded. "LEO, uh, Benham was going to take over the coercion from me, but then he changed his mind and told me to keep doing it. I don't know why he changed his mind."

"All right, fast-forward to the end, after the snake immobilized Councillor Hayes," Natalie said.

"Right, well, the snake turned into that other gentleman, though I didn't realize at the time he was also a LEO, since he wasn't wearing a uniform." Dr. Sabourin identified Jon with a wave of his hand. "I assumed he might be a LEO since he talked about coercing Councillor Hayes and since both Natalie and LEO Benham evidently knew him, but I wasn't sure of anything. I just realized that Doug was dead, and then it was clear this was a surprise to everyone. When LEO Benham suggested that the other gentleman might have suffocated Doug, I was able to use a form of magic I use a lot during surgery to determine that Doug had no broken ribs and there was no sign of bruising around the neck. I couldn't tell what the cause of death was, though, on such a cursory examination, but it wasn't strangulation. I still don't know what the cause of death was."

"Thank you, Doctor. LEO Forrester, would you please take the stand?" Natalie said next. As Jon strode up to the stand, his double row of silver buttons gleaming on his chest, Natalie reflected how very different a person could appear based on his clothing. His usual appearance of jeans and a rumpled T-shirt did not present nearly as authoritative an image as his current attire. A row of three insignia of some kind on each shoulder seemed to denote a higher rank than the uniform worn by LEO Benham, but she was not familiar enough with LEO ranks to know what it meant. He was carrying a small blue notebook.

Is it okay if I tell everyone you're a metamorph? she asked silently. *It's kind of key to the story.*

No worries. Most of the people here already know, he answered, giving no visible clue that the mental exchange had taken place. His solemn demeanour seemed entirely at odds with the fun-loving personality Natalie had come to know.

"As many of you are aware, LEO Forrester is a First Circle metamorph," Natalie told everyone in the room, dividing her attention between the Arch-Mage and the jury box of councillors, as well as their distant colleagues in Switzerland. "In the course of investigating and attempting to protect the various people involved in the situation on Sunday, LEO Forrester assumed various forms, including that of a bird, a dog and a truly terrifying boa constrictor. I'm not yet sure myself how Councillor Hayes died, but that snake practically scared me to death, and I wasn't the focus of its attention."

There was a ripple of laughter in the room, though somebody was coughing as though he had inadvertently swallowed his chewing gum.

"Now I have a confession to make," Natalie said, glancing backward toward Dr. Sabourin. "At one point, I wondered whether Dr. Sabourin might be a suspect. Sorry, Doctor. But all along, I had assumed it was likely either someone high up in LEO, who could alter the prison records, or at least someone who had practice and experience with coercion, which means a LEO or a doctor. LEO Forrester, you told me that you had valid reason to believe the doctor was not a suspect, but you weren't able to tell me why not at the time. Could you now explain that part?"

"Certainly. When Dr. Sabourin appeared on the scene, LEO Benham and I both noticed that he had the yellow aura around his head which indicated that he had been a victim of coercion, likely fairly recently, but also likely fairly briefly given that it was already noticeably fading."

"I did?! Sorry," the doctor apologized for his interruption, his face reddening slightly.

Jon nodded. "As you may recall from the doctor's memory stone, my lord, there was a point just after his daughter ran after her friend when the doctor saw an Asian security guard who was evidently wearing an illusion. He briefly lost control of that illusion and was clearly a white man. In the next second, he disappeared, and the doctor wondered if this was some kind of magical ability he had never been aware of before."

"I was puzzled by that myself," the Arch-Mage commented.

"I repeated that part of the stone myself, several times," Jon continued. "And then I noticed that the doctor's daughter also disappeared from sight at the same time, and in fact the other person, a non-mage carrying a box, also *appeared* apparently out of thin air. I can only speculate, but I believe that the supposed Asian security guard, whom we now know was Councillor Hayes, actually effected coercion on the doctor at that point, left the scene, and removed the coercion so smoothly that the doctor was unaware of any loss of time."

Dr. Sabourin's mouth had fallen open in surprise.

"But I did not notice any sign of coercion about the doctor in any of the other memory stones that I experienced," the Arch-Mage commented. "Did it fade so fast that I just failed to notice it?"

"In a manner of speaking, my lord. It is a little-known fact, kept mostly confidential by LEO, that when a person operates coercive magic, any signs that that person has been coerced disappear. This is also why Councillor Reeve has never been seen to bear signs of having been coerced. It is my theory that every time Councillor Hayes coerced Councillor Reeve, he then made her coerce somebody else in order to hide any evidence of his actions."

"So if you coerce me and force me to coerce somebody else while I'm under your control, I have no yellow aura? But presumably the person that I am coercing would have the aura?"

"That is correct, my lord. So, since the doctor coerced Councillor Reeve to become unconscious, his own aura disappeared. Ms. Reeve did, of course, have a yellow aura when she arrived in Neekonnisiwin, but since it was soon clarified how and why Dr. Sabourin had coerced her, that was not a source of alarm."

Natalie looked over at Constance Reeve and saw that her mouth formed an *O* of surprise as she digested that information. She also seemed to collapse in on herself as she presumably thought about the further implications. Natalie had once before thought one would never guess she was past seventy given her elegant appearance and bearing, but today she looked about ninety. In spite of how much she had disliked Constance, even before the mental attack that had launched her Complaint against the councillor, Natalie felt terrible for the older woman. Though she had an abrasive personality and was far too much of an isolationist, she had served the mage community as best she knew how for many years, but it seemed likely that that was all going to end in scandal, disgrace and utter humiliation.

Her attention was pulled back to Jon as he continued.

"An investigation of Councillor Hayes' home was made yesterday, and a hidden room was located in his basement. Two rooms, actually. One was a rather securely locked cell with a window so small that not even a child could squeeze out of it; the other was a small office which contained a desk and a filing cabinet. There were several notebooks in the filing cabinet, filled with notes about various magical experiments, many of them coercive in nature. Some involved animal subjects, but unfortunately, although nobody is named, it seems apparent that some of Councillor Hayes' experiment subjects were human."

"Mon Dieu," the Arch-Mage said in a sickened tone.

"It would appear, my lord, that Councillor Hayes knew more about coercion than anybody. The notes suggest that Hayes had learned how to operate the magical abilities of others. In order to test this, I volunteered to be coerced by LEO Chief Turner. I'm told he did manage to make me change form."

Oh wow, what else did he do to you? Natalie asked silently.

I don't know, he won't tell me, Jon grumbled, though again his face betrayed nothing of the silent exchange. *Gerry seems to think it was very funny, though.*

"His notes also made another fact quite clear, my lord: Councillor Hayes developed a complex set spell, which he later placed upon himself, after experimenting with many animal subjects first. The spell ensured that his own heart would stop if anybody ever used coercive magic on him, except if that magic was medical in nature." Jon handed the notebook he was holding up to the Arch-Mage. "The relevant portion is marked with a bookmark, my lord."

The Arch-Mage read silently for a few minutes and then looked up, his expression faintly nauseous. "I take it you are claiming that you did not kill Councillor Hayes, LEO Forrester?"

"On the contrary, my lord. I think there can be no doubt that I did kill him," Jon admitted. "But not by accidentally strangling him while in the form of a snake as we first suspected. I used coercive magic to subdue him. I was intending to cause him to lose consciousness, similar to the way that Dr. Sabourin had done to Councillor Reeve. I admit I have never before used coercion to cause unconsciousness; usually I use it to make someone I am arresting co-operate and do as I wish them to do. I assumed that I had succeeded in this new application of that magic when Councillor Hayes became limp in my, ah, coils. It was not until several minutes later that Dr. Sabourin realized that Councillor Hayes was dead."

"Chief Thibault, I believe LEO Forrester is most directly under your jurisdiction. Do you concur?"

"I do, Your Lordship," the European chief said soberly, rising to his feet as he spoke. "I believe that LEO Forrester's use of coercive magic in effecting the arrest of a very volatile and dangerous suspect was clearly well within appropriate procedure."

"Very well," the Arch-Mage said thoughtfully. "I wish it to be understood by all present that the more extensive knowledge of coercive magic that has been discussed here today is highly confidential. The less that is generally known about coercive magic by those who are not authorized to practise it, the better."

"There might be a counterargument, Your Lordship," Jon said, frowning.

"Oh?"

"If Councillor Reeve had had a clearer understanding of the effects of coercion, perhaps she would have realized a long time ago that there was a more ominous explanation for her memory lapses. If they have been going on for five or six years, that tends to suggest that the murders we have become aware of may only be the tip of the iceberg."

"And if more people knew how to do it, we might well have many more situations like this on our hands," the Arch-Mage pointed out grimly. "Clearly it is not a simple question. But then none of this is simple." He paused to gather his thoughts for a moment. "I am a little concerned about convicting Douglas Hayes of a possibly very significant number of extremely serious crimes without further investigation. There is no concern anymore about preventing further attacks since he is dead. But I believe further investigation is warranted before he is posthumously convicted of these crimes. These are extremely serious allegations, and as you said, LEO Forrester, the murders we now know of may be the tip of the iceberg. Do not misunderstand me: I do not have any doubt that he was the instigator of Sunday's events, and I think it is extremely likely that he is guilty as suspected. But I believe a very in-depth investigation must be conducted to find the full scope of the crimes, and the full roster of victims and attempted victims, to the extent possible, and also to see if there is any collateral harm that can now be resolved. It occurs to me that it is entirely possible that there may be people in jail convicted of crimes they did not commit or that they committed while under coercion."

Natalie thought about the scope of that investigation with some trepidation. It would have been so much easier if Doug were still alive, if he could have been forced to reveal the facts. In spite of her anger at the way Seth had refused to allow her to participate in the investigation, she had reluctantly recognized that the regulation made sense and that making exceptions could cause other problems. Certainly it seemed like a career with LEO would be more interesting and challenging than simply providing transportation services. Her attention was pulled back as the Arch-Mage continued.

"Councillor Reeve, I will require you to assist with that investigation and be completely honest and open about every single memory lapse that you can now remember, including when it took place and, if possible, where you were both before and after the lapse.

"Conversely, we cannot postpone informing the mage world that one of the councillors has been killed. It is therefore my intention to make a public announcement that Councillor Hayes was killed under suspicious circumstances and that his death is being investigated and leave it at that. I will require everybody involved in this matter to keep these events confidential until the investigation is complete. It will then be the subject of a full trial. Does anybody have any objection?"

"No, Your Lordship," several people said quietly.

"Did Councillor Hayes have family who will need to be informed?" The Arch-Mage directed his question toward Constance.

"No, Your Lordship," Constance replied, her voice still shaky. "Doug was never married and has no children, as far as I am aware. He was born into a non-magical family, and when they discovered that he was a mage, when he was 16, they abandoned him. He came home from school to find the house empty of all belongings. His father had quit his job and left no forwarding information. He never heard from them again."

"Oh my God." Natalie sucked in a shocked breath as she contemplated what that must have been like.

The Arch-Mage raised his eyebrows. "I suppose we can then understand why he would have had such strong feelings of hatred toward non-mages," he noted grimly. "Very well, let it be heard and recorded that the interim decision of this court is as follows: Constance Reeve, you are hereby charged with being an accessory to murder or murders, the total number unknown; attempted murders and using coercive magic against numerous victims."

At the look of horror and outrage on her face, the Arch-Mage held up a hand before she could interject. "Constance, I do think it is extremely likely that you were a victim and not in any way part of the criminal activities. It may well be that you will be exonerated of specific criminal intent or deliberate wrongdoing in these actions, as it seems entirely likely that you were under the coercive control of the late Douglas Hayes while these crimes took place. It is not my intention to put you in jail or even on house arrest. But I will require that you do not leave Neekonnisiwin until given leave."

His face then hardened as he continued. "Even if you are found to be innocent, however, you are found to have been lacking in the required degree of objective judgment in your role as councillor, in that you failed to recognize signs of coercion in yourself and hid those signs from others as a result of your fear of a perceived medical condition. If any medical, mental or spiritual condition, or indeed even a crisis of conscience, interferes with your obligations as a member of the Council of Mages, it is your clear and unequivocal duty to step down from that role. A very high degree of responsibility is required of a leader of the global community of mages. I will accept your resignation and maintain the confidentiality of this matter while an investigation is under way, should you choose to voluntarily resign."

Constance raised her chin, but it was clear that it was not her usual gesture of defiant arrogance but only an effort to keep from crying. "I do voluntarily resign, Your Lordship," she said in a near-inaudible voice.

"Your resignation is accepted. Chief Turner, please place the Convict's Curse on Ms. Reeve. Ensure that it will be undetectable to any mage or non-mage provided Ms. Reeve remains within Neekonnisiwin."

"Yes, Your Lordship," Seth said quietly. He faced Constance and traced a complex pattern in the air with his prism in front of her. The air appeared to shimmer briefly around her.

"LEO Jonathan Forrester, you are exonerated in the matter of the death of the late Douglas William Hayes, formerly a member of the Council of Mages. In this regard, you are found to have executed your duties in a wholly proper manner, and you are to be commended for it."

"Thank you, Your Lordship," Jon murmured.

"Dr. James Sabourin." The doctor didn't speak but looked at the Arch-Mage with a wary expression on his face. The Arch-Mage took a deep breath. "I am prepared to exonerate you, Doctor, for your actions in coercing Councillor Reeve. However, I want it very clearly understood that this was an extremely unusual situation and that being acquitted of this crime does not in any way indicate that the use of coercion outside of the usual regulations is going to become more lax."

"Yes, Your Lordship."

"Now, pending the outcome of the full investigation, we are left with only one serious problem to be addressed urgently."

The occupants of the room glanced at each other in confusion.

"Canada now has no councillors," the Arch-Mage pointed out, smiling slightly at the obvious evidence that nobody had picked up on this fact. "Until a duly constituted by-election can be held, I exercise my discretion as Arch-Mage and appoint Natalie Benson and Seth Turner as temporary councillors. Do the two of you accept this responsibility?"

Natalie's mouth had fallen open. It was several moments before she could contain her shock.

Seth rose to his feet. "I thank Your Lordship, but I do not think I can do it," he said with a sigh. "As you have just indicated, we have a *lot* of investigation ahead of us to uncover everything that went on, and we don't even know how far back we need to go. LEO is short-handed as it is. I cannot do my job as chief and also be a councillor."

"I see. We will have to come up with a second candidate. Ms. Benson, do you accept the appointment?"

"Yes, I accept," Natalie said slowly. "I never wanted to be a politician, but then I'm kind of out of a job right now. I'm not living in Neekonnisiwin, though," she added with a frown. "I'm not a small-town girl, and I never will be. I'll commute from Toronto."

"As you wish, Councillor Benson. Court is dismissed."

Epilogue

MAGICAL MURDER AND MAYHEM
AT THE LEGISLATURE

Queen's Park, Toronto – Canada Day festivities at Queen's Park were disrupted by a series of violent magical attacks carried out by parties unknown. RCMP Officer Robert Halliday was on hand when Member of Parliament Daniel Baxter collapsed of an apparent heart attack. After being revived by a self-confessed mage, who claimed to be a Toronto paramedic but refused to identify herself, Mr. Baxter was rushed to Toronto General Hospital, where he remains in serious, but stable, condition. The alleged paramedic informed Mr. Halliday that Mr. Baxter had not experienced a genuine heart attack but had in fact been the victim of a magical attack, though she claimed that she was not the attacker.

Shortly thereafter, witnesses report that an altercation involving numerous parties took place among the vendors' trailers. Oddly, these events appeared to take place in

357

absolute silence. A security guard was violently assaulted, knocked off his feet and rendered unconscious by a young unidentified female who did not actually physically touch him. The same female then proceeded to attack a young man who may also have been a mage. The remains of a gun were found at the scene, so twisted and melted that it was inoperable, and incidentally it was impossible to dust for fingerprints. It is believed that the young man was able to destroy the gun in an ultimately futile attempt to defend himself.

Once the first attack failed, the young female mage conjured an oversized canine, thought to be a grey wolf, the largest species of wolf currently in existence, of an estimated weight of 150 pounds. The canine knocked the young man down and attempted to rip out his throat. Again, the young man was able to deflect the attack. A man wearing the uniform of a Toronto police officer stood by and observed events, making no effort to intervene.

An elderly woman was seen to wander into the scene, where she was immediately attacked by the alleged Toronto police officer. Shortly thereafter she was again attacked, by a tall black man who struck her on the back of the head. This man was wearing the uniform of Toronto EMS and was with the mage paramedic who purportedly resuscitated MP Baxter.

The security guard, regaining consciousness, attempted to contain the situation, but he was immediately attacked by one of the mages, possibly the same one who had conjured the canine. The attacker this time was a boa constrictor, larger than any such snake as they actually exist. The snake squeezed its victim to death before disappearing.